Molly Hawkey

Isla Morley grew up in South Africa during apartheid, the child of a British father and a fourth-generation South African mother. She was one of the youngest magazine editors in South Africa, but she left country, career, and kin when she married an American and moved to California. For more than a decade she worked for nonprofits, focusing on the needs of women and children. Now living in the Los Angeles area, Morley shares a home with her husband, their daughter, two cats, a dog, and a tortoise.

COME
SUNDAY

COME
SUNDAY

ISLA MORLEY

PICADOR

———

SARAH CRICHTON BOOKS

Farrar, Straus and Giroux

New York

www.picadorusa.com

Picador® is a U.S. registered trademark and is used by Farrar, Straus and Giroux under license from Pan Books Limited.

For information on Picador Reading Group Guides, please contact Picador.
E-mail: readinggroupguides@picadorusa.com

Grateful acknowledgment is made for permission to reprint lyrics from "Come Sunday" by Duke Ellington, copyright © 1966 (renewed) by G. Schirmer, Inc. (ASCAP). International copyright secured. All rights reserved. Used by permission.

The Library of Congress has cataloged the Farrar, Straus and Giroux edition as follows:

    Morley, Isla.
        Come Sunday / by Isla Morley. — 1st ed.
           p. cm.
        "Sarah Crichton Books."
        ISBN 978-0-374-12687-2
          1. Daughters—Death—Fiction.   2. Life change events—Fiction.
        3. Bereavement—Fiction.   4. South Africa—Fiction.   5. Honolulu
        (Hawaii)—Fiction.   I. Title.

        PS 3613.O75518C66 2008
        813'.6—dc22

                                            2008038829

Picador ISBN 978-0-312-42977-5

First published in the United States by Sarah Crichton Books, an imprint of Farrar, Straus and Giroux

First Picador Edition: August 2010

10 9 8 7 6 5 4 3 2 1

TO BOB AND EMILY

GOOD
FRIDAY

ONE

A bad sign, my grandmother would have muttered, looking heavenward. She would not have had to say another thing and Beauty, nodding, would have taken off her apron and her starched *doek* covering her peppercorn curls and headed out the back door into the African night with its sick moon. The Cape veldt was different at night, alive with the wild smell of *fynbos*; a thing with its own heartbeat, its own snorts and threats. Children were called in from its heat at dusk, long before the earth cooled and its worn paths began to vibrate with the invisible steps of the ancestors and the menacing Tokoloshe, long before the moon would rise over the *kopjes* in the east. But under a bad moon, no one went in the veldt—not even the ancestral spirits. Only a *sangoma*, a witch doctor, whose magic her old white madam had come to rely on. Beauty Masinama, grounded in the tradition of the Ndebele nation, knew all about lunar tidings. My grandmother, a woman whose superstitions grew up in the crack between her Christian faith and the lore of her Scottish ancestry, knew about them too.

Beauty would have walked into the bush with measured haste, to the foot of the *kopje* over which the sickly moon rose, to the source of her *muti*, her medicine. Tracing her steps back to the farmhouse before the moon had completed its arc, pigskin bag filled with twigs and rocks and bones and feathers rattling with each step, Beauty would have chanted a

3

liturgy as ancient as the hills themselves. Only after she had laid out her wares in an elaborate tapestry on the back porch and kindled the blood of the long-deceased with her invocation under the moon gone bad would she go into the madam's room with her early-morning tea tray and reassuring, toothless smile: all would be well. Maybe.

∾

IN AFRICA THERE are good moons and bad moons—moons that foretell of bounty and fortune: the long-awaited birth of a chief, a wedding, a visit from relatives, rain. Eclipsed moons, yellow moons, upside-down sickle moons are bad—famine, crop failure, war, sickness. Moons with gossamer halos—nooses, the *sangomas* call them—mean only one thing: death. People in Africa will go to great lengths to stem the doom of a bad moon. But here in Honolulu, a half spin on its axis, the world is bright with fluorescent bulbs and can barely be bothered to look up.

It is a cool night and the heavy clouds are spilling over the mountain behind us, right on schedule. Solly is eager to go back inside, forgoing his leisurely round of leg-lifting for a quick pee against Mrs. Chung's mailbox. Attaboy. I look up once more at the moon and its ring before both are blanketed with clouds, and feel a twitch of foreboding and a longing for one of Beauty's spells.

I WAKE UP to a stiff neck and a throat that feels like it has dry ice stuck in it. Every inhale sears my throat and I quite expect steam to come billowing out my nose on each exhale. My left eardrum pounds and I can hear, for brief moments, the sound of blood flowing in my head. Just then Cleo marches into my bedroom and snaps to attention next to my side of the bed. "Mommy," she orders, "put this on!" "This" happens to be her purple bathing suit, an item decidedly inappropriate for a spring morning, chilly by Hawaii standards.

"Darling," I croak, squinting through puffy morning eyelids still crusty with sleep, "don't you think it's too cold to wear that?"

"PUT IT ON!" she commands.

"Let me get up; hold on a moment," I say, knowing that this is a battle I do not have the stamina to win.

"Put it on, put it on, putitonputitonputiton!"

"Please!" I swivel around and glare down at her, totally awake. "Do NOT start whining."

"Can you put it on?" she persists, and I wonder whether three-year-olds have selective hearing like the husbands of naggy old women.

I shiver barefoot, hold out her bathing suit so she can slip one foot in one hole, then the other, and try not to feel as though my watermelon head is about to roll off its stand. Before I can pull the straps up over her shoulders, she yanks them out of my hands. "I can do it!" she insists.

"Fine," I say, and reach for my robe. One foot finds the slipper. "Goddammit, Solly," I hiss, because instead of bunny fluff there is only the soggy mess of an indoor dog's sacrificial kill.

"Mommy!" Cleo reprimands. "You took the Lord's name again."

"Don't tell your father," I grunt.

When I get downstairs, Greg is still asleep on the couch and I roll my eyes for the benefit of the unseen entities that may or may not inhabit the lonely spaces of my house. Today is Thursday, the last day of my vacation, and I am not looking forward to returning to the world of editorial deadlines. I feel the resentment rise like bile: for just one morning I would like Greg to be the one to drag his tail out of bed and hup-hup-hup to Cleo's endless list of orders. I bang the microwave door on purpose and he wakes up and says, "Huh, what?"

The hammering sound coming down the staircase is Cleo in my silver high heels, which were in fashion the last time they saw the light of day, possibly last century, and the pounding on the parquet floors makes Greg frown and rub his brow. "Cleo," he calls.

"Morning, Daddy," she coos.

"Cleo, do you think you can take Mommy's shoes off for now?"

"Will it wake the neighbors?" she asks.

"Yes, it might," he answers. "It woke me up and it will most certainly wake up the cat."

She grins sadistically as she spots Pilgrim curled up on the rocking chair, in hibernation mode. She thuds over to him, more determined than ever to keep the heels on, and says, "Pilgrim! Wake up!" and then she roars at him and the poor feline lunges past her before she can grab him. I place a warm mug of milk at her place at the table and fix my own cup of tea and a slice of toast.

"Did you hear the thunder last night?" Greg asks.

I shake my head in reply. "But I saw the bad moon before we went to bed."

"It started about one o'clock," he continues, ignoring my comment. Greg doesn't like it when Africa seeps through me, as though he were a missionary watching his converts go native. "I couldn't go back to sleep, so I stayed up for a while. Bet there were flash floods down in the valley," he says, passing me on his way to the refrigerator.

"Got your fingers crossed?" He means about the new garage roof and its first test. I nod.

"What's wrong?" he asks.

I point to my throat.

"Oh, you got it now," he says. I am the last one to get a cold, having nursed Greg and Cleo through theirs for the past two weeks. "That's terrible," he says, and fixes himself a bowl of cereal. I look at him while he sets his bowl down and empties the last of the orange juice into a coffee mug.

"What?" he says, looking up and seeing me stare at him. "Did you want some?" Before I have a chance to nod, Cleo is back with a pair of dirty pajamas from the laundry room.

"Mommy, put this on," she says, already tugging at her bathing suit straps.

"No," I say, "those are dirty. I didn't wash them yesterday."

"But they are clean," she argues, and thrusts them toward me.

"Cleo, they are dirty and they are your pajamas; you don't wear them during the day."

"Put them on!" she insists.

"Look," I say, pointing to the front of the shirt, "those are yucky, dirty stains; and smell that. See, it's stinky too."

"I don't smell anything. I like these."

"No," I say, wondering why it is that I am debating with a toddler. In the half-breath interval it takes for her to whiplash her head and convulse her body as though it had just received an enormous electrical pulse, I think, What am I doing wrong? Are we too lenient with her? Is she becoming the typical precocious preacher's kid? How do you insist the Fifth Commandment be complied with by a child who requests her own time-out? I hate myself the instant I listen to the voices of the women's church auxiliary take up their seats in my head and with downturned mouths say, *And she's the minister's child! It's because the mother was raised in Africa, by the natives, you know.*

"But I like them!" Cleo cries, and, quick as a leak, big tears plop over her eyelids and land on her chin. My goodness, but the passions do run deep in this one.

I take a deep breath while Greg's contribution to the kitchen debacle is his usual halfhearted, exasperated "Cleo!" to which she seldom responds.

"Look," I say, trying to find the compromise, "you can wear pajamas today if you want to. Just not these." And then, in the familiar parlance of preschoolers, I say, "They're so stinky they will make you puke!" and wrinkle my nose.

It works. She smiles conspiratorially, "Puke! Ugh! They are so stinky they will make me poop!" And then she laughs mischievously because she hopes to get away with saying her favorite word without its permissible context of the bathroom. We go upstairs while my tea gets cold and undertake the laborious task of choosing just the right pajamas for the day. She decides on the ones that are too small for her, the pair I forgot to take out of her closet and put in the Goodwill box. But I cannot object again. So she squeezes into the shirt with the sleeves that come up to her elbows and the pants that are now pedal pushers. My old pair of pantyhose pulled over her springy blond curls passes for a wig and the pink purse clutched under her armpit completes the ensemble.

"I'm ready, Mommy," she says. "Where are we going today?"

"How about to the table so we can have breakfast?" I suggest.

"I had breakfast already."

"What did you have?"

She mouths something inaudible, which is a sure sign that I will disapprove.

"What?"

"Mints," she whispers, and I follow her eyes to the empty box of Tic Tacs on her bedside table.

"You ate them all?" She nods. "Cleo, that's not breakfast. You need to eat," I say.

"No I don't!" is her reply as she waltzes out of the room, flinging one pantyhose leg over her shoulder.

"I am going to lose it with this child, Greg," I announce as I pin my whining daughter to her seat at the breakfast table. She immediately quiets and I feel her seal pup eyes, wide and dark, on me. Ignoring the tittle-tattle old ladies wagging their fingers and chanting, *Not a good mother,* I continue, "If she says 'no' to me one more time . . ." and I can't finish. Then what? Then I will beat her the way your mother has been insisting we do since she was ten months old? Then I am going to throw the mounds of toys I have yet to pick up at you, you in your insulated world of Scripture readings and sermon notes? But none of the "thens" take into account that I have to face myself in the mirror each morning, so they turn to "whens," as they usually do: when Cleo gets a little older she will be more cooperative; when Greg has more time he will be able to help a little more; when I start to feel better I will have more patience.

"Let me handle this," Greg offers. He puts down the paper and takes off his reading glasses and peers at Cleo, who will not look anywhere but at my face. She is inches away from crumpling like a discarded tissue, not liking it when her mommy is cross, which is too often these past months. I know she is scared, and for one delicious, sadistic moment I feel pleased at having the upper hand.

"Cleo, listen to your mommy, okay?" instructs Greg with the kindness of a benevolent guru and a matching amount of detachment. She blinks and looks at her hands in her lap when I return her stare. "You have got to be nice to your mommy, sweet girl, okay? She's not feeling well today." She nods at him and he says, "Good!" and then to me, on a winning streak, "I have to leave pretty soon; what would you like for me to do?" It is a patient question, one anxious to redirect the squall. A question that elicits the opposite effect, stirring up the storm in my teacup.

"I don't know why I have to be a bloody thundercloud before anyone listens to me," I say, taking quantum leaps that Greg has learned to follow. How quickly the insolence of a three-year-old can come to represent the civil disobedience of all humankind does not strike me as silly, and if it does Greg, his face does not betray him. I cannot simply say, "How about you fix her breakfast while I go take a bath," which is what I know he can safely deal with. Greg chews on the corner of his lip because he knows he cannot say anything that will help, and takes a furtive look at his watch.

"When did I become everyone's flunky?" I continue, restacking the piles of dirty dishes. "Why is it I seem to spend all my time picking up after everyone else? Why is it that when I ask you and Cleo very nicely to put your stuff away and tell you that my tolerance for the debris in this house is reaching an apex, nobody listens? Nobody hears me, nobody answers me; if I didn't know by looking in the mirror, I would think that I didn't exist!" My throat is seared with the effort of a straining pitch.

"I am sorry, Abbe. I'll do better, I promise. I'm over the worst of this flu bug and have some energy to do my share around here." As if doing his share is the answer to all the unnamed things that stand between us.

He gets up and pulls me into his arms. "Come on, cheer up. When I come back from the office, I promise I will help clean up and do a load of laundry."

My tirade is not about to be petted back into its kennel. "But I thought you were going to take the day off." I muffle away into his shirt and the smells of day-old cologne, and he hugs me tighter.

"You're right. Just let me make a few calls, then."

The words and fever drift away like the spray off easterly blown waves.

We feel the clamp around our thighs as Cleo joins our embrace and all is forgiven. "Jesus says, 'Love one another,' " she recites. And I rub her head and say, "That's right, darling, and we love one another by being nice to each other."

"And kind," she adds, the litany complete.

"And kind," I agree, seeing the little old church ladies vaporize.

Cleo makes patterns on her place mat with the cereal I give her while I load the dishwasher. "You got plans for the day?" Greg asks.

"I promised Mrs. Scribner I would take her to the hairdresser around eleven."

"You're not required to do that, you know; it's not in the Preacher's Wife Manual, is it?"

"That's not why I do it."

"I know, I know. You're recruiting for the Abbe Deighton Lonely Hearts Club."

"Go ahead and mock me; see how funny it is when you are all alone one day with no one to listen to your clever ideas and laugh at your lame jokes. See how you like it when your idea of companionship is when the cable guy comes to sell you channels you don't want."

"I hope you're not trying to tell me something," he jests.

"I am being serious. It's not just that she's lonely; it's that she's treated like an outsider and I can't stand that."

"Abbe, no one lets her in because she's crazy and she smells bad."

"It's not funny, Greg. She's doing her best just to hang on; the least we can do is give her some small encouragement not to let go."

" 'We' meaning me, you mean?" Suddenly Greg's tone is defensive.

"No, that's not what I mean," I protest, although I do not think it would hurt Greg's ratings, ailing as they are, to spend less time at the office and more time in the field, so to speak.

"Okay, so I guess you don't want me to call in sick for you?" he asks, and I shake my head. "All right, then. 'The time has come, the Walrus said,' " he quotes, heading for the front door.

"What walrus, Mommy?" asks Cleo.

"Dad means he's going to check whether our new roof kept the garage dry."

The two-car garage and workshop, up until a couple of days ago, functioned alternately as a cistern and a sieve, seldom as a dry shelter for the car. It has been patched so many times that instead of being flat it sagged in the middle so that the birds bathed atop while buckets were positioned beneath it. We made do with buckets until Greg had the gumption to ask his mother for a small loan to help pay for a new roof. He insisted it was a loan, but I am the one who pays the bills each month and who notices that there is never a little row of numbers on our bank statement we can theoretically call "savings," or which can go toward reducing our indebtedness and my mother-in-law's righteousness. We will not be able to pay her back the two thousand dollars for roofing materials, just as we have not been able to pay back the airplane tickets for the family get-together last Christmas or her contribution to the down payment on our house. Not unless the church decides to pay its minister a salary roughly comparable to that of a car dealer. Maybe that is what Greg should consider doing: trade in Jesus and start selling Jaguars to aging symphony supporters. Bet he would have more takers than he does now.

I am picturing Greg taking the elderly for test drives when he skulks back into the house, slamming the door behind him. He collapses on the couch with an exclamation: "We should have hired professionals!"

"It didn't work?" I ask. Jakes and a friend recently paroled from prison just spent two days reroofing the garage. "A piece of cake," they had said.

Greg shakes his head. "It's worse."

Of the two of us, it is typically me who holds the glass-is-half-full policy, so when my husband makes understatements, as infuriating as they often are, they always give me a measure of hope because things seldom turn out to be as bad as he assesses them to be. Just how bad can a bad moon be, I wonder, charging out to the garage to see. The smell of damp and mold is overpowering when I open the door, and then I notice little tidal pools everywhere: between Greg's tools, next to the storage closet, around the car. What used to be water-stained ceiling tiles is now mush the consistency of porridge on the roof and windshield of our car, and on the tool bench. Water is being siphoned through the garage door opener. Turds are floating around in the cat tray. Two thousand dollars washed away. Two. Thousand. Dollars. I look up where the ceiling once was and see right through to its exposed underbelly, where it is still leaking although the rain abated hours ago.

Walking out of what will soon be a rust heap, I head for the ladder still propped up against the wall on the south side. Before I mount it, I spot at the head of the pathway next to our mailbox a small yellow box. What on earth? When I approach it, I can tell that it is a box of sandwich bags, and adjacent to it lies one of its bags sealed with something in it. Crouching down, I pick up the bag, and it suddenly becomes apparent what its contents are: dog turds.

I look around. There are no neighbors out on this drizzly morning, not that there ever are, but for a moment I think perhaps someone must have dropped the parcel while walking their dog. That is before I remember that no one walks a dog with a box of Ziploc bags. In fact, no one walks a dog around our neighborhood association, a little cul-de-sac of six homes ruled as though it were East Berlin. Certainly not since Mrs. Chung, the Kaiser, bolted billboard-sized NO TRESPASSING signs to the entry of the private driveway the day after I gave the homeless guy who sleeps on the bus stop bench (West Berlin) some food. It can only be one person. Kaiser Chung!

"Do you know what this is?" I spit, holding high the offending bag as I barge back into the house. Greg lifts his head from the back of the couch, and before he can answer I say, "Dog shit, Greg. It's dog shit!"

I hear a sharp intake of air. "Mommy, you said a bad word." Cleo is anxious to inspect my parcel, while Greg looks at me uncomprehendingly. I march over to the phone, flip through to the back of my address book where the association's homeowners are listed by last name and telephone number. Punching the numbers, I feel the scorching move from the back of my throat into my lungs as I prepare to address the president of the association.

Her answering machine comes on after four rings, after four separate speeches have blazed a trail through my mind. "You have reached the Chung residence. You may leave a brief message after the third beep," cackles Mrs. Chung's scratchy voice. I hang up and dial Gillian

Beech's number. "God bless," she answers before the phone has completed its first ring.

"Gillian, Abbe here from across the way. You got any idea why I have a bag of dog excrement and a box of Ziplocs by my mailbox?"

"Oh, dear Lord. I told her not to do it, but she has been complaining about your dog for weeks." Gillian doesn't need to name the specific "she" to whom she refers; it is pronounced as a proper noun, thereby confirming my suspicion: Mrs. Chung. "She's upset about him—ahem—defecating on her front lawn. I told her to just talk to you about it, that we are all mature Christians, amen?"

"Gillian, our dog is enclosed in a yard. It's our lawn he *shits* on," I say, choosing a word I know will set Gillian's sanctified soul on edge.

"Yes, well, she's very upset."

"You know she is mad at me because I won't stop giving Mr. Tom food."

"Yes. Well. She feels that this sort of thing encourages the, um, how shall we say? The undesirable element. And most of us agree. You did receive the memo about the spate of burglaries, didn't you?"

I ignore her question. "The only undesirable element in this neighborhood as far as I'm concerned is a busybody who tries to pass herself off as a do-gooder."

"Might I suggest we pray about this—" Gillian begins, but I cut her off.

"You tell her that she can gossip all she likes about my dog and his bowel movements, but the next time she so much as puts a toe on my property I'll have her cited for trespassing and she can see how it feels. Oh, and you can tell her, since she's so intent on preserving excrement, that I am returning this particular sample to her for safekeeping."

"Well, I think it best—" Gillian begins, but I hang up before she gets any further.

Greg is still sitting on the couch when I get back from depositing the offending materials on Mrs. Chung's doorstep. "How can it be leaking worse after a new roof?" I demand. He stands up, retrieves the newspaper from the table, and heads for the bathroom. "Good question!" he says.

Why is he not making calls? I wonder. Why is he not dressed, keys in hand, ready to drive to somebody's house and give them hell? There seems to be no apparent plan of action, which I find intolerable, even with a head cold.

"Greg! What are we going to do?" I ask, standing at the closed bathroom door.

"I don't know," is his muffled reply.

"Can you call the roofing company?"

"They are going to tell me that there is nothing wrong with the product and blame the installers."

"Well, whose fault is it?"

"I don't know." His sigh is audible.

"Aren't you going to call Jakes?" I persist, sounding even to my own ears as though Greg were to blame.

"Give me a minute, okay?" he says.

I am about to remind him that two thousand dollars has just gone down the toilet when Cleo nudges me.

"Mommy, can you fix her?" she asks. Barbie's head is in one hand and her body in the other. This is exactly what I feel like doing to someone, definitely my neighbor, possibly Jakes, increasingly my husband.

"Not right now, Cleo. Daddy and I are talking," I say.

"But Mommy, she has an owie."

"I said, not now," I reply.

The toilet flushes and Greg reemerges. "Abbe, just calm down."

Which is what does it. The argument is explosive and brief, and Greg picks up Cleo, who begins to cry, and takes her and the decapitated Barbie out to the garden. Upstairs, I slam the bedroom door, take two slugs from the NyQuil bottle, and get into bed. Pulling the covers over my head, I do the arithmetic, but every calculation ends with us further in the red.

IT IS PAST NOON when I wake up, my cheek damp in the pool of drool on my pillow. My eyes are swollen and my head feels thick with fur, but I get up just as the guilt seeps through my feet like the chill of cold cement. Downstairs, I follow Cleo's happy tune outside. Greg is sitting on the porch swing watching her take his nappy Russian hat for a ride in the doll's stroller.

"Don't leave that on the ground, Cleo, or Solly will chew it," I call to her. "Hi," I croak at Greg. "Hungry?"

"You just missed Cheerios and ice cream." He smiles, and in this small exchange we acknowledge each other's white flags.

"Mommy!" Cleo rushes over and hugs my knees. "We don't eat boogers," she announces.

"No, we don't."

"We don't hit," she adds. "And we don't say 'stupid.' "

"That's right."

"It's not polite." Her list of commandments is an attempt to cheer me up, and they do, even though I know she will break at least two of them before sundown. She rushes off, pleased with my improved mood.

"You get your calls made?" I ask.

"Some of them. And I called Mrs. Scribner to tell her you were sick," he says.

I nod my gratitude. "I thought if I just lay down for a few minutes . . ."

"We'll get it sorted out," he assures me.

"Mrs. Scribner's hair or the roof?"

"The roof is probably easier, don't you think?"

"You're terrible," I say, lifting his hand and putting it on the back of my neck.

"Thank you, thank you very much."

HEATING UP last night's spaghetti for lunch, I pick up the kitchen phone, do the math to calculate California time, dial my brother's number, and turn on the TV with the volume down low. Oprah is interviewing a sad, white-haired middle-aged man. Members of the audience are crying.

"Spenser residence," is my brother's clipped answer.

"Oh good, I'm glad I caught you," I say.

"Sounds as if you caught something worse than me."

"It's a cold. It's Greg's fault—he passed it on to us."

"Hey, I know it has been a month since you asked me for those photos, and I apologize for being such a sloth. I haven't forgotten; I will get up in the attic and look for those boxes this weekend, I promise." Rhiaan is my last living relative and the self-appointed family archivist. Apart from my grandmother's farm, about all we have left of our family heritage are those boxes of photos that were once at the bottom of my mother's closet.

"Keep your knickers on. That's not why I'm calling."

"So to what, then, do I owe the privilege?" Rhiaan always pretends it is my fault we do not communicate more regularly, but the fact is, when I do call it is often to be told by Cicely that he has requested not to be disturbed.

"I want to talk about the farm."

"At last you want to sell it," he guesses.

"Do you always have to know what I'm thinking before I do?"

"I do—it's my job."

"We need the money," I confess, picturing him cringing.

To his credit, he refrains from offering assistance from his own coffers. "I don't know how much a fifteen-acre farm in Paarl is worth these days. A lot more if it were closer to Cape Town, I suspect. And the exchange rate isn't exactly in our favor, but I should think it would add up to a couple hundred thousand dollars all told. Would that do it?"

"It would, but you don't think the curse—"

"Abbe! No one takes curses seriously, certainly not real estate agents. I think you should call the trustee, what's his name?"

"Slabbert."

"Right. Call Slabbert, tell him to put the word out there. Tell him to set the price high and see if anyone nibbles."

"And the kids?" My grandmother's farmhouse, abandoned for years after her death, is now the venue for a group of orphaned African children to learn things they will probably never live long enough to apply. Almost all of them contracted HIV/AIDS from their mothers.

"The school was never supposed to be a permanent deal, you know that. This will force them to find a proper school instead of a dilapidated farmhouse. For all we know the Department of Health is probably trying to shut it down anyway."

"So you are all for it?"

"I'm never going back there, if that is what you are asking. And I don't imagine you will either, will you?"

"No."

"Then there you are. Go for it. In my opinion we have hung on to it for too long. It's time. It's more than time."

"Rhiaan?"

"Hmm?"

"Thank you."

"What for?"

"For always looking out for me."

"*Si vales valeo*: If you are well, then I am well."

Before I hang up, I ask if he is writing again.

"Just a slightly immovable writer's block to deal with first. Nothing a bottle of Glenlivet and my wife's undaunted cheer won't cure. But you take care of that cold now—let the preacher take care of you for a while. And give that gifted niece of mine a well-appointed Snoopy kiss."

After hanging up, I turn up the TV's volume. The white-haired man is the author of *Under Currents*, the true-life story of a freak boating accident off the coast of Maine that cost him the lives of both his sons, his marriage, and his career in the attorney general's office. The strangest thing, he remarks, is that his wife told him not to take the boys out sailing that day, even though the weather was the finest it had been in a month. "She didn't have a premonition, or a bad dream," he explains to the talk show host. "She didn't even say that she thought something would go wrong. She simply asked me not to go. 'Don't take the boys out today,' she said, but I didn't listen. The boys didn't even say goodbye to her, they just waved from the truck."

"Do you believe in omens?" Oprah asks.

Just then Pilgrim yowls from somewhere below the kitchen window, which sets off all the neighborhood dogs and sends an electric current of fright through my body. I rush out the back door and down the path to the gazebo, calling him to stop because his quarreling sounds like the tortured cries of a frightened baby. Just then I see the offending streak of black fur run out from under the gazebo and into the safe confines of Mrs. Chung's yard, and the superstitious flash of bad luck prickles my skin.

"Pilgrim, get in the house!" I scold our tribal tabby with his bottle-brush tail and ears pinned low, emerging triumphant. "You're too old for this!"

I look up when I hear the low growling of the heavens and see the dark clouds pulling together again over the mountains. Another storm.

"Can I watch TV?" Cleo asks when I get back in the kitchen. There is a commercial for laxatives, and I know there is no chance I can go back to the show.

"No, love," I say, "TV rots your brain."

"What's a brain, Abbe?"

"Cleo, don't call me Abbe, call me Mommy."

"But I like to call you Abbe."

"Yes, but nobody else can call me Mommy—only you; it's a very special name for me. And a brain is something that makes you smarter than your silly cat, who doesn't know that he is too old to be getting in fights."

"Fighting is bad," she says.

"It is indeed."

"Can I watch TV, just for five minutes?" she asks, but I pretend not to hear.

"Just two minutes, Abbe?" she implores.

For one horrible moment, I think my "Okay" is going to come out like Pilgrim's screech, but Greg walks in and hands me the largest red hibiscus I have ever seen, so instead it ends up like the gush of air from a deflating balloon.

While Cleo watches a purple dinosaur lead a bunch of one-dimensional children around a cardboard yard, I fold laundry at the dining room table. I cannot stop thinking about the father and the tragedy that made his hair turn white. What's a couple thousand dollars, a roof that leaks, a few rusty tools? I live in a house on a hillside of Honolulu with a daughter who recites Scripture and a husband who doesn't beat me. So what if he is the constant, peripheral blip on my radar to which I seldom steer? Is it really that bad that we have lost sight of each other over the great swell of laundry, the never-ending chatter of a demanding child, a mound of bills, and the plight of a declining, fussy congregation? There are worse things than tedium; just ask the man with white hair. Tedium, it seems, can be remedied, perhaps with as little as one earnest dollop of will and a smudge of lipstick. Throw in the pair of strappy silver high heels and we just might have the makings of a stellar night out. It might just be all it takes.

Putting away thoughts of perished sons entombed in the wintry waters off the coast of Maine, I send a hasty e-mail to the executor of my grandmother's estate and then reach for the phone. It is Jenny's number I am first inclined to dial. Cleo's godmother and the first among my friends would have been more than happy to babysit a few months ago, but lately she has complained of backaches and fatigue. Even so, I can't help but wonder if she is standoffish because of our differences on the matter of disciplining Cleo. Jenny, having the clear advantage of being both parent and teacher, issues advice as if the world of parenting were always black and white. My problem, she reported at the New Year's party after we all had just endured one of Cleo's fits, was that I "didn't follow through." I knew better than to argue, especially after all the champagne, and I certainly knew better than to cast aspersions on her expertise, but dammit, why did it always have to be *my* fault? On the way home in the car, Greg had said my lecture to her "was uncalled-for," and I knew it, which is why I called her the next day to apologize. Of course she forgave me, but her back has been sore ever since.

Now is not the time for another one of Jenny's excuses, so I call Theresa instead. She answers after five rings and instead of saying hello I hear her holler, "You made that mess, you clean it up or, so help me God, your ass and my hand are going to have a tête-à-tête!"

"Teaching the children French now, are we?" I tease.

"What's up, *tita?*" She laughs, and I hear her take a deep drag on a cigarette. I am the palest of all my friends by several palette shades, scrawny by comparison with her, and certainly far from the picture of what comes to mind when locals refer to women as *titas*. Theresa, by virtue of her size, is entitled to call me—or anyone else—whatever she wishes. A hair shy of six feet, she makes dwarves of her friends. She is built like a swimmer although she has never learned to swim, and when she dances with her husband, Jakes, it is often she who leads. Still, she is by no means a tomboy. Theresa favors dangly earrings, polished nails, and outrageous handbags. She is the only one of us who wears makeup, often adding to her ample cheeks a neatly appointed beauty spot. "Hey," she adds, "I liked your article in the magazine on the *mahu*. I think I recognized a few of my cousins!"

Theresa is Samoan but is on what she calls "a self-imposed exile from the tribe" because, she says, "they are all stupid," by which she means the old customs cramp her style somewhat. Her exile has involved marriage to Jakes, Annie Lennox–length hair, a wardrobe sans muumuus, and children who do not know the tongue of their parents' land. When she removes her small oval spectacles and ties her T-shirt (WILL TRADE HUSBAND FOR WINE) into a knot above her belly button, she is quite beautiful. Never the shrinking violet, Theresa dances at parties that are meant to be sit-down affairs and breaks into song after as few as two mai tais. Her mother, who has imported Samoan culture all the way from their little island in the South Pacific to Theresa's cramped semidetached in Kalihi, shakes her head and mumbles every time Theresa wears her white Bermuda shorts to church. Wearing shorts to church? Her mother should be lucky she shows up at all.

"Can you watch Cleo tonight for two or three hours? I want to take Greg out to a movie," I ask.

"Sure!" she croons. "Going to fool around with the preacher man, are you?" Theresa told Jenny and me that after sixteen years of marriage and three kids, she and Jakes still have sex every night. We have made allowances, therefore, for her one-track-mindedness, and try not to stare at Jakes at every church potluck.

"Fat chance! Can I bring her by at six-thirty?" I ask. "I'll feed her first."

"No, no, we're having pizza tonight, bring her for dinner."

"You're the best."

"That's what Jakie says!"

"By the way, tell him the roof leaked and to come by when he has a free moment."

"You know, I swear that man is good for one thing, and one thing only! Oh hell, I've got to go, the boys are having a food fight!"

I hang up and look for Greg, who is in the garage cleaning up the mess.

"We're going out tonight. I'll pick you up at six!" I tell him.

He is surprised, and a bit pleased. "What's the occasion?"

"You and me being an old married couple, that's what," I say. "Theresa's going to watch Cleo."

"Can we sit in the back row and make out?"

"Only during the trailers," I say.

It is six-thirty when I pack down the layers of tulle of Cleo's pink tutu so that I can buckle her seat belt. "We're late!" I snap as Greg lifts up the garage door.

"Mommy, it's okay, don't be mad," Cleo says. Immediately chastised, I take my seat and give myself the mental talk about not sabotaging the fun before it has started.

"I'll get you there in time for the trailers," smiles Greg as he pats my knee and backs out of the garage. I have to unbuckle my belt, get out, and pull the door down manually. I glance over at Mrs. Chung's front doorstep and notice the box of Ziplocs and the bag of dog turds are gone, but as we drive past the house the blinds of her living room window swing slightly from where she has no doubt been peeping. The storm clouds fold over the hills again and the town below looks like it needs to be wrung out.

The island is least appealing when it is overcast. When the sun is shining and the cartoon clouds cast big shadows on the evergreen mountains, Hawaii has the most chance of living up to its reputation.

You can overlook the congested neighborhood streets where the single-wall construction houses have given up even elbow room. You can put up with the potholed roads, the rust-stained buildings, and the crumbling lava-rock walls because just an arm's length away are the brightest rainbows you'll ever see. Crane your neck past the high-rises in Waikiki and you will see an ocean whose colors defy adjectives. Look close enough and you'll see, among the folds of the Pali Mountains, ribbons of waterfalls. But on damp days like these, there's no masking the deterioration, no sun to keep at bay the creeping edges of third-world neglect.

The worst of it is summed up on the street where Theresa lives. Downhill from us, wedged in the valley, is River Street. A misnomer, it is nothing like the picture its name conjures. No quaint plantation houses with sprawling backyards sloping down to a willow-tree-lined stream. Just cramped shacks jammed in a one-way lane that dead-ends by a ditch filled only with litter and a few old tires. Not even a trickle, even after the rains. It is a shantytown street hiding behind the store-fronts of Mr. Woo's Laundromat and Phuong-Thai Takeout. River Street is the back-alley neighborhood that could have been imported from District Six or Soweto. The slouched bodies that stand in the doorways are not black, however, but mostly Asian. The slope of their shoulders and the weary looks of hopelessness are the same as those of township people, ghetto people, people hanging on by their finger-nails.

Greg stops the car in the middle of the street because there is no parking place at house number 121, a house the size of our soggy garage, a house with two front doors. 121B is open, and on the front step that doubles as a porch is Theresa's daughter Tess hanging over the railing. She sees us and with a sticky hand pushes back the sweaty black strands of hair from her face and cries out, "Hi, Cleo!"

I follow Cleo up the stairs and watch the two girls embrace. Cleo, a year younger than Tess, is the same height. They examine each other's outfits and immediately exchange shoes. When Cleo insists on wearing the frilly pink dress Tess refuses to take off, a scuffle ensues. I begin insisting Cleo mind her manners, but Theresa sweeps Cleo into her arms, twirls her high in the air, and says, "Come, now, a princess like you needs something with a bit more pizzazz, don't you think? Come look what Auntie Theresa bought for you today." She latches Cleo to her hip and reaches for the shopping bag on the couch. When Cleo peers in, she exclaims with delight.

"I want to try it on!" She grins.

Theresa winks at me.

"Thank you," I say.

She shakes her head. "You just go have a good time now, you hear, and don't be rushing back."

"We won't be later than nine-thirty," I promise. "Greg's got to get up for Good Friday. You coming to the service?"

"Nah, too morbid for me. I'll go to both services on Easter to make up for it, how's that?"

"Deal."

"Go, already!" she orders me out.

I bend down. "Cleo, have fun; be a good girl, okay? And remember to put your hand over your mouth when you cough. Now give me a kiss." But she ignores me. "Kiss?" Instead, she takes Theresa's hand and asks her to help her put on the dress.

"Bye, baby!" I yell out the window of the car, but the two girls are already immersed in the world of princesses and monsters and purple nail polish. I roll up the window and Greg and I are sealed in air-conditioned silence, suddenly strangers.

"Got your sermon ready for tomorrow?" I ask.

"Oh, I guess. Nobody wants to hear much about executions just two days before Easter. Theresa coming?"

"Nope."

"See what I mean?"

Greg pretends he isn't perpetually disappointed with his flock, even though it doesn't afford him the same courtesy. Continuing its decline in membership and income, the church has started to look for a scapegoat, and the pastor who had been packaged and delivered to them with such promise has become the obvious candidate. Greg's defense, if he had the will to offer it, would be to point out the congregation's lukewarm commitment to the faith, its country-club approach to the Gospel, its cut-and-paste theology. Instead, he has increased the church's budget, sparking severe rows over a spending deficit, so while the budget continues to grow like a fatted calf, it seems Greg is all but taking a knife to his own throat.

Even though what would suit Greg more is a position in headquarters, something requiring the production of surveys and charts and reports with words like "strategy" and "benchmark," he should, in my opinion, be putting up more of a fight. Or if not a fight, then at least a show. Instead, each Sunday morning, when he preaches to more vacant pews than occupied ones, I can see him straining and stumbling through his sermon as though lugging the deadweight of a gargantuan corpse behind him, not an inspiring picture of the Body of Christ. The congregation's routine lack of enthusiasm is perfectly suited for only one service a year: Good Friday. It's ironic that no more than a dozen will attend tomorrow.

We do not speak again until we are at the theater, and then only to debate briefly the options. The romantic comedy wins and we take our seats, several rows from the back. Greg reaches for my hand, and for one bizarre moment I feel like grabbing his face and kissing him with the zeal of a sixteen-year-old.

It is a silly movie, and it ends with all the predictable charm of apple pie à la mode. For two hours we have pretended to be lovers on a date, a feeling that is remotely familiar. "We should do this more often," says Greg as we make our way back to the car.

"We should kiss more often," I say, and immediately regret it because it sounds like an accusation.

"Like this?" Greg kisses the way he shaves, the way he first prepares, then delivers, sermons. Meticulously. And there is nothing wrong with a meticulous kiss, but it is a dirty kiss the day calls for, and only when I smother his best intentions with a mouth bent on foul play is he aroused.

"A brazen hussy," he says. "Want to come to my place and see my etchings?"

"Why not?" I answer.

The car clock says 9:25 when Greg starts the ignition.

"We're going to be late," I observe.

"You say that too much."

The roads are shiny with rain and the windshield wipers flip-flap against the downpour.

"Think she's asleep?" asks Greg. Neither of us wants to think about the roof and what the garage will look like when we get home.

"Wired, more like it."

I check the time at every red light and stop sign.

At 9:52 we turn onto River Street, and even before we reach their home I can tell something is wrong. Lights are on in all the houses and every door is open, like gaping mouths. People are standing in groups under umbrellas on either side of the road, and they stare like deer at our approaching headlights.

"Greg?" I frown, feeling the lurch in my chest.

On the porch of 121B, Theresa's mother stands with Tess on her hip. The child looks frightened while the old woman keeps watch, stroking her hair rigorously. A police car blocks the street and an officer is talking to the Korean woman who lives at 121A. Something is very wrong. And among all these faces I notice only one missing: Cleo's.

TWO

I am out the car before Greg has stopped it completely, trip-ping up the stairs to the old woman.

"Where's Cleo?" I ask, panic swelling in my throat. "What happened?" I look into her shrunken eyes, but she can only shake her head.

"WHAT, for chrissake?" I shout, but the officer is next to me now and asks, "Reverend and Mrs. Deighton?"

Ignoring him, I clutch at the old woman, and Tess begins to wail while Greg steps around me and says, "Yes?"

Theresa's mother moves her mouth, garbling sounds I cannot un-derstand. Impulsively, my hand rises to slap her because I think she is hysterical, when from behind me the words "accident" and "car" and "hospital" embed themselves in my flesh like leeches. I swing around to the officer, who has taken off his hat, and cover my own mouth. "No, nononononono . . ." I shriek, and turn wildly wanting to run.

Greg grabs me. "Get in the car, Abbe, the policeman's going to take us to the hospital." A uniformed hand holds open the back door and I tumble into what seems like a black hole. As the siren begins to wail, it is into this deep chasm that I begin to pray. "Please, God, please, please let her be okay." The faces lining the streets are hollow.

The robotic voice on the car radio reports that Cleo has been moved from the emergency room to the ICU. I clutch Greg's hand and squeeze it hard. I look into his face, white with shock, searching for his assurance—she's in the ICU, that's good, right? She'll be okay, won't she? But he says nothing, eyes locked ahead, the desperate expression of a man with his head held underwater by an invisible hand.

The police car's digital clock blinks 10:06 when we pull into the emergency room parking lot.

Maundy Thursday, I think suddenly, the night Jesus went up to the olive orchard lit by a pale moon to pray. *Remove this cup from me.* The night his closest friends fell asleep after they dutifully promised to keep watch. There is no moon when we step out of the police car and into the bright light of the Queen's Medical Center foyer. But I need Beauty to walk out into the dark and retrieve from its bowels the offerings that will turn a bad moon good.

We run down a long, sterile corridor to the elevators. I stand and look at the round numerals light up: 8, 7, 6. A century goes by before the vault doors open, another universe collapses on itself before they close. The fourth floor is deserted, and we run down another hallway, heading for the double doors with a sign saying AUTHORIZED PER-SONNEL ONLY.

"Cleo Deighton," Greg says to the male nurse behind the desk. "Where is she?"

"Mr. and Mrs. Deighton?" he asks, to which we both nod. "She has just been taken down to the OR. Let me call one of the physicians to come and talk to you."

"Please," Greg says, reaching across the table and grabbing his arm before it can reach the receiver. "How is she?"

The man, plump and rosy-cheeked, looks around for help. Seeing no one, he smooths his hair and replies in a soft voice, "She has sustained significant brain trauma and loss of blood from an aortic tear. She's in critical condition, I am afraid, but we have managed to stabilize her blood pressure so the surgeon can operate." He looks at Greg. "I am sorry, but you will have to talk to the attending physician to find out more."

"Jesus, oh Jesus," I whisper, trying to assemble Cleo with "brain trauma" and "aortic tear."

"Where is she?" Greg asks.

"Second floor. There is a waiting room on the left when you come out the elevator. I will call the OR and let them know you are here. There is a couple already down there—the people who came in with her."

In my recurring nightmare, I am required to dial 911 but keep getting the numbers mixed up. Such a simple task, yet one I find impossible to complete. It is into this dream Greg and I now lurch, hoping to find our daughter in a hospital of endless corridors. The second floor is quiet, dimly lit, and abandoned except for the waiting room, which we race by without noticing.

"Pastor," calls Jakes. He has completely filled the doorway with his broad tattooed frame, jet-black hair pulled back in a paisley bandanna. "Pastor Greg, it's terrible," he says, and starts to weep as they embrace. "Abbe, I am so sorry," he says, breaking from Greg's arms to hold me. Without waiting for the question, he begins to explain, in gushes, what happened. The girls had just finished eating their pizza when they went out to the porch. Theresa went to the sink to wash the Cinderella dress, upon which Cleo had spilled her soda. Jakes had just walked to the fridge for a drink and was returning to the living room when he saw a flash of pale skin whiz down the front steps, out from under the porch light into the dark night. The pale naked body he saw, not the yellow kite that had caused its pursuit. He had called to her, he says, and walked to the screen door in time to see her squeeze through the two parked cars and dart into the road, where the kite's short-lived flight had come to an end.

"The guy hit his brakes . . ." Jakes says, and does not finish his sentence. "The others are in the chapel praying, got to just keep praying." He shakes his head and moves back into the room and over to the left-hand corner by the fish tank where he kneels. *Stay awake and pray that you may not come into the time of trial.* No sooner have these familiar words run across my mind when from the ceiling come the words, "All personnel, OR2, Code Blue, Code Blue."

. . .

"WHERE IS MY DAUGHTER?" I cry, long before the two coats reach us. One of them is Cleo's pediatrician, Dr. Demalka, her Dutch skin almost translucent in the fluorescent light. The first person to weigh Cleo, to measure her head, to count her toes and fingers. Who only two months ago gave her a fistful of stickers for being so brave at the annual checkup for putting up with four shots without crying. Her face looks zipped up, tight; she is not the doctor we know. I see her nod at the gray-haired man next to her and suddenly I am deeply afraid of her. Don't say it. Don't tell me. Don't speak. God, don't say a word.

"Reverend and Mrs. Deighton," the other coat says.

We are two tall trees now, Greg and I, root-bound in a pot of rotting soil, bending and straining toward the other but not quite touching, waiting for the ax to find its mark.

"I am very sorry," Dr. Demalka says. "We did everything we could. She didn't make it."

"Don't say that, don't say that, DON'T SAY THAT!" I scream. Somebody is holding my arms, I cannot tell who. The narrow tunnel of focus fixed on Dr. Demalka's face becomes a dark, yawning cave. With my hand on the wall steadying me, I manage to ask, "Where is she?" The cavernous night from the plains of Africa rolls out in front of me, pinpricks of light filling my eyes. "Don't touch me, let go! Get your fucking hands OFF ME!" They belong to Greg.

"God, God, God," he keeps repeating, crying, through the sobs. He lets go. The floor is cool where my forehead bends to meet it, while a pool of tears collects in front of my knees: "No, no, no, no."

"Where is she? Where is my daughter!" Greg demands somewhere above me. *They have taken my Lord and I do not know where they have laid him*, says the voice inside my head, and I am all the Marys aching to hold the stolen body.

Somebody lifts me and we pass the crowd of mourners standing outside the waiting room. One of the heads turns to watch us as we pass, a hand pressed against her mouth. It takes two blinks to recognize her: Theresa, held up by Jakes on one side and Jenny on the other. They all look like they have just awoken, eyes rubbed red from sleep and shame, aware that they have failed in only one simple thing: to keep watch.

It is into a room with glass walls that we are led. The tomb is dimly lit. Cleo is lying on a narrow bed, a white blanket pulled to her chin as if to ward off the chill in the air. Greg reaches under her, lifts her into his arms, and settles her into his lap on the floor. Kneeling next to him, I lean over to stroke away the blond curls and kiss her white forehead, feeling the last beams of sunlight retreat. A deep, long moan covers the air and Greg begins chanting her name.

"Give her to me," I tell him. "She's getting cold."

"Don't hold her," he whispers, shaking his head. "Baby, don't hold her."

And then I know he is trying to save me from something awful, the evidence that some terrible monster in the night, the Tokoloshe from the veldt, crawled under the sheet and robbed Cleo of her body.

"Let me have her," I insist.

∾

THEY WERE THE SAME HANDS that held Cleo, bundled and quiet, up to my face three years ago. She was only minutes old, but already she seemed wise. "This is your mommy," he said to her. "Mommy, this is Cleo." Arms strapped to the operating table, body numb from the anesthetic, I looked at my child, swaddled in white, and croaked a teary "Hi." No more than a whisper away, she peered at me through the oint-ment-clouded eyes, and in the haziness of the new world I knew she recognized me. Maybe it was the sound of that hushed greeting in a voice as familiar as the inside of a womb, perhaps the invisible cord that tied us together so that no words were necessary, no sight.

So light she was when I held her for the first time hours later, after the incision was stitched neatly together and the spasms and retching of the drugs had subsided, long after the emergency equipment had been packed away. So light. Yet the weight of her tiny frame made an indeli-ble mark on me, like an embosser on rice paper. I let her sleep on my chest for hours, sending the nurses and their concerns back to their station. My anchor she was, securing me to the settled moment of the rise and fall of my chest, to the soft purr of her snoring, to the perfectly populated world of two.

❧

"WAKE UP, wake up, wake up, darling," I beg, tucking the blanket around her, frowning at what now feels like crushed eggshells where a firm hip used to be. My anchor has been wrenched loose and I am adrift.

"What have they done? Greg, what have they done to her?" I ask, but he is on his feet, anger flashing across his brow as the surgeon returns.

I peer down into her face, the usual flush on her creamy cheeks now gone. Her golden curls are mussed, except for one perfect spring across her brow. I slip one hand under her head, to cup that golden crown one more time, and touch what feels to be caked mud. As her head turns with my palm, I see it is blackened dried blood. Greg's clipped words are running away from him and I hear a voice far away, on the moon, say, "Increased swelling in the brain . . . was stabilized . . . suddenly crashed . . . too late to operate . . . everything we could . . . ," and I think they can leave now, all of them, and Cleo and I will stay here, like the ashy figures of Pompeii.

They drone on, Greg getting louder, the other more apologetic, until I turn around and shush them harshly.

"Tula tu tula baba tula sana, Tul'umam 'uzobuya ekuseni." I begin to sing the African lullaby Beauty once sang to me, rocking my girl as though through a bad dream. *"Sleep, baby, sleep, tomorrow your mommy will be with you again."*

PAST THE DOORWAY I see the others still knotted together, Theresa and Jenny. Sensing my glare, Theresa turns her head, still leaning on Jenny's shoulder, and looks at me. *See, my betrayer is at hand.* She straightens up, lets go of her friend, and across the chasm seems to say something. Her hands clasp together—are they begging or praying? I swing back to Cleo as her arm falls from the blanket. That soft hand that used to reach for mine is limp, and her nails are the color of a twilight sky.

"A pianist's fingers," Theresa had said when she and Jenny came to the hospital the day Cleo was born and unwrapped the blanket to examine their prize.

"Save your pennies then, because you're going to help pay for piano lessons," I said.

"She's going to make the world cry one day with her beautiful music," Theresa said.

"Or for writing the next *Gone With the Wind*," I added.

"Whatever she does, she'll make us cry!"

"CAN THEY SEE HER?" Dr. Demalka asks as she enters the room, but before Greg can answer I hiss, "Nobody sees her. Tell them to go home."

Home. My home is gone now. This is home; let the ashes fall from the heavens and settle over us in this sterile, infinite home. Far away there is a wail of an animal caught in a snare. When Greg touches my shoulder, I realize it is me.

Cleo's lower lip is crooked, weighted to the right as it always was when she was asleep or when she was scared. Exactly how it was when she was born.

"Cleo!" I cry, calling into the abyss, calling her back from the void; a loud clear call. "Wake up, Cleo; open your eyes, darling; it's time to go home."

But she has gone to the burial grounds of drowned boys and crucified Lords.

THREE

When Cleo starts to stiffen, face-first, my hold on her relaxes as if it knows that she is more resolute on being dead than on coming back to life. Concrete-cold she is. Greg places her back on the bed, helps me out of the armchair where I have cradled her, arranges for the ride back to the house. I stand for a long time beside her bed, checking still for the briefest flickering of her lashes, unwilling to say goodbye, to walk away, to leave her, as if leaving her again will exact another great price. It is only five steps to the door, and after I have made them I turn around again to watch my daughter, lying as though on an altar. Greg's hand grips my shoulder and suddenly I lean into him, clutching his shirt, the world tilting.

The dark sky at the tip of the horizon is becoming gray, as though the day will wake up to a 1920s black-and-white talkie. A different policeman drives us home, and when he pulls into the small cul-de-sac, I can't imagine why it is that everything looks the same. Even the shaking of Mrs. Chung's blinds where she has stolen a glance. Our garage door is up and someone has parked our car to the left and put buckets to catch the leaks on the right. The officer sees us to the front door, mumbles, and then retreats to the sound of Solly's fierce barking. The front door is unlocked, and a vase of ghost-colored lilies is centered on the telephone table alongside the keys and a note with my name written on it. In the kitchen Jenny is washing yesterday's dishes. I walk into her soapy arms, which fold around me and try to contain the shaking.

Gently, Jenny leads me upstairs and helps me into bed, then hands me Cleo's stuffed rainbow turtle, Tow-Tow, and puts a box of tissues next to my pillow. She opens a small brown paper bag, the sound loud and annoying. I shake my head when she retrieves from it an orange prescription bottle. She puts it down on the nightstand ("If you need it") and reflexively I think about putting it higher, out of Cleo's reach. Instead, I sit up, twist and turn the childproof lid, pop two tiny pills in my mouth, and swallow. When I lie back Jenny picks up the discarded clothes from the chair and begins to fold them. I watch from a few light-years away as she softly pushes drawers back in the bureau, puts strewn jewelry in their boxes, picks up Greg's socks, and tosses them in the laundry basket. Tucking everything away. It is when she bends to the abandoned pair of strappy high heels that I say suddenly, "No." She looks at me and reaches instead for the pantyhose lying next to them. "No," I tell her again. "Just leave them. Please." I want to picture Cleo as she was yesterday morning, clip-clopping around in my shoes, pantyhose pulled on her head, finger pointed in command. Her last morning. I choke on the thought and wish never to awaken to one again.

Sleep does not come, not the sleep I want. Not oblivion. Through the haze of exhaustion, I keep stirring, hearing Cleo sing on the deck outside our bedroom or call to me from her bed. Through lashes weighed down by leaden eyelids, I see her shadow sweeping across the foot of the bed, in hot pursuit of Pilgrim. When my eyes are sealed tight, Cleo is underwater, drifting away like kelp in a current. One time she is climbing into bed with me, patting my face, pressing her nose against mine, but my arms are strapped down and I cannot embrace her.

I do not know what time it is when I get up. Jenny, in keeping with her tradition from Jamaica, has covered the clock on the wall with an old pillowcase. There is a tray of uneaten food next to the bed and crumpled tissues like paper roses strewn around it. I open the blinds and not day but a starless night peers in: an impenetrable curtain that separates me from my mother, my grandmother, and now my child. For a moment I think I might go downstairs, where an amber glow keeps watch and the voices of late-night TV drone on. Greg will be down there, on the couch; Jenny too. The thought of even the most banal verbal exchange makes the dizziness return, so I go pee and climb back into the dark sea.

Day and night blur into an endless gloaming from which I cannot escape, not even with the help of the contents of this little bottle. Has it been a day? A week? A month? The pills are yellow. The color of cowardice, I think as I swallow two more and replace the bottle on the nightstand. Why is the song about a yellow ribbon on the old oak tree? Why do the bumpers of cars have yellow ribbons that say SUPPORT OUR TROOPS on them? Blue ribbons are more appropriate for boys out fighting a war, for the color of their lips and nails when they are zipped up in their body bags. Blue for the code that signals no vital signs, blue for the music of inconsolable lamentation. Yellow is the color of desert sand before the blood of the fallen soaks into it; the color for mommies who cannot get up when their children are stuck in icy drawers in cold cellars. Yellow is the color of bile, the lingering hue of a bruise. The color of a kite.

Blue was always Cleo's favorite color. The first color she learned to name. Cinderella wore a ball gown of the sweetest shade of cerulean blue, a replica of which Cleo wore every other day. In the tiny Catholic chapel at the retreat center where Greg once conducted an ecumenical worship service for those living with HIV/AIDS, she went up to the statue of the Holy Mother and with almost reverence stroked her blue tunic.

"What's her name?" she asked.

"That's Mary, Jesus' mommy," I answered.

"Is she sad?" she wanted to know, glancing up at the Holy Mother with her downcast eyes.

"I'm not sure," I said after a pause.

But I know now. I know that Mary's grief is a thousand fathoms deep, where blue is so dense it becomes black. So vast is her sorrow that she cannot speak but only part her robe and reveal the crimson heart that in its stubbornness will not cease its beat.

"WHAT DAY IS IT?" I ask when I walk into the kitchen, squinting out at the sheets of rain.

"Sunday, honey," says Jenny, cleaning the oven.

It has been two days, then, which makes it Easter Sunday. But there is no resurrection today, the timing is all wrong. I am standing in the midst of the empty tomb, but there is no angel asking, *Why do you look for the living among the dead?* and no gardener calling my name.

"Did you get some sleep?" Jenny asks.

I shrug. "Where's Greg?"

"In the garden," she says. "He hasn't slept much."

"How about you?"

"Here and there," she says, and smiles weakly at me, her coffee-colored face dim.

"Rhiaan called, and someone from your work—he wouldn't leave his name. Also, several people from church. I wrote it all down on the pad. I told them you're not up for company yet."

"Thank you," I say, taking the cup of coffee she has just poured.

"I called most of the people in your address book and a few others Greg made a list of. He called his family."

We sit at the kitchen table and peer into our mugs, silent enough to hear the mynah birds arguing on the porch.

"If you would rather me go home, I will. I don't want to intrude," she says. "I want to do what's helpful."

"No, please don't leave; I'm glad you are here."

We each take an end of the quiet, as though it were a tablecloth that needed laying.

"I wanted to see her," Jenny says finally, looking up. "I wanted to hold her one last time." And suddenly she cries and I realize it is the first time in the ten years we have been friends that I have ever seen her weep. Isn't this the part where I apologize for refusing to allow her to hold Cleo in the hospital? Where I say sorry? She wipes her nose with the back of her wrist, and I picture her sitting at the table holding Cleo in one hand and eating with the other. "She was my baby too."

"Yes," I muster. "Yes, she was."

Everyone wanted a piece of Cleo when she was a baby. The women at the church, young and old, lined up to hold her, passing her from one bosom to the next, leaning into her smell and taking deep breaths. Sylvia Horton almost had one of her hyperventilating spells the Sunday Cleo smiled at her, and ran into the choir room for rehearsal an uncharacteristic ten minutes late. She might not have hurried—only the three old tenors sat there, britches up to their rib cages, gumming their way through the music sheets—the warbly sopranos and altos still lined up to see Cleo smile at them from Jenny's cradling embrace. But Jenny had wanted more than a piece. Maybe it was because her nest was still warm from Leroy's flight to UCLA, her second son to leave the island. Maybe it was because Cleo was the little girl she'd never had.

"The other mother," the women at church called her. Taking leave from her teaching job, Jenny moved into our home the first few weeks of Cleo's life. She gave Cleo her first bath, showing me how to hold her with one hand and wash around the little clothespin attached to Cleo's navel with the other. She prepared an old Jamaican remedy that eased Cleo's colicky cries and gave me herb tea supposedly to make my milk sweeter. Her omnipresence that first month eased our transition from couplet to trinity, and forged a thick-as-blood bond between her and Cleo of which everyone was envious. Even me. After Jenny returned to her own home and went back to teaching her first-graders, she insisted every Friday was her time with the baby. So we would drop Cleo off at her boxy two-bedroom cottage after I had nursed her from both breasts, and go to the mall, aimless and dazed. Cleo-less. Looking at other people's babies and our watches till it was time to pick her up again.

But in the last few months the Friday ritual had ceased. I tried not to chalk it up to the New Year's Eve incident because we had been friends too long for that to change things and also because Jenny started taking care of the retired high school principal who had first hired her twenty-five years ago, taking a risk on a poorly educated but keen Jamaican girl running from her past. Now the old man, living alone and without family to help him, was forgetting to eat and bathe, and lucky for him, Jenny was a believer in repaying debts. Five nights a week she walked to Mr. Finnegan's house on the slope of Diamond Head, finding him often naked and disoriented, sometimes soiled, in his leather chair. She helped him wash, cooked him a modest meal, and then read Dickens or Auden till he settled enough to go to sleep. Then she walked back home and waited for the ritual to repeat itself the next day.

The worn look of a housemaid had etched itself on Jenny's face since then. Her mother's face, she had told Theresa and me a few weeks ago, stared out from her bathroom mirror each morning, and her mother's back began to make her limp almost imperceptibly. "Hey, girl, if that's all you inherited from your mom, you got off light," I had told her. The doctor told her otherwise: she was not to lift anything heavier than ten pounds, no children. What he had not told her was the effect the carrying out of his orders was to have on Cleo. Cleo began to miss riding on Jenny's hip, and would frequently beg to go to Jenny's house. Just last week I had called. "When can Cleo come visit?" I asked. "She's nagging me about going to your house."

"I can't do this weekend, Abbe. My back is acting up something terrible," she said. "How about next weekend?"

"Okay," I said, feeling as though into my cupped hands a copper coin had fallen.

And that is why when Jenny sits opposite me at the dining room table across the stack of unopened cards and talks to me of "my baby" that I come close to grabbing her arm and clawing my way through the layers of flesh and fat to the bone. It is your fault, I want to say. You and your crooked back! Next weekend never came and now there would be no next weekends! You, who hand-stitched her baptism gown and took her up to the chancel while Greg murmured holy words and sprinkled ordinary water, are to blame too!

"It's my fault," she suddenly confesses, as though she had read my mind.

"What?"

"The night before the accident, I woke up and saw a woman standing in the corner of my room. I asked her who she was and she just stood there and pointed to the picture of Cleo on my dressing table. Oh dear Lord, Abbe, it must have been Cleo's grandmother. She was coming to warn me, but I didn't listen."

Without saying a word, I get up from the table and go to the shelves in the laundry room, from where I retrieve the old photo album of my family. A chill pricks my skin. I return to the table and open it to the first page, where a young bride, unsmiling, stands next to a surly boar of a man on the steps of the Cape Town courthouse. Chosen to conceal the swell of her belly, her outfit is as stiff as their pose. Jenny hesitates, then shakes her head. "No, not her."

It is the barking that startles me, not the knock at the door. "I'll get it," Jenny says, and I sit and stare at the young woman who would first become Rhiaan's mother and then mine. There was a time when she smiled, although it would be years ahead, but for the life of me I cannot recall whether it had ever been captured on film. Gillian Beech's high-pitched jabber pollutes the quiet: "I don't want to be a bother. I just wanted to say how very sorry we all are—you know, the entire neighborhood association—and how much we will miss the little girl. We are all praying for the family. Please tell Reverend Deighton and his wife that if there is anything we can do . . ."

Thanks issued, the door closes and Jenny walks in with Easter lilies that have no doubt come from Gillian's church, a Pentecostal runt in the industrial park of Kakaako. There is no available space on any of the tables, so she puts it at the foot of the stairs. I watch her move around my house like it is hers, with the same familiarity she had when I'd sat on this same chair and nursed my newborn baby. She comes back to the album and flips through what could be construed as a journal of my mother's misery. "There!" she says, pointing. "That's the woman!"

My mother is older in this picture, no longer the frightened bride.

It has something to do with the passage of time, the bearing of children, the bearing of things heavy enough to round the shoulders. But she is older too. Rhiaan assures me there are other family portraits in the boxes in his attic, but this one to which Jenny points is the only one I have. Captured by my grandmother with my mother's new Instamatic, a Christmas gift from Rhiaan, we seem as we were. My father, standing behind my mother, has lost half his head (thanks to my grandmother's careless framing), and his mouth is cemented in a line as straight as a mason's level. Rhiaan, next to him, has avoided the same fate by bending to where I sit on my mother's lap, his fingers finding my ribs. I am blurred by the action of swinging around to counterattack, my left foot hooked around my mother's leg for balance. Of the four, hers is the only face fully captured, holding dead center. I imagine my grandmother trying to coax a smile or even issuing a stern command—" 'Sakes alive, Louise, smile! You look as though you've seen a ghost"—and then giving up, snapping the picture and forever immortalizing the moment just before our family unraveled for good. I have wondered often if my mother looked that way because she knew what was ahead, felt it a long time coming. Or if that day she looked not into the lens but into a mirage where all good things dissipated the closer she got.

"I don't believe in ghosts," I tell Jenny, as I do each time she relates one of her wacky visions.

"Neither do I," she replies. "But that doesn't stop them from showing up on my doorstep from time to time."

"You sure it was her?"

Jenny nods. "Back home people believe the spirits show up to warn us, sometimes to bring comfort. Sometimes just because there is unfinished business."

"But why would my mother pay you a visit and not me?"

"Maybe she knows you don't want to see her."

"That's dumb," I say.

"Perhaps." But Jenny knows what a ball of twine my feelings for my mother are. Maybe she did come to warn Jenny, or maybe she was the angel at the tomb of a child long gone.

LATER IN THE AFTERNOON, when Jenny is folding the body-warm clothes from the dryer, I walk into the family room, sit down on the couch, and watch TV. Greg is sitting on the floor, knees up, elbows propped on top of them, hands cradling his head, a cup of coffee slimy and cold in front of him. He turns, sees me looking at him, crawls over, and sinks his head into my lap. He weeps loudly, and I feel my hand lift as though by a system of pulleys and then fall down on his head, a gesture automatic and removed, ten miles from my screeching heart.

Evening takes forever to come, the twilight unusually long, the blazing sky spectacular in its farewell. Greg is asleep on the carpet in front of me; Jenny covers him with a quilt.

"Can you eat something?" she whispers. I shake my head and she says, "You should eat something."

She sits down at the kitchen table, the light still off, and I sit opposite her. There are six dishes of food in front of us: a congealed whole chicken, a quiche, a Jell-O salad, a box of donuts, a tub of rice, and a big bowl of chili. The table is set for three, with plates and knives and forks and glasses with melting ice cubes and napkins and salt and pepper. The place at the head of the table—Cleo's place—is bare. I put my head in my cold plate and gasp: I cannot go on.

"I am going to stay here again tonight," Jenny says, and I nod, feeling sorry for her because she has suddenly become a ninety-year-old woman, babysitting two bodies of inertia. She must tow me to the table to the bathroom to my bed. Deadweight.

"Want a couple more?" she asks, holding the little bottle of pills as I collapse in the disheveled remains of a troubled bed.

"I am afraid to sleep," I say. "I keep forgetting, and then I wake up and it starts at the beginning again."

"I know," she says, and slips two pills into my hand and passes me the water.

"Jenny?" I say, getting onto my bed with an armful of Cleo's dirty clothes from the laundry basket.

"Mmm?"

"Will you lie down next to me?" I ask.

"Sure, honey." She eases herself under the cover of Cleo's quilt and accepts the tiny top, still fresh with Cleo's scent, that I hand her.

"Do you think you might see her?" I whisper.

"I'd give anything to see her again, but I just don't think so. That little girl of ours, knowing her, has just too many things to do."

"I hope you are right."

The last thing I hear is Jenny's soft breath and the abrupt sniffs as she swallows her tears, closing her eyes on my empty room.

OCCASIONALLY, as the hours rot away, there is the weight of another next to me, sometimes the sound of a small groan, or the slight shift when the bed is mine again. Greg, I imagine, comes and goes, but I do not have the strength to turn over to check. It is, I know, not the weight of my child. I suppose days are going by because there is always a different arrangement of food petrified on the tray beside my bed whenever I step over it on the way to the toilet. Sometimes Jenny insists I sit and eat a few bites, and when I have the stamina I tell her no. Otherwise I nibble a bit of this or that so she will go away with her Madonna eyes. Other times it is Greg, who never tells me to eat but just sets the food down and sits on the floor, leans against the closet door, and props his head up with his hands. His hair, I notice, is turning white, like the hair of the man who lost his sons off the coast of Maine.

Today I have to get up, he says, because we are going to talk about the funeral. It is not enough to hold your dead child, to pray without ceasing for Death to jab its crooked finger at your heart, to replay the events of her last living day a thousand times, changing every possible thing you said a thousand times more. No, now we are required to plan a funeral wherein the promises of God are read to the faithful. Closure, they will say. A final goodbye. But it is a charade, a charade in which my husband expects me to participate.

. . .

WHO DECIDES how best to bury a child? Who sets the protocol, the list of choices childless parents must make? Did the clergy do it or the pasty-faced owners of funeral parlors? All these questions with their multiple-choice answers amount to nothing, circumventing the only choice parents wished they had had: that she lived. Instead, we are called upon to pick hymns, to choose the appropriate wood stain for a half-size coffin, and to decide from a hundred just the right bulletin cover. Some choices, I notice, have already been made: that banana bread is served on the china we use only for company instead of store-bought cookies on paper plates; that a pot of tea accompanies it rather than coffee; that we will assemble in the living room instead of at the congested dining room table.

The little delegation of funeral professionals has arranged itself in my house, as out of place as the gaudy bouquets alongside them. I am instructed by an anorexic middle-aged woman with a precisely bobbed Purdey hairdo and Siamese-shaped eyes to look through a folder of plastic-clad bulletin covers. She sits across from Chuck Burton, an army chaplain and Greg's longtime clergy colleague.

Did you ever watch *The Avengers*? I feel almost compelled to say, but don't. Is she the Avenger, the one come to mete out judgment and reverse the wrongs?

"This one is nice," Purdey says, and I see that her teeth protrude way past her lips. In a former life Jenny and I would have exchanged only glances, no hint even of a smile, enough to say, See, it could be worse—you could have your problems *and* look like that. This time I gaze down, following her twig-thin finger. "Nice" is rays of light beaming through gilt-edged clouds. I dutifully turn the plastic page. "Nice" to Purdey also happens to be monarch butterflies circling springtime flowers. I turn another page.

"Do you have anything in black?" I ask, tired already of the charade.

"Abbe," says Greg softly. I consider changing my name. But the Avenger is not offended. She looks at me sympathetically—she has been through this many times—but does not pat my knee.

"This one," I say in gratitude for that absent act of artificial affection, if nothing else. It is a picture of a shadowed canyon above which a lone eagle flies. According to Purdey, it is not merely "nice" but "perfect."

Greg has written a poem that he will read during the service. The poem will be recited after the first lesson from John 14 is read, Chuck explains. The ubiquitous tray with the uneaten banana bread and the teapot centers our gathering, but the smell of it and that of the flowers is suddenly overpowering, nauseating. I look around and the house is just too damn neat, not how I remembered it with Cleo's toys strewn everywhere. It is a set, and I wait for someone to yell "Cut!"

"Alex will be co-officiating and he will read the second lesson," explains Chuck. Reverend Alexander Takamura is the superintendent of Hawaii's calcified collection of Methodist churches. He is Greg's boss or Greg's pastor, depending on what mood he is in. Lately he has been in the "boss" mood, meeting with Greg two times in the last few weeks to discuss complaints he has received from undisclosed disgruntled parishioners, a.k.a. Kelsey Oliver. Greg is nodding, listening to Chuck outline the order of worship, with his face turned to the west and the gusty trade winds blowing in through the louvered windows. Chuck warbles on and Greg does not interrupt, not once.

". . . What do you think, Abbe?" asks Chuck.

I look at his nutmeg-brown face and fail to recall what specifically I am called upon to have an opinion about. "I'm sorry," I say. "Could you repeat that?"

"Do you want to open the mike for anyone who chooses to share remembrances, or would you prefer to limit it to a few predetermined folks?"

Both men wait for me to answer, as though there might be a grand prize behind my reply. A trip for two to the Cayman Islands, ladies and gentlemen.

"I don't know," I say, but they keep looking at me; I have not answered correctly.

"Limit it," I say, and Greg lets out a sigh while Chuck nods and

44

says, "Yes, I think that's probably a good idea so the service doesn't go too long."

This exercise is for my benefit, I suddenly realize. I get up. "You decide the rest, okay?"

"Please, Abbe, don't make this any harder than it already is," Greg pleads.

"No, that's fine, Greg. Let's just pick the hymns and I can do the rest. Okay, Abbe?" Chuck suggests.

I sit.

"She liked 'The Wheels on the Bus,' " I say without rancor, but Greg looks out the window again and for a moment I want to say, Forgive me if I don't feel like singing praises to the Great Almighty right this minute. But instead I say, " 'Jesus Loves the Little Children.' The first song she learned to sing." The first song I taught her how to sing. Purdey purrs her approval.

"That's a thought," says Chuck. "What if we sing just children's hymns?"

While he and Greg select two others from the hymnal the blood drains from my face and the stars that have been absent from the sky these past few nights suddenly collect in my eyes. The smell of the African bush fills my nose and cicadas ring in my ears.

Greg is fanning my face with Purdey's binder when I come to. "She needs to eat something," he says. Once I am lodged on the couch, propped with pillows, Chuck picks up a piece of the banana bread, breaks off half, and hands it to me. The symbolism of this tiny gesture is not lost on me; he might have said, The Body of our Lord broken for you. I take it and eat it reluctantly, and without thanks. "There is one song," I say. "*Siyahamba.*" I had been trying to teach Cleo the song in its original Zulu, and although she could get some of the words, she much preferred the actions: marching around the house, just as the song instructed, in the light of God.

After they leave, Greg and Jenny watch the evening news and I move to the dining room, not bothering to turn on the light. Between the baskets of food and the flower arrangements, at the center of the table is still that lone white envelope leaning against the vase of now wilting lilies. I pluck it from its station, sever the seal, and pull out the card. Scrawled, as though carelessly, at the bottom of the note are four impossible words: *I love you, Abbe.* Not in the hand of the Reverend Gregory Danforth Deighton, the writing of curls and flourishes, but no less recognizable.

FOUR

West Park Funeral Home looks like a cross between a Best Western and an interstate rest stop, and straddles the corner of Park Avenue and Pikake Street. Inside, the decor is Hawaiian whorehouse, which strikes me as a beautiful irony since all the two-bit hookers in Honolulu stake out their stilettoed turf on the four corners of the bustling intersection outside. A receptionist who greets us as if we are about to check into the honeymoon suite tells us to take a seat. Just as we do, an elderly woman with ashy hair walks out to meet us and identifies herself as Joan Avery. She's shrouded in the smell of magnolia flowers and quite sincerely says to us, "I'm very sorry for your loss." Mr. Osaka, the man with whom Greg has dealt for the last two days, has been called away on an urgent matter, she apologizes. Someone else just died, I think. Someone else's son or daughter.

Would we like to see Cleo, she wants to know.

I turn to Greg and say, "Can I have a few minutes alone with her?"

He looks surprised but nods, and I follow the drifting scent of Mrs. Avery down the corridor. Before she opens a narrow wooden door, she turns to me, eyebrows raised, and asks quietly, "Are you ready, dear?"

WE NEVER DID CUT Cleo's hair. Greg's mother sent a little teddy bear box from Neiman Marcus on her first Christmas. It had "Baby's

First Curl" written on the bottom. You could never tell whether Greg's mother was just plain thoughtless or if her actions teetered on malice. Everyone knew that a peach had more hair than Cleo, and it was not until her second birthday that anything close to a curl became evident. But one of the things you could count on in life was that every time Greg called Ohio, his mother would ask in her high-pitched acerbic tone, "That baby of yours got any hair yet?"

At three, however, Cleo's head was covered with corkscrew curls tipped with blond, none of which we could bear to cull. So the box is still in her room on the shelf, empty. At night after her bath, she would have me wet her hair and then brush it so that for a minute or two it would be straight and long, reaching well past the constellation of freckles at the base of her neck. Sometimes, after it had dried back into springs, she would cry and pull at her hair in frustration, "Long, Mommy; I want it long." The pantyhose wig was my attempt to help out.

Cleo, with a halo of curls, lies perfectly still in the coffin. But she does not look like she's asleep, the way they say dead people do. Gone is what she is, as though spirited away by Africa's mythical Tokoloshe, leaving a papery skin that doesn't quite fit what remains. Her cheeks are not as rounded, and her chin is pointy where it was once plump. She is wearing the Easter dress Jenny bought for her a month ago—the one embroidered with blue butterflies on the hem—and only the straps of her blue faerie wings pressed beneath her are visible around her shoulders. Her hands are folded on her chest. Although the second lid covering her torso and legs is closed, I know her feet are bare, as they always were.

"Do you have a pair of scissors?" I ask Mrs. Avery, who is waiting to be dismissed.

"I'll be right back, dear," she says, and passes me her handkerchief.

"Cleo," I whisper, "it's Mommy." I touch her forehead, which is frozen, and my hand withdraws as if it has been scalded.

The quiet is one I have not known before. It is not the crackling, hissing sound of the reef forty feet below the snapping waves at the surface. Nor is it the shushed quiet of Greg's sparsely attended chapel services or the quiet of the sandstone caves deep in the Klein Karoo. It is crypt-quiet, a silence abandoned even by angels, where my tears plop noiselessly on a dust-colored carpet.

"Darling," I whisper, "Mommy's here."

I do not hear the door open when Mrs. Avery returns with the scissors.

"Take as much as you want," she says gently, guessing my intention. "No one needs to know."

She hands me an orange coin envelope and glides out.

Where to cut? I caress Cleo's hair, stringy now like the texture of corncob silk. There must not be an obvious gap where the curl has been lopped off. It cannot look like a hack job, even though she won't be able to look in the mirror and reprimand me for it.

"Darling," I tell her, "Mommy is going to cut a piece of your hair so I can keep it. Okay?" I cry, wipe my nose with Mrs. Avery's lace handkerchief, and then steady my trembling hand. Snipping off a small whorl behind her left ear, I leave the long one that was the first to grow at the nape of her neck. It falls into the envelope, which I then fold and tuck in my purse before Greg knocks once and walks in.

WHEN WE GET HOME, Rhiaan is the one who opens the front door, and I step into his outstretched arms, the arms of a home long gone. "I miss her so much," I cry.

"I know," Rhiaan says.

"I would trade everything for one more day."

"Yes," he says, rubbing small circles on my back.

When I lift my face from Rhiaan's shoulder, a wet spot as big as a map marks the place. From his shirt pocket he extracts a small notebook, its cover folded behind a page where words once were. Now they are inky flowers.

"Sorry, Rhiaan. I've ruined your writing."

"Here." He smiles, getting his handkerchief out. "Wipe your nose; the writing was ruined before it even hit the paper." A closer look at my brother reveals a face much older than it was the last time we saw each other—not quite a year ago at the Fourth of July reunion. Much older than his seven-year lead on me. A face that speaks of loss. Up till now we have all just thought it a phase, writer's block—surely no one is immune—but now I wonder if Rhiaan has been mourning the loss of something dear himself. The very thing that gives him identity, purpose. Years ago, in an interview published in *The Literary Review*, Rhiaan was asked to name his greatest fear. "Running dry," he had said. I would have guessed "Losing Cicely," or at least "Losing one of my children." But losing inspiration for Rhiaan, I learned, had to be a kind of hemorrhage where eventually all that would pass through his veins would be the whistling wind of the high desert. It is a terrible thing, then, that my spent tears have made blurry patches on what was an attempt.

Rhiaan's burnt-orange hair, shaggy since boyhood, is now cut close to the scalp and looks like the veldt after a bushfire. He takes off his spectacles to rub his eyes and stretches up to embrace Greg. This brother of mine, famous around the world for his eloquent poems, his ability to capture in couplets the depths of a suffering nation, has no words for a suffering father. Instead, he shakes his head and then rubs the top of it as though to put out the last of the cinders.

"Cicely didn't come?" Greg asks.

"Couldn't get a plane out of Paris in time," he explains, answering Greg, as he so often does, by looking at me. "I'm mad as hell at her for going in the first place, but that's another story. But she does send all her love and her sympathies, of course. You know Cis—she's never going to be able to forgive herself for missing the funeral."

"And the kids?" Greg is asking all the questions I have forgotten to ask.

"They're at some horse-riding camp in the Sierras this weekend. I left a message at the lodge where they are staying, but I'm going to try calling them again a little later."

"We are really pleased you could make it," Greg thanks him.

Looking at me, Rhiaan says, "I wouldn't be anywhere else."

After we have had tea and nibbled on the platter of cheese and biscuits Jenny prepared, Rhiaan goes outside to smoke his pipe and escape

Greg's earnest attempts at conversation with him. Rhiaan has never said he doesn't like Greg, nor has he ever, in the slightest way, done anything that might be construed as dislike for the man I married. It could well be that the aloofness that characterizes most of my brother's social interactions applies to his dealings with Greg. I haven't ever asked, in part because I have never wanted an answer, and Rhiaan has never volunteered.

The rain is coming down in vertical sheets and Rhiaan huddles under the awning and stares out at the storm hanging in the harbor.

"Your newscasters are calling it 'a storm of biblical proportions,' " Rhiaan says.

"Don't you just love the media? To them just about all the Bible is good for is its 'proportions,' " I respond.

Rhiaan nods. "When it can be good for so many other reasons— doorstops, paperweights, dumbbells—"

"Oh, stop!" But it does elicit a smile, an arrangement of muscles that feels to my face as foreign as a mustache.

For a while we hear only the sound of rain pummeling the deck.

"I keep having the feeling that if I had had more time I would have become a good mother," I wonder aloud.

"You *were* a good mother—even by biblical standards," Rhiaan offers, taking a deep draw on his pipe.

"But what about by Cleo standards?"

"Hers too." Seeing how unconvinced I am, Rhiaan continues, "Remember last year when we all went down to the beach and Cleo wanted to get in the water?" She hadn't turned three yet and the little waves frightened her even when I held her hand and tried talking her through them. How frustrated she became when the other children skipped over them and kicked at them till they were blue and shivery. "It was so hot and everyone else went in to cool off, and what did you do?" he asks.

"Well, I didn't want to force her to go in . . ."

"You dug that great big hole and tried to make her a swimming pool, even though all those buckets of water you hauled kept getting sucked up by sand. You must have done that for hours—I don't think I have ever seen you that determined! And we all swam and sat in the beach chairs and drank beers and watched you."

"It's what any good mother would do."

"My point exactly."

Somewhere far-off there is the sound of a child crying. Automatically I stop, cock my head to the side, and listen to hear whether it is the cry of the child I love. "You think Mom was a good mother too, don't you?" I ask, recognizing that it is not.

He nods. "She did her best."

"With you I think she did. But I think her best left the day you left for college." Rhiaan, who had matriculated a year ahead of his peers and was accepted at Rhodes University on a full scholarship, was seventeen when he left home. I was ten. Grahamstown might as well have been another country and not the nine hundred kilometers northeast of our doorstep, as far as my mother was concerned. Where before she interspersed her domestic responsibilities with outings for us, sometimes to my grandmother's farm or to the library or even once or twice a year to the local theater, after Rhiaan left, an outing for the two of us was an ice cream from the vendor outside the grocery store before heading home. She went into hibernation during the long months Rhiaan was at school, spending her evenings either composing letters to her son or rereading one of his. If before my father treated us like rearranged furniture around which he had to navigate, after Rhiaan left he took up target practice with my mother in his sights. She was to blame, whether it was because he had misplaced his car keys, or because a check bounced, or because he was passed over for promotion (again). Most especially, though, she was to blame for her son's bleeding-heart liberalism.

Although my father never went to the trouble of voting, he was a staunch supporter of the National Party. On the topic of politics, he had only one argument. "Take a look at the rest of Africa," he would say, "and then try telling me it's a good idea to give the *kaffirs* their way!" This logic, passed from father to son for several generations, had done a good job of carving out a rather nice life for white South

Africans. Sure, you had to put burglar bars on your windows and se-
cure your property with walls and German shepherds—a small price
to pay. But what kind of price was it when your own flesh and blood
thumbed their noses at your beliefs, at the way of life they were expected to inherit? Rhiaan, like a lot of white teenagers of his generation, started questioning the government's policies, and when they
didn't get the answers they were looking for they challenged its tactics.
Fathers all over the country were taking it badly. "The army'll sort
them out" was often the general consensus. *"Kry all daardie civvy kak uit."*
And my father believed this would have worked for Rhiaan if our
mother had not done a good job of filling his head with the notion of
college. She encouraged Rhiaan's creative pursuits and his growing objections to apartheid with all that listening!

It was anticipated that black boys would grow up to be trouble-
makers, recruits for the feared *Umkhonto we Sizwe*, but when white kids
caused trouble with their college campus sit-ins, their threats of civil
disobedience, the fathers of South Africa were quite at a loss. "This
country is going to the dogs," my dad would snarl, watching on TV as
SADF troops fired tear gas into the college crowds, "and it doesn't help
a goddamn inch when *kaffir*-loving Commie buggers like your son en-
courage these terrorists! Think they know everything! Well, let me tell
you something, when he goes into the army they'll knock the bloody
shit out of him. That's what he needs, not some limp-wrist professor
spoon-feeding him a pack o' lies!" Did she ever argue with that? All I
remember is her serving dinner, washing the dishes, and cleaning the
counters, and the more he fumed the more she scrubbed. She would
stop only when Rhiaan came home from varsity with a sackload of
laundry and a fistful of poems for her to glue in a scrapbook.

"I don't know that I would agree with that," Rhiaan now argues.

"You weren't there, Rhiaan. Things changed; *she* changed."

"I was still around, just not to the same extent. But Mom and I
talked on the phone. She told me things."

"She told you things you wanted to hear."

"That's not so. Mom told me things she couldn't tell anyone else.
Not Dad, not you." And it is always like this when we speak of the past:

Rhiaan rewriting our family history from my mother's letters. If I so much as hint that she might have been less than honest with him, he gets very quiet and looks as if I have jabbed him with a hatpin. The most we have been able to do is concede that each owns a piece of our mother, a piece that, try as we might to make it otherwise, does not line up snugly with the other.

"All I am saying is she didn't have to tell me anything; I was living with it," I say.

"I think part of being a good mother—a good parent—is choosing between which things you tell your children and which you don't. You are not going to blurt out things to your child, even if you think she is old enough to understand, when there's a damn good chance it is going to pull the rug out from under her."

"It's just better to have secrets then, is it?"

"Would you tell Cleo all your secrets?" Sometimes people mistake my openness for transparency, but not my brother. Rhiaan knows there are places I tuck things away, and behind labels like "openness" is as good a place as any.

It is an unfair answer to his winning question, but I give it anyway: "Well, we will never know, will we?"

"Come here," he says, and I feel my brother's arms close around me, concluding the first conversation I have had in days. Maybe it is because Rhiaan is threaded through my past that I can talk to him, or maybe it is because I know he is not going to respond with any religious platitudes.

Jenny walks out. "Don't hate me for this, but I have lunch ready—if you'd rather wait, that's fine with me. It will keep." Rhiaan rubs his stomach. "And I think your husband might need some reinforcement."

"Oh?"

"He's on the phone to your mother-in-law and it doesn't sound good."

It never does. "Give us a few minutes," I tell her.

"You're lucky to have a friend like Jenny," Rhiaan says when she has gone back inside. "Wouldn't Dad be pleased to see you finally have a black woman in your kitchen fixing your meals?" He means it as a joke, as a dig at our father's racist ways, but it just resurrects all the old feelings.

My father, an impatient man even at the front end of a twelve-hour day, became unrestrained after Rhiaan left for college. There were brooding silences that lasted for weeks, interspersed only by the rat-a-tat-tat of his curt insults. If my mother made the mistake of speaking during the eight o'clock news broadcast, if the chicken curry wasn't hot enough, if she started to doze off in front of her plate at the kitchen counter, my father would deliver an insult as though he wished, rather, it were a well-aimed kick in the gut. "For chrissake, Pet, I shouldn't have to eat leftovers when you have been home all day!" That was his nickname for her: Pet.

Sometimes the silences parted for a season of unpredictable patterns. Rages that could go on all night just because someone had left a glass to sweat on the dining room table. My mother would slip into my room late at night, sometimes waking me, just to tell me my father wasn't angry at me; he had a lot on his mind, that's all. Her reassurances never once worked. Fathers should tidy the world for their daughters; they should stack the good and bad into neat piles. But Harry was a Karoo tornado, perpetually rearranging things so that cars hurtled down U-shaped bends, mothers got wrapped around gin bottles, and brothers got blasted into kingdom come.

When East Coast people move to the islands they often say, "Oh, I miss the seasons." They do. Even the blizzards that can cause fifteen-car pileups, or hurricanes that can whip up waves big enough to drown a city. I know what they mean. My father's raw, unceasing seasons don't touch me here, and even though I have filed away those remembrances that can make a heart tip out, I have to admit the sheer force of his windy moods made our hair stand up, made us feel glad to be alive when the storms abated.

"Grandma used to say that it always rains on the day a good person dies. I bet not one cloud passed through the skies the day Dad died."

"You still mad at him?" Rhiaan squints over his smoke at me.

"You aren't?"

"It is seldom a productive thing to be angry," he replies.

"You haven't answered my question."

Rhiaan stares out at the harbor. The navy has brought all its vessels into port except one, which cuddles the coastline like an orphan. He taps out his tobacco and finally speaks. "For a long time I felt responsible for what happened to Mom. As you said, I was the one who left, but her misery was apparent even long-distance. He was a mean bugger, I'll give you that, but I always blamed myself for being such a disappointment to him. So, to answer your question, if I was mad at anyone, I was mad at myself."

It seems impossible that this golden-child brother of mine, guilty of nothing, has assumed someone else's load. "So he got off scot-free when he was the most to blame."

"You think that he didn't end up paying in some way?"

"I think he got to do exactly what he wanted, whether it was disowning you or beating up on Mom or ignoring me. I think he fractured our family and blew us all in different directions. Maybe it's just me, but I think he should have had to pay a price for that."

"Maybe he did."

"He up and died is what he did."

"Well, you are the religious one—maybe he got to pay his price after that."

"I'm not so sure."

Rhiaan lifts his eyebrows at the ambiguity. "Come on, let's go in."

༄

THE BOOK with its red cover had lain on the coffee table in front of my father for three hours, from the time my mother had set it down next to his coffee cup when he came home from work, right through the eight o'clock South African newscast of the bombings along the country's railways, to when my mother announced my bedtime. "Aren't you going to read Rhiaan's poem, Dad?" These might have been the only words anyone had spoken all evening, and a response to them did not seem likely. But I did not want to go to my room, close the door, and spend the rest of the night pinned to the other side of it, waiting for his reaction. I could be like that, standing between him and his TV, braving his wrath.

"Dad?"

"Louise!" my father barked, leaning left to look past me. "Your daughter has learned to nag almost as goddamn good as you!" Again I stepped in his line of sight. Snatching up the book as though it were a puff adder, he glared at my mother, who had come to collect his dinner tray, dish towel draped over her shoulder. "This is your fault!"

It took a long time for him to read it although the poem was only thirty-six lines long. I allowed for the fact that my father had never completed the eighth grade. Perhaps he had to read it several times to understand it, being a newspaper reader who liked things spelled out in who-what-where-when-how fashion. Perhaps he was letting it sink in: that this son, despite his father's prophecies, had made something of himself. Most certainly he could not deny that it was good; "brilliant," some bigwig professor of literature at the Witwatersrand University had called it. You can hope such things, as you might hope goldfish will fly in gilded flocks, even when you know better.

My father's reaction did come finally. As the book took on a trajectory headed for the wall, he issued not a review but a verdict: "I'll kill that little shit!"

All over the country white kids were popping up, overnight like mushrooms on a compost heap, with their protesting questions. Questions quickly turned to demands, demands to action. "Power to the People!" *"Amandla!"* "One Man, One Vote!"—taunts that the old folk said warranted tear gas. "You go to university to get an education!" they said. But then they called the military in to teach them a different kind of lesson. Fathers watched their sons trade in their loyalty to the *Vaderland* for a rebellion that spilled like gasoline on a slope of matches. Our father watched Rhiaan pick up his pen as though it were an AK-47, as though it were aimed at him.

It was too late for my mother to call Rhiaan, to warn him, to suggest he delay his visit to us—the train carrying our guerrilla-poet had already left the station and was bound for the tiny town of Paarl, for the fist my father had in mind for him. The year was 1981, and it was the day the Commies inadvertently saved my brother's life. A group of apartheid dissidents blew up a section of the railway tracks Rhiaan's train needed to complete its journey. So grateful was I that I vowed to become a Red myself. Had Rhiaan arrived as scheduled, in the middle of the night, and not as he did a few days later via car, he would have certainly been greeted with my father's murderous mood. On the other hand, with all the fists flying, there might not have been room for my father's words. Perhaps my dad's arm would have swung and delivered its message, and Rhiaan—knocked out cold—would have awoken to my father's remorse. Instead, as it turned out, Rhiaan came home three days later, in broad daylight, to something worse.

My mother was the first to greet him, having kept vigil at the living room window for much of the afternoon. When Rhiaan's roommate's car pulled into the driveway, she let out a yip and ran out while I followed close on her heels. He was different somehow, and although he hugged me just the same, I felt shy around this grown-up brother. "What's the matter," he asked me. "Cat got your tongue?"

The All-Blacks, having ignored the Gleneagles Agreement, which preached an international sports sanction against South Africa, were giving the Springboks a thorough beating in the first test match. It could not have had a worse effect on my father if he had been the captain of the rugby team himself. When the three of us tumbled into the house, he was standing at attention in front of the tube, shouting directions at the referee, who had apparently just awarded another penalty to the New Zealand side.

"Hello, Dad," Rhiaan said.

I had not noticed, until he raised his arm in our direction, that clasped in my father's grip was the red book.

"What the bloody hell do you call this?" he demanded, a scrum of one. Didn't *we* need a referee?

Rhiaan looked at the floor and rubbed the back of his head, but did not answer.

"I'll tell you what it is," my father continued. "It's Commie bullshit, that's what! You think I'm stupid?"

Rhiaan was quiet.

"I said, do you think I'm fucking stupid?"

"No, I never said—"

"Don't interrupt me! This is *my* house; I do the talking around here!" My mother came to get my hand and guided me into the hallway, where we still had a view of the muddy rugby field and the battlefield in front of it. For weeks I had been waiting for that duffel bag to come home, to be opened, to be handed from it a treasure my brother had picked out just for me. But now it sat zipped up like my mother's mouth, ready to leave, at Rhiaan's side.

"It's a poem, Dad. It's just a poem."

"It's a bloody disgrace—that's what it is! Let me tell you something, *boetie*, I have put up with your attitude and your superior ways for years, but the thanks I get is this piece of shit! It mocks me and everything I stand for, do you hear me?"

"It has nothing to do with you, it's about—"

"It has *everything* to do with me! You fuck with my country, my boy, you fuck with me." I was beginning to wonder whether our neighbors could hear, whether they had turned down the volume on their TV sets for a better earful of the match going on in our house. My father opened the book to the page where Rhiaan's poem was printed, ripped it out, and crumpled it. "That's what I think of your poem and that's what I think of you. Now clean out any other Commie bullshit from your room and get the hell out of my house! You aren't any son of mine." Wiping the spittle from his mouth with the back of his hand, my father sat down in his recliner and picked up his beer just as the Springbok running back scored a try.

"Harry," my mother gasped.

"Don't start, Louise, or by God you can leave with him."

My mother didn't leave—not in any physical sense, at least. Instead, after Rhiaan had left, she picked up the page from the floor and taped it back in the book. Later that day she picked up something else—a very tall glass of gin. When Rhiaan left the country a year later along with a phalanx of political refugees just after his twenty-first birthday, it was a long season before I saw the glass empty.

∾

INSIDE, JENNY IS cleaning out uneaten food from the refrigerator while Greg paces in the kitchen with the phone to his ear.

"Greg's mother apparently can't make it to the funeral," Jenny warns. "Something about the old man."

Greg is chewing on his thumbnail, a dead giveaway that his mother is bulldozing her will through yet another conversation. On one of his about-turns, Greg sees me staring at him, waiting for him to stand up to her. This is the moment. You can do it! Tell her: tell her that her granddaughter is dead and if she had a kind bone in her body she'd get it on a plane and fly it over here.

I wait.

Greg turns from my scowl and mumbles, "I know, Mother. It's okay."

I head upstairs, walk into Cleo's room, reach up to the shelf for the teddy bear box, and throw it in the trash. In my bedroom I retrieve from my purse the envelope with Cleo's curl. The lone curl in my hand, weightless as a dandelion tuft, is so unlike my dark, heavy hair. Hair that used to fall to my waist when it wasn't tied up in a ponytail, hair that now lies in a Ziploc bag in the bottom of Greg's sock drawer. From it, I get a strand and put it in the envelope with Cleo's.

I wonder if there are other reasons why women cut their hair themselves. Reasons that are different from the one that compelled me that last morning of our summer vacation. Waking up to the great divide that had come to characterize our marriage, I felt an androgynous desperation that morning. Invisible and undesirable, I was far from the happily-ever-after ending into which bridal couples are supposed to step. While Greg and Cleo were peering into rock pools outside our hotel room, I peered at my aging face and wilting hairdo. I was beginning to look like my mother. Something had to be done. I found the craft scissors Cleo and I had used to make collages the day before and returned to my post in front of the mirror. Pulling my disheveled ponytail to one side for a clearer view, I hacked and hacked until the whole thing came off in one butchered bushel. Look at me now, I wanted to shout. You can't ignore me now!

There was a feeling of exhilaration the moment those two feet of matted hair fell to the floor, as though I had shed the deadweight of a decade. "Oh, babe," Greg said sadly when he and Cleo returned from the beach. "What have you done?"

I couldn't help but grin. "I like it," I said, insolent and panicky both.

"What did you do that for?" His frown was mixed with concern.

I could not remember my rehearsed answer. It had something to do with wanting to make a change, not just to myself but to us. My steady argument, the calm voice of reason, was suddenly mist on a cool morning, and all I could picture was a portrait of me and Greg with the faces of Louise and Harry Spenser. Greg wasn't the vengeful, brutal Harry, to be sure, but I could not shake the sense that I was morphing into my mother, right down to her neglected fingernails and low expectations. I had cut my hair to put up a fight. It seemed silly to say I was fighting for my mother, that I was fighting from becoming her too. I just could not think, when my husband was asking me about hair, how I was supposed to answer him about marriage and how, without any intention on anyone's behalf, it had become so disappointing.

"I like it!" Cleo declared. "Cut mine, Mommy," she said, reaching round for that tiny curl.

"Darling," I told her, "princesses have hair like yours; it's too perfect to cut."

I set the envelope in my treasure chest where I stashed yesterday's card so Greg would not inadvertently read it, thinking it a message of condolence only to find another man's profession of love to the preacher's wife. Instead of rereading it, I reach for my mother's old airmail letters, bundled together with an elastic band. From the stack I pull the top one, her last one, and scan it for clues. There are twenty letters, one written every week from the time I left South Africa till the time she died, and ever since, I have always wondered if she knew she was dying, if she knew this was to be her last goodbye.

She writes of the irises blooming, the apricot tree outside my bedroom window covered with silky buds, the neighborhood gleaming from spring cleaning. She mentions how her old friend Muriel came by to help her spruce up the house the week after my father's funeral (*It was good that you didn't come*). They rearranged furniture, hung new curtains in the kitchen, put up some new pictures. There is a wish for a happy Thanksgiving—what was to be my first (*I never could get you to eat turkey at Christmas—maybe American turkeys taste better*). And then two paragraphs—one of regret, the other of advice—with barely a space between them. *I wish there had been more happy times in our family,* she penned. *I wish more than anything that this last year had turned out different. However, things do all turn out for the best, my girl. I never used to believe that, but I do now. Don't ever let life get the better of you. Sometimes it dishes out bitter stuff, but as they say, "What doesn't kill you makes you stronger." I hope you will remember that.* She ends by writing she is proud of me and she loves me (*with all my heart*).

Rhiaan knocks and enters my bedroom with two mugs of tea.

"What's all this?" he asks, sitting on the corner of the bed.

"Oh, one of Mom's old letters. I've often wondered if she knew she was going to die . . . What do you think?"

"It's possible, I suppose, but not likely."

I go on. "There's this one line that puzzles me, like she had a total change of heart. She says things always turn out for the best. What were her letters to you about?"

"She wrote mostly about Dad and how she pitied him because he had missed out on so much of my life, so many of the good things. I read them every now and then, when I need some inspiration. It was her greatest gift to me—that she could only ever see promise in me. Isn't that how all mothers see?" he asks.

I nod. "Last week Cleo told me she wanted to be a mother when she grew up. She wanted to have babies, 'possibly five,' she said. And I was so looking forward to the day when I could watch her deliver them, and then love them one by one. And yes, as you say, see in them all their promise. I can't bear it, that she's gone and I'm left with nothing. Nothing. Just one little curl." I retrieve from the coin envelope her golden tuft. "See this? It's all I have of her. And to think it was dead long before she was."

"There," he says, holding me. "There now."

"The worst part is that I didn't get to say goodbye to her. I didn't get to tell her how proud I was and how much I loved her and to say sorry for all the times I yelled at her for not packing up her toys."

After a while, he pulls from his pocket a pen.

"Why don't you write her a letter and tell her all that," he suggests.

When Rhiaan leaves, I get off the bed and move to the writing desk at the window. I pull out the drawer with my stationery and extract a crisp blank page. *Dear Cleo*, I begin, and the words begin to flow. When I am done, I retrace my words to my daughter, and notice that wedged between the lines of guilt and grief is my own brief admission of a broken vow. So I write a second letter, this time to the writer of the card.

JENNY DRIVES RHIAAN and me to West Park Funeral Home a little before five o'clock in the middle of rush-hour traffic. If Mrs. Avery is surprised to see me return after a few short hours, she does not let on. She ushers us into the same room and exits as Jenny begins to wail. Rhiaan puts an arm around her shoulder without ever taking his eyes from Cleo's face. She bends down and kisses Cleo's forehead, lingering there as though she were inhaling that sweet baby smell one last time.

After Rhiaan escorts her out, I pull from my purse the letter I have written for Cleo, folded into a square. I lift up her hands just enough to slide the note on her breast beneath them.

"Goodbye, sweet girl," I whisper. "I am going to miss you so much." Mrs. Avery shakes my hand on the way out and I tell her that there will be no more visitors for Cleo, that they may close the casket. We step out of the catacombs, past the bustling weekend trade of painted flesh and stilettoed heels, and into an endless stretch of Good Fridays. On the way to the car, we pass a mailbox in which I deposit the second letter, the one to the man who imagines himself in love with me.

FIVE

It is the phone that wakes us, piercing the dark with its insistent shrill. When I push Pilgrim off my legs and turn over to look at the digital alarm, it reads 5:15. My heart pounds because I imagine it is someone calling to tell me my mother has died. But then awake, I remember that that nightmare is over and another is about to begin. Today is Saturday, the day of the funeral. Someone in another room answers. Somebody from the mainland calling, no doubt, someone who doesn't know the time difference.

Saturdays used to be for getting up late and having pancakes soggy with syrup, and then taking two hours to pack a picnic and get ready to go to the beach. Saturdays were for wading out in the shallows with all the other mothers and their toddlers, learning to share the sand bucket and leftover sand castles. Saturdays were for taking long naps, still salty from the seawater, and for waking up to sunburned shoulders and a sandy bottom.

On those rare Saturdays when it rained all day over the hills of Honolulu, Cleo and I stayed inside and watched *Sesame Street* videos back-to-back and built tents out of stale-smelling patchwork quilts. Saturday dinners were leftovers or takeouts, whichever was easiest. And each Saturday rolled on by, one after the next, without special acknowledgment of their extraordinary power.

Saturday. Sabbath. (*When even the closest did not return to the tomb.*) We were good at observing the Sabbath, Cleo and I. Not Greg. If he wasn't conducting a wedding, he was holed up in his office, putting the last touches to his Sunday sermon. Occasionally I would remind my husband that for all his fervent commitment to Christ, he was violating the Fourth Commandment. Arguing that the Sabbath was a workday for him, he compromised by taking Fridays off. So he would, for a few weeks, clear his calendar of meetings and spend Fridays with Cleo, sometimes picking me up from work for a quick midday meal at Buster's. "Good Fridays," Cleo called them, delighting in having her father to herself. For her, Saturday would come all too soon, as it does for me now.

Frank Tucker, the church's lay leader and Greg's closest ally in the church battles, has come to drive us to the church in his ugly brown Cadillac. It is the first time I have seen him in long pants and lace-up shoes, and with his sailor's windswept gray hair neatly pressed into place. There had been talk of a limousine, but, thankfully, Greg had declined. A hideous idea.

It is overcast again today but not raining, as if the sky were holding its breath. The peaks of the Ko'olau Range are blanketed with dark clouds, and I am reminded of Cape Town's Table Mountain and its foggy tablecloth that frequently drapes over it. There is no pretense in the streets of Honolulu today—even the plumeria trees do little to draw attention from the mounds of trash stacked along the sidewalks. Bits and pieces of people's living rooms, bedrooms, basements, sit out on the curb rusting or rotting away, on display. High-density living has taught us there are no secrets; there is no use putting on airs. It's okay, then, to put out the corduroy recliner Uncle Kimo died in or the baby's metal crib, the cheap toys bought from someone else's garage sale. You jam people in tight enough and soon it's even okay to hang wet underwear from balconies as though they were Christmas garlands.

With its blazing poinciana trees, the old church seems almost regal until a closer look reveals the peeling plaster, the rusty sign, the gum-pocked sidewalk. The car pulls up in front of the church and Frank opens my door, gives me a quick, crushing hug when I step out, and then drives to the basement parking lot. Greg finds my hand and leads me up the stairs and into the cavernous, nauseatingly fragrant space that is Makiki United Methodist Church.

Jenny enters from the side door with a Tupperware box and heads to the reception table to set up the display. Someone has already erected a framed picture of Cleo and draped around it a purple orchid lei. It was my idea to arrive this early—before the casket, before the crowd—but when I see the big floral arrangements and the center table at the chancel, I know it is a mistake.

"Greg," I say, feeling my stomach turn itself inside out, "let's go wait in your office."

The church offices are located adjacent to the sanctuary, above the fellowship hall on the second floor. Greg opens the door and flicks a switch so that the air conditioner starts to hum. He leaves the lights off and opens the blinds enough to cast long, horizontal shadows on the carpet. I lie down on the couch, and he sits in the small chair next to me. On the table is his grandfather's Bible, which he picks up, flipping through its skin-thin pages. He begins to read aloud, sputtering as though something were lodged in his throat, and I do not have the will to stop him:

"Hear my prayer, O Lord; let my cry come to thee!
Do not hide thy face from me in the day of my distress!
Incline thy ear to me;
Answer me speedily in the day when I call!
For my days pass away like smoke,
And my bones burn like a furnace.
My heart is smitten like grass, and withered;
I forget to eat my bread.
Because of my loud groaning my bones cleave to my flesh.
I am like a vulture of the wilderness, like an owl of the waste places;
I lie awake, I am a lonely bird on the housetop.
My days are like an evening shadow; I wither away like grass."

The moment he reads the *"But,"* I know what is coming, and I lift my hand to cut him off. He does not see it. *"But thou, O Lord,"* he reads, *"art enthroned forever."*

I say abruptly, "Stop. Please." Greg glances at me briefly, then reads on silently to himself while I picture myself, wings tucked tight, perched high up on a rooftop overlooking a smoggy city. The dry wind screeches over the chimney pots and threatens to topple me over. The nest and the baby bird have long since been blown away. I am a lonely bird; I am a lonely bird.

AND NOW the warm trade winds blow through the church, stirring not feathers but flyaway hairdos. One woman has the gall to wear a hat, her fingers becoming clothespins. Does she think she is attending a tea party, perhaps? I see when she tilts her head against the breeze that it is Buella Baxter from the magazine. Buella, whose rebellion against her southern upbringing brought her to the islands two decades ago, will relinquish neither her accent nor her knack for making everyone else feel underdressed, even in a church that, I would be willing to bet, she has not stepped in since her last wedding. Buella, married three times, is mother to none. "Can't stand the little urchins!" she is fond of announcing. "Can't see what all the fuss is about," she said when our boss, after a decade of trying to conceive, got pregnant. Without an ounce of humor, Buella sent the poor woman a condolence card and boycotted the baby shower the editorial staff threw for her. Most days we laughed off Buella's outrageousness, and when it became unbearably insensitive one of us would tell her and she'd spit a cuss and be done with it.

Shortly after I started working for the magazine, Buella adopted me as part of her coven. When she found out I was the wife of a preacher, she pronounced her almost psychopathic loathing for all things religious and made me promise not to genuflect or pray in public. "I am not Catholic and I'm not Charismatic," I told her, but it was only after she saw that I was not the reincarnated version of her evangelical great-aunt that she felt reassured.

"Good morning, Reverend Mother," she would call out from her desk when I walked by to pick up my mail each morning. Often she would use her pet name for me in the company of others and flounce off, scarves and jingly jewelry trailing, leaving confused expressions and fumbled explanations. At first I liked her little nickname for me, but a few months ago, while folding laundry late at night, I realized what the moniker said about the person I had become. One word relating to my husband, the second relating to my child. Somewhere between preacher's wife and toddler's mother were the unnamed, unknown parts of me. An Abbe of the blank space, the person of the synapse, the imperceptible pause between those two words. And now, with a rush of regret, I realize that I am no longer "reverend" or "mother," and the two definitions have taken the junction with them.

The first two pews are roped off, but fortunately Rita and Frank, and old Mrs. Scribner with her toy poodle assuming her regular Sunday morning post, ropes or no ropes, have taken some of the seats reserved for family. Michael, Greg's younger brother, and his wife, Martha, have flown in from Ohio with their three sons, and take up the front row with us. Mike's suit is a size too small for him, quite possibly the one he wore on his wedding day ten years ago. Martha, a woman who has modeled herself after her biblical namesake with an impressive exactness, has made sure all her boys are wearing matching plaid shirts and have their hair trimmed like hedges. She leans over Rhiaan— a buffer—to me and touches my knee. "Those are from Mother," she says, nodding to the two unsightly bouquets that stand like sentries on either side of Cleo's casket. "She wanted to be here."

"No she didn't," I reply tartly, to which she responds by clearing her throat. For a moment I imagine the saints of departed family members seated among the living; the ones I miss most—Mother and Grandmother—and those I do not know. It is all I can do to stay seated in the pew and not lurch toward the coffin, bear down on it with all my weight. You cannot have her, I want to shout. Go back to your graves, the lot of you!

I look across the aisle at the five rows clothed in black, the Samoan choir. At the director's signal they rise like a swarm of hornets to their hive, and even the wind seems to retreat at their deafening voices. The words are indecipherable, but the melody weaves its familiar thread through the crowd. Behind me people begin singing along in English "Abide with Me." Their song seems to rock the church as though it were a cradle until we are all gently swaying, swaddled in song.

The rocking dislodges the last few bolts battening down my composure. When I careen forward, two hands—Greg's on one side, Rhiaan's on the other—anchor me to the pew. Chuck, in his Easter ensemble, moves to the lectern and reads from the open Bible: "*At that time the disciples came to Jesus, saying, 'Who is the greatest in the kingdom of heaven?' And calling to him a child, he put her in the midst of them and said, 'Truly, I say to you, unless you turn and become like children, you will never enter the kingdom of heaven. Whoever humbles himself like this child, he is the greatest in the kingdom of heaven. Whoever receives one such child in my name receives me.' "*

"Let us pray," he says. "O Lord, who yourself did weep beside the grave and who are touched with the feeling of our sorrows, fulfill now your promise that you will not leave your people comfortless but will come to them. Reveal yourself to your afflicted servants and cause them to hear you say, 'I am the resurrection and the life.' Help them, O Lord, to abide in you through living faith, that, finding the comfort of your presence, they may have sure confidence in you for all that is to come. Amen."

I straighten up, accept Rhiaan's handkerchief, and stare out at the courtyard. A mother has taken her fussy child outside and is pointing to the plumeria blossoms on the tree. I do not recognize her. Two little boys chase after each other, hands shaped as pistols.

It cannot be that she is no longer here.

Chuck nods at us and for one wild minute I cannot remember what I am supposed to do. But Greg gets up and walks to the mike, unfolding his piece of paper. He reaches inside his jacket pocket for his glasses, slips them on, stares down at the page, and then glances quickly at the crowd. He looks down again and says, "Eleventy-twenty: A poem for Cleo."

"When you count as high as eleventy-twenty . . ." he begins, and then pauses. Blinking hard against the shifting tides in his eyes, Greg repositions his mouth and begins again. Go on, I urge him silently, but he does not speak. Way behind me someone coughs. Greg's hands begin to tremble and he lifts off his glasses and rubs hard against his brow as if clearing a windshield of splattered bugs. When his shoulders begin to quake he folds his little piece of paper into a tiny square and slips it back into his pocket. Chuck puts his arm around him and guides him off the chancel. He sits down next to me, finds his crumpled handkerchief, and mops up the sorrow. "I can't," he whispers. The organ pounds out the opening bars of "Jesus Loves the Little Children," not taking no for an answer.

Putting love away, Emily Dickinson writes in her poem about death, and as I stare at Cleo's coffin I figure my love has been put away in that small box. *We shall not want to use again / Until eternity*. Sealed up tight with decorative latches, it is a box one strong man could surely hoist onto his shoulder. While Greg sniffs and wipes and fidgets with his father's pocket watch, I turn to look at him and suddenly think, There's no leftover love, nothing to be warmed up and served to you. And fleetingly I feel sorry for him. Peering out through the fogged-up window of my own grief, I see that Greg has lost his child too. And then, just as quickly, he becomes a blur.

The Reverend Alex Takamura reads the second lesson in a thespian voice and then Chuck, in Greg's pulpit, begins his homily. The words buzz around. I see his mouth moving and I hear sounds, but it all seems to come out like a badly dubbed movie. What does he have to say about Cleo? Is he saying anything about her? Maybe it is a prayer he is saying, or a Scripture verse. I try to listen closely but keep being drawn back to the coffin. A box. That she should be lying in there seems all wrong, and suddenly I recall the ghoulish story Beauty told me of the albino girl with the crooked back whose family had once lived on my grandmother's land. The land that had swallowed the native girl, still alive in her box, because the white doctor had pronounced her dead. You can still hear her scratching some nights, especially during a full moon, Beauty told me. I sit and stare, waiting for the box to wobble slightly, straining beyond the blah-blah-blah to listen for the sound of nails against wood.

Chuck and Alex beckon to Greg, who joins them at the coffin. Laying his hands on it, Alex says, "In infinite wisdom and love, our Lord has received the innocent spirit of Cleo. We therefore tenderly commit her body to its resting place in the sure and certain hope of a glorious resurrection unto eternal life, through Jesus Christ our Lord."

Amens recited, benedictions pronounced, Greg and I now stand like store-window mannequins while a long line of people take their places to bestow on us their tidy condolences. Teary faces, pulled long like Edvard Munch paintings, crowd in on mine. Cleo's preschool teachers, the bedraggled clump of widows, the parishioners, the Rotary Club board members, the neighbors I all recognize, but others just come and go without names. And suddenly here is the unexpected guest. Sal takes my hand and kisses the back of it so tenderly I feel like I have splintered into a thousand shards of light.

❦

"ELIZABETH DEIGHTON, meet Salvatore Mariotti," said Buella on my first day at the magazine, "art director and resident Italian stud." When he stood up from his chair and came around to the front of his desk to shake my hand, it was as though he had stepped off the page of a Barbara Cartland paperback.

"Watch out for Buella." He laughed, taking his spectacles off and hooking them into his dark, curly hair. "She is fond of building reputations that are impossible to live up to."

"But you do your best, don't you, darling?" she retorted. "This one is spoken for, by a man of the cloth no less, so try not to incur the wrath of the Almighty, won't you?" she said, spiriting me away before he could say another word. "Charming but harmless," she said of him as we wandered to the next office. "He's still pining for his ex. A nasty piece of work, rumor has it, who dumped him for a wealthy divorce lawyer. You fill in the rest of the blanks—it's all too cliché for me."

"It's not cliché, it's sad," I said.

"It's sad because it's cliché, silly girl."

After that, every morning on his way to the coffeepot, Sal would pause in my doorway to give a smart bow as if he had just concluded conducting an aria. Sal in faded jeans and a shirt that always looked slept in, with black eyes casting dark shadows beneath them, could smile the saddest of smiles, a smile that made you want to run for your first aid kit.

"How goes the war?" he would ask, meaning the deadlines and their casualties lying in scrappy piles on my desk. Or maybe he never meant that at all.

"The barbarians seem to have the upper hand," I usually answered.

After a few weeks he started coming in, as if the desire for conversation was enough to make one happen. Sometimes it was only when he got to my desk that he realized he had nothing to say. And I would apply the energy it took to jump-start a dead battery just to find a way to reply. Instead of exchanging any words then, we would look at each other the way mothers tell their children not to look into the sun.

Sometimes he would pick up the galleys of an article I was proofing and make a comment, and we'd keep it light. And then one time he picked up a book from my stack.

"Nietzsche," he said. "You read Nietzsche?"

"When I'm having trouble sleeping," I joked.

"A man who fell in love only once, with a Russian girl sixteen years his junior."

"I didn't know he married," I said.

"He didn't. She turned him down and later became involved with Freud. Salomé was her name, perfect for a woman who caused him to lose his head, don't you think?" It seemed to me then that Sal was speaking of himself and his own Salomé.

A few days later, Sal returned to my office with a book under his arm.

"I come bearing gifts," he announced, handing me the book. I opened it to the page with the bookmark. It was Raphael's painting of the Transfiguration of Jesus.

"Are you religious?" I asked, drawn not to the ascending beatific Lord on the mount, but to the demonic expression of the boy's face at its foot.

"A lapsed but well-intentioned Catholic," he replied. "See, our friend Nietzsche used this painting to explain one of his philosophical concepts. He believed the world was divided between the Apollonians and the Dionysians. Apollo, the god of light, represented reason and self-control. Dionysius, on the other hand, the god of wine, stood for intoxication and passion. And pain."

"I think I can guess in which camp he would put his dear Salomé."

"And himself." Neither of us was looking at the painting anymore.

"What about you?" I asked. It was a cheeky question, one that sprinkled crumbs into the forbidden forest, and one we could both pretend was meant for the birds, the way we could pretend we were talking about philosophy and not people losing their heads.

"All Dionysius around you, I'm afraid." He said it straight-up, eating the crumbs just as I had intended. It's a game that children play, getting lost, just for that one delirious moment when you're in the middle of something unfamiliar, where you have to smell and taste and guess your way. Sal was looking at me, unblinking: had he guessed right?

There was no finding the way back by flipping the book's pages, but I did anyway, to the page featuring Moreau's painting of Salomé's dance. I have since looked again and it is indeed the Baptizer's head served on a silver platter, but at the time I could only see Greg's. When I returned Sal's look, it could only have been with Salomé's eyes.

All Dionysius around you. It was a dare, not a compliment, but nevertheless it confirmed that for someone I had ceased to be invisible. That I might be something other than mother, wife, baker, candlestick maker. That I might, if I were painted on one of Raphael's cream canvases, be the siren whose plaintive song caused men's ships to be dashed upon the rocks. It had not occurred to me then how closely my feelings might have resembled my mother's.

"She's a beauty," he said a few mornings later, returning the framed photo of Cleo to my desk. He touched things on my desk, lifted books, stroked picture frames. Everywhere were his hands, claiming, to begin with, the inanimate parts of me.

"Do you have children?" I asked, digressing.

"No, but my wife—my ex-wife—and I talked about it. She said she didn't want children, but I thought she'd come around . . . She has now, with her new husband," he said, and his hands ceased moving, came to rest in a clasp in front of him. "They say children change your life one hundred and eighty degrees. Is that true?"

I rolled my eyes in reply and nodded. "Yes. And when it's not dizzying, you sometimes see that one-hundred-and-eighty-degree turns mean better views."

"Ah yes."

❧

"I AM SO VERY SORRY for your loss, Abbe," Sal now says. "This is for you." Pressing into my palm a tarnished filigreed heart, he explains, "It was my mother's." It is heavy like a stone, and when I spring open the latch, the locket reveals a tiny pen-and-ink drawing of Cleo's face. A view from a thousand miles away.

"Didn't you get my letter?" I ask.

"Please," he implores when I look up at him, ready to return the gift. "Take it."

Dizzying views. They don't have merry-go-rounds anymore. Why is that? Playgrounds are static these days. Everything is safe, bolted down, rustproof. They're paved with squidgy material so if there is a landing to be had by anyone, it is a safe one, no harm done. I'm all for that. But in exchange for safety we have given up merry-go-rounds. Cleo never knew the thrill of a merry-go-round. She never knew what it was like to hang on to a metal bar, one foot cemented to the circular wooden platform, the other kicking up speed till everything spun crazily, hanging on tight to keep from flying off. There were no thoughts of landing on hard concrete, of getting concussed or having the wind knocked out of you. There was only spinning trees and the blurred horizon, the still air suddenly whipped into froth; and the pull. A tug so hard it turned your knuckles white with the fighting of it. A tug that wrapped its invisible arms around you, its one hundred invisible arms, and tried pulling and prying you from that speeding platform. It was a pull that made the

74

cells in your body pop with excitement, that made something race around under your skin, made percussion instruments of your internal organs. And instead of screaming in fear, you could only laugh, hysterically, the way you weren't supposed to, inches away from being splattered. And when the world slowed down and the risk of falling ebbed, you stuck your foot back out on the earth and pushed and pushed and pushed till the world went around at a dizzying speed again. This time you'd risk a little more: lean out from the platform, tip your head back, close your eyes, and let the day contract into a single great battle between holding on and the tempting desire to let go.

That's what Sal was. My merry-go-round.

Each time he came by my office, I heard that platform creak as I stepped on it. Each time I put out my foot and gave a tentative push. When he left, everything slowed, everything became so infuriatingly solid, immovable, predictable once again. Things didn't move. Objects didn't fly about. Not the cabinets or the desk or the house. Or Greg. Dear bolted-down, rustproof, net-protected Greg.

If Greg was a piece of playground equipment, he would be the sandbox. It is hard to get hurt in the sandbox, and I had loved that about him right from the start. After my father, it was all I ever wanted in a man. If not happy, I might have been content within those boundaries if someone hadn't had to go pointing out the merry-go-round.

There's been a death in the family, is what I thought when Sal and I were in the janitor's closet. I was expecting sparks, not tears, but tears there were, surprising tears because there was nothing to cry about. A man was holding me with the tenderest of looks. And, not speaking, he reached across the spinning gap and wiped them with his thumb, the way he would wipe his own tears. And there it was again: There's been a death in the family. Shh, he whispered, even though no one was making a sound. Perhaps he was shushing the wind that had gathered speed around us, which was lifting our hair and setting it in arcs. And even when his lips were so close that even the wind couldn't squeeze through, he called for quiet, so close there was nothing round about his eyes—they had flattened to an escarpment, the end of which I couldn't see. And I did not make a sound. It was my body who was the family, and there were bits inside it that had climbed into their graves. Bits that didn't even have names, so there were no tombstones. But all at once they rose up like the swirling skirt of a girl on a merry-go-round, and I let them rise and rise till modesty spun off and sailed away with the breeze. After his lips left mine I still had my head tilted back, so he came back, and we rode around one last time.

Jostled along the conveyor belt of mourners, Sal is gone. I shake hands and stumble into people's embraces, and all I can recall is that last stolen moment Sal and I shared—his whisper ("Do I dare hope?") so faint it might easily have been misheard had it not been offered by his lips in my hair. A thief I was, or worse, because of that moment, stealing what had no business being mine.

Mrs. Avery approaches me. "We will now move the coffin to the hearse, Mrs. Deighton, if you would like to follow us." Her companion, a man I do not recognize, directs Greg, Rhiaan, Frank, and Chuck to take their places at the four handles. I look around frantically for Jenny but do not see her, and the overwhelming sense of jet lag assails me. Quickly Mrs. Avery reaches out for my arm and I accept her help with dry gratitude.

We follow Cleo, riding on the men's shoulders, down the long aisle and out the back of the church. Cleo always loved to ride on Greg's shoulders. Sometimes he forgot to bend when walking through doorways, and her sharp cry would make me want to kill him.

"It's just not right," I say, shaking free the tears, watching love walk away.

"No, dear, it certainly isn't," Mrs. Avery quietly replies, tightening her grip on my arm. It is a second loss, seeing Cleo put in the hearse, hearing the doors slam behind her. She goes, and I shall not see her again. As the hearse slips quietly into the crowded lane, I hear my grandmother's voice just as surely as if she were standing behind me and whispering the words: Hold a button, Abbe.

GREG AND I SHUFFLE to the church's fellowship hall, modestly decorated and overcrowded, just as the rain comes down.

"Who was that?" Greg asks.

"Who?"

"The guy wearing a tie."

I search Greg's face as though it might have the answer. Doesn't he know? Hasn't he seen a thing?

❧

SOMETIMES I felt as though I had watched too much of my parents, as though they were a never-ending daytime TV drama bound to give me square eyes. But sometimes I think I was not watching closely enough. I cannot say, for example, how long my mother slaked her thirst with the gin bottle. It might have been my entire fourteenth year or it could have been a month. Nor can I say I know the moment she started smiling again. The little things I noticed did not seem like any big deal, certainly nothing that was about to lead to her branding. She no longer took naps at the kitchen counter beside her untouched dinner plate; she started growing her nails; there was the new hairdo (a permanent for her reed-straight hair) and a new dress. And oh, one other thing: her laugh. That was new. She laughed at things that weren't even funny—my knock-knock jokes, my grandmother's backfiring Morris Minor when it drove up our street, the cat's antics with her feather duster. But I never stopped to think about it until I came home from tennis practice one day and found her spilling that laugh all over the phone.

For one thing my mother did not spend much time on the phone because my father always clanged on about the bills he had to pay each month. It did not seem to matter when the call was on someone else's dime. And also, my mother did not have many friends. Any friends, really, except for Auntie Muriel, who only came by when there was no chance of running into my father. But that afternoon my mother giggled like Natalie Chandler did each time she walked up the school stairs while a row of eighth-grade boys lined up below for a view of the valley up her skirt.

My mother was on the phone when I put my racket away, when I came out of the kitchen with a sandwich, and when I came out of my room after doing my homework, all the while soaking the conversation with that burbling brook of a laugh. She was still on the phone when my father blasted through the front door, plum-faced. We would hear soon enough how he had been trying to call home for two hours to tell her that he had finally gotten the promotion, to cancel dinner because this was a night for Bender's Grill. But first there was the business of the phone to attend to, and the business of the laugh.

"Who the hell are you gabbing to?" he yelled, my mother pale as her freshly hung wallpaper.

She let the receiver slip from her ear to her heart. "It's no one, a friend," she answered.

"Well, which is it?" he spat. My father, apparently, had been watching my mother more closely than I had, because before she could answer he grabbed the phone from her and yelled "Who is this?" in such a manner as to indicate he knew exactly who it was. My mother tried reaching for the cradle to disconnect the line, but he flung her hand aside.

The No-One-Friend evidently answered because my father's rage blistered like canker sores.

"Listen here, you mealymouthed faggot, don't think I don't know what's going on! I told you before, you talk to my wife and I'll fuck you up. You hear me?" And then, by way of demonstration, he banged the receiver against the telephone table a few times and replaced it at his ear.

"I am going to say this one more time: You don't ever, fucking never, talk to my wife again. You stay away from her or, so help me God, she's going to read about you in the obits. And I'll be the one laughing then!" The phone, having enjoyed its last moment of function, was ripped from the socket and hurled against the wall.

There was no trace of a laugh on my mother's face when my father spun around to meet it.

"Dad," I cried. "Dad, please!" If he knew I was standing at my door on the other end of the hallway, a witness, would he not quit? But there was no quitting: Louise Spenser's face had to be taught a lesson. The blow, fierce and hard, was over quickly, but the one word that had accompanied it lingered long. *Whore.*

∽

"ABBE, who was that man?" Greg asks again.

"No one, a friend," I mumble, grip tightening around the locket. Cutting my hair, and the million other things I have done to keep from becoming my mother, have not worked, it seems.

"What did he give you?"

"Oh, it's nothing."

"What is it?"

I open my palm and Greg lifts out the locket, pries it open, and peers at his daughter's face. After a pause he looks at me and, without speaking, returns the locket to my hand. There is no backhander, no name-calling, even though I wish there were. Call me a whore, call me Salomé, call me something! Instead, Greg steps out of my circle to accept a cup of coffee and is instantly pulled into the gravitational field of his parishioners who need consoling, this the day of the Sabbath.

ORDINARY TIME

SIX

Sparrows carry the souls of the dead, Beauty used to say. Sitting on the rocking chair, looking out the sliding glass door to my balcony and the bird feeder Greg fills now that the storm has passed, I watch the sparrows haggle and jostle around it like old women at a church rummage sale. Why Beauty, whose toothless face is as clear as the sky from which those fidgety birds have descended, must haunt me I cannot fathom. Why her and not the bouncy-haired sparrow of a girl I once, a long time ago, yesterday, called "my child," I do not know. Nor why I can picture her hands busy at the task of wringing a chicken's scrawny neck now that her spells are no longer needed.

Their wings flutter and they hop about, sometimes over one another, and there seems to be great injustice in the transaction, for the fat ones feast while the forlorn-looking ones are penned out. I hope the souls of the departed are a little more cordial and accommodating. And suddenly the sparrows are joined by a couple of cardinals, the male sending the others scattering, making room for his mate.

The house is empty, Rhiaan having left before sunrise for his flight back to California. Jenny has returned to her routine of taking care of first-graders and Mr. Finnegan. The roofing contractor (a licensed one this time) and his team have left in their pickup trucks, taking the last of our line of credit with them. Only the smell of decaying bouquets and Greg's insufferable patience take up space.

"The mortuary called this morning," Greg announces, walking into the bedroom. "We can pick up Cleo's cremains tomorrow."

"You go," I say, watching the sparrows bide their time on the balcony rail, the cardinals' apparent disinterest.

"Come with me, Abbe," he pleads.

I turn to look at him and his face threatens to collapse on itself. Slowly, deliberately, I shake my head and turn away. His sigh is a flutter of wings.

"We are going to have to talk about this, you know," he says, walking to the rocking chair, scaring the birds from their meal.

I look ahead and blink.

"About what to do with her. About what to do with her ashes," he presses.

"Yes, I expect so."

"Well?" he asks.

"Well, what?"

"Well, what are we going to do? Where are we going to spread them?"

"I can't have this discussion now," I say, seeing the first bold sparrow return to the feeder.

"So you want me to just bring them home and prop the box next to the sugar bowl till you are ready to talk about it? Is that what you want?"

"Greg, please."

"No, Abbe, not this time. You don't get to always have it your way."

"Who the hell are you to talk to me about my way?" I shout, facing him. "If I had it my way, she would not be dead. Do you understand? If I had it my way, your church members would not be clogging up my refrigerator with food that's fit for a Fourth of July picnic. And if I had it my way, you would not be standing here right now provoking me into a conversation I do not want to have."

We stare at each other, blinking at the heat of an unearthly fire, until he turns away and walks out of the room. When I look at the feeder, all the sparrows have returned to peck at the cardinals' leftovers, and I rock again, slowly, for the souls of the deceased.

SHE STEPS into a dark swamp, where the trees are up to their knees in water. The reeds are sharp and the mud smells bad like boiled rot. She doesn't like the dark, she doesn't like forests, this is going to scare her, I think. "Cleo," I call to her, but she cannot hear me. "Cleo!" I call louder over my own terror. She is lost; I can tell because she looks around and then walks a little deeper into the darkness. From behind I try to speed up, to reach her, but even though she is very scared now, taking very few steps at all, I still cannot get closer. I reach out my arms, stretching across the abyss: "Cleo!"

I wake up and pull at my hair, crying out into the silence of the room. Greg runs up the stairs, turns on the bedside light, and holds out his arms. "Shh, shh," he whispers. "It's only a dream. Shh."

"I couldn't help her," I stammer. "I was trying to get to her, but she couldn't hear me. She was in some kind of hell, Greg, and I couldn't save her."

"It's only a dream, babe," he whispers. "Come downstairs, come have some dinner."

It is not the middle of the night but only seven-thirty, and Greg has just settled down for his evening vigil in front of the television.

"Anything on?" I ask.

"No," he says. "I have come to believe that this is one of the things we can rely on in life: that there will be nothing on television."

I sit down in his chair and he brings me a tray with a plate of cheese and biscuits and an apple cored, pared, and peeled the way Cleo used to eat hers. We watch sitcom reruns, deadpan through all the one-liners, and Greg answers the phone each time it rings. Patiently, he says the same things over and over again: No thank you, we don't need anything right now; yes, it was a moving service; thank you for your thoughtfulness; yes, see you Sunday.

"You're not honestly going to church on Sunday," I say, incredulous at the thought.

"Yes, I am. In fact, I'm going to preach," he says to the TV.

I frown, stare at this man I suddenly do not know. "What?"

"It's what I know to do, okay? It's how I process things," he says.

"These are not 'things'; this is mourning—there is no 'process-ing.' "

"If you don't mind, I would really rather not argue about seman-tics. I am going to church on Sunday, I will be in the pulpit, and I would very much like it if you could come with me," he says.

"I am not about to go to church and face all those people and sing praises to God," I say.

"That's what I thought. And I completely understand."

I am about to say, Understand? There is nothing about this that any-one can understand, but catch myself. Semantics. I begin to tremble, and realize that it is not Cleo walking into the swamp, losing her way. It is me.

When the phone rings for the fourth time, I tell him to leave it, but he picks up anyway, and rather than the usual acceptances, I hear him say, "Yes, this is Reverend Deighton, who is this?"

"I'm sorry," he says, "I cannot hear you very well; could you speak up?" I look over at him just in time to see his eyes glaze over.

"Who is it?" I whisper, but he gets up and leaves the room.

"Yes," I hear him say over his shoulder. And then, again, "Yes."

Fifteen minutes go by but Greg does not return. I put the tray of half-eaten food down, get up, walk through the kitchen to his study, and find him sitting quietly on his chair in the dark.

"Who was that?"

He looks over at my quivering face and delivers the answer for which I am quite unprepared.

"Mr. Nguyen," he says.

"Who?"

"The driver."

What I know of the driver is that he owns a white Toyota Corolla, older model, impeccable but for the slight dent on the left-hand side of the bumper and a missing headlight. I know he lives alone in a cinder block house at the cul-de-sac of River Street. That his only family is a son in Los Altos, California. And that he has never been cited for so much as a moving violation.

Involuntary manslaughter, the police had first said (nothing in the books about childslaughter), and then changed their minds. No evidence, I overheard the officers tell Greg in our hallway, of negligent driving. He had not been drinking, or speeding; it was one of those random, no-fault accidents. Unaware that I was standing at the top of the stairs, they continued their report, although I heard Greg twice invite them to sit in the living room and drink some coffee. "The driver has no priors. Hell, Reverend, the man has not even been ticketed before." The voice sounded apologetic. There was a pause and I imagined them to be standing around, shaking their heads in amazement. Was it then that Greg offered them coffee a third time? "The skid marks corroborate what the witnesses testified. The strange thing about it," the officer said, "is that the old man keeps hanging around the station. Every day. I swear he's disappointed we haven't arrested him."

"What does he do there?" Greg asked.

"Sometimes he adds something to his statement, but mostly he just keeps giving us the same details. One of us usually has to tell him to leave; otherwise he sits out in the waiting area for hours."

What I know about the driver, perhaps better than anyone else except maybe for Mr. Nguyen himself, is that he, like Theresa, like me, is getting away with murder. That there is no such thing as a no-fault accident.

"WHAT DID HE WANT?" I now ask Greg.

"I'm not really sure. He offered his condolences," Greg replies, still stupefied. I put my hand over my mouth to smother the erupting scream. "He said how sorry he is, that he would never be so bold as to ask forgiveness."

"What did you say?"

"I can't remember. I don't know if I said anything." He frowns, trying to recollect.

I sit down on the floor, lean against the doorpost. Minutes go by.

"He sounded so . . ." Greg begins, and pauses again, shaking his head. After a while I get up and turn around to head out. ". . . damned," he says. "He sounded like a damned man."

∾

MY MOTHER knew what it was like to be damned, and if on a morning after waking up she temporarily forgot, my father would find a way to remind her. After the day the telephone left skid marks on the wall and Mr. No-One-Friend stopped calling, my father did not repeat the word that had turned his "wife" into a "whore." Which is not to say he had changed his mind on the matter. He cut up her purple frock, dumped the hot rollers into the trash can, and replaced the telephone with one that came with a lock and key, while my mother's fingernails went back to being chipped instead of painted.

Ever since the earth was formed my father had the same schedule—off to work by seven, home by six for dinner, Wednesday nights ten or eleven depending on when he got kicked out of the pub, weekends mostly fishing in the afternoons and playing darts at the pub in the evenings. But after the incident (which in my mind came to be known as "the last laugh" because of my father's new best phrase, "Who's having the last laugh now, hey, Louise?"), you could no more predict his timetable than you could an earthquake's. It had surely cost him the offer of promotion to foreman, leaving work at two or three in the afternoon without permission or an hour before clock-out time. But my dad had more important things to check on. My mother, for instance.

She had come to pick me up from school one day, not too long after the telephone incident, and she told me we were making a quick stop on the way home.

"Where are we going?" I asked. "Can we get an ice cream from Pick 'n' Pay?"

"We aren't going to the grocery store," she replied.

"Well, then where?"

"I am stopping by the City Hall to pick up some papers."

I didn't have time to ask her what papers because I was leaning

88

over my seat to reach my backpack for the uneaten banana in it when I noticed a familiar car behind us.

"Isn't that Dad's pickup?"

My mother, checking her rearview mirror, sighed. "Not again." And that's how I learned that this was not the first (nor was it to be the last) time my father followed my mother. She turned left at Main Street, and instead of heading east for the municipal buildings, she headed west. I swung around to check and, sure enough, my father made the turn and kept right on coming.

"Shouldn't we stop? Maybe he wants to tell us something?" I suggested, but my mother kept driving, both hands clamped to the steering wheel, muttering under her breath and shaking her head.

By the time she turned onto R45, the road that led to my grandmother's farm, my father's truck was so close to our bumper that it appeared as though we were towing him.

"Mom," I said. "Slow down." I glanced at the speedometer—100 kilometers per hour, the needle still arching its back. Instead of watching her speed, she glanced from her rearview mirror to the road and back again. Within minutes we were in the farmlands, the road veering past the vineyards headed for Dead Man's Curve.

"Mom, the sign says fifty!" She barely tapped her brakes, then carved up the curves till she got to the hairpin bend that had totaled more cars than the Kyalami Racetrack. I prayed that ours would not be one of them. But she eased up, eyes so fixed on the road that she did not notice, as we rounded the bend, that my father had tied us for first place. With the truck window rolled down, he gestured for my mother to pull over.

"Not today, Harry," she whispered to herself, and stepped on the gas.

I saw a flash of black the same second I felt its impact on my mother's car. Only then did she hit her brakes, skidding to a stop on the road's gravel shoulder. It was a hard blow, one that should have killed the animal, one I wished had so we might have been spared its loud, agonized wailing. I looked first at my mother, slumped over the wheel in defeat, and then behind me to where my father was getting out of his truck and making his way to the middle of the road, where the whining dog lay. I got out in time to see my father wrap it in his windbreaker and lift it off the center line. "Get back in the car, Abbe," he said. Out of nowhere a man who identified himself as the dog's owner appeared, his own pickup at the foot of the driveway on the opposite side of the road. The dust had not yet settled from where he had come, the farmhouse at the line of trees.

The dog was big—a bull mastiff, the man told my father. "Always chasin' cars; too dumb to know it would be the death of him one day," he shouted above the noise. My father laid the dog on the man's flatbed and they talked as old friends.

"Helluva sorry about this," my father apologized. (So that's what it sounded like.)

"Aw, that's all right," the farmer said. "He's a tough bugger—probably just a busted leg, by the look of it. I reckon you should worry more about that car over there."

"My wife," my father explained. "Tell you what, give me your number and let me help out with the vet bills if this guy over here survives."

Numbers exchanged and apologies issued, the farmer got in his truck and drove his dog, still yowling, down the road. My father, ushering me across the street, went to my mother's side of the car where she was still heaving silent sobs on the steering wheel. I climbed in the passenger seat, expecting to hear my father's biting insults.

"You okay to drive home?" was all he asked, and when she nodded he closed the door so quietly you could barely hear it click.

When my mother finally pulled a U-turn and headed back for Paarl, my father was long gone, but you could see my grandmother's water tower on the horizon behind us. I wanted to exonerate her. "He just came out of nowhere, there wasn't anything you could do, Mom," I said.

"I could have killed him," she replied. "I could have killed us." Lesson: Could-haves carry just as much weight as gone-done-its.

After dinner that night she asked my father for the telephone key and the number the farmer had written on the back of his cigarette box.

"I called him already," my father told her. "The dog's going to be fine once his leg heals. He'll probably be out chasing cars in a couple of weeks."

But she persisted till he gave in. She called the farmer; she must have told him "sorry" a dozen times. And still that wasn't enough. She called the next night and the one after until my father refused to give her the key. But for her it seemed that enough sorries could not be said, sorries that would ease her guilt for a dumb dog's leg or for the guilt that drove her to take Dead Man's Curve at ninety in the first place.

My father did help pay for the vet bills, working overtime to do it. But he did not spend one dime to have my mother's fender mended. So it sat there, lopsided with its dog-shaped dimple, a visual reminder for my mother that absolution did not come for free and someone else had paid her price. The point everyone seemed to be missing, however, was that if it hadn't been for my father pulling up alongside her, distracting her from the business of driving, she would not have hit the dog in the first place. To my mind, he was just as culpable.

❧

"HE'S GOING TO KEEP CALLING," I tell Greg.

"I don't think so."

As if Greg had not spoken, I shake my head. "He can't keep calling."

"Abbe, he's not going to call again. All right? Just forget about it."

But I feel as though I am approaching Dead Man's Curve with someone else's foot strapped to the accelerator. "What if he calls again? What are you going to tell him?" We peer at each other as though two drivers in two separate cars . . .

"I'm not going to tell him anything, because he isn't going to call!"

THE THUNDER WAKES ME and I feel the headache creep up my neck and over the top of my head to settle on my left eyebrow. Greg is still asleep in the other chair and does not stir, even though the room gets day-bright before the next big bang. I get up from the sofa, turn off the TV, and head to the kitchen, but I stop at the dining room table where Greg's Bible serves as a paperweight for his sermon. Sunday tomorrow. I sit down, pull the pages free from their weight, and begin to read.

I have been back to before the beginning of time, when the earth was formless, and darkness covered the land. A cold, uninhabitable nowhere of a place, I want to tell you. Where chaos and calamity are the order of dawnless days, where ears are deaf to the Creator and marbled eyes are white from crying. There is not much to see and not much to know. All that is is the Eternal Absence, invisible yet more real than breath. And Death is all there is to know . . .

As most of you know, our daughter Cleo died a little over two weeks ago on the cusp of Good Friday, the night Jesus knelt under an olive tree. "Remove this cup from me," he prayed, a cup that offered no sustenance; a poisoned chalice that promised only death.

By noon the next day, it was not a prayer but a plea he offered. "Eli, Eli lama sabachthani—My God, my God, why hast thou forsaken me?" Jesus was already on his way back to the beginning of time when darkness covered the face of the earth. Abandoned first by his friends and then by his God, Jesus seems to be shouting down the canyons of time, but all that comes back are the seemingly indifferent echoes, the sound that Absence makes.

I shouted down those empty canyons the night Cleo suffered. Please, I begged, let her live. Most certainly the purest prayer I have ever uttered. A wish I felt sure would be granted. After all, was I not a faithful servant, had I not served the Master these past twenty years? Was it not true that Jesus, after being beckoned by the synagogue ruler, rushed to the bedside of his daughter to summon her from the grip of death? I believed, I want you to know; I truly believed. "Your faith has restored her," I was waiting to hear. Instead we were told that she had suffered, then rallied briefly, suffered a little more, and then finally died. Alone.

Oh, I know those Scripture verses—thank you to those of you who wrote them in your kind notes. Indeed I have recited those same words many times to grieving family members. Some of you here today have heard me say them to you. "Weeping may endure for the night but joy cometh in the morning," declares the psalmist. "Blessed are those who mourn, for they shall be comforted," promises our Lord. But where was my God when I needed him more than ancient words which roll off the tongue a little too easily? Where was God when the young man he called "Son" cried for help? Where was Cleo's God the night she stepped out onto a narrow street, lit only by looming headlights? And why couldn't God grant this one small prayer? Why couldn't God spare her? It is not as if I were asking for world peace, an end to hunger. What difference would it have made in the grand scheme of things?

After many hours, after repeating these same questions over and over again, I was reminded of a different dark time. Not the pure dark, the cold dark before daybreak when the stone was rolled away. (I, like Thomas, had missed Easter, so could not shout "Hallelujah, he is risen," could scarcely believe those who declared it that Sunday.) No, it is the dark night that John describes at the end of his Gospel when the disciples are fishing on the Sea of Galilee. Casting their nets all night in hopes of even the smallest morsel to sustain them, they catch nothing. When they are about to give up, they spot someone, a shadowy figure standing on the beach. Squinting into the darkness, they cannot tell whether it is friend or foe. They draw a little closer and the darkness is dispelled ever so slightly in the small embers of a charcoal fire. The stranger tells them to cast their nets once more. And they do, and you know what happens—their nets nearly burst from the weight of the fish. When they arrive at the shore, the stranger has cooked them breakfast, and in the sharing of the humble meal, in the tiny glow from a breakfast fire, the fishermen see it is their friend.

The miracle of this story, you might be tempted to think, is the catch. No, dearly beloved, the miracle of the story is the existence of that small glowing coal, made by one who gently blew a small spark into a beachside hearth, who dispelled the darkness and ushered in the dawn, who offered this time not a chalice but a hot meal.

As for us, it is our emptiness that draws us to that small flicker, our hunger that stretches out our hand. Only when we accept the humble meal from the stranger at the shore will we recognize the Light of the World. Like the disciples, we will be filled long enough to see the farthest edges of the *horizon tinged with the merest hint of color. Our prayer—"My God, my God, why hast thou forsaken me?"—finally becomes a profession of faith: "My God." Then we see how salvation comes in insignificant and easily overlooked acts, in bite-sized portions. It sustains us not for all eternity, as we might prefer, but only for a little while, until the edges of hunger narrow in again and the darkness settles over the earth.*

What then of faith? It is the bravery of going about our tasks with one eye scanning the shore for that small charcoal fire and for the oddly familiar stranger calling us to "Come, eat."

It is a communion mediation, I realize. Greg's spindly flock will collect around the altar rail, eager to peck at the crumbs. Cupping their hands, they will wait for Greg to break off a morsel of the loaf and drop it into their hands: *the Body of our Lord, broken for you.* They will dip it into the cup when they hear him pronounce: *the Blood of the Lamb, shed for you.* They will receive the morsel of grace, of forgiveness, for cussing or lying or lying down with another man's wife. Forgiveness, whether they ask for it or expect it or even deserve it. And Greg will bestow it on anyone who is beggar enough to kneel in front of him, even those who come with someone else's blood on their hands.

I look over at my slumbering husband, head tipped forward as though bowed in prayer. Mr. Nguyen will call again, and when he does I know Greg will not be able to send him away empty-handed. The last caller's number is still stored in the phone's memory. I dial in the instruction to connect me to the number. It rings for a long time. Just as I am about to hang up, a phlegmy voice croaks out a bewildered "Hello?"

The beating in my ears is like the flapping of birds' wings.

"If you ever call my house again, I will kill you myself," I whisper. Slowly, quietly, and without waiting for his response, I return the receiver to its cradle.

SEVEN

"Jenny called," Greg announces when I come downstairs. "She said you haven't returned her phone messages." It is midmorning, the shadow of the mountain retreating from the harbor and already halfway up our hill. From this vantage point, I can see the H1, unraveling from Ewa through the congested sprawl of Pearl City to downtown, along which cars are strung like abacus beads. The freeway deposits most of them into the clogged tributaries of town. Honolulu, on a bus tour, is exactly what the brochures depict—a mix of modern and turn-of-the-century architecture, built around spidery banyan trees and ancestral burial sites.

It's a city as noisy as it is fragrant. With the windows open, I can hear the distant hum of traffic, the sirens, a radio turned to Krater FM, but it is the smell that's distracting: overripe mangoes and papayas rotting in their trees. The houses on the street below us have the sun already beating down on their roofs, but we are still shaded. There are no trade winds today, and the sun-bleached palette of summer is unrelenting.

"She's worried about you. You should call her," he suggests. I manage a polite nod. There is still some milk in the carton that hasn't soured, which will be my breakfast.

"Want to go out and get some brunch?" Greg asks. Before I can answer, he says, "Abbe, you need to get out of the house; it's been two months."

"Seven weeks," I correct him. "What's that?" I ask, seeing a writing pad scribbled with notes on the far corner of the dining room table.

"Some stuff for church," he says guiltily.

"The church is filling her place."

"Excuse me?" It is a warning I do not heed as Greg picks up his paperwork and tucks it under his arm like a security blanket.

"You can't substitute her with the church."

"It helps, all right? It helps me get my mind off things; it gives me something to do. It's not a substitute."

All I do is roll my eyes, but he says, heat rising up his neck, "Don't go off on a tirade now, because I do not want to hear it." I don't recognize the voice of the man who stands in my kitchen any more than I recognize my own reflection, and he would not recognize a tirade even if I had the inclination to share one with him.

"Keep your mind off things? Like your dead daughter?" I ask with icy calm.

"How dare you!" Greg shouts. "Don't you ever, ever say that to me again, do you understand?" Instead of waiting for an answer, he marches out of the house, grabbing the keys on his way. The door slams like a slap and I shout into the silence of the house, "Your dead daughter! Your dead daughter! Your dead daughter!"

I walk into our bedroom, sit down in my closet, and close the door. Anger makes the thoughts piling up in my head snap like dry twigs, as though the devil is preparing kindling for a bonfire. I want to beat my arms against the walls till they too splinter. This fury is my new companion, taking up the vacancy that sleep has left. It makes me want to smash plates, to scalp books of their bindings. When I close my eyes, wild horses beat their hooves in panicked flight across my chest. There is no walking away from it, slamming the front door on it. How do I tell Jenny with her thoughtful concern that I have become mad with the bristling of unsubsiding rage? That I am the rabid, mangy dog at the end of the street, baring its teeth at imaginary threats, jerking and jumping and frightening the children who wait for Atticus Finch to come home? That there is nobody who, in mercy, comes to peer at me down the barrel of a borrowed rifle, finger poised to end my misery. Just a long road sided by houses where nice folks play out their parts in suburban Technicolor. People who see me coming and herd their children back indoors and peer out through lace-covered windows: Crazy!

Suddenly Solly barks, hearing the garden gate open. Oh God, Greg's back, I think, and I consider hiding in the closet till he goes away. But the doorbell rings and an unfamiliar male voice hollers an impatient "Hello!" I dredge myself out of the shoe pile and make the long journey down the stairs to the front window, shouting at Solly to stop making a racket. A fidgety tattooed man in a brown uniform stands next to a box that is four feet high. "Delivery," he says when I open the door, and then he sees me and grows very still. Even his frenetic gum-chewing ceases.

"You have the wrong house," I say, not calling Solly in, not apologizing for the barking.

"1886?" he says, reading his gadget.

"Yes, but there are six houses at this address."

"House C?" he asks tentatively. "Deighton?"

It is my turn to look afraid. What has come?

"Would you mind putting it in the living room?" I ask, taking his clipboard to sign. He hesitates, as though I might deliver a well-placed rabid bite, then lifts the package and takes a wide berth around me, the monster with hair like sprigs. A burnt bush, that's what I am; a singed remnant, smoky and brittle. Not the burning bush Moses encountered, the kind that makes you remove your shoes and bow your head and avert your eyes. "I Am," declared the unconsuming fire. No. Ravaged by the Great I Am, I make people turn away. Yesterday it was Gillian Beech with the agenda for the annual homeowners' association meeting and her campaigning for Mrs. Chung's resumption of the presidential seat. The day before that, Greg's secretary, Betty, with another casserole. They come and go, with their downcast eyes; So sorry, they say, or nothing at all. Just those marshmallow faces. Why don't they burn? How come there are no singed places around their edges, no smell of sizzling hair?

The UPS man leaves without saying a word, and without looking back.

And there it has alighted, a box the size of an oven, in the middle of the living room floor. Kneeling down and turning my head sideways, I read the label: COTTAGES 4u. The smoldering coals in my belly begin burning again. Cleo's dollhouse.

A plastic dollhouse. Now, that's something that doesn't leap into flames. It has small parts that can choke a child under two, warns the label, but it is not combustible. I had packed away every button, every washing machine quarter, the month Cleo was born. I all but nailed shut the kitchen cabinets under the sink long before she could crawl. Every time I found a pushpin Greg left lying in the study, I picked it up, centered it on my palm, and ceremoniously walked it over to him. His carelessness could do her in, I implied, but only ever said, "We need to be more careful." After reading a magazine article about how a child had strangled herself on the blind cords while her mother was putting on the kettle, I became a cord vigilante too. My house became a yacht with all its sheets knotted down in place. There was no way she could hurt herself. It was impossible.

∾

GREG AND I have called on parishioners whose houses take on appearances. Appearances that say, All is right with the world. Clutter-free countertops, carpets vacuumed till every fiber snaps to attention, gleaming toilet bowls, for-show-only couches, lampshades still wrapped in plastic, and fireplaces stocked with unused candles—dead giveaways of things running amok, if you ask me. The smell alone can make me panic: the smell of trapped air, windows kept closed for the fear of neighbors' wandering ears. Air breathed in and out, over and over again, siphoned through pinched lungs, lungs used for shouting or crying or, worse, squeezing it all in.

Houses like that make some women envious, and had I not lived in one when I was sixteen years old I might be one of them. Because

when you have lived in one you know that it is all an act, a façade behind which a demon runs loose.

My mother never picked up those important papers from City
Hall. Instead, she stayed at home, day in and day out. It was as though
she were punishing the house, disciplining it in the hopes that what
took place in it still had a chance of being "normal." She beat the cush-
ions till they swelled; she struck the rugs with the broom till they
coughed up big clouds of dust. With the duster she lashed out at the
corners of each room whether a web had been brave enough to occupy
it or not. Every inch of the house took a beating, and even though it did
exactly as she wished, things only got worse.

For one, we ate less, at least she and I did. With my mother's
household allowance cut, there were no longer bowls of fresh fruit on
the table. Sandwiches of ham and cheese were replaced with ones of
jam. The fridge, once stocked with cheese and sausages, housed mostly
my father's beers and eggs from my grandmother's farm. We took to
eating food out of boxes and cans, sometimes for weeks in a row till my
father would complain.

"Christ, Louise, if I come home to one more macaroni and cheese
dinner or one more goddamn Vienna sausage, I'm going to spit!"

"We can't afford anything else with twenty rand a week, Harry,"
my mother protested one night.

"Well, maybe if I had taken that promotion instead of having to
take charge of you, we might have more money, now wouldn't we?"

And just like that she left the table to go slap the sheets on the
clothesline while my father yelled, "Tomorrow, by God, I want a roast
on my table!"

The following day, before she sent me off to school with her sad
eyes, my mother asked me a favor: "Could I borrow some money?"
Other kids got pocket money, but I only ever got money for birthdays
and Christmases. Still, I had saved enough for a new tennis racket. She
saw the look on my face. "Ten rand," she pleaded. "Just enough for a
small leg of lamb. I'll pay you back, I promise."

That night, while my mother, the lamb, and I waited at the dining room table for my father to come home, the house took on a smell that to this day can make me break a sweat: burnt meat. It was close to midnight when he came home. My mother was still seated at her chair at the table in front of her ruined dinner. He was loud enough that I woke up and opened my bedroom door in time to see him pick up the lid off the roasting pan and peer at the meat shrunk to the size of a tennis ball. Then he looked at my mom and said in a billowy cloud of alcohol, "What would your fancy boyfriend think of you now?"

I closed the door on his laugh and wished with all my might that it would be his last.

∽

MY HOUSE, you could say, suffers from neglect, but it is a premeditated neglect. Stuff piles up in the corners where the geckos hide their eggs, the windowpanes are streaked with dirt. Rather than burnt dinners, the air is full of the smell of dead flowers, of the stagnant water in which they wallow. It is to this home, where there are no appearances, where things seem exactly as they are, that Greg returns at seven o'clock, the time I get up from my afternoon nap.

Heating something in the microwave, he comes to hug me as I walk in, a gesture that now strikes me as peculiarly out of place. "Dinner is nearly ready," he says.

"I'm not hungry."

"Eat something, Ab."

"I did already," I lie, and he knows it because there are no dishes in the sink.

I can tell he has been crying, and for a moment I can't think why. But then I look over at the dollhouse sitting in the middle of our living room, the dollhouse with its decorated bedroom and en suite bathroom.

"What should we do with it?" he asks.

"Leave it there," I say, and it comes out contrary.

"Why don't we give it to . . ." and I know he's trying to think of a child he knows, but the names do not come. "Charity?"

"Why don't we keep it?"

"It just doesn't seem right," he says after a deep silence.

It is the longest conversation we have had in days, since Sunday, and I am already tired out.

"Leave it where it is," I insist, and walk out of the kitchen.

My grief is a bully, I notice—people cave in so easily at its obstinacy. I don't need to say much, but its weight and size make them back off. It is not a good idea to keep Cleo's new dollhouse in the living room, God knows we have enough reminders that she is not coming back. It isn't good for me, it isn't good for Greg, but good is not the point; good is taken away and all the best intentions amount to nothing.

I cannot stop and think about how I make other people feel, because there is too much feeling in the world. I am afraid of them, with their suffocating blankets of feeling. I only want them to stay away. Greg, I imagine, knows this too, but when the two of us come head to head, it is usually my bully who prevails. So the dollhouse stays up, and tomorrow, I think, I will set up the miniature kitchen.

❧

GREG BOUGHT ME a dollhouse once. I told him long ago how I had wanted a dollhouse as a child but never got one; instead, my father handed me a tub of bulky LEGOs more suitable for a toddler, and left me to build my own box of a house into which my dolls could never fit. We had been married five or six years when I found a receipt from a place called Gardens and Paradise on Greg's desk for $180. He hadn't brought anything new home, so that night, when we were getting into bed, I asked him about it.

"You snoop!" he accused, smiling. "It was supposed to be a surprise for your birthday," he sighed.

"Right."

"No, really."

"What is it?"

"Can't you just wait for your birthday?"

"No."

"Okay, it's a garden gnome," he said. And I laughed so hard, but then I saw the crushed expression on his face. I had hurt his feelings.

"Honey, a garden gnome?" I frowned.

"Well, it's not just your common garden-variety gnome," he explained. "Its hat is also a birdbath."

I snorted.

"I thought you would like it," he said miserably.

"I will," I lied, and snuggled into his chest. "I'm sure it's very nice."

But the next day, after I swore Betty to secrecy in the print room while she ran off copies of Sunday's bulletin, I told her her boss had bought me a garden gnome that doubled as a birdbath. "No!" she said. And we laughed till the tears ran.

The big box arrived a week before my birthday and Greg let me open it that afternoon because it was no use waiting. And there it was, a beautiful Victorian dollhouse in the sweetest shade of lavender, complete with a shingle roof and wraparound porch. I immediately burst into tears.

And then he bought us a life-sized dollhouse when he knew Cleo was on the way. Borrowing from his mother and using the proceeds of the sale of a small plot of land in Ohio that his grandfather had left him, Greg exchanged the rent-free parsonage for an indigestible mortgage on the little two-story chalet perched on a hill overlooking Honolulu. It was met with a mountain of disapproval by the church's finance committee. "Why pay him a housing allowance when the church owns a perfectly good parsonage?" Kelsey Oliver grumbled. A retired financier, Kelsey Oliver was a short, stocky man with glasses that made him look like an owl. He had a slight limp, from an injury during his service in the Korean War, but walked with a briskness that was hard to keep up with. Always arriving late on Sundays, as though the invocation and hymn-singing at the beginning of the service were mere preamble, Kelsey would slip into the second-to-last pew next to his old friend Warren May and talk throughout Greg's sermon. Then he and Fay, his wife who seldom spoke at all, would leave before communion to take their places in the parking lot, the site of many unofficial meetings to which Greg was never invited.

It was Kelsey and Warren who ran the church, who made the big decisions. It had always been that way. And then Greg had to show up and insist he have a say. He wanted to do things differently. Now, it's one thing when a minister makes a few changes to the Sunday bulletin—heck, he might even get away with introducing a few new hymns occasionally—but anything that involved spending money was downright meddling as far as they were concerned.

"There are two types of people," Greg told me after spending the better part of the evening at a finance meeting trying to convince the members that the parsonage, rented out, could fetch a price more than enough to cover his housing allowance. "Those with a mentality of scarcity and those with a mentality of abundance. As Christians, we ought to be operating with the latter."

"Oh, like the 'The Lord will provide' and all that?"

"Hasn't he?"

"I'm beginning to think the Lord is a miser, Greg," I told him. "His staff get paid like clerks and treated like errand boys."

"No, I think you're confusing the Lord with Kelsey," he replied.

"Well, who has more clout around here?"

Church members remembered how Kelsey had spared the church from bankruptcy in the seventies, raised the money to repair the sanctuary's collapsing balcony in the eighties, and led the crusade to build a monstrous new organ in the nineties whose bellows the termites had already made good work of. He had outserved three pastors, two district superintendents, and a couple of bishops, and there wasn't a doubt in anyone's mind that he would outserve Greg too.

It seemed to me, then, that the dithering group of old-timers had a collective will mightier than the Lord's. Greg didn't find this nearly as troubling as he should have, not until that group turned its squinting attention from bean-counting to Greg's bullet-point plan for church growth.

It is fair to say it wasn't entirely Greg's plan but one that resembled similar plans all over the country that were credited with the transformation of dwindling congregations to multimedia centers attracting the masses. Just before Cleo was born, very much in the mood for new birth, Greg preached a sermon and distributed a one-page document outlining his plan for the church's revitalization. If some of the church members had been cold and unintentionally unwelcoming before, now, with Kelsey's vocal opposition to it, determined rigor mortis set in. "We don't have but a handful of youth in this church anyway," Kelsey declared, objecting in the all-church meeting to what he called an unnecessary expense of a youth pastor.

"That's the problem," Greg retorted, straining at the effort of collegiality.

"Can't see why you don't have Deighton do the youth program," Kelsey barked at the chairman of the staff-parish relations committee.

"It's *Reverend* Deighton," said Gregory, pried away from his usual ledge of self-restraint, crumpling in one hand his one-page plan.

Some said it was tampering with the way things had always been done, but it was that single aggressive gesture that made people swing their heads—and their votes—from Greg to Kelsey Oliver for the last time.

❧

IT MUST BE SATURDAY, because when I get up and pass the bay window I can see Greg in the garden, trimming back the halekonia, careful to leave their red-clawed blossoms. I put the kettle on and walk out the front door, down to the mailbox to get the midweek paper. Just as I head back to the house, I hear Mrs. Chung's screen door open and her shrill voice call my name: "Mrs. Deighton! Mrs. Deighton!"

The ill feeling stiffens my neck and I know that what is to follow will surely be a complaint.

"What is it this time?" I snap. "The wind chimes, the cat, the bird feeder? Did someone park the wrong way in the parking stall or is our mango tree dropping leaves in your yard again?"

Her rickety-stick frame slows from a trot to a hobble and she holds out a white plastic bag as though it were a white flag. "Please," she says, "I would like you and the Reverend to have these." She approaches me cautiously and hands me a bag of oranges. "They're from our tree." And before I can thank her, she is headed back to her screen door.

Once inside, I stack the oranges in the fruit bowl with the two overripe bananas and open the card that is taped to the outside of the bag. A short, impersonal note of condolence is typed below the card's preprinted message. What kind of person types a condolence message? I wonder aloud. The kind of person who accounts for each orange on her tree and shares them with no one. "She's too stingy to eat them," I used to tell Greg each time I saw her standing with her notebook making an inventory of the oranges in her tree. Today she has given us eight of her finest.

I am unpacking the dollhouse's living room set, marveling at the miniature rug and matching pillows, when Greg sits down on the floor.

"I met with the district superintendent yesterday, Abbe," he says.

"What about?"

"Seems that Kelsey and his recruits don't think I'm up to par. They have asked that I be transferred to another church." Funny how rumor travels faster than news. I have been waiting for the official word on the subject for months, ever since Jenny heard from someone that Kelsey was recruiting church members for a coup. Nobody was questioning Greg's commitment to his calling or had any quarrel with his doctrine; it was that silly plan that was going to sink his ship. They said they were not opposed to change, it was the price tag attached to it.

"When?"

"Apparently they wrote a letter to the bishop before Cleo died, but Alex didn't have the heart to tell me till now."

"No, I mean when do they want you to go?" Somewhere a voice is telling me I should be more shocked, to muster, at least, a little outrage.

"First of July," he says.

"But Greg, that's a month from now."

"I know. It's not going to happen. Alex says the bishop and the cabinet have made all the appointments for the year already, but it will probably mean a mid-appointment move, if they can find us a church."

"And where might that be?"

"Well, that's the thing, Abbe. It's not likely to be in Hawaii."

I arrange the TV set, the bookshelf, and the floor lamp.

"Maybe they can find us something closer to Rhiaan and Cicely," he continues. "Maybe it's not the end of the world."

"But what about my work?"

"Are you going back to the magazine? I just assumed you were going to resign."

"I can't move, Greg." And that's that.

Move. God knows I cannot muster the strength to drive to the grocery store; California is hardly an option. And the house, with its imprint of Cleo all over it. There cannot be a new house. There has to be her room and her closet with her little clothes hanging in it.

"It's not going to happen for a while . . . Maybe we'll get lucky; maybe something will open up here. But wherever it is, we are going to get through this together." The microwave pings. "Now come and eat lunch with me. Oh, where'd the oranges come from?"

"Mrs. Chung's tree," I answer.

"You are always on at me for stealing them," he says.

"She gave them to me."

"Miracles never cease," he says, shaking his head.

Yes they do.

EIGHT

I have taken to watching clocks. There's the digital one on the nightstand of what used to be Greg's side of the bed, the one whose alarm used to wake him at five-thirty on Sunday mornings—but no more, not since his insomnia dispensed with all that. And not since he stopped sleeping in our bed. Sometimes, when I have spent an afternoon castigating my former self for dressing up a crush in True Love's clothes, I think it is because of that filigreed locket. Other times, when the jagged edges of self-recrimination cannot be dulled even a little by the yellow pills, I believe Greg's absence from our bed is because Cleo's death has decanted the curdled illusion that Greg and I were a couple. When I hear Greg weeping outside my window where he tends the orchids that stubbornly refuse to bloom, I feel sure it is Cleo's absence that has wedged between us, every bit as palpable as a lover. And while the red digital numbers flip over themselves, I wonder why I did not spend more time thinking about Cleo and less about the jilted leftovers of another woman's marriage, which is what Sal has now become. Guilt stains my thoughts, like the nicotine-tainted tips of my father's fingers.

An antique clock is mounted on the wall to the left of the dressing table mirror, and because it never chimes is more decorative than functional. Before, its hands would be frozen on the same time for months, even years, for lack of attention. I wind it every other day now. There is also a clock in the guest room in which Greg pretends he has not moved, although his clothes are draped on the back of the chair and the debris from his pockets is strewn on the bedside table. Located inconveniently on the high shelf, the clock requires that I bring in the rattan chair from the hallway and get up to wind it.

They are all Greg's clocks, except the one in the dining room in the glass display cabinet that was my mother's twentieth-anniversary gift to my father. It is the only thing of his I have. Greg used to keep his clocks going; companionship, he called it, an old habit from his decade-long bachelorhood. But now I have assumed responsibility for them, and it is the only thing I am diligent about.

The kitchen has two clocks, both built into the appliances—one in the microwave and the other in the oven. I watch them both whenever I am in the kitchen, which is seldom. The one on the VCR I finally figured out how to set, but there is no setting the grandfather clock that Greg's mother gave—it either goes too fast or too slow, but either way, it is of its own choosing. It is the only inanimate object about which I have harbored homicidal thoughts, chiming as it did boldly off-key and off the hour, often just when I had rocked the baby to sleep. When it chimes now I long for the baby's cry that used to accompany it.

The poets write of time standing still when someone dies. It is not true. Time comes alive and takes up space. Time-past and time-to-come compete for turf in my ticktocking house. Every second mushrooms; every minute is counted in deliberate increments. Hours march steadily, calculatedly, through the afternoon like the Night Marchers on their ghostly patrol through the valley. The colon blinks like a heartbeat, as though it can push blood through the veins of a pallid day.

Greg does not approve of my clock-watching. He draws in a deep, nasally breath each time he sees my clock-winding ritual, steadying himself like an arrow drawn tight on a bow, the epitome of restraint. What he does not know is how the clocks all tell me the same thing: I am alive and she is dead. I have lived four thousand four hundred and twenty hours since she died, four thousand four hundred and twenty hours when I wanted to stay asleep, be unconscious, die. A captive to time, I am the mute witness to past events as they unfurl around me in uninterrupted and overlapping sequences: accidentally closing the car door on Cleo's finger, staying late at work too many evenings, walking out of Cleo's room when she cried for me to stay and read one more book.

Cleo's is the only room where there are no clocks, where time is neither kept, marked, nor marching. At the threshold of her room, I watch the way the light comes in through the blinds. If I have gotten a late start to the day, like today, the sun shines in through the south-facing window and almost reaches her bed. If it is before ten o'clock, the light spills in through the east window and her bed is bathed in light. After taking stock of all her toys and her pajamas still lying in a crumpled heap at the foot of her bed, I sit down next to Mimi, her first doll, at her rightful place on the pillow. It all stays the same, as though Cleo has been hurried off to day care and will return anytime. Only the shadows and light move, and the dotted line of ants that have taken up residence around the discarded lollipop stick on her bedside table.

Today Pilgrim is sprawled out on the sunny spot next to her tea set, having left another gift on her bed: the remains of a ghost-colored gecko. Startled at the shattering of quiet by the ringing of the phone, I walk downstairs to answer it. It is twenty to twelve, according to the grandfather clock.

"Hello?"

There is only a wide silence on the other end.

"Greg?" I ask, knowing immediately it is not him. I hear the deep inhale that can only be a drag on a cigarette, and the breath-hold that follows while the nicotine does its job.

"What do you want, Theresa?" I ask crisply.

My name comes out in a rush of wind, a reed shaking in a stiff breeze, "Abbe . . . I just want to talk."

"There is nothing to talk about," I tell her.

"Please, Abbe; please don't hang up." We are both quiet while I watch the granddaddy big hand snap up to the next minute marker.

"I can't do this on the phone," she finally says. "Can we meet some-where?"

"I don't think so."

"We are leaving Hawaii, Abbe. We'll be gone at the end of the month. I would like to see you before we go. There are things Greg said in his sermon about forgiveness and grace, and I just thought—"

"You will have to talk to Greg about those things, not me."

"If I can just—"

"I'm sorry, I have to go. Please don't call me again," I say.

"Abbe—I loved her too . . ."

I put the phone down at the same time Granddad begins to peal.

Greg hadn't told me that they were still attending services, and I wonder now if he had to shake their hands at the door after each service. Had he talked to them? Had he served them communion?

I sit down at the table and begin to cry. Yes, she had loved Cleo. Shortly after Cleo was born, when the call came that my grandmother had died, Jenny and Theresa, with Tess on her hip, drove up to our house to look after the baby while we grieved. Greg and I walked to the top of the hill where the houses were expensive and the view stretched from Diamond Head to Waianae. When we returned a couple of hours later, a pot of chili simmered on the stove, the dishes sat soak-ing in sudsy water, and a pink-faced Cleo nursed at Theresa's breast. "Whoa, slow down, little one," Theresa was saying. As I watched my little girl draw at her nipple, I felt my own milk let down and my guard go up. For a moment I wanted to snatch my baby from her bosom. She's not yours! I had the impulse to say. You have your own children! But nobody was stealing anything. My child had been crying from hunger, there were still tears on her cheeks, and I had been away, steal-ing moments to attend to my own needs. Theresa had let Cleo cry as long as she could bear it.

I watched and marveled at how easily the lines between mother and child blur. In what was then a tender moment, I felt that we were all mothers to all the children of the world, and whose womb bore whom did not matter much. But it does matter when the one from my womb has gone and left a carapace for a mother in her aftermath.

. . .

GREG COMES HOME and sets about making sandwiches for lunch. When he sits at the table across from me, he begins the laborious task of starting a conversation. It follows the same predictable route: He tells me something I pretend to care about. I do this by blinking instead of staring at the clock. It is never about anything important, usually something to do with the church: Mrs. Freemount's kidneys; Betty has booked him for another wedding even though he told her he wouldn't do any more; the trustees chairman trimmed the poinciana trees too much so that they now resemble baobabs; the front page of the church newsletter misspelled Al Firth's name in the birthday list so it appeared as "Girth," which is particularly unfortunate given the fact that Al hastily regained all the weight he lost on his yearlong zero-carb diet.

Today it is about Mrs. Scribner's dog, Puffy. Puffy has been on the prayer list longer than Mrs. Freemount, well over a year, for one or another health reason, and was even trotted to the chancel for an anointing during the biannual healing service. Liver cancer, the vet said. Advised to end the dog's misery, Mrs. Scribner could not bring herself to make that one last trip to the veterinarian, so we added her name, along with Puffy's, to the weekly prayer list.

"Puffy died," Greg says.

"She had him put down?" I ask, feeling sad for the old woman losing her only companion.

"Actually, he fell from her balcony. Eighteen stories. She said the condominium manager called yesterday afternoon to ask if Puffy was with her and she told him that he was taking his usual nap on the lanai, but when he asked her to check and make sure, she found only his chew toy on the blanket."

"Oh my gosh, Greg, how terrible."

"She says the little guy committed suicide because she didn't have the guts to end his suffering. She's very distraught."

"Did you go visit her?"

"That's where I've been all morning. She has him in her old knitting box, covered up with an old sweater."

"What is she going to do with him?" I ask.

"She doesn't know yet. I suggested she bury him in the church's memorial garden, but she said she'd think about it. She told me she didn't think she'd be coming to church for a while."

When Greg leaves for the office, I get out the shoe box marked "church photos" and dig around till I find the one I am looking for. Greg is holding up Puffy in one hand and laying his other on top of the poodle's fuzzy white head. "Blessing of the Animals—1999," is written on the back. It is not the nervous little mutt that stands out in the picture, or Greg's wide smile, but the beaming background that is Mrs. Scribner's proud face. In a notecard, I write, *We will miss Puffy*, and then a hasty postscript, *I stopped going to church too*. I enclose the photo with it, pop it in an envelope, and walk it down to the mailbox, past Mrs. Chung's peering eyes.

I know why Mrs. Scribner doesn't want to go to church. The lead weight of those well-wishings and good intentions only serve to take a drowning woman farther into the depths. The things people said were not lifelines but chum thrown into already treacherous waters. The sharks circled, the monsters of the deep rose up to clasp thrashing feet, while all the while polite ladies in their Sunday best cut tea cakes into perfect squares and tch-tched not quite out of earshot.

Mrs. Scribner knew what the people at church said behind her back. That she had gotten soft in the head ever since her husband, Alfred, had died. That she had no business bringing a dog to church. It was sacrilegious, some gossiped, after Carolyn Higa swore she had seen Mrs. Scribner bite off a corner of her communion wafer and feed it to Puffy. Mrs. Scribner knew they were not her friends, although they expected her to attend every women's auxiliary meeting, and pouted when she didn't. Puffy's death gave her a reason to finally stop participating in a ritual in which she had long since stopped believing and for which she finally had no energy. I knew all too well about that. However, death, I was coming to realize, replaced one set of rituals for a set all its own. Like winding clocks and counting the hours.

. . .

112

IT IS FIVE MINUTES TO SEVEN, Greg is leaving for church, sermon packed, wearing his lace-up shoes and smelling of cologne. It must be Sunday again. Tiptoeing around our room, retrieving his clerical collar and his belt, Greg does not know I am awake. I pretend to be asleep so he won't give me the awkward kiss goodbye and I won't struggle to find a suitable valediction: Good luck, God bless? What are the things ministers' wives ought to say to the fathers of their dead children?

I breathe evenly and pretend to inhabit the wind-burnt plains of my dreams.

When I hear the front door close, I get up even though it is too early. There is still steam in the bathroom, and the mirror is fogged up. I rub it viciously and stare at the haunted face that gazes back at me. I know this mood; my only mood. Hollowed out by grief, I ought to manicure my coiffure, arrange it around the bleakness that might be mistaken for a face. I look in the cupboard and find the shears, plug them in. In a few swift sweeps I hack off my hair. It falls in matted clumps in the sink. There. I stare at my reflection. I look like a convict. I am a convict. And I cry. Sunday morning, the Christians are gathering to sing "Amazing Grace." And won't it sound so sweet when they sing "that saved a wretch like me"? I am truly lost.

THE PHONE RINGS just after I have brewed my morning tea and I let the machine get it, but when it rings again I imagine it is Greg with something urgent to say. Something he has forgotten to take with him to church—a poem photocopied from one of his books, the last page of his sermon.

"Greg?"

"No, dear," I hear the woman say, "it's Pearl Scribner."

"Mrs. Scribner, how are you? Is everything all right?"

"Yes, dear. Well, no, not really. I have been cooped up in this apartment for a week and the only thing I can think of to do is go to church."

"Yes?"

"Well, the thing is, my dear, I feel rather peculiar going by myself.

There was always Alfred, you know, and after him—God rest his soul—there was always Puffy."

"It must be very hard not having him around anymore," I offer.

"It is, thank you, dear. You know all about it, I am sure. But the thing I am trying to say is I was wondering whether you could find it in your heart to accompany me . . ."

"I don't have the car this morning, I'm afraid. Greg has already taken it," I say, the excuse quick in coming.

"I was thinking of picking you up," she counters. And I am quite at a loss. "Are you there, dear?"

"Yes, Mrs. Scribner." I pause again.

"Well, will you?"

"It seems that there is just one other problem," I say, rubbing my prickly head. "I have just chopped off almost all my hair."

Without skipping a beat, she says, "I have the most excellent hat. Wait right there."

Mrs. Scribner's most excellent hat is wide-brimmed with a blue gingham band, and scares the hell out of the cat. "It matches your trousers," she says, and opens the passenger door of her little Fiat. "I think you should keep it." We talk about Puffy and how he could not stand little children or men, and we laugh about the day he took a nip at Kelsey Oliver's ankle. All too soon we are at the church, where Mrs. Domingo pounds out the prelude on the organ with the vexation of a woman doing her laundry by hand.

I sit with Mrs. Scribner in her usual spot, second pew left of center. Several people in the pew behind dust us with attaboy pats. Greg is visibly surprised, and during the opening hymn comes to embrace first me and then Mrs. Scribner. It is difficult to concentrate on Greg's sermon, so it is only after the offertory, when the Wai twins—shooed from the front pew by Helen Wai—hand out bookmarks to the men standing in the aisles that I realize it is Father's Day. Ikaika, seeing that his sister has covered all of her assigned territory and much of his, looks around desperately to offload his stock. Spotting some of the members who are pointing behind him, he spins around and dashes in inspiration to the four men sitting in the choir loft. On his way down

114

the chancel steps, he stops next to Greg's seat to give him a bookmark, then hesitates, and the look of pure turmoil is visible to everyone. He looks over at his mother and, seeing her nod vigorously, hastily hands Greg a bookmark and rushes back to the front pew, sliding down as he sits.

One by one the parishioners come up to me, their brows sloping, their Emmett Kelly mouths, their sympathies tucked up like handbags. No one mentions Mrs. Scribner's excellent hat or my hair. They smother me with hugs.

"We miss Cleo so much," "A precious angel," "So special." Sylvia Horton can only cry and shake her head apologetically as though it were covered in cobwebs till Jenny, coming to the rescue, ushers her into the choir room. Among the faces crowding closer is Theresa's. It is an old face, with dark smudges beneath her eyes. Seeing her intent, the determination to talk to me set on her mouth, I sneak out the side exit and head for the ladies' room on the second floor of the administration building, the one no one uses on Sundays.

I stare at my reflection. If I half close my eyes, the hat makes me look like a madam on the deck of a ship, out for a leisurely stroll in the midday sun. But when I lean across the sink, eyes wide open, there is a vacant gaze shadowed by heavy lids . . . the look of a madwoman. Not for the first time I think I look more and more like my mother. I try to picture the next few minutes, try to plan a way around Theresa's purpose, when Carolyn Higa walks in with a reed of a woman in tow. Built like a wrestler, Carolyn is both despised and tolerated as the church bully. Today she is wearing a fuchsia muumuu and white pumps that add another inch to her almost six-foot stature. Her stringy gray-streaked hair is rolled up into a bird's nest of a bun and is decorated with a spray of fake hibiscus flowers. The scent of cheap perfume assails me.

"Morning, Carolyn," I say, pulling at the paper towel dispenser.

"We didn't expect you this morning, Elizabeth," she says (the only person who uses my full name) with her characteristic bluntness. We have not talked to each other since the day a group volunteered to assemble Christmas gift bags for the homebound members and she told poor Sylvia Horton off for putting the angel ornament in the wrong corner of the bag. "There is no need to be rude, Carolyn," I told her. "She should do it right or not do it at all," Carolyn fired back. "If you find it that intolerable, perhaps you should go home," I said, sticking to my guns. "Well, if that's the way you feel, I think I will," she replied, and stomped out. Except she did not go home but marched the ten steps from the church library to Greg's office door, where she interrupted his sermon preparation to tittle-tattle for the better part of an hour.

"This is Lily Otai, a friend of mine from the YWCA; Lily, meet Elizabeth Deighton—our minister's wife," she introduces us, and we shake hands. Quivering neighbors and browbeaten tennis partners are frequently the people Carolyn pesters into accompanying her to church, a function that corroborates her self-appointment as chairperson of the evangelism committee.

"You came with Pearl?" Carolyn asks.

"Yes."

"At least we don't have to put up with that mongrel in church anymore," she trills.

My shorn hair begins to itch around the brim, bristling like centipedes. I throw the towel away and head for the door, but she steps in front of me.

"I know we haven't always seen eye to eye," she says, "but I am sorry for your loss."

"Thank you."

She turns to her companion and explains, "Their daughter is with the Lord now." And to me she nods in agreement with herself. "He always takes his favorites to be his special angels." Having uttered her obituary, she steps forward, tree-trunk arms untangling to gather me up. The itching is intolerable now and I snatch the hat from my head and point it at her. "Don't say that again! Ever! You know nothing about it!" I blast, and push past her and Lily Otai, whose mouth has dropped open like an unlatched purse.

I hurry out to the churchyard just in time to see Mrs. Scribner's car make a left into the Sunday brunch traffic.

It is three miles from the church to the house the way Greg goes, taking the direct route up Nuuanu Avenue. But today, on foot, I take a detour and weave through the narrow streets around Punchbowl Crater. Halfway up, instead of turning left in the direction of home, I veer right on Puowaina Drive, past the row of flags to the entrance of the caldera. The sign on the lava rock says NATIONAL MEMORIAL CEMETERY OF THE PACIFIC. I put Mrs. Scribner's hat back on, even though I walk in the shade of the shower trees in full bloom, and find a place among the graves. Something as close to Sunday worship finally begins.

GREG IS DOZING in the lounge chair on the deck, still in his collared shirt and pants, oblivious of the tiny blossoms the pepper tree is depositing in his hair. He wakes as soon as he hears the gate latch. "I was worried about you; I drove up and down every street to try to find you."

"Did you call home to wish your dad Happy Father's Day?" I ask.

He nods. "What happened with you and Carolyn?"

"I can't do it, Greg. The people thing. I am not going back," I say, stepping out of my shoes before going in.

"People don't know what to say," he offers quietly.

"Then why can't they just shut up?"

The truth is not that I want nothing to do with the people but that I want nothing more to do with Carolyn's God. The God who plucks up little children from their earthly nests and sets them on heavenly errands; the God who gives life and then snatches it back. The Stingy Bastard God.

Greg's God is worse—the God who is off somewhere else, darning socks or stringing beads or in his parlor counting all his money, certainly not doing anything useful like saving lives. If there is any God I want, it is Jairus's God, the God who not only led the poor father through the crowd to the miracle worker but did something neither he nor his wife could do, something entirely useful: made their little girl, pale and without a pulse, rise up from her deathbed quicker than you could say "abracadabra."

"They mean well," Greg says, following me into the bedroom, watching silently when I take off Mrs. Scribner's hat and reveal my prison do.

"Tell me who means well, Greg. Is it people like Carolyn who think I should move on because it was the 'Lord's will'? Or is it God who means well?"

"I am not suggesting that it was God's will that Cleo died, if that's what you're asking. And angry as I am with God, I don't for one minute believe that God's heart is not broken too."

"Well, what use to me is a brokenhearted God?" A hand-wringing God who weeps outside the window of the world, massaging his temples, heaping burning coals on his head? Neither the God who mourns at gravesites nor the one who deploys winged toddler-cherubs to find parking spaces for people who recite just the right prayers has any business paying a visit on my grief. "I'm done with Manifest Powers and Transcendent Almighties, Greg," I announce, during what is to be our last theological conversation.

"Don't say that. Don't mistake God for the people who profess to know his will," he pleads.

"In that case," I retort, "I am done with them too."

SOMEHOW it is dark again, and I haven't noticed the afternoon growing old, just that I can no longer make out the photo clearly without switching on a light. It is 8:33; you have to love digital clocks for never rounding off. The photo I took was outside our front gate, next to the jack-o'-lantern. Greg, dressed as the White Rabbit with a plaid jacket, a waistcoat, and bunny ears, is kneeling next to Cleo-as-Alice. He is looking into the camera, but she has reached into his pocket, retrieved his grandfather's pocket watch, and is pulling on it with an adamant expression. Her mouth is open, poised in the defining word of a two-year old: "Mine!"

Trick-or-treating down the lane, careful to cross the street before we got to Mrs. Chung's yard, it was Greg who carried the basket and

Cleo who held on to the watch, dangling it from its chain like a pet. "I'm late, I'm late, for a very important date," they chanted as they skipped. Finding the old frame tucked behind the stacks of recipe books that are never opened, I replace our wedding photo with this one of Greg and Cleo. When he is asleep in front of the TV, a John Wayne Western, I put it on the table next to the spare room bed, where he will see it later.

NINE

The whirring of the vacuum cleaner wakes me. Thursday! I pull on my robe and swallow against the resentment rising like heat off the blacktop at the thought of the cheeriness that shimmers at the bottom of the stairs.

"Mor-ning," Petal, the new uninvited, unwanted feature of my empty life, shouts in her singsong voice, and turns off the vacuum. "And a happy birthday to you," she coos, planting a kiss on each cheek, European style. "Ooh, look, your hair's growing out." Petal's driver's license, if she had one, would indicate that she was born "Penelope Oliver" a full two decades after it was fashionable to wear ankle-length patchwork skirts, denim vests, and leather thongs. Peering out from beneath bangs that part like a vaudeville curtain, she gushes on, "Reverend Deighton told me what the flowers were for. He's *such* a lovely man. Look, there's a card too. Granddad should really get to know him; life's too short for spats, don't you think?" By "Granddad" she means Kelsey Oliver; by "spats" she means his castration of Greg. I tried getting Greg to explain exactly why he was hiring Kelsey's granddaughter. Was it for political gain? To have the moral upper hand? "It's passive-aggressive, Greg!" is what I eventually accused him of, an accusation he was vehement in denying. "It has nothing to do with getting at Kelsey," he protested. "It's what I believe: someone needs help, you help them, whether it's your friend or foe or your foe's granddaughter.

You don't think about how it is going to appear. I couldn't care less if Kelsey sees it as a sign of weakness." Problem is that I saw it as a sign of weakness. Just for once I wanted Greg to stop turning cheeks as though they were cards in a deck and start delivering a few blows back. But instead, here I am, listening to Petal talk of life being too short for spats while I am called to march toward a battle by a bugle only I can hear.

Petal whips along in her inimitable lisp, "I wish I had known before I came, because I would have made you a present. A necklace, maybe . . . moss agate is the *perfect* crystal for a Gemini. I made this one; do you like it?" She points to the necklace around her neck, a heavy rose-colored stone wrapped in a disheveled web of silver wire. "I am getting better at it; one of these days I am going to sell them at a craft fair; don't you think that would be lovely?"

Kelsey brought this girl-woman to church the Sunday after she arrived from England, jet-lagged, pale from the English winter, and still shell-shocked from her mother's untimely death. Apparently Kelsey's oldest son, the Oxford professor, seemed ill equipped to deal both with his own grief and that of his hippie child. So Petal had sold her camper van parked on the downs of the English countryside the week after her mother's funeral and bought herself a one-way ticket to her grandparents in Hawaii before they could launch their objections. Almost four months had gone by, and rather than showing interest in returning to England, Petal is settling into the aloha lifestyle with a vengeance. Grandfather Kelsey, not one to put up with excuses, has apparently insisted she start earning her keep, and if it means mopping floors and scrubbing toilets, then so be it. Even if they are the parson's.

"You sit down and I will bring you a proper English breakfast," she says, and skips off to the kitchen, humming the refrain of "Yellow Submarine."

"I'm not hungry," I say, but she swats at my objection with a dish towel.

"You can't start your birthday on an empty stomach." Today she has on a pair of purple linen pants and a tie-dyed halter top. Arranged over one shoulder and around her waist is an Indian silk scarf. She has on an ankle chain of bells that jingle with every step. Greg warned me that she was a cliché in motion—the paisley clothing, crystal jewelry, and canvas tote with pocket-sized star sign guide and diary. He said he could tell the first time she came to church that she would be a vegetarian, consider herself "spiritual but not religious," practice yoga, burn incense, and roll her own cigarettes. He is wrong about only one thing, as she bites off a piece of crispy bacon and brings me a plate. "Don't be unkind," he had warned me. "We're going to help her out." And I agreed only because I knew what it was like to lose a mother.

"Jeff's asked me to move in with him; isn't that lovely?"

"On the boat?"

"Yes, there's enough space for the two of us, and that way we can save up for a proper place when the baby is born." Greg forgot to mention our new housekeeper was pregnant.

"Has he found a job yet?"

"He's found the perfect job, actually. He's a bartender at Tiki's on the weekends, which gives him time to work on his invention during the week. He's going to start applying for the patent soon. Oh, Abbe, you would really love him. He's scrumptious. I think he's my soul mate. I think it was meant to be."

She sets down the vase of yellow roses in front of my plate of food and hands me the card. "Didn't you feel that when you met Reverend Deighton?"

"Meant to be," so that notion was still around. There are still daisy petals making girls silly with their love-me / love-me-nots, letting them believe love and fate are folded into a corolla. If I ever thought Greg was meant to be, it was only after Cleo was born, when she was clearly meant for us. But when I met him, on one of my first assignments for the *San Luis Obispo Bee*, there was nothing of fate in the encounter. His church had just been vandalized, a crime uncommon in the happy-go-lucky town. The vandals had broken the stained glass windows of the sanctuary and had tagged the side of the building with the words "Fuck the church!" When I went to interview the pastor, I was expecting something of my father's retaliatory fire. Instead, Greg was calm and forgiving. He said he intended to leave the slur up on the wall for a while, to give his parishioners a chance to see someone else's point of view. Nobody in their right mind thinks tagging is a point of view. "You think it's okay to say that kind of stuff?" I had asked him. "I wouldn't have put it that way myself," he had replied, "but there are definitely times when the institution has cared more about the preservation of its white walls than about the people those walls often keep out."

I quoted him first, then kissed him later. In between, I was drawn to a man whose nature was so unlike my father's, whose feathers remained so unruffled that my father would have thought him a chicken, plucked and ready for the pot. Yet in the foggy winter, when the hills greened and the vineyards promised new wine, our romance simmered like a pot on low heat. There are many ways to cook a romance, I told myself. It doesn't always have to be boiled.

"I a-dore roses," Petal says. Whatever Petal says is accompanied by gestures so distracting it requires great effort to stay focused on her face—a meringue with scalloped lips and a shiny peak of a nose. "They remind me of my mum. She used to fertilize them with the manure from the stables next door. Made a right pong, it did, but she always had the sweetest-smelling roses. There's a—what do you call it?—a moral to that, isn't there?"

"My mother grew roses," I say, remembering the rows of bushes my mother tenderly planted alongside the driveway of our house, having spent weeks digging out the rocks. The idea of a rose garden and the money to finance it was her birthday gift from my grandmother, a firm believer in the therapy of hobbies. They were just bare, thorny sticks when they came in the mail. Nothing at all like the pictures of blossom-laden bushes circled in her catalog. But over months, with pruning and care, they grew chest-high and heavy with blossoms. It was enough to make you give hope just one more chance. If the smell of burnt dinners and cheap soap still assailed our home, at least it was mingled with the scent of roses with names like Mary Marshall and Lilian Austin. My mother was literally growing her friends.

"Really?" exclaims Petal. "What star sign was she?"

"I don't know—she was born in September."

"Virgo—unhappy people, usually, aren't they? Mum was a Capricorn, a real homebody. Earth signs are usually the ones who like to garden."

At first gardening was something my mother did to get out of my father's way, especially on the weekends, especially when he would come back from the pub queasy and bad-tempered. But then it became something else, something that seemed to take her far, far away. I would watch her from my bedroom window tending the calla lilies, trimming back the African daisies and the king protea. She would leave the roses for last, where she would spend most of her time. By the time she lay down her pruning shears, there would be spent blossoms in plump piles beside her. Sometimes she would come back in only after the sun went down, scratched up and sunburned, with a look that almost matched whatever it was she felt the fateful day she sat laughing on the phone.

"Do you miss your mum?" she asks.

"Every day," I reply.

"I wish my mum were here to see my baby when it's born," she says, and, like a cloud crossing the sun, the cheeriness is sopped from her face.

"C'mon, then, you haven't opened your card," she says suddenly, blinking back the darkness.

To the moon and back, is penned in Greg's careful cursive.

"What does it say?" she asks, and I hand her the card. She frowns, "What does it mean?"

"It's something he promised me a long time ago," I reply, remembering the night thirteen years ago when I was packing up, ready to leave San Luis Obispo and its finger-pickin' folksiness for a real job on a real newspaper. How deliberate our lovemaking was, as though we could slow down the night, keep the dawn from creeping up over the frosted windowsill. "Don't go," he had said. And when I argued about the merits of following my lucky break, he proposed. "Marry me," he said. "Then I'll follow you wherever you want to go, even if it's to the moon and back."

Petal stands the card on the table next to the roses. "He's a Taurean, isn't he? I dated a Taurean once. People always think of them as being bullheaded, but they aren't. They are very loyal, and they always keep their promises." She tucks her henna-dyed bangs behind her ears and I see that with her topaz eyes this tall girl-woman is on the fence of beautiful. "The bullheaded ones are the Aries, like my grandfather. Mum said that's the reason why Daddy never left England to come back here—he needed to put a continent between him and Granddad."

"What does your grandfather have to say about your moving in with Jeff?"

"He's not happy about it; he doesn't think Jeff is mature enough to be a father, but he just needs to get to know Jeff better, that's all. Jeff is going to be a brilliant dad."

"Mmm," is my only comment, and I take a bite out of my toast.

"It's my birthday next month and I'm going to have a big party and invite all my new friends."

"That's nice," I respond, suddenly feeling much older than my thirty-seven years.

"You must come, Abbe. Jeff and his friends are going to bring their guitars and we're going to build a big bonfire on the beach and have a cookout." She goes to the fridge, retrieves from it her lunch box, and sets it down across from me. Sitting down, she unwraps a roll and dips it into a cup of vanilla-flavored yogurt. "I'm always hungry. Got to keep my little Blossom happy," she says, patting her belly. She is already starting to show and celebrates each week with a new craving. A fortnight ago it was canned tomatoes (halved, not diced, she was quick to point out; "Isn't that so weird?") with brown sugar. Who can guess what it will be next time she comes?

I sit watching her mouth form words, occasionally hearing what sounds to be a lecture on the evils of modern-day cleaning agents. I am just about to excuse myself when she abruptly changes course. "Soon I will have to quit my job," she says with regret. "Jeff says I won't have to work when his invention is patented because we will have plenty of money." Jeff's invention is top secret, she's told me on a number of occasions, but it is going to make him a millionaire because every bar owner is going to want one.

"What about your family, Petal? And all your friends back home?

Don't you think you should get back to England before the baby is born, so they can help you and support you?"

"But I have Jeff now," she says.

"Right," I say, pushing back from the table.

"Don't you think your husband should come first?"

"Yes, but Jeff isn't your husband," I say, and she looks like I've just slapped her.

"What about you, Abbe, are you going back to work?"

"They've offered to throw some freelance work my way until I decide, but I don't know yet. Depends on whether your grandfather gets his way and we're kicked off the island."

"I feel awful he's been so rotten to Reverend Deighton, I really do. But maybe a move someplace new will be good. As they say, 'A change is as good as a jest.' "

"A *rest*," I correct.

"What?"

"It's 'A change is as a good as a rest,' " I repeat. "And I've been having my share of that, although it hasn't done a damn bit of good."

She starts to giggle, then laughs and puts her hand on her belly. I smile wanly and finally get up.

"Abbe!" she shouts, and grabs my hand. "The baby just moved!" In one shattering moment, with my hand pasted to the warm hill of her stomach, I feel the gentle nudge in the heel of my hand. My grief parts like the Red Sea, long enough for me first to feel the leap of new life, and then the thundering hoofbeats of despair gaining ground.

Solly barks suddenly and we both jump. The doorbell chimes and I move to answer it, leaving Petal with her hand on her belly and peering into the space between the atoms. I open the door and there stands Jenny, holding a very pink cake. "Happy Birthday, old lady," she says, and gives me a kiss, then quickly sees the brimming tears and says, "What's wrong?"

I shake my head as though to say, Tell you later, and take the cake. She follows me in and I say, "You remember Petal, Jen. We've just felt the baby move."

"How wonderful," Jenny says.

"I think it's a girl, but Jeff thinks it's a boy because it moves so much," says Petal.

"Do you have names picked out?" asks Jenny, putting her hand in the vacancy that mine just left.

"We're not telling everyone, but I'll tell you if you promise to keep it a secret." She waits for us both to nod our vows of silence. "It's going to be Blossom if it's a girl, and Budd if it's a boy. In honor of Mum. Aren't those the best names?" she asks.

Jenny lights the lone candle and insists I blow it out. "Make a wish," she says. "A good one." Petal picks up her bucket and mop and heads for the stairs. "Aren't you going to have cake?" Jenny offers.

"No thanks, I don't eat anything with food coloring."

Jenny slices the cake and we eat standing at the sink.

"Is it that she is just young, or have I turned into my mother?" I ask.

"Having never met your mother, I cannot answer that, but I can say with relative confidence that you have turned into mine!"

"Were we ever that age?" I sigh.

"The good Lord knows I wasn't," she snorts, and I remember why Jenny is my friend. "I was raising two babies and a good-for-nothing husband at that age, and working two jobs to pay for his good-for-nothing ass! What were you doing?"

"Oh, nothing as risky as getting my navel pierced or boycotting cake icing," I say. "I guess I was falling in love with Greg. Probably was risky, if I knew then what I would eventually have to give up."

"You mean, losing Cleo?" she asks.

"No, I mean losing me."

Jenny shakes her head. "You've always seemed 'all there' to me. And he's always struck me as a good man."

"He is," I agree. "I knew the first time I met Greg he was a safe bet. He was going to be everything my father wasn't—he was going to love me and stick by me and never leave me. He was going to wake up every morning and be exactly the same man I went to sleep with the night before."

"Nothing wrong with that."

"Unless you don't mind dying of boredom."

"You think that's fair?" Jenny asks.

"I don't know. It's just that Greg has spent a decade hoping and praying I would be the perfect preacher's wife, who doesn't get her back up so easily. That I would turn out to be the superwife and the supermom. And every time I'm not, I swear Greg leaves me just an inch. You add up all those inches over time and see the miles you come up with." I can't say I have given this theory a lot of thought, but as I say it I know it is at least one version of the truth.

"But he loves you, girl," Jenny adds, insisting on a happily-ever-after.

"He loves me most when I'm least me," I counter. "When I don't 'take things personally,' when I'm not out fighting lost causes or fighting back." Or giving up. Greg is equally uncomfortable with this side of me, but for the same reason—because it is driven by the same tip-the-scales passion.

When Jenny says, "I don't know, honey," I don't argue; I change the subject. "I feel old today. Older than Mrs. Worthington," I say. Althea Worthington, whose age no one knows for sure, has outlived a husband, both her children, and the doctor who all but signed her death certificate fifteen years ago when they found the first lump. Althea, who appears always to address your navel because she does not have the spinal agility to stand fully erect, whose root-bound fingers clasp around her great-grandson's arm each Sunday as he helps her make the circuitous route from the car to the sanctuary to the communion rail to the cookie table and back to the car. Althea, whose remaining obligation—which some say keeps her alive—is to water the sanctuary's potted plants, has more fight in her than me. "When I'm dead and buried," she once instructed me, "hire someone who knows how to take care of plants; don't leave it to that bunch who work in the church office." "I think you are going to outlive us all, Mrs. Worthington," I told her, to which she smiled with obvious pleasure.

"That reminds me," Jenny says, and digs around in her handbag. "There's a card from the women in the auxiliary. And last Sunday Mrs. Scribner gave me this to give to you." She hands me a little box wrapped in last year's recycled Christmas paper. Inside is a key ring with a polished nut suspended from it and a note that says, *I don't need this anymore. Happy Birthday.*

"What is it?" Jenny asks.

"An acorn." I smile. "My grandmother used to stash them all over her house. They're for luck and longevity."

"Did it work?"

"She did live a long time, but I would have to say her luck ran out before she did. Right around the time my mom died."

We finish our cake, and Jenny rinses the dishes.

"I don't know how the world works anymore," I say. "Life was easier to bear when I thought there was meaning to it, when there seemed to be reasons for why things happened or didn't happen. When life was one great algorithm. But it's not. Bad things happen, good things happen, then more bad things happen. There's no logic to it."

"Honey," Jenny says, and holds me tight. There is only the humming of the fridge, which gets empty and filled without any effort on my behalf, the ticking of my mother's clock, and the everydayness of my quiet house. The nagging thought that every fourteen or fifteen days Petal will use my spare house key to let herself in and remind me that there are barbecues on the beach and budding fetuses in the wombs of other women. That the world is filled with people who aren't dying, like Mrs. Worthington, or who want to die, like Mrs. Scribner; people who walk straight up, and dance around bonfires, and have babies and name them after rose parts.

After a while, I pull away and Jenny and I nibble at our cake crumbs.

"Can I fire her for being cheery?"

"Why, sure, honey, but then that just leaves Carolyn Higa to gossip about."

GREG COMES HOME exactly at five o'clock, just as Petal has folded the last of the towels fresh from the line. I put down the stack of mail and greet his hesitant smile with a tepid "Hello."

"Brought you a present. Well, two actually," he says, and from behind his back produces two wrapped gifts, each tied with a bow.

"I want lots of presents for my birthday," says Petal.

"I'll remember that."

"Oh, Reverend Deighton, I didn't mean it like that." She blushes. "But you are coming to my party, right?"

"Sure," he says as I unwrap the presents—one a book of collected poems by Emily Dickinson, the other an anthology of South African liberation music.

"Thank you," I say, and turn my cheek so he can pester it with a kiss.

"You're welcome." And then to Petal, "Are you ready?"

She says goodbye to me and lifts her box of cleaning supplies. "Let me get that," says Greg. And he turns to look over his shoulder. "I made reservations at the Bamboo Lanai—we'll head out as soon as I get back so we can catch the sunset."

That gives me an hour, long enough for a poem and a bath. I open the book at random:

Mine enemy is growing old,—
I have at last revenge.
The palate of the hate departs;
If any would avenge,—

Let him be quick, the viand flits,
It is a faded meat.
Anger as soon as fed is dead;
'Tis starving makes it fat.

"SHE HAS an inexhaustible supply of cheeriness," says Greg, putting down his menu and glancing around for the waiter.

"It's a front," I say without looking up, debating between the oriental chicken salad and the linguini.

"Covering her grief for her mother, you mean?"

"Maybe. Or maybe she's hiding something."

"Oh, come on, Abbe, the girl's as transparent as glass."

The waiter comes over, apologizes for the long wait, and takes our order.

"I don't think so. It's almost as though she's trying too hard."

"Maybe to get over her mother dying," he repeats.

"Possibly."

The restaurant overlooking the harbor is busy at this hour. Several teams of paddlers are slicing through the turquoise water in their outriggers. The yachts dawdle at the harbor mouth like reluctant children called in for supper. Along the boardwalk, tourists are out with their cameras, waiting for a yacht to sail in front of the dipping sun, while behind them flows a stream of runners, rollerbladers, and cyclists. Nobody pays any attention to the person with the wobbly shopping cart making a marathon of his own, each trash can a rest station.

It is a long time before the pupus come, accompanied again with the waiter's apologetic shrug. I am already tired and ready to leave, the heat from the day lingering on the evening's damp breeze. The spot just above my left eye begins to vibrate, and then the flare goes off somewhere to my right. In the flashbulb instant that I feel the vibration of the oncoming migraine, I see a man at the table closest to the kitchen looking not in the direction of the setting sun but directly at us. Or rather at Greg.

"Do you know that man?"

"Who?" Greg turns.

"No, over there—by the kitchen. The old man sitting by himself." It's his stoop rather than his face that makes him appear old.

Greg flushes and half raises his hand in salutation.

"Someone from church?" I ask.

"No one you know," he says, too quickly.

"He keeps looking at us," I say, digging my finger into the corner of my eye, blinking against the flashbulbs. "Why is he staring at you? Who is he?"

"Shall we go?"

"What? Our order hasn't arrived yet."

"Let's go, Abbe; you don't look well." He folds his napkin and puts it on the table, careful not to glance in the direction of the lone diner.

"No, Greg, *you* don't look well. Who is that man?"

Greg lifts his hand and flags the waiter, who rushes over. "The bill, please. We have to leave."

"Your entrees will be out shortly, sir, sorry for the wait," the waiter apologizes.

"Who—is—that—man, Gregory?"

"Sorry, it's not you," my husband explains to the waiter, ignoring me. "Emergency."

"What the hell are you going on about? What emergency?" The waiter rushes off, but Greg stands and comes around to my seat.

"Who, Greg? Who is he?" I demand. Both the man's eyes and hands flicker and fidget. But for the patch of dyed black hair, he lacks color, as though he had been put through a strainer. Where his lips ought to be there is only a thin line, like an old scar, a mouth that has been stitched closed. His hands keep fidgeting and when I focus on what they are doing I see that he is making origami from a stack of cocktail napkins. They are red, and at first glance it appears as though the man has sat down to a pool of blood.

Suddenly I know the answer before Greg gives it.

"Mr. Nguyen, Abbe. That's Mr. Nguyen," whispers Greg, steering me toward the register where the waiter hands him the bill and Greg's wallet opens, credit card ready. The hammer in my head now keeps time with my heart and all the chatter of the waiting area ceases. The candles on the tables suddenly are acutely bright and I can hear the fans whir overhead like choppers.

Greg is bending over the receipt, glasses on so he can sign it, when I feel, for the first time since before Cleo died, the undeniable gravitational pull of will. Each step is deliberate, measured, and quick, quick enough to bring me to the table of the man before anyone can stop me.

He looks up at me and around the wrinkles is the smallest of smiles, the dawning of a greeting or an apology, but before his lips part even wide enough to form a word, I say, "You should be locked up, you know! Locked up!"

Suddenly Greg clutches at my arm. "Abbe, please!"

"You're a murderer, do you understand?" I snarl.

"Madam, we must ask you—" the maître d' says.

"Murderer!"

And before they each take an arm, I reach out and strike his face with one backward swing of my hand. The electrical current that has been bothering my eye and setting off the flashbulbs rushes out of my arm, leaving it limp and hot.

"Jesus!" someone says. "She's crazy!" another voice says. Someone else comes to assist the man, who has laid down his head among his crumpled creations, while I am jostled to the exit amid Greg's flapping apologies.

∾

MY MOTHER did not know she had watered her beautiful rosebushes for the last time when she came in one Sunday afternoon, happily complaining of a sore back. Placing the yellow roses in a vase for the dining room table that I had been told to set, she had been humming. I remember she was humming because it was I rather than she who heard my father's car gear down before it turned into the driveway. She'd been humming since the previous day when the tobacco-scented journal arrived in the mail from America with a note from Rhiaan marking the page upon which his new poem was printed.

My father had seen it despite her attempts to conceal it, but who was to know whether he actually read it? If he did, then surely he would have thrown a few dishes or slammed a door, because *Swartland* was "Commie bullshit" of the first order. But there had been no rampage, and we were off the hook. Or so we thought.

It was the squealing tires that cut short my mother's humming, that made us both run to the living room window in time to see my father's pickup flatten her rosebushes one after the other before skidding to a stop two feet away from where we stood. And it seemed that we had been glued in place then, hearts plastered on our faces, the last bars of the hum floating above us, while the variegated petals settled on the lawn. My mother's face was a bald stump from which the petals had been plucked. But it was my father's face that surprised me most, for in all the months I could remember I had not seen him laugh with such malcontent abandon.

She should have slapped him; *I* should have slapped him instead of watching him kick the dismembered blossoms on the ground. Should have slapped him when he came inside, petals still stuck to his work boots, and said, "Christ, Louise, your roses have fucked up my fender!"

❧

I SIT AT THE DINING ROOM TABLE, gleaming from homemade wax, and pluck the petals of each long-stemmed dethorned rose. The ice pick has removed itself from my left eye, but something is still worrying the corner of my peripheral vision. The old man's face keeps getting in the way, and the feeling of his face on the back of my hand. It is only when I come to the last rose, when the table is overlaid with fragrant petals, that it comes fully and forcefully into focus, as clearly as the deliberateness of my father's rampage: Gregory knew Mr. Nguyen.

TEN

By the time Greg comes down to the kitchen for his monastic breakfast, I am waiting for him at the table. Before he can express his surprise that I am up before the city lights have turned off, I hand him his morning paper. Instead of reading the headlines, he scans my face.

"At what point did you and the man who killed our daughter become friends?" I demand.

"At what point did you start having an affair with someone else?"

"Jesus, Greg. The man killed Cleo. He drove his car into her body and ended her life. He ended *our* lives," I say, ignoring his question but feeling the panic beginning to well.

"This is something you need to understand, okay? It was an accident. He didn't intend to do it; he didn't wake up one day and plan to hit a pedestrian. He didn't plan to hurt Cleo or destroy our lives. If anyone's been doing any planning around here, it's you!" Blame, for Greg, is new and he tries it on like the latest clergy stole he ordered from a catalog.

"Accident, yes, accident. It's what everybody says. But an accident means it wasn't anyone's fault, and Cleo's death *was* someone's fault, Gregory. It was that bastard's fault. And it was Theresa's fault. And God knows it was my fault too. Intent does not matter. What matters is that we pay. And he has to pay. Except you want to get him off the hook.

135

You want to be his buddy and his priest and his savior! So that you can feel good, and you can say your prayers at night and tell God what an almighty good deed you did today!"

"You don't know what you're saying, Abbe."

"Oh, 'Forgive them, Lord, for they know not what they say' . . . You think you can wrap yourself up in your religion so you don't have to be real."

"Don't lecture me on being real! You think you are real because you sit in this house, day after day, week after week, winding clocks and staring at photos? You think you're being real because you won't leave the house, or come to church, or go back to work, that you can't do one nice thing for someone else, say one nice thing to Petal. But listening to the man who has killed my child, watching him weep and beg, that's not real, right? It's not real trying to forgive the man who least deserves my forgiveness? What I know is real, Abbe, is that that man's debt is so big we can never collect on it; all we have a chance of doing is to forgive it."

"*You* forgive it, Greg. You get on with your business of forgiving sinners and playing God."

"It's better than playing the fool," he mutters, turning away, spent.

"And what's that supposed to mean?"

"Why don't you ask your boyfriend?" he replies without looking back. I realize neither of our questions, the ones that started this exchange in the first place, has been answered.

THE THREE-STORY OFFICE COMPLEX of Kahako Publishing Inc. is fronted with date palm trees and orange bougainvillea, which bloom despite persistent negligence on the part of the occupants, who never look out their blinds-drawn windows. Today the cluster of bums whose belongings are normally piled in the corner of the front entrance are being shooed down the road lined with black film crew trucks by two security guards. A starched-looking woman with horn-rimmed spectacles blocks the entrance to the lobby with a sign that reads QUIET PLEASE! FILMING. I look beyond her to the cameraman and the faux reception desk to which he is aimed. The sign hanging beneath it says CARSON P. FULLER ASYLUM. Someone in a beret (who wears a beret in Hawaii, for Pete's sake!) shouts "Action!" and suddenly a man in a white coat tries to placate a very large, hairy fellow who apparently has not noticed that the gap in his hospital gown affords a rather unflattering view of his derriere. Just as he begins foaming at the mouth, Beret Man shouts, "Cut! Is it too much trouble, ladies and gentlemen, to find a hospital gown that wasn't made for a GODDAMN MIDGET?"

I slip past the chaos and enter through the door whose sign above it I still recognize: PERSONNEL ONLY.

"Well, look what the cat dragged in," exclaims Buella with a little applause when I stand in front of her desk. After being enveloped by layers of burgundy scarves, I suffer through her scrutiny of my outfit, which today is jeans and a T-shirt. Judging from her expression, as though she has caught a whiff of something unpleasant, I know that Buella is disappointed to find not even one adornment.

"Fitting that I should return to work on the day it's become a loony bin," I say, hoping to distract her.

"Oh, darling, it's all very exciting! They're filming the season premiere of *Across the Border*. Did you see Roan Mitchell? He has raised the estrogen level in this place by a few hundred pints. He's beautiful, but my God, the man has an ego—he had the nerve to ask me if I wanted his autograph!"

"Did you get it?"

"Of course not! I asked him if he wanted mine!"

"Jean in?" I ask, looking at the closed door.

"Yes, but she's meeting with the printers at the moment. I'll buzz you when she's out. Abbe, it's wonderful to have you back." As a postscript, she adds, "Oooh, you are going to make the Italian Stallion's day!"

Seeing my face, she laughs and waves her hand dismissively, "Oh fergodsake, everyone knows the man is sweet on you. It's not a chargeable offense."

My office smells like my grandmother's old closets, of decay, of neglect. Tying back the curtains so that the light can dispel some of the gloom, I watch the suspended sparkles of dust. Someone has stacked my work into orderly piles and the desk calendar is still on February. After wiping the dust from my desk and the file cabinets, I take my potted plant—its Valentine's Day ribbon garish compared to the starkness of its brittle branches—and head for the large trash can next to the Xerox machine. But Sal is suddenly planted in my doorway. "Buella said you were in," he says, gesturing with his thumb over his shoulder.

"Come in," I say. "Have a seat."

"I remember that," he says, glancing at the deceased plant. It appeared on my desk the morning of the fourteenth with a card signed simply "Your not-so-secret admirer."

"Didn't hold up as well as the locket," I remark, showing him the single adornment tucked under the crew neck of my T-shirt. He seems pleased, yet struggles to find a comfortable note nonetheless.

"Well, I won't stay. I just wanted to say . . . well . . . What I was going to say was, 'Welcome back,' but what I really wanted to say was—"

"Please, Sal. Don't," I interrupt before he goes on.

"You're right. It's just that I can't stop thinking about that day and I know things are different for you now. But how I feel about it—about you—is still the same."

"Let's pretend it never happened, okay?"

"Yes, but it did happen."

"Please, Sal. I just can't."

The same dogged expression returns to his face. "I feel like I've lost you even before I had you."

"You never had me, Sal. It was just a kiss."

In the old days, before Cleo died, it might have taken something as small as a kiss to change things, but now that's not how it works. Death changes things, not carbonated kisses and fingers sticky with want.

"If it was just a kiss, then why did it feel like a promise?" he asks.

"Maybe it was—I don't know."

"Maybe you just need some time. I didn't come here to rush you or pressure you, I—"

I shake my head. "Sal . . ."

"I see," he says, and instead of waiting for my apology, he stands up and walks out of the office, the sparkles of dust colliding in his wake.

I turn around and look out my window to the courtyard below, where the film crew is gathering. Men with tool belts are laying tracks for the camera while the man in the white coat signs the autograph of a drooling teenage girl. Behind them, Buella is pilfering something from the crew's concession stand.

"Temporary insanity," I say, although there is nobody to hear my confession. There couldn't be a more suitable place for filming a segment for a fantastical TV show, for manufacturing artifice and dressing up unreality so only the desperate are willing to think it's real. It is what Kahako Publishing pays us to do each issue, by whatever means necessary. Which has led to moments of insanity, at different times, for each of us. Was the moment with Sal my moment of insanity? Had my mother become insane when she fell for the man on the other end of the phone? Wasn't it insane to act as though another man could kiss away the bruises of an abrading marriage?

Buella buzzes me. "Jean's free for a minute."

"A story a week, that's the deal," Jean says when I enter. Not "Welcome back," "We missed you," "It must be tough," but "Come in for the editorial meetings and long enough to catch up on e-mails or calls. Or don't. I don't care. Just make sure Peter gets his five hundred words Tuesday before noon so he doesn't come in and give me hell."

"Thank you, Jean," I tell her.

"Pff," she grunts, and waves away my gratitude as though it were a bad smell. "You're a good writer, Abbe. Just glad we're not going to see that talent go to waste."

I turn to leave.

"One more thing . . ." she says.

"Yes?"

"You have anything to do with Sal quitting?"

"What?"

"He quit. Five minutes ago. His resignation—such as it is—is scrawled on the back of this," she says, holding up a postcard. I don't need to look closer to know it is a picture of Raphael's *Transfiguration*. "Now, what the hell is this supposed to mean?"

"I haven't got a clue," I lie.

THE WALK UP THE HILL takes twenty minutes, half the time it takes to wait for the next bus. Tomorrow I will take the car and Greg can ride the bus! By the time I turn onto our street, my heart is pounding from the exertion and puddles have collected all over my T-shirt. The ambulance is parked the wrong way in the street, between Mrs. Chung's house and ours, and my first thought is, Cleo! and the ancient voice reminds me gently no. Mrs. Chung's door, always closed, is now open so that her house seems like a discarded cardboard box. Suddenly two men rush out carrying a stretcher while a woman in uniform rushes to get in the driver's seat of the ambulance. Mrs. Chung stands in the empty doorway wringing her dish towel as though it were a neck.

After the ambulance skids down the street and around the bend, I consider walking quickly to our gate, pretending not to have intruded on a very private moment. But then she turns my way and her old turtle face, pinched perpetually in a grimace, now looks punctured and afraid. I walk down her path.

"Mrs. Chung?" She seems not to notice me, casting a long shadow that reaches her before I do. "Mrs. Chung, it's me, Abbe Deighton from next door. Are you okay?"

"Ronnie fell off the ladder. He fell," she says, as though explaining to herself.

"Mrs. Chung, I think you should sit down. Here, let me help you . . . May I come in?"

Mrs. Chung's home has the odor of bitter things—petroleum floor polish, almonds, hospital wards. The parquet wood floors and the ball-and-claw furniture in her living room compete in their luster. The shelves on the west walls are bare save for a few framed photos and a cloisonné vase with no flowers. The dining room table, with its crisp crocheted white tablecloth, is laid for dinner although it is only barely past three. I might as well have walked into my parents' house.

Mrs. Chung sits down at the setting closest to the kitchen. "My son always wants to do things himself. I told him we should have hired a painter," she explains. There is a kettle on the stove but no dishes in the sink. The kitchen looks as if it has never been used.

"Would you like me to make you a cup of tea?" I ask.

She nods and points to the cupboard in the corner. "Ronnie said it's cheaper to do it yourself than hire someone else who is only going to cut corners."

There is a box of green tea among the shelves of assorted pill bottles.

"His father," she says, glancing at the ceiling above her, "is always telling him he's no good, and that is why poor Ronnie always tries too hard. And now he's gone and broken his neck."

It has often been a source of speculation between Greg and me why a middle-aged man would be living at home with his parents, apparently unemployed. A mental case, I thought, given his gene pool. I even looked up Ronnie's name on the sex offender watch site to see if it was listed, just in case. It wasn't.

"Doctors can do amazing things these days; they can fix anything," I say, the words ringing false even to my own ears.

"He's going to be scared," she says. "Ronnie has never liked hospitals." I hand her a cup of microwaved urine-colored tea.

"Do you need a ride down there?"

"I can't leave my husband till five, after he's taken his pills. I'll be okay to drive, and by then Mrs. Beech will be home from church and she can ride with me." I try not to feel offended by this. After a few sips, she seems to regain her focus and looks around, at me in her house, as though she has awoken from a dream. "I think I will call the hospital now," she says.

As she ushers me to the front door, I notice the pictures hanging on her hallway wall. One is of a much younger Ronnie, smiling in such a way so his teeth don't show. The other picture, obviously taken at the same time in the same studio, is of a young woman with Down syndrome features. "Who is this?" I ask.

"That's Mai," she replies. "My youngest."

"I don't think I've seen her before."

"No. She died many years ago."

"I didn't know . . . I'm so sorry."

"You don't ever get over losing a child," she says, staring at Mai's picture. "But losing them both would kill me."

"I am sure Ronnie is going to be fine," I say.

Standing in the foyer of her house, I see that Death makes skeletons of the ones left alive, and when I look down to take her hand, I notice it is identical to mine. Related we are, by our dead children.

"Thank you, Mrs. Deighton. And goodbye," she says, the cool lid of cordiality snapping back firmly into place.

All I can think of in reply is, "Remember to eat."

∽

MY MOTHER STOPPED EATING after Mary Marshall and Lilian Austin were flattened by my father's truck. She set the dinner table with three places each evening, cooked macaroni and cheese or shepherd's pie, but never took her place. If she ate at all, it was a diet of Mint Imperials and apricots from our tree. Soon all her housedresses hung like Halloween costumes and she took to wearing leggings and baggy sweaters that came to her knees. She seldom went anywhere, and when she did we would have to call the neighbor's gardener to help jump-start the car.

My father mocked her about eating like a bird, and I stopped going to Cindy's house for sleepovers because I was dead scared she was either going to croak or fly the coop. To torture us both I tried convincing her to eat. Not once did I call my grandmother or our family doctor or write to Rhiaan about what books called "anorexia." And I certainly never mentioned it to my father. Insanity elicited from each of us an unspoken agreement, a complicity—We are all in this together, just as long as nobody involves an outsider. Only once did I try to tell Cindy what was going on, and when she said things couldn't be "that bad," I thought she must be right.

The other thing about which none of us spoke was the matter of my mother's indiscretion. It had been almost a year since my father had yelled down the phone to my mother's lover and still I was curious: Who had he been? Had my mother forgotten him? Had he forgotten her? Had it really happened or had I dreamed the whole thing up?

"I'm going to run away!" I told my mother one Sunday afternoon when my father left for the pub. "I'm going to run away if you don't start eating, Mom!"

"I do eat, Abbe," she replied, clearing the table. "Besides, where are you going to run that I won't find you?"

"I know some places, I do! Maybe I'll run away to America, like Rhiaan!" She stopped in her tracks then, and came over to where I sat pouting on the couch. Hugging me in her sharp, bony-bird arms, she cried, "Oh, baby, now don't go saying that; please don't go saying that." She rocked me as someone might worry a stake till it is set firmly in the ground.

"Mom?" I finally said. "Did you love that man?"

She didn't say "Who?" or "Hush up" or anything I imagined she would say. So long was her answer in coming that I knew she had chosen her words with the greatest of care. "I love you and I love your brother; that's all that really matters."

❧

I FIDDLE WITH THE LOCKET, running it back and forth across its chain. It could not have been Sal's dark looks or his height that reminded me of the blue gum trees lining the street on which I grew up that did it. That made me kiss him, that made him feel that he'd extracted a promise. It could not have been his baritone laugh or his chivalrous manners or his freshly pressed scent. Something else, something beyond appearances, something quite invisible, pulled me to Sal. Something on him that smelled of misery, or loneliness. Of kinship. Of someone who was waiting to be delivered from his own brand of insanity and introduced to something—anything—else. Even if it just turned about to be *my* insanity. There is no escaping unhappiness, there is only sharing it. If I had promised Sal anything, then, in that kiss, it was only to make him a witness to my same-same existence. Same-same as his, as Mrs. Chung's, as my mother's. All same-same.

"I said something nice to Petal today," I tell Greg when his head pokes in the door, tentatively, as though a brick might be launched his way.

"Excuse me?"

"I called her this afternoon to see how she is doing."

"And?"

"I told her she reminded me of an E. E. Cummings poem, coura-geously breaking all the rules." What I didn't tell her was there would come a time when she would be forced to move along in brisk, neat sentences with the punctuation marks all in place. That there might even come a time, God forbid, when the cruelty of life would strip her, as it had Mrs. Chung, to a haiku poem. Lean and tucked in tight, and smelling of almonds. "You said I couldn't say something kind to her."

"I shouldn't have said a lot of things, Abbe."

When I don't reply, he turns to head out of the room.

"I didn't sleep with him," I announce hastily.

Greg moves back into the doorway.

"I wanted to. I would have." Greg lifts his hand for me to stop, but I ignore it. "I wasn't playing the fool, Greg. I was unhappy. I know you don't think this is any kind of solution, but I wasn't thinking about you or church or even Cleo. I kissed him because I wanted to find out if there was something that could make me happy, even when I knew ten-to-one it wouldn't. Do you understand?"

Greg's sigh of a million lonely nights echoes through the room. "I met Mr. Nguyen for coffee after he called the house that night. I thought it would help me. I never expected that it would help him or that there would be more meetings."

"How many times have you met with him?" I ask.

"Several."

"How many?"

There is a beat. "Several."

There are five names I want to call Greg, but I remain silent.

"I swear, Abbe, I never intended it to turn out this way. It just sort of happened." After the words are out I realize I might have said them to him about Sal.

We stare out the sliding glass door beyond the deck and today's droppings from the birds to the sun, a small orange orb landing on the ocean. The sun is sinking, Cleo said once, panicked that it might never come up again. And we laughed at her furrowed concern. But it seems tonight, with the clouds streaked with pink flares, that she might just be right.

Greg is the first one to break the silence. "Did you love him?"

"I don't think it matters anymore." And what is left of my deceit goes the way of the sun.

ELEVEN

I am awake when the phone rings at 5:10, having wormed my way through only five lines of mediocrity, the noon deadline chasing my heels. Kelsey Oliver, crisp and curt as though he has been up longer than God, is down to business before I can finish my greeting.

"Petal has gone into labor. Kapiolani Hospital, third floor. She has requested you and your husband's presence."

"She's early," I say.

"Obviously," he replies. "When should I tell her to expect you?"

"Tell her we will come right away."

"Right, then."

"Kelsey," I say before he hangs up. "Her father coming?"

"Norman cannot take any more time off from work until the Christmas break. We are presuming she will be home by then." Punctuating his remark is an abrupt click.

"A bit of a cliché, going into labor on Labor Day, isn't it?" I say, watching Greg run from the closet to the bathroom and back again, gathering items as though the house were burning down.

"Not as cliché as having that loser dump her just in time," he replies, and rubs the fatigue from his eyes. Jeff has exited the stage on cue, failing only Petal's expectations. Greg, on the other hand, is the understudy, only too eager to pick up his lines. "What is she going to need?"

"Not a Bible, I know that much," I say as he crams his grandfather's Bible into his shoulder bag.

"I thought she might like to hear a few psalms."

"Do we still have any of the lollipops left over from last year's Halloween? She might like those," I suggest, picking out a few CDs. "And put in a pair of those woolly socks your mother sent you for your birthday—they'll finally get some use."

Kapiolani Hospital is wide awake by the time we arrive—nurses bustling in and out of rooms with blood pressure monitors, bothering groggy-eyed patients with thermometers and the spryness of a clambake. A chirpy nurse at the maternity ward station points us down the hall to Petal's room just as Kelsey and Fay walk out of it. He nods a hard-boiled greeting in Greg's direction and tells the nurse that he and his wife will be back at lunchtime.

"Miserable bastard," I murmur, and try to paste on an elastic smile when we enter her room.

Petal is wide-eyed with fright. Her skin is flushed and her brow prickled with sweat.

"It's too early," she says, clutching my hand. "Something's going wrong."

I look over at the nurse who is reading the printout of her contractions as though she were scanning the NASDAQ composite. She shakes her head and smiles.

"No," I tell Petal. "No, everything is fine. Babies aren't like trains, Petal. They don't care about our schedules. They come when they're ready."

The force of an unseen entity seems to strike her with such vigor that she bolts forward, eyes bulging, her hand suddenly a vise.

"It's all wrong," she wheezes through the contraction.

"Don't push," the nurse instructs her. "Breathe deep breaths. That's it. That's it."

Slowly she releases her grip, eases back against her pillow, panting.

"I wish my mum were here," she whimpers. "It's not right that Blossom will be born with no family."

"We'll be her family," says Greg, as easily as oil poured on troubled waters.

Feeling the surprising flood of sympathy, I say, "You just worry about delivering that baby and we'll figure the rest out later."

I send Greg on a mission of gathering ice chips for Petal and a caffeinated soda for me before he makes any more promises, and sit at the edge of the chair holding her hand, waiting for the baby-train to arrive.

∽

CLEO NEVER DROPPED, and a week after she was due Dr. Urukawa announced that he was going to induce labor. It was not at all what Greg and I had imagined, what we had prepared for: my water breaking in the middle of the night; Greg scrambling for the overnight bag, patting himself on the back for keeping the gas tank full even though it was only four miles to the hospital, rushing back inside to put out some dog food for Solly before driving with cautious haste, hazard lights on, to the hospital. That was how it was supposed to go. Instead, we were marched from the doctor's office to the ultrasound department to the registration desk, where we were ordered to sit down and sign papers in triplicate while the registrar clickety-clacked our insurance details into the computer, her squirrel cheeks bobbing in time with her gum-chewing.

The African way is to have a midwife, relegating the husband to the outside corridor where his job is clear: pace until further notice. Pacing, then, goes on for a few hours if the expectant father is lucky, days if he isn't. But a continent away, Greg, ill equipped to deal with my birthing fears, was up to the task of being a makeshift doula and a stand-in for the matriarchs in my family. "She's not ready," I kept telling him, but all he did was wipe my forehead till I feared it gleamed like alabaster, breathing on my behalf through each contraction. There was an order to the universe, an order knotted together by delicate threads of timing. Who could know the effects of disrupting that, of imposing a man-made schedule on an infant's introduction to the world? What if our baby was somehow altered by doctor's orders? What if she was meant to be the Sabbath child but sentenced to the woe of a Wednesday's child? And then I heard those first mewing sounds, and the panic drifted away like the smoke of freshly lit cigars.

"I'll never let anyone hurt you," I whispered. "I promise."

✦

BLOSSOM IS BORN, as her mother predicted, without any family present, just after her great-grandparents leave for supper at five, and twenty minutes before Greg and I return with one of Cleo's quilted baby blankets.

"Isn't she lovely," Petal cries when we enter the room. "I did it, all by myself." It seems that we have made her an impossible promise—to be her family—one we have already broken.

We nod and stare at this new child from the void left by another.

"See, there was nothing to worry about," Greg says. "Here, let me hold her." He scoops up Blossom with the nervousness of a new father and blinks back the tears.

"Well done, Petal. You're a brave and clever girl," I say, watching Greg fan out the baby's fingers.

"Mum would think so, wouldn't she?"

I nod and hand her the blanket. "Most definitely."

Greg offers me the baby, but I shake my head quickly and he passes her back to Petal. "She looks just like you," he says kindly.

When he leaves to buy flowers and balloons, I put on a CD. "What do you think—is it too soon to introduce Blossom to Enya?"

"Abbe?" says Petal when I sit down again, a pale tremor on her lower lip.

"What's wrong?"

"Can you keep a secret?"

✦

MY GRANDMOTHER told me once that a secret shared was as a sorrow spared. I suppose she told me that because she knew I was keeping secrets, secrets about what had been happening in our house. But even before my mother's hair started to grow out white, my grandmother could tell for herself that things were bad. She didn't need me to give her a précis. All you had to do was take a good look at Louise Spenser and you would know it was no secret that she was digging her own grave. It amazed me then how grown-ups can look and look at a thing till their eyes go buggy, and still not see.

As if to spare us the effort of all that looking, my mother spent less and less time in the communal rooms of the house. She gave up her chair in front of the TV during my father's standing ovation when the new state president—P. W. Botha—was elected. "About bloody time!" he said when the president declared a state of emergency. When, I wanted to know, was someone going to do the same for our household?

My mother spent the rest of her evenings in the guest room, where she would sit for hours in front of her sewing machine, threaded and idling. I would do my homework on the bed, the bed I knew she slept in after all the lights were out, just so I could be with her, the way one might keep a stone company. Sometimes, instead of doing algebra, I would watch her pin and repin the hem of a curtain she had no intention of hanging or the lining of a dress she had no intention of wearing. It was as if even the smallest act of permanence, the act of stitching, was too great a risk, too large a commitment.

One night, when my father was working the graveyard shift and I was supposed to be asleep, I drew near the guest room door. It was the sound of melancholy that had brought me to it, that kept me listening at its side to the awful sound of my mother's heart breaking. And then, as though speaking to a friend, my mother prayed. "I know I shouldn't say it, Lord," she whispered, "but it sounds nice to be dead, to be tied to a stone at the bottom of the lake." Apart from grace at my grandmother's table, never had I heard my mother pray, let alone such impossible words to a God who was as remote as the man in the moon.

"Deliver me from this hell," she bargained, "before I send myself to another."

It was an admission of intent every bit as intractable as a suicide note. And I had no idea what to do with the hearing of it. Rather than barging into the room and getting her to reverse her words, to extract from her a reassuring promise, I crept into my cold bed and shivered long after the sheets warmed up. I did not tell my father, eating his reheated dinner at the breakfast table the following morning, and I did not ask to borrow the telephone key to call my grandmother and tell her. When my mother handed me my school lunch and money for the bus, I did not even then let on that I knew her secret. "Bye, Ma," I said as I had a thousand other mornings, careful not to cling to her or cry. Even when my physics teacher snapped at me for not paying attention, I could only respond by imagining my mother wading, Woolf-like, into my grandmother's wintry lake with rocks pinned neatly into the hem of her dressing gown. The secret I was really keeping was how I was failing to do something to prevent it.

Sometimes I think it is much easier to keep a secret than a promise. As long as they are stored out of sight, secrets give the world a much better chance of making it through the day unscathed. You make a promise, on the other hand, and you are just asking for trouble.

❧

PETAL'S BIG SECRET is that Blossom's daddy is not Jeff but a Sagittarian from Scotland who promised to be so much more than the one-night stand he ended up being. And, as it turns out, it is no more a secret than it is a surprise.

"I told Sue—the nurse; she's great. She says what matters is that I'm Blossom's mommy."

"Who else knows?" I asked.

"I told Grandma Kay last month, only because she was so sad when Jeff and I broke up."

"I thought he dumped you."

"Well, it was more of a mutual agreement."

"Oh."

"I suppose she told Granddad already, because he has been more grouchy than usual."

"Is there anyone who doesn't know?"

She shrugs.

"It's not really a secret, then, is it?"

"Well, my dad doesn't know yet, and Reverend Deighton," she says.

"And are you planning to tell either of them?"

"I sort of was hoping you could help me with that."

IT IS DARK when Greg and I get home. In the cupboard above the refrigerator is a bottle of Johnnie Walker someone gave Greg when Cleo was born. It has never been opened. I get it down and pour it in the mug on the draining board.

"You okay?" he asks.

The first swallow is an antiseptic, the second an anesthetic.

Before the third, I lift my cup to him. "A toast," I say. "To Blossom."

When Greg gets in the shower and as the fragrance of his shampoo wafts through the room, I kneel down and lift the skirt of the bedcovers. It is a reach for the shoe box, but my hands locate it without me having to look. I pull it out, lift the lid, and stare at the heart-shaped koa box. My hands enfold it. "Baby," I cry, "my sweet baby," but all I seem to have are the ashes of a broken promise.

LENT

TWELVE

Summer in Hawaii takes forever to end. By the tail end of December it becomes a terminal condition, with its smell of decay—rotting mangoes, mold, sweat—that even the fans cannot dispel. It trudged right through Advent and Christmas, its thermometer never once dipping. There is no relief from the dizzying glare; from the sticky lethargy there is no escape. Today the cloying Kona winds coat the air with grime, obscuring the view of the Waianae Range. And the hours drag on till I get bored with the clocks and their melancholic shuffle. Rinsing the few dishes in the sink, I watch Ronnie—his neck brace no apparent hindrance to the task of pruning the orange tree—and dream of brisk temperatures.

Cleo never knew winter, and it was difficult explaining it to her when we read her Christmas books. To Cleo, cold was swimming in the ocean at Waikiki Beach in January or the chill you get from eating shave ice too quickly. Cold never fell out of the sky like pigeon feathers or stacked up on the fence posts. One Saturday last December, when we were both bored and itchy from the heat and the candy canes had all melted into sticky gobs on our brown Christmas tree, I cut a hole in my old down pillow and ushered Cleo into the middle of the bathroom floor. To her delight, I climbed up on the bathroom counter, stretched my hands up to the ceiling, and shook out the feathers while she twirled and danced beneath them.

"Aden!" she shrieked when the last one floated to the floor. I cut up Greg's pillows and two old couch pillows with foamy stuffing before she had had enough. Later that night, when we read *The Night Before Christmas* I told her that snow was as soft as mommy kisses, as light as angels' wings. I told her I loved her more than all the snowflakes in the world.

Greg comes home from church soggy and tired. Heat rash streaks his neck and he walks to the freezer for the ice pack. "How was your day?" he asks.

"Oh, the same. Jean wants me to do a travel feature for the February issue. Buella found a stray kitten she's named Liberace that she wants to palm off on me. You?"

"Not without a few surprises," he says. "Mrs. Scribner took me to lunch, for one thing."

"Oh?" Mrs. Scribner has not invited me to attend church with her again since the incident with Carolyn, but she has dropped off two more hats with hatboxes and the calling card of her Korean hairdresser. Last week she came by to show me her new Maltese poodle, an excitable pup who peed on the carpet when Pilgrim hissed at it.

"She's decided about Puffy's ashes," he says.

"The memorial garden?"

"Nope. She's going to sprinkle them at the golf course."

"She can't do that, can she? Isn't it illegal?" Mrs. Scribner and her late husband, avid golfers and members of the Honolulu Club since the day it opened, were exempt from the no-pets policy. Some said it was their money, some that it was lifetime membership. Whatever it was, their canine companions were known to travel along in the golf cart, retrieving Mr. Scribner's ball if it wandered too far from the fairway, which was often, as Mrs. Scribner tells it.

"She's going to get a cart and dribble a bit of his ashes at each hole."

"They're not going to let her do that!"

"That's why she's not going to tell them. The plan is to do a leisurely nine holes with her pastor just before closing time."

I cannot get used to an uninterrupted conversation. Cleo would get so frustrated when Greg and I talked at the table, so intent on our conversation about work or church or theology. She would get louder or start playing with her food or stand up on her chair and jump. Sometimes she would just holler at us, "Stop talking!" And we would exchange a look of resignation and turn our attention to true north.

"You said 'a few surprises'; what else?" I ask.

"The district superintendent called today . . . There's a church they want me to consider."

"Oh?"

"In California. Just north of Fresno. The guy there just had a heart attack. They've got an interim, but they need to fill the position by conference time, so Alex is suggesting we go up and take a look around. See if it's a community we could get along with. I thought we could go visit Rhiaan and Cicely while we're at it."

"I thought you were going to hold out for something here," I say, irritated at Greg's obvious excitement. If California is the cool-cat state, then Fresno is its hairball. Air you can gag on, heat that makes turncoats out of shade, ninety-nine square miles of boredom. Come conference six months from now, and it will still be too soon.

"I know," he sighs. "I told Alex you didn't want to move. But he's not sure any appointments are going to open up on Oahu." My terror must be apparent, because he says, "Tell you what, let's not worry about the church right now, let's just plan on a trip to Tahoe."

"I don't know. I will have to take time off work . . ." Here we go again, his face seems to say. "Maybe you should go without me; maybe we could do with some time alone."

This time Greg is adamant. "No, Abbe! I am alone most of the time; I'm sick of being alone. I am doing my best not to lose you altogether. Please, please, let's go. Together." I see a drowning man before me, someone who looks vaguely like a man who was once my husband. I nod and whisper, "Okay."

CHRISTMAS HAS PASSED without trees and twinkle lights, carols or fuss. No magi with their morbid gifts of embalmment. Somewhere beyond my walls people celebrated the birth of a baby, forgetting it is a stone's throw from Golgotha. Now it looks as though New Year's Eve will go without fanfare too. Greg and I watch a foreign film about Japanese samurai and kiss chastely at ten o'clock before going to bed. "Happy New Year," we each say sadly, and lie waiting for the old year to go quietly to its grave. After a few minutes, Greg's hand reaches for my waist and he shifts himself into the curve of my back. We are still a long time, side by side, till I feel the small, cold lump of flesh swell against my buttocks. His hand cups my breast and only a stale sense of resignation rises up to meet it. The gesture is doubtful; a question more than a plan. If I wait long enough without moving, Greg's straining penis will lie back down obediently and he will fall asleep holding no grudges.

Greg's return to our bed went without comment, just as his departure from it had. After months of retreating to separate rooms, covering our grieving hearts with separate sheets, we once again share the same bed, tucked into our familiar hollows without footnotes. And there are no speeches now, in the pause between my rejection or reception of his advances. Thinking that sleep might be coaxed more quickly, I turn to him, and invite him onto my body. Beyond his measured strains, his face buried in my hair, I watch the east window. It has started to rain. Good. There won't be many fireworks tonight.

After a quiet shudder, Greg wriggles apart awkwardly and I return to my side. "Sorry," I hear him whisper, and I smile my okay, even though it is too dark for him to see it. A minute later he snores softly and I think, No need for sorry. I offer a body not meant for loving anymore, a hag's bony embrace.

THE CLATTER OF PANS wakes me up to the first day of January. Greg is cooking pancakes, and I wonder if we are now expected to return to all our prenatal rituals. When I enter the kitchen the teapot is already full, ready for pouring into the teacups only ever used for company.

"I spoke to Rhiaan—we're on! And I just booked our tickets—we have enough frequent flyer miles for one free round-trip." He seems almost happy.

"When are we leaving?"

"January twenty-sixth, returning the thirty-first."

Exactly one month before Cleo's birthday.

He puts down a plate of pancakes, pours me a cup of tea, and says, "You need to put on some weight; it almost felt like I was sleeping with some other woman last night."

"You were," I say without rancor.

I am hungry this morning, so I eat what he puts in front of me, and I can tell by the way he sits straight up that he feels like we have a chance.

"Perhaps we can go skiing," he chitchats.

"I don't know how to ski," I reply, seized with portents of misgiving.

"I'll teach you, and we can stick to the bunny slopes."

"Maybe we can just see how it goes," I say, and then, because he starts to look concerned, "We can read books by the fireplace and sip hot chocolate, how's that for starters?"

It is only these minuscule kindnesses that I am now capable of, in between the waves of cataclysmic cruelties. And how often I seem to confuse the two. Perhaps Greg is right, that by going on a trip we might find our way back to each other, as we have done before. That what we need is the company of family and a good dose of fresh mountain air to remind us of our vows, to keep from becoming my parents, and his parents, and the countless lost couples who have worn down the marital path with their resigned treading, striding along in step but lost to each other. "Till death us do part," we promised. Yes, but hadn't that time come?

Greg rises from the table and says, "I've got a wedding this afternoon; I don't suppose you want to go with me, do you?"

Sunday, January 1, stretches out before me, a mirage of never-ending horizons.

"I'll go," I say, surprising us both.

And now a mother-in-mourning on the first day of a year already old with loss, I must find something to wear to face a bride.

GREG HAS NEVER LIKED conducting matrimonial services, and seemed self-conscious even participating in our own. "I prefer funerals," he would tell people. "They stay dead." People loved that gag, chuckling with delight at his rare impudence, not believing he was actually serious, which of course he was. He didn't like working with brides, the ones on their first go-round, with their exhausting picture of the perfect day; or the brides' mothers, who doled out instructions and dollars in equal measure till the day was whipped into a frothy illusion every bit as rich as the tiramisu at the end of the buffet line. Or even the brides on the second, sometimes third, go-round, who knew enough to have prenups and exit strategies. Allergic to hairspray and gardenias, plentiful even in those with Motel 6 budgets, Greg is always runny-eyed and red-nosed in the bridal pictures. But brides and allergies aside, what annoyed Greg the most was the ease with which covenants were made and blessed, and then broken.

They stay dead is all I can think while the bride lip-synchs her vows. Greg gestures to remind her to look at her betrothed while she repeats them, not at him, and the audience shudders with a delighted tee-hee. I look around the church. Same crowd that shows up for funerals, only a little more bored perhaps. The living stay dead too, apparently.

I was three months pregnant when I first pictured Cleo's wedding. Saw her floating in my grandmother's wedding dress, a dress whose fibers carried the traces of genealogy, one that was layered in promises for each of its would-be wearers. Each of whom, as it turned out, chose something else—my mother a maternity-friendly suit and me something that didn't involve costly alterations and a psychological overhaul. But Cleo—she was surely destined for the dress, leapfrogging over our failures to claim the promises of a happily-ever-after.

"But it's going to be a boy!" Jenny argued when I told her about my vision.

"No it's not."

"Well, if I'm wrong—and that has happened once before—tell the preacher to start saving, because it's going to be a big wedding."

The congregation stands and applauds dutifully. The bride and groom, having tripped through their lines, look happy the ordeal is over. Swooshing past me in a shimmering gown obviously not her grandmother's, the bride beams directly at the cameras.

I walk against the flow of well-wishers, toward the chancel where Greg is collecting his notes and glasses. Not looking up, he takes the mike off the stand, unplugs it, and winds up the cord. We are both at a loss, strangers again.

An earnest little man shuffles up with his hand already extended. "Reverend?" he calls to Greg. "I just wanted to say that was a very pleasant service . . .," and then when Greg looks at him and he sees Greg's red-rimmed eyes, he becomes apologetic and embarrassed.

"Pardon me," he says, and makes an about-face from what he mistakes for sentiment rather than allergies. But then I notice I am the one who is mistaken, that Greg, perhaps reminded of the one wedding he will never conduct, is welling up.

"Do you have to go to the reception?" I ask. "Can we skip it and just go home?"

"Give me a minute. I'll find the best man and let him know."

Greg walks away from me looking like a man huddled beneath an umbrella that has blown out the other way.

When we get home, I ask him to get the trunk down from the attic.

"What do you want from it?" he asks.

"My grandmother's wedding dress."

When he comes back with the chest, I open it up and dig to the bottom till my fingers find the package. The tissue paper around it has yellowed and in its folds are cockroach egg cases, but the dress remains intact. It smells of old things, dead things, of books that haven't been open for a hundred years. It is the dress of Miss Havisham, the dress for a corpse, and as it unfolds, ghosts seem to fly about the room.

"Greg," I cry, "let's burn it."

For a moment he is confused and then he nods, and suddenly I want to burn other things too, to make an offering to Cleo, so that the embers might fly up to meet her. In her room, from her bed, I retrieve Tow-Tow the Turtle, still soiled from being dragged all over the place. I reach for the dress Jenny hand-stitched for her baptism, but Greg says, "Please, Abbe, not that." So I take her favorite pair of pajamas and her pink blankie instead. A big fire, is all I can think. A raging inferno big enough that the neighbors will complain and the fire engines will come, a fire big enough not to be doused by a torrent of tears.

Greg suggests we put everything in the old wheelbarrow and I tell him we should wait until nighttime. Midnight, perhaps. A new New Year.

He finds me when I am rummaging through his bureau drawer and shows me the wooden train he made from a kit for her. Yes, I nod frantically. "Good."

"My dollhouse," I tell him, "let's burn that too," and he is off to get it.

I find my bag of hair, still in its ponytail; the stink alone will offend the gods. I add it to the pile and keep rummaging. Behind my jewelry box are my mother's rabbit-skin gloves—the only thing I have of hers besides her worn gold band and her dentures, which replaced the real teeth my father knocked out. One glove is gnawed at the opening where Solly chewed on it before I salvaged it, but its rescue means nothing now. It will burn and be no more.

With the load piled into a neat flammable tower in the living room, I look for Greg. He is in the study, the journal open on his lap. He started writing Cleo an open-ended love letter the day after she was born. Snapping the book closed, he hands it to me for the pile. "What about photos?"

"No. No photos," I say. But I remember the needlepoint of Peter Rabbit my grandmother did for me, still hanging by Cleo's bookshelf. Heirlooms burn the best. And then I go to our bedroom, take my pillow collected with night terrors and tears, and pluck from it a handful of feathers.

We sit a long time and look at the heap. Greg brings me a beer, and it seems that this is the first time we have truly done something together since Cleo died.

For all my fury at the world for spinning on its axis, despite all my rage at the old people who have the nerve to keep on living and breathing and abluting next door to the home of a dead child, I call Mrs. Chung and Gillian Beech with an apology. I tell them both the same thing: Do not be alarmed, no need to call the fire department, my husband and I will be having a bonfire in our backyard tonight. Sorry for the disturbance. Yes of course, they say. Not a problem. Will let the other neighbors know.

So at 9:25 p.m., when we are too impatient to wait for midnight, Greg stacks up everything on the rusty green wheelbarrow and pushes it beyond the banana trees. After a squirt of lighter fluid, he throws in a lit match.

I am unprepared for the blaze, for the heat that makes us both back up. There is just a trickle of fear along with the question of turning on the hose. The dress—four yards and a hundred years of romantic illusion—is the first to burn, and then it is too late to stop it. I know this about fires: they have a life of their own and they pretty much don't give a damn who got them started. Or who gets burned.

∽

IT DIDN'T MATTER that my mother started the fire that almost burned down our house. Only why. It might have been an "honest-to-God mistake," just like she said later, but I wondered if she didn't mean to, in a volcanic moment of defiance, burn up the house and its rotten contents with it.

I would not have been at home when the fire started if Mrs. Beasley from two doors down had not seen me walking to the store for my mother's jar of tartar sauce and offered to give me a ride on her way there and back. What my mother knew would be a forty-five minute errand, if I took an extra ten minutes to sneak a read of the latest comic book, turned out to be a little less than quarter of an hour. Long enough for the crackling and spitting oil on the stove to tire of its unattended pot. I heard, when I walked back into the house, the soft *poohf* it made when it leapt out of the pot and we watched the shiny flames climb the checked curtains like a cat after a lizard.

"Jesus Christ, Louise!" my father yelled, running into the kitchen. As he barked orders at me to bring wet towels and cursed till I felt sure hell had come to swallow us up, my mother stood rooted in one spot like a witch tied to her stake. That's when it first occurred to me that this was no accidental kitchen fire, but arson. I watched the orange and black shadows writhe and twitch on the hallway wall like some kind of monster. By the time he had put out the fire, the monster had turned the house into a black cloud, my mother into a lump of coal, and my father into a white-hot poker.

It took a week to wipe away the oily black grime, but nothing was the same after that fire. If anything, it seemed only to blaze on in my father's chest. It was he who needed my grandmother's lake, its waters to lap at the edges of his infernal anger. If I thought before, having overheard my mother's ghastly prayer, that she had a death wish, after the fire I became even more convinced. The only question unanswered in my mind was by whose hand the wish would be granted.

❧

THE HAIR AND FEATHERS have made the air pungent, and I wonder what burning flesh smells like. It was wrong to burn Cleo. Just plain wrong. We should have buried her. But somehow it did not seem right to put her in a hole in the ground either. Greg preferred a burial plot, a place that marked the spot, a place he could visit as he would a decrepit relative in an old-age home. He had buried our old dog, Jingles, in the backyard of the parsonage next to the bird of paradise and claimed it had been therapeutic. Maybe it was. I would see him when I was washing dishes, sitting out there in the corner of the yard on the lava rock, muttering away like a vagabond. When he came in for supper, his face damp and doughy, I would think it was nothing but dragging things out. I never went to the spot where Jingles's rotting corpse lay in Greg's old backpack. I couldn't bear the thought of our old companion packed down there like a clod of soil. And then we moved and renters occupied the parsonage, and Jingles was forgotten. So what good was that?

Cremation, then, had been my decision, my only decision, and it has turned out to be something far, far worse than what Greg wanted. Ashes. Ashes had sounded almost reverential at first. Fitting, like Ash Wednesday: so solemn and holy. The minister—holding the bowl, finger cocked as though on a trigger—awaits your remorseful approach down the center aisle to the altar. And then, eyes lowered, you feel his finger take aim, lining up with the crosshairs of your forehead. Scratch. And then another scratch. Back in the pew, you watch the other people walk by, examine their smudgy crosses, wonder if yours looks blurred too. That the ashes are smeared—and the next morning wiped entirely away on the pillow—is a little disappointing. For one bold, blind moment, you want the world to know what a phony your life turned out to be, that upon the illusion is at least one distinct blemish. *X*, okay, marks the spot. A welcome respite from the Jolly-Rogering of Christmas and Epiphany, Lent somehow makes room for the deep black brand that has been there all along. Sacrificing, Lent leads you to believe, will erase it.

Living without Cleo is a lifetime of Lents back to back. So ashes seemed fitting. Then. But I was unprepared for them being *her* ashes. What came home, in the little heart-shaped koa box, was not the holy dust of burnt palm fronds and wood chips, but gravel. Bits of Cleo's ground-up bones, coarse as pebbles, seared white. Not ashes that inspired acts of attrition, but ones that reminded me of all I had given up. Little more than a saltshakerful. People don't tell you these things when you are about to burn your child.

It is all too much: to think of Cleo's hair burning, to remember my father's combustible tendencies in the weeks that followed our house fire. And now he is dead, buried alongside my mother in their unvisited graves. And Cleo has no grave.

Greg comes to me from the other side of the fire when he sees me pull on my hair and bend over, the scream just a silent rage. He cannot help me stand upright, so we crumple on the hard cement in an awkward embrace. "They stay dead," I cry out. "They stay dead!"

In the distance, we hear the fire truck's siren.

THIRTEEN

Ten minutes till touchdown and still I can't think of 14 across: *Pope's lovers* (6, 7). I guess that rules out NUNS. Whoever picked up the airline's magazine before me has scribbled in LARK in 5 down, giving me L as the second letter, but still I am drawing a blank. It is the word that runs away with me: *lovers*. "Lovers" means passion, passion transgression, transgression a price. Not a good note with which to start a vacation, so instead I close the magazine, tuck it in my backpack, and imagine Cicely's face awaiting our arrival. Cicely, a woman who comes without a price tag.

No matter how hard I tried, even on my best days, I was never able to match Cicely's enthusiasm for life. Leaping from Yuletide to Easter to Thanksgiving as though each Hallmark holiday were a stepping-stone (with tasteful decorations to match), my brother's wife has avoided gloom with enviable good nature. Which is not to say that Cicely's life of privilege, bequeathed to her by her parents and then doubly assured by her husband, has numbed her to the plight of others less fortunate. Cicely, who visited South Africa but once after she married Rhiaan, had reportedly cried for days after seeing the puddles of street kids outside the stores, high from glue, burn-scarred hands cupped for coins. She became so passionate about these orphans that she started a campaign half a world away that had sent thousands of dollars in aid.

It was easy to see why Rhiaan was in love with her, then and still, after seventeen years of marriage. Rhiaan, a celebrated South African poet in exile, had drawn large audiences in the seventies, mostly female. Groupies, Cicely called them, as if Rhiaan were the lead singer in a rock band, as if she had not been one of the good-looking girls vying for his attention. It had been her good looks that won him over. Her good looks, and her good, bright heart. First he, and then the rest of us, got caught up in the gravitational pull that was Cicely's overflowing enthusiasm. An unlikely match, some said—this poet of dark thoughts of a dark land and the luminous child of Marin County's wealthiest couple. Looking at them confirmed it: Rhiaan, shorter than his wife by several inches, freckled and bespectacled, burnt-orange hair; Cicely, with the improbable assemblage of parts that made her both lean and endowed, topped with a cascade of now dove-gray hair that fell well beyond her shoulders.

Rhiaan had loved Cicely from the get-go with a lack of caution we had never seen as children growing up. If anyone in our home had once loved, it must have been guarded, private, as though suitable for a lavatory. Punishable even. And Cicely, who read the old poems and still cried, returned the favor by birthing twins who are each a perfect braid of their mother's wholeheartedness and their father's sagacity. Claude and Francine, required as teenagers to treat Cicely's devotion to them as a public humiliation to be endured, privately adore their mother.

Rhiaan meets us at the baggage claim looking tired because he had to drive the sixty miles of slippery blacktop to get to Reno's airport and then had to mark time for another hour for the conditions to clear enough for our plane to land.

"Hello, sis," he says, hugging me hard, his jowls giving way to dimples. "Hope you're ready for snow." I put on the pink down-filled parka Cecily has sent along with him; my denim jacket, the warmest thing in my closet, is no match for the brittle air.

"How did an ugly bastard like you wind up with my beautiful sister?" he asks, patting Greg hard on the shoulder. It is an old joke: Rhiaan openly envious of Greg's height and easy good looks, far from an ugly bastard.

"The weather report said high twenties today," Greg chats, warming his hands at the blast of hot air from the car's heater.

"Cold enough to freeze the balls off a brass monkey," Rhiaan replies.

"Not to mention mine," adds Greg, snickering like a twelve-year-old.

"How's the writing?" Greg asks. "Magazine publishers as fickle as book publishers?"

"Oh *ja*," Rhiaan confirms, "and as tightfisted." He mentions, without enthusiasm, that an anthology of his old poems is coming out in the summer, but even the publisher is less than optimistic, committing to a small print run. The lectures, he explains, are the bread and butter.

From the backseat, I tune out Greg's chatter and watch the winter I have been waiting for drift by the car window. Stripped of color, the world finally feels a little more habitable. The clouds are heavy with gloom, casting their gray pallor on the snow-covered mountains, the meadows like gaps in a row of decaying teeth. There are no traces of summer, no promise of spring—just skeletal trees and their sepulchral shrouds, stark and comforting.

When the car slows I awake just in time to see that "bread and butter" is yet another renovation to their stylish bungalow and a second Lexus parked out front. Cicely opens the front door before Rhiaan has turned off the ignition, and waves. She looks thinner, but this is often my first thought when I see her after a long absence. Only on one occasion did Cicely speak of her high school bout of bulimia, admitting that even as she approaches fifty she still occasionally succumbs to her habit of old.

"I'm so sorry I didn't make it to the funeral, Abbe," she apologizes as we embrace, and I muffle a reply in her fragrant hair. "We should just give up going to France for vacations. Each time we go something dreadful happens." Last year, if memory serves, their cat ran away. She grabs my hand and pulls me in. "Come, I've got something for you."

Their home smells of cedarwood and roasting meat, and the familiar sounds of *kweto* music come from the stereo. The house is streaming with upper-class debris, and we have to step over a mound of East

Coast newspapers to enter the living room, where the fireplace blazes beneath Cicely's perfectly decorated mantel. Out their picture window is a sprawling view of the lake and the steep mountains sliding into it on all sides. The lake looks bad-tempered today, dark, its surface bothered by the gusty north winds.

"Where are the twins?" I ask.

"Claude is spending the weekend with a friend, and Francine is only back from her class trip on Tuesday."

Leaning against the chaise lounge is a package. "It's for you, Abbe. I hope you like it."

I pull the paper off and beneath, framed in koa, is a watercolor in summer hues of Cleo and me.

Cicely has painted us from a photograph taken at the Fourth of July beach barbecue. Worn out from the sun, Cleo had insisted I pick her up. Cicely has captured the faint glow of sunburn on the slopes of Cleo's cheeks as her head rests on my shoulder, the afternoon sun dappled on her arms, which are slung like pendulums from my neck. Although only my back is visible to the viewer, the comfort of holding a sleepy child is unmistakable.

"Oh, Cicely," I whisper.

Suddenly she looks panicked; has she done the wrong thing? Greg assures her quickly, "It's beautiful, Cis. You got her exactly right." He hugs her and then puts his arm around my shuddering shoulders.

I look and look at that sweet face gazing heavy-lidded to the horizon, my face turned into her hair. I can still smell her, the sweat, the smoke from the barbecue in her salt-stiff curls. Still feel the weight of her in my arms, her head heavy in the dip of my shoulder, the one last muscle in her arm to keep the bucket from falling from her grip.

"I wanted to finish it months ago, but with all the holidays, it has been slow going."

"Thank you," is all I can say, and summer then threatens to flood the room.

. . .

NIGHT ARRIVES EARLY in the afternoon, the saggy-bellied clouds swaying low over the lakeside cabins. Greg has slept through dinner and I watch as Cicely draws a quilt over him, tucking it around his broad back. Rhiaan has gone to bed early too, with a headache Cicely says plagues him a lot of the time.

"It's not a tumor," she says, on the bright side, and hands me a glass of wine as we sit at the kitchen counter. "He had a scan done and everything is normal. Physically there's nothing wrong with him, so now the neurologist is recommending a psychiatrist."

"Is he depressed?" I ask, wondering if the Hebrews were right—that the sins of the parents are visited on their children. Does the inevitability of that fate catch up with us the minute we are distracted from our struggle against it?

"Oh, you know your brother. He's a poet. He'd be the first one to tell you that misery is an art form." The concern is etched around her smile. Suddenly she starts to cry, and it is so surprising to see her anything but glass-half-full jolly it takes me a moment before I embrace her.

"Have you talked to him?" I ask.

"Sure. We talk, or at least I talk. He makes me feel like I overdramatize everything, but the last time we spoke about his work he said he felt 'redundant.' Now you tell me how I am supposed to take a statement like that?"

"Is it writer's block, you think? Have you read anything of his lately?"

"There have been a couple of poems, but that was a while back. I thought they were good, but it doesn't seem to matter what I think, and now, to be honest, I'm just too afraid to ask. Maybe you could get him to show you something. Maybe you could talk to him about writing, and about seeing a professional."

"Rhiaan is not likely to see a shrink, Cis, you know that. It's just not how we were raised—stiff upper lip, and all that," I reply. And just for an instant Cicely can't keep the contempt from her face. Contempt for the broken children from their broken family in their broken backwater country messing up the otherwise sunny landscape of her preordained bounty.

"Maybe that's part of the problem," she says.

"Maybe you're right."

She looks wrung out, and pats at her cheeks with a leftover napkin before returning to the tasks of domesticity. "What about you and Greg?" she asks. "How are you two handling the trials?" Cicely does not need an acute skill of observation to notice how I shrug Greg off like a shawl on a humid evening.

"Not good," I say. She nods, and waits for more. "Greg might tell you otherwise. He's buried himself in the church, and I avoid it. I suppose he feels this weekend is our last hope."

"A little bit of hope never killed anyone," she answers, identifying her ally.

THE WORLD IS PLUMP with snow when I get up and the flakes drift down, as though they have all day. The pine trees have cotton-ball branches, and from the eaves dangle icicles. The only sign of activity outside is the smoke drifting up from the chimneys. Inside, Greg and Cicely are sitting on the floor by the window, piecing together a puzzle the size of the coffee table. Thick in conversation, Cicely sees me before I have a chance to eavesdrop.

"Hello, Abbe, how did you sleep?" She hurries to the kitchen and pours from her cat-shaped teapot a mug of fresh tea.

"Okay." What I don't tell her is that I have spent half the night hearing her words over and over in my head—*A little bit of hope never killed anyone*. It is hope that will pull Rhiaan and Cicely from the quicksand, as it always does. But what did hope ever do for my mother, or for Cleo? What can it possibly do for me and Greg? "Where's Rhiaan?" I ask.

"Out in the shed. He's converted it into an office, but it's more like his cave. You must take a look."

I put on the parka and Cicely's boots and walk along the cleared footpath to the shed.

"Brought you some tea," I announce as I step into the warmth. There is a small potbellied stove in the corner and a rolltop desk that looks as though it comes from Bob Cratchit's office. On top of it is the Olivetti typewriter. Pinewood-lined walls are shelved with books and framed photographs: Rhiaan with Nadine Gordimer and J. M. Coetzee, Rhiaan shaking hands with Desmond Tutu, Rhiaan sitting with a group of African children outside a rondavel in the middle of the sticks. The small black-and-white photo in the pewter frame gives me pause: Rhiaan as a boy standing on top of a ridge next to our father.

"I haven't seen this one before," I say. "Where is that?"

"Eastern Transvaal. Just outside Nelspruit. Ever go to God's Window?"

I shake my head.

He takes a sip of tea. "They say from the escarpment you can see all the way from the Lowveldt to the front door of the Almighty."

"Was it open?" I ask, and Rhiaan laughs. "Just wondering if the Almighty has an open-door policy." When Rhiaan smiles he looks nothing like my father, but when his face succumbs to gravity, the likeness is eerie.

"I don't remember him ever smiling, do you?" I ask, noticing how in the photograph my father does not have his arm around his son, does not even stand close enough for their sides to touch; how the view of all creation yawns between them.

"There were times," Rhiaan counters.

"Like when?"

"Like when you were born," he says, and I am reminded that Rhiaan's memories are not my own. "I remember him having a big barbecue when Mom came home from the hospital with you, and all his buddies from work came over to have a look." I feel a twinge of delight—maybe there were times he wasn't the bogeyman. "And then he got as pissed as a fart and left a helluva mess for Mom to clean up!" He laughs, and I roll my eyes.

I sip my tea and change the subject. "Cicely says you're going back to receive some fancy award?"

"Oh, I haven't decided yet. They're opening an apartheid museum in Cape Town and they have a wing dedicated to the artists of 'protest works,' whatever that is."

"You're not excited."

"To tell you the truth, I am tired of talking about the past. It's gone, it's done; whether I like it or not, there's no going back and changing it." Is my brother giving me advice? "You've got to lean with all your might against the boulder of the present and wedge it loose, even if it means you have to watch it career into your neatly built idea of the future."

There falls between us a soupy silence. After a while he looks up from his mug. "So what are you up to these days, Ab? How are you doing?" He squints, rubbing the spot between his eyes.

"Well, let's see. I get up before noon most days, write a few hundred words of nonsense they keep printing in the magazine, and count the hours before I can go back to bed."

"Don't ever underestimate what a courageous thing it is to get out of one's bed each day."

"Speak from experience, do you?"

"My wife been talking to you?"

I nod.

He gets out his pipe and tobacco pouch. "She makes too much of things."

"Depression is a serious thing."

"Cicely always worries about those things over which she has no control rather than letting things run their course. She calls it depression so she can speed up the process with a Prozac-inspired happy ending. But I think we have to hold out for the real thing."

"She says you are working on some new poems. Got anything you could show me?"

From a binder of loose sheets and newspaper clippings, he extracts a page. In single-spaced Times New Roman is an untitled poem.

Waste not your woe, O Breath
upon the wooden grain you
mistake for flesh.

For kindness rather a spark proffer
Not to singe or maim and
with regret hastily smother;
Not for spite, nor shame,
nor pity for rhymes untold.
For perhaps one last blaze
a towering glory,
a phase, this pyre will trade
an ashy mound.

What scars, what charry husk
then, tempting sorrow Coeur;
What kindness then to puff
and words shall be no more;
Only wind and scatterlings,
across the rooftops I shall soar,
bid adieu to telluric shores,
and bonjour, upon winged hope,
to birth, to life once more.

"It's lovely. It's so tragic, and suicidal, and hopeful."

He grins. "Glad you like it."

I get up and give him a hug, and then return to my seat. "Give me a copy, will you?"

"Only if you pinkie-promise not to show it to Cis. She'll surely have me committed."

"Only if you pinkie-promise not to set yourself on fire!"

He holds out his little finger and I reach over to clasp it with my own.

Just then a cold gush rushes in as Cicely opens the door. "Come on, you loafers. Let's go find some snow!"

Before I leave, I browse the shelves for a book. Rhiaan has always organized his library the way an aspiring Don Juan might organize his lovers: autobiographically. Books he fell in love with at school sit in the shelves next to those that seduced him in college. There are the early-exile books, the pre-Cicely tomes, and a rather sparse section that he says are for the books he read when his children were very little. Every ten years or so he adds a new classification, and although this system works quite nicely for him, it is a bugger for guests who perhaps want to find a light historical novel or a saucy romance. You have better luck choosing a book by its cover, which is what I do now, running my hands along the spines till they come to rest on the faded yellow back: *The Works of Alexander Pope.*

"*That* Pope!" I exclaim. "Of course!"

THE AFTERNOON LIGHT passes across the pages of my book, then dims until I can read no more. "Roast lamb and new potatoes, with mint sauce," announces Cicely. "To remind you of home." My sorrowful sister-in-law of the night before has given way to the one who punctuates the day with meals and merriment.

"Sounds good," I fib.

When we gather around the dining table, decorated with tea lights and a potted poinsettia, Rhiaan's place is empty.

"Rhiaan is going to eat later," she says. "He's not feeling too well at the moment." But no sooner has she made the announcement than he comes in and sits down. Frowning, he turns off the overhead light so that we are illuminated only by Cicely's candles. "Anybody mind?" he asks.

"Ambience," jokes Greg. "It's what makes an entrée cost twenty dollars more in a fancy restaurant."

We pass the platters, scooping generous portions on our plates, if not for appetite's sake, then for Cicely's, while she fills the wineglasses, careful to skip over Rhiaan's.

"I think I will have some wine, my dear," he insists, and without fuss she fills his glass. The conversation turns from the weather forecast to plans for skiing and then, without warning, to Lent.

"What are you two giving up for Lent this year?" asks Cicely. "You always give up the most unusual things."

"Ah," sighs Greg, pleased to gnaw on the idea.

"I remember when you gave up guns." She laughs.

"Hey, have you ever tried sitting through the news without seeing a gun of some sort? It was the longest forty days of my life!" says Greg.

"I am going to give up dieting," Cicely announces, and we all laugh. "What?"

"Dear God, woman, that's about as necessary as giving up vacations to Baghdad!" exclaims my brother.

"Okay, Rhiaan, what's your big sacrifice?" she retorts.

"Don't ask me to give up pork rinds," he jokes. "My comforts are few and far between."

"I thought I might give up nostalgia," Greg interjects, turning the air serious.

"Say more, young man," says Rhiaan.

"It seems to me that the older I get, the more I yearn for my past. For the neighborhood I grew up in, the little community events, my old school pals. I suspect that if I went back there I would still feel nostalgic. So it's a deceptive thing, isn't it? Nostalgia traps you into believing the past was better than what's up ahead."

Could he have said anything worse? If it weren't for Cicely's earlier salute to hope, I would stand up right now and say, You jerk! The past *was* better than what's ahead because the past had Cleo. It is these abstract theoretical constructs of Greg's that drive me to despair. He might as well have said, "I'm giving up memories," or "I'm giving up Cleo."

Cicely does not bang him over the head with the pot lid but nods, listening intently while I assassinate the peas on my plate. It is when Rhiaan speaks that I look up. "It is nostalgia for the things that will not come to pass that is better to give up," he says. "A homesickness for the home you do not yet have."

"Careful, Rhiaan. Sounds like you're dancing dangerously close to theology," Greg jests.

Rhiaan shakes his head. "I'm not talking about the eternal home to which you and your flock feel assured of reaching. What I'm talking about is the absence between having potential and having fulfilled none of it."

"Oh, thanks a lot," says Greg with an embarrassed laugh.

"Speak for yourself!" Cicely scolds her husband.

"Oh, but I do, my dear. Hear me out. It's when you look back and realize that the thing you did all those years ago is probably the best thing you ever did and are ever capable of doing, and that no matter how much you try, you are not ever going to be able to capture the glory again. The irony, of course, being that back then you were too young to enjoy it and now you are old enough to realize it had little to do with talent or effort on your behalf." And to Greg: "No offense, old chap, but it seems to me that rather than give up nostalgia you should give up the notion of achieving happiness altogether—"

"See? *This* is what I am talking about," Cicely interrupts, looking at me.

"No, wait a minute, let me finish—my wife thinks I am morose, but I propose a more noble quest. Not for happiness but for identity. Strip away all that fetters it, all the bells and whistles, till there is only self."

"Till there is only a selfish, miserable old goat!" flashes Cicely. She pours another glass of wine for herself.

"That, my dear, will be a matter of opinion, of which the pure identity will have no need."

It might as well be a tableful of tomcats for all the bristling. In an effort to inject levity, Greg says, "Sounds to me as though you are talking about a midlife crisis."

Rhiaan snorts his pleasure. "Ah, if it were only that simple. Then we could purchase our sports cars, have our fandangos with minors, and be done with it."

At which point Cicely leaves the table and heads for the kitchen.

"What about you?" Greg asks, turning to me. "You are very quiet."

What I want to do is recite Rhiaan's poem. "What's there to give up when all I ever wanted has been taken from me?"

The banter ceases and for the moment we all become occupied with the task of heaping tidy piles of food onto our forks, till Cicely returns. "Homemade apple pie," she announces. "Who's for à la mode?"

When dinner is over and the dishes are soaking, Cicely asks me to join her for a dip in the hot tub. The air is frosty, the sky punctured with stars, and the water a scalding welcome. It is one of the things I love about this place—the absence of human-generated sound. Although there are homes tucked among the pine trees all along the lake and up into the foothills, you don't hear much. In summertime, they even insist the boats creep out of the keys. In winter, when the boats and vacationers are hibernating, nothing but nature has a say.

Cicely talks about the quilting guild of which she is not only a member but the president, mentions that their prayer quilts are being sold online to raise money for the AIDS orphans in South Africa. She talks of accompanying Rhiaan on his trip—if he goes—and volunteering at one of the orphanages for a month or so. "The babies need someone to rock them," she said. "Goodness knows I can rock a child."

"You could do just about anything you put your mind to," says Greg, walking out to kiss us each good-night. After he has left, and while I am still choosing something to say, Cicely turns to me and says, "He's a wonderful man, Abbe; if I were you, I wouldn't let him go." She gets out, wraps herself in her gown, and darts back into the house.

I switch off the jets and close my eyes to the quiet. After a while there are discernible sounds: the lap-lap of the tub's water, the occasional rustling of trees, and then suddenly a *hoo-hoo-hoo-hoo*. On the roof of the shed alights a screech owl, its gray plumage a perfect camouflage. It is still there when Rhiaan opens the sliding glass door and steps out onto the veranda.

"See the owl?" I point out to him.

"Ah yes, she's a regular visitor."

"Granny told me a story once about an owl. This beautiful woman called Blodeuwedd who had been made out of flowers to marry a man who didn't have a wife."

"*Ja*. And then she fell in love with another man and killed her husband, and for her punishment the gods turned her into an owl . . . She told me that one too."

"I always felt sorry for Blodeuwedd. I always pictured her husband being someone like Dad, impossible to live with, which is why no earthly woman would marry him. No wonder she fell for someone else."

Rhiaan nods.

"What I haven't been able to work out," I continue, "is whether things would have turned out differently had she not gone down that path." Had *I* not gone down that path.

"You mean, whether she was to blame?"

"Yes."

My brother prefaces his axioms, as he always does, by lighting his pipe. Only when there is a steady glow in the tobacco nest does he say, gently, "Blame is another excellent thing to give up for Lent."

GREG AND CICELY leave only after I convince them I would much rather look at the snow than go out and play in it. The advanced slopes, then, will be their choice today, and Greg can't hide how pleased he is at the idea. Rhiaan is working in his studio, so I settle on the chaise lounge with Mr. Pope.

It is the sound of chopping that diverts my attention. I head outside and around the side of the house, following the noise to where Rhiaan is splitting firewood.

"I thought you were working," I say.

He smiles. "I am. I do my best work with an ax; ask my editor." He stands a log on its end, lifts the ax, and swings it till the blade finds its soft center. *Thwack.* Again he reaches for the pile for another log. *Thwack.* I hate the sound, the sound of nursery rhymes: Jill tumbling down the hill, Humpty-Dumpty breaking to pieces; the sound as the bough breaks just before the cradle falls. It is also the sound of a kitchen table felled by a madman, the seams of the world as they are ripped asunder.

❧

COMING HOME FROM TENNIS PRACTICE, I watched my mother, overbloomed in her pink chenille gown, wincing at the insults my father hurled at her: liar, bitch, whore. After running out of expletives, he flung the soiled dishes she had so neatly stacked instead of washing till it seemed a flock of porcelain birds had taken flight in our kitchen. "You think you can leave me? You think you can just walk out of my house? You think you can just go and I won't drag your skinny ass back here again? Is that what you think?"

My mother didn't answer him but rather turned to me and beseeched me to go to Mrs. Folliett's house. This time she did not even bother with a reason: tartar sauce, a cup of sugar, a barrel of gasoline, a box of matches. "I'm not going, Ma," I protested.

"Someone's got some fucking sense around here!" he spat.

"Harry, please—"

"Please? Please? You don't 'please' me anything! It's about time she knew about her mother, about what a lying little whore she is, about how she was just going to up and leave her own daughter for some prick without so much as a goodbye."

Looking at me again, she pleads, "I wasn't going to leave you. I wasn't."

"You going to lie to your own goddamn kid now, Louise?"

When all the dishes had been smashed against the cupboards and the air was thick with cussing, my father thundered out the back door. I picked out the shards from my mother's hair while her gaze fixed on the stain Mr. No-One-Friend's unattended cigarette had left on the Formica kitchen table. The stain might as well have been a damp spot on a mussed bedsheet for all its testimony. "You weren't going to leave me, were you, Mom?"

Before she could answer my father was back, this time with his ax. In one deft blow—*thwack*—he chopped off the corner of the kitchen table and the burn mark with it.

"Teach you a lesson," he muttered, padded-cell crazy. "Teach you to bring another man in my house and have him pack your bags!" Wild, he swung the ax over his shoulder and above his head, his eyes scanning the room for its next mark. And I watched them come to rest on my mother at the moment she sank to her knees.

I did scream then, as if all I was ever born to do was become a single, piercing siren.

CICELY KISSES ME GOODBYE while Greg loads the picture and the bags in the trunk of Rhiaan's car. In place of blinding cheeriness, Cicely shows signs of resignation. She will never leave Rhiaan, and I am glad, but I can't say the same for myself. Greg wants to give up the past the way cocksure people give up smoking. Which seems to leave me with only two choices: either I give up the past too, or I give up Greg.

"I never understood why Ma didn't leave him when she had the chance," I tell Rhiaan as I hand him the pink parka at the airport.

"She found a way in the end, don't you think?" he asks.

"No," I say, "I don't think she did."

He rubs my head, shakes Greg's hand, and watches us till we pass through the security checkpoint.

Greg steers us to two empty seats in front of the departure lounge's TV set. He watches the news while I think about the passion that binds my brother and his wife, a bedrock that cannot crack from the weight of humdrum, or even, I suspect, from catastrophe. It occurs to me now, in a flash, that the kind of love I once sought is the kind that is not found but rather stumbled upon when the gaze is fixed on something else. The kind of love Mr. Pope's lovers knew all about. I retrieve from my backpack the airline's magazine and open it to the crossword puzzle. Fourteen across: *Pope's lovers* (6,7). Eloisa, Abelard.

FOURTEEN

The garage door is open when I drive up in the car, and Greg is stacking the cardboard boxes with his office books in the left corner even though it is raining hard outside. The new roof inspires that kind of confidence now.

"I didn't think you would make it home this early," he says when I get out. "They have shut down the Pali Highway to one lane because of a huge rockslide."

"It wasn't raining that hard when I left the office, but the traffic is crazy. You'd swear we were having a blizzard."

"Did your boss like your Tahoe travelogue?" Greg asks, changing the subject, following me inside the house.

"Oh, I guess," I reply. "I think she likes the advertising it generated." Greg brings out the basket of laundry and starts folding it while I sift through the mail.

"It's her birthday week after next," he says.

"Yes."

"I've been thinking . . . a remembrance service might be a nice way to commemorate it."

"Yes, I suppose so."

"And that it could be the right time, you know . . . to spread her ashes."

"You have a place picked out?" I ask curtly.

"Let's not make it like this, please, Abbe."

"You do, don't you? Where?"

He gives up. "I thought the beach by the lighthouse. The time we went shell-collecting, remember?"

"Yes."

"Maybe we could recite some poems and say a prayer."

It is a watery grave, then. We think it is quiet under the waves, but when they roll over it sounds like the distant beating of thunder on the Highveldt when the rains herald the arrival of summer. And in between, the perpetual rustle, like cicadas in the bush.

"You can't go on keeping her under the bed," he says.

"You're probably right." I think of Rhiaan's "ashy mound." *What kindness then to puff / and words shall be no more.*

I ARRIVE AT WORK bleary-eyed from lack of sleep and Buella follows me to my office with a report that the city's sewer system has burst in several places, the one closest to us at Bishop Street and Nimitz Highway.

"Most of the staff can't get into work. You might say we are well and truly up shit creek now," she scoffs.

The TV is on in the staff lounge and the reporters are telling viewers to stay off the beaches and out of the water, now contaminated. There's a report of two hikers missing, presumably a result of new waterfalls.

"Speaking of shit creeks . . . ," she says, handing me a postcard. "This is from the One Whose Name Shall Not Be Spoken."

On the front is a picture of New York at night, on the back Sal's hastily scribbled note. It is addressed to "the Belle of Kahako High." "See, it was me he was really secretly in love with!" she teases. The note says that he's getting married again, to a chorus girl named Charlie. At the bottom, a postscript: *Tell Abbe that Dionysius beats Apollo 2-to-1.*

"What the hell does that mean?" she asks.

"It means he's giving love another chance."

Buella reaches over to answer the phone, "Abbe Deighton's desk, may I help you?"

"For you," she says, and waves goodbye with her postcard.

"Hello?"

"Elizabeth, Carolyn here. I got your work number from Jenny, I hope you don't mind."

"What can I do for you?" I ask, already bristly about the chorus girl.

"Some of the ladies at church want to have a reception after the event and I thought we should check with you first."

A rummage sale? The annual women's auxiliary meeting? "What event?"

"The remembrance service next Saturday, of course. Even though it's not going to be at church, Lou and I thought we could have the reception at Sylvia Horton's house, since she lives on that side of the island."

I can't be sure if I reply before dropping the phone down on its cradle. Picturing Carolyn standing on the rocks, flagging the group of well-wishers into a neat pattern of assembly for a good look at my girl's ashes, is almost too much to bear. I dial Greg's office, but Betty says he has gone over to Petal's place to talk about the baptism. The number she gives me rings until I hang up on Kelsey Oliver's answering machine. Jenny comes to the phone after I insist the school secretary page her.

"Did you know about this?" I demand.

She doesn't answer for a beat. "Didn't Greg speak to you about it?"

"He mentioned a service but not a tea party for Carolyn and company!"

Jenny's apology rolls into an explanation and then a hasty defense. Nobody, she says, really planned it this way—it just sort of took on a life of its own. It is probably going to be only thirty or so people, even less if the damp gets the better of everyone's arthritis.

"I should be so bloody lucky," I snap.

"I will gladly call them all and tell them it is going to be a private ceremony," she says. "Nobody will hold it against you."

"It's just that I—I don't know, Jen—it's not a spectator sport, that's all."

"You're right. How about a compromise: whoever you want goes to the beach, and the rest joins in at the reception." She thinks she has mediated a settlement, but the only thing to feel well and truly settled is Sal's marital status. It's unmistakable—his giddiness—even if it weren't confirmed by the postscript. Sal has chosen the dance of Dionysius, and he's going to take his chances.

I SPEND THE WEEKEND keeping track of the reports about the weather, the contaminated water in Honolulu Harbor, the roads pock-marked with potholes, the flooded houses on the Ewa Plains. Everyone wants the rains to go. Everyone except me. But go they do. Today, five days before the service, the skies are clear and a rainbow straddles every valley from Pearl City to Hawaii Kai. Blooming a month early, the shower trees decorate our street, and Ronnie is out on the ladder again, clearing out the eaves. I call Buella and tell her that I won't be coming into the office, that I will be working at home today.

The keyboard sits quiet and the computer screen blank. The words are not coming today, only thoughts of birthday parties in the park, mothers who are happy with the forecast, calling friends: "We're on for Saturday." Wedding coordinators, glad not to have to face "Plan B," will give the brides thumbs-up for beach thongs. And the nurse aides at Belmont Village will wheel out the comatose along Kuhio Boulevard for a whiff of fresh air. Cooped up, my grandmother used to tell me. "You've been cooped up too long." And she would shoo me out of the house and into the garden, where I didn't have a clue what to do. Which gets me to thinking about children in boxes, in coops.

I rush upstairs and reach under the bed for the treasure that used to be my child. It is only when I feel the rucksack beside the box that the idea comes, quick as a beetle from under a rock. Pulling them both out from under the bed, I mentally check off the plan's bullet points. The box, wrapped in my favorite old T-shirt, and the water bottle fit together snugly in the backpack. I throw in a snack bar, and before my head clears and the edge dulls against acrimonious voices shaming my plan, I run out of the house. Mrs. Chung calls out a greeting and I wave hastily, and instead of turning right to go down the hill to town, I make a left.

There is nothing to mark the head of the south Nuuanu Trail, set behind the water tower, so if anyone hikes it it is bound to be a local or someone who has stumbled upon the Division of Forestry and Wildlife's outdated brochure. Several years have passed since we last hiked the trail, and even then not all the way to the ridge crest but to the halfway point, where the lookout under the monkeypod tree gets you a view of the city in one direction and the Ko'olaus in the other.

The trail is muddy in many places, with puddles of water in the dips of the path, and earthworms, half drowned from their water-logged burrows, litter the way. A gaggle of Hawaiian nene is startled by my intrusion and quickly crosses the path and disappears into the bush. The morning is limp with humidity by the time I reach the lookout, but it seems too soon to stop. And too late to stop. Turn back, says a voice, and for a moment Greg's sad face flares up, and I almost do. But then there is Carolyn's face—or is it the Lord's face? I can't seem to tell them apart, so I press on.

There are parts where the trail is completely lost, covered with rocks and deadwood, and it is purely by accident that I find it again. Mosquitoes flicker about and the forest is tangy with the smell of mold. After climbing over a boulder that has come to rest against the trunk of a koka tree, I see that the path heads suddenly and steeply downward. Giant ferns with curlicued fronds elbow for room next to plants with bathtub-sized leaves. Spiraling around each tree trunk are pothos vines, and mossy monkey tails hang from the branches. The trail widens as it flattens out, and what I thought was freeway noise be-comes the unmistakable sound of rushing water. I follow it past a patch of bamboo and over the hollowed trunk to where it has tumbled from a ledge two hundred feet above the rocky pool. The mist catches the sun so that it streaks down in rays as if from a children's picture book. The spray is so luminous and light that if you had never seen snow, you might believe this was it.

Opening the backpack, I grasp the box and stumble over the boulders, black and slippery, to the veil of the falls. The pellets of water plaster down my hair, and I have to rub my eyes to see the scrap of blue between the treetops. In this cleft of the earth the roaring, soaking downpour shakes free as though the heaven-sent leak cannot be patched, and the long wait ends. I lift the lid, and with one shake, Cleo is an ashy mound no more. She is free.

> *I shall soar,*
> *bid adieu to telluric shores*
> *and bonjour, upon winged hope,*
> *to birth, to life once more.*

"WHERE HAVE YOU BEEN? I was worried . . ." Greg says when I walk into the house. "What have you been doing?" He points at my legs, muddy and scratched, dotted with mosquito bites.

All the way home, I have thought of what to tell Greg. Perhaps that children were not to be cooped up, perhaps recite the line from Rhiaan's poem. But with each step, the words came no closer.

His face is furrowed with concern, his frown deepening when I cannot reply. "Sit down." He ushers me into the living room. "What's going on?"

For a moment it is a horrible thing, a treacherous thing I have done. Ebullience makes way for guilt.

After a long silence, when I am convinced that the grain in the wood floors is not going to reconfigure into the script I seek, I look up at him.

"I let her go."

He is tempted to rush at me with questions, but stops and frowns, spying the backpack at my feet. Grabbing it, lifting the flap, he finds the koa box. He knows before he lifts the lid, and begins to shake his head. Like me, Greg has come to know the weight of her in the box, knows now that the box has an unbearable lightness.

"No, Abbe." He shakes his head, and shakes it till I think he must be sick from dizziness. "No!" He hurls the backpack across the room, sending the lampshade crashing to the floor. "SHE IS MY CHILD TOO!" Greg's face is swollen in anger, his fists clenched, and when he looks at me he might as well have an ax in his hand for how closely he resembles my father. "God damn you, Abbe. God damn you!"

❧

IT WAS THE DEATH OF HER, having hope. People die for things far less audacious. I have never figured out what made her go from the woman of suicide prayers and unstitched seams to the one who was hopeful enough to summon the help of a man who smoked Van Rijan plain. Was it because neither a gin bottle, nor Dead Man's Curve, nor a pot of boiling oil did the trick? I don't know, but one thing I did know: from the moment my mother lifted her scrawny neck to look me in the face, she was as good as dead. And hope had done it just as surely as my father's ax meant to.

A neat row of neighbors lined our side of the street; women who stood elbow to elbow, aprons lifted to conceal their gaping mouths or to cover the wagging tongues, I could not tell which. Mercy wasn't what my mother wanted, even if the housewives rustled from their orderly kitchens were ready to give it. "Pity's for cripples," she said, ushering me into the car before my father's truck returned. "Don't ever let anyone make a cripple out of you, Abbe."

She turned the key in the ignition and the car gave a dry heave. Again she turned it, stomping her foot on the accelerator in her own private tantrum. Just as she banged her hand on the steering wheel and sniffed at the tears she had been trying all this time to keep from spilling, the faces of Mrs. Folliett and Mrs. Beasley and the two widows from across the street peered through our windshield.

"Let out the hand brake, Mrs. Spenser," instructed Mrs. Folliett. My mother did as she was told and slowly the car moved backward, out into the waiting street. When my mother turned the wheel so we faced the hills and threw the transmission in gear, we felt the weight of the women's collective will shift to the back of the car, where it leaned and heaved and panted till the darn car sputtered to life. If my mother had looked back, as I had, she would have seen the housewives slowing to an idle in the middle of the street, watching us with something as close to envy as I have ever seen.

Later, at the farm, after Beauty had made up the beds in the spare room with wind-whipped sheets, I told my grandmother what had happened. And then I cried the bone-marrow-tired cry for which sleep is the only cure. When I awoke to the predawn crows of the roosters it seemed impossible that the previous day had only just passed. Had I not awoken to a better story or a future more far-off? Was I still to face the question of What now?

My mother's bed was both empty and made, and for a horrible minute I wondered if she had, in fact, run away without saying good-bye, just as my father had accused her of attempting to do. Hastening through the farmhouse, I found her neither in the bathroom, nor in the kitchen. Beyond the back door was my mother's car, still parked next to the outhouse, and beyond it the chicken coop, where the silhouettes of Beauty and my mother bent to the task of collecting eggs. Shivering more from relief than cold, I drew nearer to their hushed voices just as they rounded the coop and headed behind it to the wattle tree, where the chickens too stubborn to roost on racks lay their double yokers.

"I need your help, Beauty; I don't know what else to do," I heard my mother say. I was only a few feet from them, seconds away from when they would turn and see me against the rising sun.

"Don't worry, miss," Beauty promised. "We going to help you make it all better."

How? is what I wanted to ask. How was an old *sangoma* going to fix a white woman's worries? How was a maid too poor to do anything but clean house going to remedy a wrong so set in its ways? But before I could ask anything, my mother turned around and saw me. Noting the absence of a dressing gown and slippers, she scolded me back indoors as though catching a cold were the greatest of our worries.

That afternoon my mother made me a promise I later found out she could not keep. "It's only for a few weeks," she said, unpacking my clothes from the suitcase but not her own. I was to stay at my grandmother's house while she went back home and "sorted things out" with my father. There was no arguing with her; the gin-riddled mother of the spare room was one of steely resolve, if only on this point: I was not to return with her.

"It's not safe for you to go back, Ma," I begged. "He's going to kill you."

"Nonsense!" she snapped. "Your father is ill, Elizabeth—very, very ill. I'm going to see he gets what he needs. And then I'll come back for you." Only her hands gave her away, trembling as she smoothed out the collars of my shirts.

Yes, but what was it *she* needed? Surely not the home where her kitchen table was chopped in two. And what about what I needed?

Her admonitions did not stop me from pleading, even when I stood on my grandmother's red *stoep* to watch her load her suitcase in the trunk of the car. "She doesn't want to go back there, Grandma; make her stop!" I begged my grandmother. What my mother *wanted* and what she *needed* weren't the same thing, according to my grandmother. In her estimation it was a thing called "Gilead's balm" that my mother needed. And when Beauty, who had made one of her mysterious treks to the *kopje* earlier that day, came to the car and gave my mother a parcel wrapped in newspaper, I assumed she was being handed just that.

"What did Beauty give you?" I asked when my mother mounted the steps to kiss me goodbye. She smoothed back my hair, cleared my cheeks of their teary trails, and ignored my question. "It won't be for long. I promise."

"Don't leave me, Ma," I cried, but she shook her head firmly as if to free her hair from the last shards of porcelain and said, "I'm not, sweetheart."

Then she got in her car, turned the ignition, which started on the first try, and drove away.

FIFTEEN

Odd-numbered years, it seems, have the unenviable task of signaling an end to things. One: the end of infancy; thirteen: the end of childhood. Twenty-one and you can kiss goodbye all the excuses that come with being a minor. Twenty-nine: the end of young adulthood; sixty-five: the end of a career. Even-numbered years, though, get to flag new beginnings. Six: big school; sixteen: driving; eighteen: voting (and in my country, drinking and conscription). With forty comes the permissiveness of a midlife crisis, while sixty gets you senior menus and discount movie tickets. Somewhere between twenty-nine and death, almost assuredly on an odd-numbered year, spouses set aside marriage vows, write carefully worded Dear Johns, pack suitcases, and hire lawyers. Both my age and my marriage are on odd-numbered years.

AT FIRST I step over the envelope on my way to the kitchen. The morning gusts have knocked over the skinny vase that nobody bothers either to fill with flowers or put away, and blown the table clear of clutter. Sunday's worship bulletin, Greg's grocery list and the coupons paper-clipped to it, the TV guide, and the envelope all form a haphazard path on the parquet floor. A bill, I think; as good a place as any.

Two sips of tea later I bend down to pick it up, and it is only after

I turn it over that my chest begins behaving like an accordion. I stare at my name written out in full in Greg's neat cursive, marveling at how closely it resembles my mother's. Greg has gone to the effort of buying special stationery for the occasion. Rather than his customary yellow legal pad, he has chosen parchment the color brides wear when honesty rather than chastity is the virtue to be showcased. Stiff at the folds, his letter is one continuous neat script. No errors. Copied out.

Dear Abbe,

I have tried and tried to reach you, but I cannot. I cannot comfort you with the right words—the words that will bring you back to me—or the right actions. I had desperately—I see now, vainly—hoped that our trip to Tahoe might shorten the distance between us. It seems only to have made things worse. "Love is not enough," you said a few months ago, and I brushed off that comment as a product of a heated argument. But I now believe you are right. Love is not enough. Not mine, at any rate.

I cannot help but wonder whether you stopped loving me a long time ago, or only after I was no longer "Cleo's daddy," even though I know it doesn't make any difference. Whatever the case, I know I cannot make you love me any more than I can get you to accept my inadequate offerings of love.

A part of each of us died with Cleo, and though we have both wished at times that it was not a part but the entirety, we are still faced with the incredible challenge of living without her. Perhaps living and loving was too tall an order. Even though I cannot yet forgive you for dispersing her ashes without me, I feel you have done me a favor. I see now that the only way to really honor Cleo's memory is not just to go on living as a function to be endured, but to live on. Fully. I don't know how I am going to do that, but I am going to give it my best shot.

I am going to take the church appointment in Fresno in June, but in the meantime, I will be in Ohio spending some time with my family. I leave next Tuesday. What you want to do about the house is your call (one that doesn't need to be made anytime soon), but I really don't see how we can hold on to it, given my additional living expenses and reduced salary. Of course, I will do everything I can to help.

I apologize for writing this letter instead of talking to you. Somehow whatever I say ends up being the thing I least intended. What I hope you will understand from this, Abbe, is that I cannot live and die at the same time; I must choose. Know that you were always my first choice.

Greg

I leave Greg's letter on the table and go upstairs to our bedroom. From the back of the closet I retrieve the two suitcases, still with Nevada tags on the handles. Among his socks and underwear, his favorite shirts and half a dozen ties Greg will need on the mainland, I pack a few of Cleo's things: the framed photo of her as a baby, the pink pocket Bible Jenny gave her on the day of her baptism, the rattle he bought her, and a couple of baby blankets. In a tiny box, the blue velvet one that has spent all these years in the corner of my underwear drawer, I place my wedding band. While the birds come to the feeder for their morning feast, I sit down on his side of the bed and stare at the circle around my finger, envelope-white where a promise once lay.

∾

MY MOTHER WAS DIFFERENT when she came back to the farm, after I had called and begged for her to come. Perhaps I expected her to look as though her head were still on a chopping block, still half dead or wrinkled from wishing it so hard. I was quite unprepared for her purposeful step and a face that didn't quite crease into a smile but looked satisfied nonetheless. It was not something I could put my finger on, this alteration, but there was one difference I identified immediately: the absence of her wedding band.

"It keeps falling off," she explained, and it was true that her hands looked like a connect-the-dots drawing. But she could not fool me: she was going to leave him.

That my mother was going to leave my father I was certain—the first time she came to visit me. By the second visit, two weeks later, I gnawed my fingernails to the quick and had my doubts. When she showed up a third time, I knew for sure that the only person my mother intended to leave was me. Better a liar than a fool, I resolved the Sunday of my mother's fourth visit.

The lie meant to punish my mother was formed as she got up at dawn, while she quietly dressed, folded something into an envelope, and then tiptoed out of the room. Before following her, I rehearsed the lie, confident that if it did not prevent her from leaving, it might very well make her feel bad enough for doing so. I peeked in the envelope she had tucked in her purse. Addressed to Beauty, it contained five ten-rand notes and nothing else. Where she had come up with the money was as perplexing as why she would give it to Beauty.

"Go back to bed," my mother suggested when I sat down on the porch swing next to her. "It's too early to be getting up."

"You're up!" I snapped back.

My grandmother, in her gown and slippers, gray hair in a single braid down the length of her back, joined us and there was no going back to bed for anyone. Not even for Beauty, who straggled out of her *kaia* fully dressed when my grandmother called to her window where the paraffin lamp stood burning. It might have made a grand picture if someone had been there to take it—the four of us collected on the red *stoep*, waiting for the day. Had I known I was not the only one to face it with dread, I might have said something else. Or perhaps I might not have said anything at all. But I was seventeen then, on an odd-numbered year, and it seemed to be a year strung with one ending after another, only for me.

"Why don't you leave him?" I asked just as the sun peeked out from between the *fynbos*.

"It's not that simple, Abbe," my mother answered, glancing at Beauty.

"Grannie left Oupa," I prodded. Even though a scandalous thing whispered in backhanded conversations—an old woman divorcing her husband after so many years—it had not been hard. Oupa, already feeble both in spirit and mind, surrendered without much of a fight and shuffled off even eagerly to Downey Homes in Constantia. "Neutered the ol' bugger," my father described it, who stopped coming to the farm when my grandmother had Beauty eat her meals with her in the dining room instead of alone at the kitchen table.

"This is different," she said.

"How?"

"In my day," my grandmother interjected, "a woman never left her husband, no matter how bad things got. You put up with all sorts of shenanigans for the sake of the children. Even when they left home and had children of their own, you put up with it because you were afraid of being lonely."

"You weren't afraid of being lonely," I insisted.

"Yes, well, one day I realized it can be quite a lonesome thing to live with someone who is no longer there." It was apparent, suddenly, that I was not alone in wishing my mother would give up my father, or whatever it was that drew her back to his whereabouts. It also seemed that my grandmother had said the one thing that would convince my mother to stay, for good this time.

Instead of agreeing, my mother turned to me and said, "We'll be together one of these days, you'll see." As though I were a child, as though I could live off "you'll see's" and "I promise's." Had my mother forgotten I had watched her, pressed between my father's moods like a flower in the pages of a thick book, go brittle? The only thing left to see, surely, was the moment she went from a dried flower to a handful of crumbs. My lie, steady as a boot, came crunching. "I don't want us to be together! So why don't you go, and don't bother coming back!"

When my mother drew a sharp intake of breath and rose slowly from her seat, her back to the glowering sun, it seemed the first draft could just blow her away.

Later, after receiving from Beauty her tin of tea or whatever it was my mother said calmed her nerves, she headed for her car. Shading her eyes from the sun with her free hand, she squinted in my direction. She would not have been able to see me, in the shade of the fruit trees, watching her from around one of the massive trunks, but she knew I was there. I both dreaded and hoped she would come to me, and kiss me and make it all better. Instead, she got in her car and drove back to the house I had once thought of as home, to a man I once thought of as father.

It was only after my grandmother had driven off to church that I went back to the house. Entering my room with the timidity of a stray dog, I searched for something she might have left behind. Would it be a book this time, or a photograph, or perhaps her perfume? I glanced around the room: clothes strewn hastily on the floor, the disheveled bed by the window, hers neatly made, a drawer of the bureau open like the mouth of a panting dog. And then there it was, on my school case. Not something of hers at all, but a new thing that was to be mine alone. A sealed envelope with my name centered tidily on the front of it.

My grandmother returned from church to find me with my head in Beauty's lap, my mother's letter still in my hand. So long had I lain there that I no longer noticed Beauty's odor—the spiky scent of wood fires and Vicks and unnamed things—or her fingers unknotting the tangles in my hair. The soft song of Africa accompanied my guilty tears. *"Tula tu tula baba tula sana, tul'umam' uzobuya ekuseni."*

"It's all my fault," I cried when my grandmother sat down on the bed next to us.

"Now, now," she said.

"It is—it's my fault she stays with him, and now she's never coming back."

Beauty lifted me off her lap and ushered me into the crook of my grandmother's arm before leaving the room.

"If anyone is to blame for her staying with your father, dear child, it's me." When I looked up at her, she explained. "Your mother came to me long ago, on a day when she had gotten between your father's hand and your brother's face. She wanted to know what to do, and I said something I have regretted all these years, something I have tried to reverse a hundred different ways."

"What did you say?"

"I never did think she should have married him, your father. He was a bad apple right from the beginning, but your mother could be a stubborn girl in those days."

"Grannie?"

"I told her she had made her bed so she had to lie in it."

I hate going away, my mother had written, *because it means we have to be separated again. And though it must feel to you as though I leave you again and again, I never do . . . I just go away. But please believe me, Abbe—I will never leave you.* The truth of it was that *we* had all left her, deserted her in some way by what we had said, by our expectations of her. The only one not to have left her was her amber-haired boy who had grown up and gone away.

∾

"I'M PICKING YOU UP AT SIX," announces Jenny in an early-morning call. "Petal is coming too; the grandparents are going to watch Blossom." Hearing my groan, she goes on, "Hey, she could do with an evening out too."

"Okay," I relent.

"It will be fun," she insists, perhaps too keenly, because she asks, "Are you going to be okay today?"

"We'll see," I answer.

In the three weeks since Greg left, not a day has gone by without a call from Jenny. If it is not before school starts to make sure I intend to get up, it is in the evening after she has fed Mr. Finnegan his saimin, changed his diaper, and put him to bed. It seems I am also part of her flock, as is Petal, for whom she babysits every other Friday. Just as she once did, and then stopped doing, for us.

I do get up. The first few mornings, it was just to double-check that Greg had not just gone away but left. For good. I looked for bits of Greg, but the house, covered with Cleo like a coat of dust, offered barely any signs of him, as though he had never quite lived here. Besides his clocks and his gray easy chair, which Ronnie has agreed to haul to the curb, there is nothing much to remind me of him that isn't attached to my memories of Cleo.

His absence does mean I have to remember more things. Besides remembering to eat breakfast before going to work, I must remember to fill the pets' food bowls. When I come home in the afternoon, I must remember to attend to the litter box and fill the bird feeder. It was a week before I remembered to clear the backyard of Solly's business, which is when I noticed Greg's orchids, withered in their pots. When I tipped out their remains behind the torch ginger whose stalks had taken custody of Greg's pitiful tomato patch, I said out loud to those things still stubborn enough to grow, "You will all just have to fend for yourselves now."

The church, according to Jenny, is fending for itself quite nicely. The interim pastor, a middle-aged woman recently graduated from seminary, has a portable electronic keyboard and the zest of the newly ordained. Some people say she is going off in too many directions—if you can call replacing hymnals with praise song sheets a direction. "She means well" is the general consensus, but there are still those who miss Greg. They did not have time to host a farewell luncheon for him, so Cleo's memorial service turned out to be their last social gathering. Jenny said many more than the anticipated thirty showed up, filling Sylvia Horton's house, her yard, and half of her neighbor's.

And today, on the anniversary of Cleo's death, I wonder who minds the date. A handful of us, is my guess—Greg and his mother, Cicely and Rhiaan, Jenny, yes; Theresa—bad with dates—no. Mr. Nguyen, if Greg still corresponds with him, yes; the clergy who officiated at her service, no. Perhaps I should have put something in the paper, for people to say, "Gosh, has it been a year already?" No, I'm glad I didn't.

No sooner have I called Buella to tell her I won't be coming in than I realize my mistake. There is a day to fill. The walk to the mailbox and back takes two minutes, even with a pause to hear Mrs. Chung's updated tally on her oranges. If I am diligent about reading the entire stack of mail, including the credit card offers, I might kill an hour. I have never been so eager. Sandwiched between the weekly coupons and the mortgage loan preapprovals is a postcard. On the front is a field of flowers; on the back an Ohio postmark and Greg's handwriting. *We'll never forget. She lives on.* The note brings with it images of Greg on a ladder, scraping off old paint from shutters, his mother coming around the corner with a soda, licking her lips in that nervous fashion of hers, saying, "Be careful now, Gregory." Of him standing up there, with a view of the fields and their spring flowers and the old highway that no one uses anymore; up there with God and the big blue sky and thoughts about Cleo living on.

Cicely calls and, surprised to find me home, stammers the sentiment she had intended for the answering machine. When I ask about Rhiaan, she speaks as though she has been let off the hook. His trip back to South Africa went well, and she thinks her decision not to go along probably accounts for part of that. He met some people who are making a film that they want him to coproduce, so that was good too. And he had paid a visit to the cemetery. Someone, apparently, had left flowers on my mother's grave. Who, I puzzled, would leave my mother flowers?

After Cicely's call there are no more distractions. There is nothing left to do but sit on the floor in Cleo's room and go through her closet. I gently lift the dresses free from their hangers, fold them along the seams to avoid creasing, and put them in the boxes left over from Greg's move. One box is going to be just for all her dress-up clothes, with their wands and crowns and wings.

It is only among her stuff where I find bits of Greg, in the things he couldn't resist buying her. Suddenly it seems wrong to pack up her closet, so I stack the empty boxes at the foot of the shelves and close the doors. Maybe another day. Returning from the linen closet with clean sheets, I remake her bed and fill the empty vase next to it with a hibiscus flower. I straighten her bookshelf. Her sketch pad opens to a crayon drawing of three people. From enormous lollipop heads sprout root-thin limbs, the tips of which have Ping-Pong ball fingers. Two of the figures have curly hair; the one whose hair is short and spiky is me. Around them are green shoots. "Lost in the Forest" is what the picture is titled. On the bottom, in my handwriting, is a written account of her story: *The mommy and the daddy are lost in the forest. They are calling and calling. The little girl finds them. She is brave and kind. She takes them home and gives them bread and honey. The End.* As if being "brave and kind" is all it takes to find the lost and fix the broken. There is only one place to which the lost and broken can go at an hour like this: daytime TV.

IT IS ALMOST half past six when Petal knocks at the door, wearing what looks like a dishcloth around a floor-length paisley skirt and a tank top with a picture of an orange on it with the word "art" printed below it.

"Jenny's in the car," she lisps, and gives me a quick kiss before I can pull away.

"You're late," I snap, feeling like a scratchy sweater my grand-mother might have knitted.

"It's all my fault. Sorry about that. Blossom got all worked up just as we were about to leave, so I had to nurse her till she fell asleep. Didn't want Granddad to be all in a tizzy from the get-go."

"Didn't know he could be anything but," I mumble.

"You sit in the front, Abbe," she says, holding open the door for me as though I were a cantankerous elderly aunt.

The car is not even out of the driveway before Petal hands me a gift wrapped in hand-stamped paper. "It's for you in memory of Cleo," she says, chewing her bottom lip. "Hope you like it." I unwrap it to find a CD, the back of which is listed with song titles from the sixties. I re-ally must roll my eyes now. "I wrote some of the lyrics down so you could sing along if you wanted to," she says, pointing to the insert.

I see Jenny glance at me from the corner of my eye, and I know she is pleading with me to be kind. *Brave and kind.*

"Thank you, that's very thoughtful," I say.

"SHALL WE HAVE WINE?" asks Jenny, peering over the top of her menu.

"Why not?" I reply.

When the waiter brings the bottle, Petal announces that she really ought not to, cupping her breasts quite unexpectedly, which I take to mean she is still breast-feeding, but Lord only knows what the waiter thinks. Evidently he sees it as a sign to move on to the next empty glass—mine—but she says, "Oh, what the heck. It's a party, innit?" and then just as quickly her smile falls. "Oh, blimey, Abbe, I am so sorry. I never seem to say the right thing."

It is as though we are locked in a game of Statues, the waiter bent over with his bottle poised at the lip of my glass, Jenny nose-up from the top of her menu, me with hand ready to remove the napkin from my plate, Petal with hers clasped to her mouth.

"No, you're right. It's not a wake. Tonight, just for tonight, how about we live a little."

The waiter, relieved, pours the wine and Petal reaches over and gives me another hug.

"To life," says Jenny, wineglass poised in a toast. "And to Cleo, who showed us how to live it."

"To life, and to Cleo," we say before Petal drains half her glass of wine.

By the time the desserts arrive, Jenny and I have both exchanged half a dozen glances each time Petal drained and then refilled her glass. We have listened to all the "brilliant" things Blossom has accomplished in the past few months, moved through a litany of Kelsey's idiosyncrasies and Fay's reasons for sainthood, and ended with Petal's decision to return to England.

"That's good," I remark. "I am sure your father misses you very much and is eager to see the baby."

She nods. "You have to go back eventually, haven't you? Can't put it off forever." Well, yes you can, I want to tell her; I have.

"Speaking of trips," Jenny announces, "I think I might go back home for a visit." When she sees what must be a look of shock on my face, she explains. "A visit, I said." While Petal nods with the enthusiasm of a plastic dashboard-mounted chihuahua, Jenny explains. "I talked to my sister the other night and she says my mother is getting a bit feeble, and you know how it is with old people. Besides, I have been waiting for something to spend my tax return on."

"I would love to visit Jamaica if I had the money," gushes Petal. "All those things you hear about—spells and voodoo—it must be a very spiritual place."

"Well now, don't go believing everything you hear. Poor's what my hometown is more than anything else."

Petal is not to be dissuaded from the topic. "Where would you go if you had the money, Abbe?"

Without hesitating, I tell her, "If I had the money I wouldn't have to go anywhere," but I can't keep the tremble from my tone.

"What's wrong?" asks Jenny.

I shake my head. "I don't think I am going to be able to hang on to the house much longer. Greg's got his own bills to pay come June, so unless I get a buyer for my grandmother's property soon, I'm going to have to sell the place."

"Where will you go?" asks Petal.

"We'll just add that to the bullet-point list of things to worry about," I snap.

Jenny, who will gladly forfeit her trip to Jamaica to pay just one month of my mortgage, is quick. "You can always stay with me."

The waiter clears our dessert dishes and I ask for the check.

"I am sure there will be a buyer—it's a nice place, right? Farms have such good energy—you know, from all the growing things."

"Not this one, apparently."

"What do you mean?"

I look over at Jenny. "She's going to love this," I say.

"What? What am I going to love?"

"It has a curse." There. When I say it, it sounds as ridiculous as it did when I brought up the matter with Rhiaan.

As though at a séance, Petal gasps. "What kind of curse?"

"Well, Petal, the bad kind."

"What was the curse?" This must be as close to pulling teeth as Petal can get.

"It was a curse on the land, that none of the trees would produce fruit until wrong was made right. I'm not one to believe in stuff like that"—and I can just see Petal's incredulous look: *Why not?*—"but the weird thing is that those trees haven't produced fruit in twenty years.

They're barren, and that's why no one has bought the farm. It doesn't have anything to do with the curse; all anyone has to do is take a look at those poor trees to figure the soil's gone bad. And what farmer is going to buy a fruit farm with bad soil?" The waiter brings our check, and for a moment there is a flurry of handbags and a race to see who can draw their wallets first. Petal stirs her coffee, sucks on her spoon, and then points it at me as though it were a wand. "Curses can be broken, you know."

On the way back home in the car I am preoccupied by thoughts of those sick stick trees. When we pull into the driveway, the house is completely dark because I forgot to turn on the porch light. Petal no doubt brings up Greg because it looks overbearingly lonely. "You must miss Reverend Deighton an awful lot."

"Actually, not much."

"I miss him," she continues. "It's too bad he had to go away."

I bend over to give Jenny a hug and get out the car. "He didn't go away, Petal; he left. There's a difference."

Jenny has to drive another thirty minutes to take Petal home. For Petal, the porch light will be on and a baby will be waiting. A grandmother will greet her, while across the ocean her father will count off the days on his calendar till it is upon his doorstep she stands. For a girl just turned twenty-four, of course curses can be broken, just as Cleo's stick figures can find their way out of the forest to a table of bread and honey—Petal, after all, is on an even-numbered year.

SIXTEEN

There are several people with blue masks and white coats standing around me as I lie on a gurney and gaze into a circle of lights directly above me. They stare at my chest, and when someone cranks open my ribs I see them remove a tiny bird where my heart should be. The bird is sticky and wet, as if newly hatched, but its eyes are white; dead. An alarm sounds and they hurry to close up the cavity, but they do not put my bird back. They have taken my bird; there is no other bird. The ringing goes on and on, and the lights are very hot, and the people have gone away. When I manage to open my eyes, the afternoon sun is blazing down on the couch where I lie and the phone is persistent in its ring. Sweaty and shivery, I put a hand up to my chest and reach for the telephone.

"Hello?"

"Abbe, it's Jen; I have some sad news." Without waiting for a response, she says, "Jakes died yesterday."

"What?"

"He died from complications after a kidney transplant. Remember his brother who was so sick? Jakes was giving him a kidney, but he never came out of ICU."

I didn't pray for bad things to happen to Theresa, so it is not my fault, is the first thing I think. And then: God is getting even, there's a universal justice at work in the world. And finally, I think, Dammit, Jakes is dead now too.

Jenny goes on, "It was just one of those flukes."

"Terrible."

"Theresa is having the funeral here," she goes on. After Cleo died, Theresa and Jakes moved their family to Utah to be near his family. Before I made it clear to Jenny that I didn't want updates on how their lives were getting along, she reported that Theresa missed Hawaii terribly. "Jakes's family are Mormons; and you know Theresa and dresses," Jenny had said. But really it was her family that Theresa missed, her sister, her mother, her girlfriends.

"When is it going to be?"

"Saturday. But I'm flying out to Salt Lake City tonight to help her." There goes her trip to Jamaica.

"Terrible," I repeat.

"I know."

"And the kids?"

"The boys are in shock, but Tess doesn't know yet. Theresa said she can't figure out how to tell her her daddy isn't coming home from the hospital."

"I'll call Greg."

"He already knows."

"He's doing the funeral?"

"No, but he'll be there." After a pause, she says, "They say they come in threes."

"What do?" But I know what she is going to say.

"Deaths."

Cleo plus Jakes. "But there's only been two."

"I know; that's what worries me."

Perhaps the best newborn photo we have of Cleo is one I have not looked at since she was alive. Pasted in the book that tells of the day she was born, the picture on page three is of Jakes. With huge tattooed biceps, rounded shoulders, and resembling a wildebeest, Jakes is cradling a bean-sized Cleo. The caption beneath says, *On the day you were born, gi-*

ants bent down to smile at you. He is not facing the camera but lost in the moment of swaddling new life.

You could say Jakes knew all about new life because he was in the midst of having one. Released from federal prison years before he had served his full sentence for grand theft auto, a newly converted Jakes threw himself headlong into acts of deep penance. "I am a different kind of prisoner now," he was fond of saying, "a prisoner of the Lord," confirming for me that Jesus always had time for people who didn't feel like they had paid enough. Every Sunday morning before the first worship service, Jakes made breakfast for the hobos from the park across the street. Every Sunday afternoon, he went back to the prison to a motley assembly of no-gooders and held a Bible study. When his students got out, they looked him up, limped to the church like mange-riddled hyenas, and lined up patiently for pancakes and bacon, and salvation sunny-side up.

One morning a middle-aged man roasted by the sun hobbled to the front of the fellowship hall and leaned heavily on his cane as he bent down into the mike Greg had just set up for the service. "I murdered a man," he confessed. Someone in the breakfast line cleared his throat, the rest of them turned to listen. "I murdered him because I never did like the look of him. Didn't like what he said to me one day, and I did it lickety-split, without thinking. But here's the thing: You take away someone's life, whether you're thinking about it or not, and your own life goes with it too. I'm a shadow here today, my brothers, but I'm here because Jakes told me about the Man who puts flesh on your bones again, breathes into you again. I ain't saying I got life yet, but I'm saying I got hope, and if it's good enough for me, it can be good enough for you."

"Amen!" one ex-con applauded. And then another. I think that must be the closest I have ever come to being saved, listening to that pock-faced, yellow-toothed Hawaiian with a cane and flip-flops giving up the glory.

And that's how I want to remember Jakes, sweeping up the human leftovers along with their scraps of hope, serving them cheapo breakfasts as though a feast for kings. Giving a kidney to his brother couldn't have been more typical of him. In exchange, God dished out death—which was typical too, if you ask me.

"I don't think I can go," I tell Jenny.

"No one's asking you to."

❧

VENGEANCE IS MINE, says the Lord. You get the regret, he might have added instead of the bit about feeding the hungry, even if they happen to be your enemies. Beauty must have got tired waiting for the Lord's hand to smite her enemies, must have just had it up to here with feeding her enemies. No one knew that Beauty even had enemies, let alone what they had done to become them. Come to think of it, none of us knew much of anything concerning Beauty: not how old she was, nor how it was that she had arrived at my grandmother's farm the year the Great Drought ended. She never spoke of children or a husband and no one, to my knowledge, asked. That she had a private life was only alluded to once or twice a year when she would walk down my grandmother's gravel driveway with a small bundle of belongings on her head and not return till a week later smelling of *shakeys*, the fermented beer sold for less than a bottle of milk. That she had any clothes other than the crisply ironed gingham dress with a starched white apron over it and her neat *doek* tied over her hair was debatable. If you never looked down past her modest hemline that would make any Methodist proud, you might mistake Beauty Masinama for a woman of standing. But it was her lace-up shoes, scuffed and worn, that spoke of muddy lean-tos and buckets for toilets, of people who didn't live on the farm, some of whom should never have dared put a foot on it.

The knitting had been my grandmother's idea when Beauty, after having a weeklong vacation, returned to the farm with paraffin breath and trembling hands. At first my grandmother warned Beauty about her drinking: "I don't want this to become a problem," she said. "Madam doesn't know anything about my problems," was Beauty's retort, and you could have knocked old Edith over with a feather when she heard it. But my grandmother was not about to give in that easily. Her second suggestion was a trip to the OK Bazaars, a local market, which was to have just the right solution, both to Beauty's bad habit and my bad attitude.

My problem, as my grandmother put it, was a matter of "cutting my nose off to spite my face." I could not separate the guilt I felt for how I had treated my mother from the anger I felt toward her, so I was going to knit them tightly together into whatever sweater pattern my grandmother had her heart set on. Who knows what complexities Beauty was going to knit together? Two pairs of aluminum knitting needles and a bucketful of yarn later, Beauty and I cast on identical rows of stitches in the hopes that with steady effort we might produce something akin to the picture on the pattern cover, to say nothing of finding solutions.

Not much more than a dozen rows later, a man who identified himself as "Stompie" came to the back door asking for Beauty. It seemed, then, that one-plain-one-purl was not going to do the job for Beauty. I watched from the kitchen window as she opened the front door of her *kaia* for the man with the yellow eyes and sloping shoulders, and then followed him inside. When they had not emerged half an hour later, I returned to my knitting alone, to replay the conversation my mother and I had on the phone the night before. If I had learned anything from my father, it was how to avoid saying sorry. Even when I had willed myself to call, to say the words I had rehearsed for days, I still could not get past the accusatory tone to anything resembling an apology. I did not want to hear how sick my father was when I asked her when she was going to come fetch me. "Take him to the doctor if he's that sick; you're not a nurse!" I had said, even though we both knew he would rather rot than be "some goddamn quack's pincushion." Besides, he could not have afforded the medical services, refusing any deductions from his paycheck to profit the insurance business. If there was anyone my father mistrusted more than a doctor, it was an insurance man.

Just then I heard the crunching of gravel and looked up in time to see my mother's car pull into the driveway. She got out, waved at me with a grin (yes, that was my mother smiling), and went around to the side of the car. Only then did I notice the passenger. Without his beer belly, my father looked almost healthy as he got out of the car and shaded his eyes against the glare of the tin roof and my wrath. But as he stood stooped in front of me, I could see the sickness strung from his mouth to the gorges where his cheeks once were.

"Been behaving yourself?" my father asked, his breath corpsey. Lovely to see you too, Dad.

If I thought his ailment might do anything to soften his temper, I was wrong. While we all sat stiffly on the *stoep*, it seemed that there wasn't one thing to talk about that did not involve my father's bodily functions. "Can't even have a decent crap anymore," he announced. "I keep telling her to quit feeding me that goddamn mush!"

By way of explanation, my mother said, "His teeth are getting loose."

"Because they aren't put to work anymore! Keep telling her a goddamn steak would sort them out!" It might have been all poop-and-porridge talk had Beauty not walked out with a tray of tea, set it down, taken her usual seat at the crook of the veranda, and picked up her knitting from the basket. That did it.

"You pay your *kaffirs* to sit around all day now, Edith?" he asked my grandmother, staring at Beauty's unwavering profile.

"Harry, please—" my mother began, but he interrupted her with his raised hand.

"Hey, for all I know my daughter does all the work around here." When had my father ever considered what I was doing?

"What goes on in this house, Harold, is none of your business," my grandmother retorted, "and if you cannot choose language suitable for civilized conversations, I must ask you to leave."

"You have your monkey sitting out here and *I'm* the one not being civilized?" He snorted, then coughed till there was no mistaking the acrid smell of urine.

Beauty stood up to leave. *"Tchini!"* she hissed as she passed my father, who was hobbling to his feet, and for one minute I thought she was going to spit at him, but she walked back into the cool of the house. It was apparent, then, that the farm was overrun with men—the one in the front with his putrid temper and soiled diaper, and the other still sleeping in Beauty's *kaia*. The only escape for Beauty was the kitchen, where she paced as though she had one foot in a trapper's snare.

"I'm sorry, Beauty. She shouldn't have brought him; I don't know why she did," I apologized awkwardly. Beauty muttered a reply in Xhosa, and I caught only one word, *hamba*—"go." Instead of packing away the dishes on the draining board, she reached for her medicine bag and headed out the back door to the beckoning hill.

∿

TODAY IS SATURDAY and my head is as clear as a scrubbed-up pancake griddle. I call Jenny and tell her I have changed my mind, that I want to go to the funeral.

"I was just headed there; you want me to pick you up on my way?" she volunteers. I can tell she is pleased.

Jenny does not have to ring the doorbell; I am waiting outside, watching Ronnie cut his mother's lawn with hand shears just slightly bigger than tweezers. Jenny is wearing a black dress and I am glad because I have on black too. "Don't wear bright colors to my funeral," I once told her and Theresa when we were sewing purple paraments for Ash Wednesday. "I can't stand it when people wear flowery prints and bold colors as if we should skip the grieving and move straight on to the rejoicing. I don't want you rejoicing at my funeral. I want you crying and wailing, and depressed for an unbearably long time."

"You'd make a good Samoan," Theresa told me.

But Jenny argued. "We rejoice because we are resurrection people." Jenny's favorite event on the Christian calendar is Easter, which accounts much of the time for her disposition as well as her faith. But to me Easter always elbows its way in on Lent, coming before there is time to shake off the weight of guilt, to strip away our regrets until good intentions finally become good deeds.

Now Jenny is quiet and pale, without a soupçon of rejoicing, and we do not talk till we get to the church. "I'm sitting with her," she announces, and I nod. Tapa cloths drape the altar rail and are affixed to the pulpit and lectern, and the same gaudy bouquets are back again. Jakes is lying in a black coffin four feet from the front pew where his widow is steadied between her two sons, their heads hung low. Jenny walks to the front, sits next to Theresa, and pulls Tess onto her lap. I take a bulletin and find a pew near the back where a few ex-cons prop each other up. Greg, who does not see me, is seated across the aisle next to Petal. The service begins and we stand for the opening hymn, but the verse is interrupted by a shriek and then angry wailing. Petal's baby, tipped over on the pew no doubt from trying to reach for a toy, has bumped her head. It is Greg who picks her up, hurrying to the foyer to minimize the disturbance. She will not be pacified, and all four verses and a prayer later, she still wails. Finally, Petal makes her way to the cries.

❧

LATE THAT NIGHT, when we were all asleep—my mother in the bed next to mine, my father on a cot in Oupa's old study—the wailing began. I thought it was a wounded animal, or a baby, until the cussing started. Looking out the window that faced the *kopje* from which Beauty late in the day had returned, I saw her in front of the chicken run, *sjambok* in hand, wild as a warthog. Before her, on his knees, was Stompie, bloodied and pleading for mercy. We ran out to the yard and watched in incomprehension as Beauty tore open Stompie's flesh with each crack of that deadly whip. Her unrelenting screams terrified me, and as I clung to my mother's arm I wondered how it was that Beauty, naked except for a tatty slip, hair all sprung out of its clips like Medusa's snakes, could be this thrashing monster.

She seemed not to hear my grandmother's reprimand or notice her audience, whose numbers had swelled with the neighboring farmhands. It was my father who sprang into action, dragging the garden hose from my grandmother's hydrangea bush to the side of the house and spraying the writhing couple like a pair of dogs. Drenched, Beauty turned her mad gaze on my father, and the murderous gleam was still there.

"*Ndiya kubetha*," she foamed.

"What'd you say, *kaffir* girl?" he demanded, throwing down the hose and pushing up his sleeves. I might have translated for him, might have said, "She says she'll beat you—kill you," if not for the deepest desire that she keep her word. And with one quick flick of her thick wrist, the wrist that had wrung chicken necks for Sunday dinners, Beauty's whip etched on my father's smug cheek a bright red gash.

It was a curse she pronounced then, though none of us could understand what she was saying at the time. But to see her pointing her finger in a sweeping arc across the farmland, to hear her angry chant and the gasps of the villagers, was enough. To my father she was just another bitch in a dogfight, but to Africa's people she was their *sangoma* calling on the might of the ancestors, and nothing could be more powerful. Vengeance, that one night in Africa, was not the Lord's but Beauty Masinama's.

⁓

I INTENDED to pay my respects to Jakes, to remember he had done a decent job of charity even if his roofing skills weren't worth a damn. But I am distracted by the sounds of Petal's fussy child, by the dormant urge to comfort a child, by the empty space where her need to be comforted should be. As I join the condolence line a few people from the end, I hear my mother saying very clearly, as though she were talking to my father on the *stoep*, Please. Be nice. Nice things are what I hear the people in front of me saying, the things you say at funerals: I am so sorry for your loss; he was a remarkable man; we are going to miss him so much; if there is anything we can do. Then I hear the blood drumming a beat in my ears, the war cry of fed-up-tired, and the urge to smite comes charging. Suddenly Theresa and I are face-to-face.

Her expression registers shock and then softens, as though she understands why I am here. We are even, she must think; we have both lost. Truce. But she is wrong and wrong again. Why the tracks of grief down the sides of her cheeks don't stop me, I do not know. Or the briefest of gestures: her hands lifting to embrace me. Surely I recognize that her eyes are empty rooms with burnt-out lightbulbs—God knows I stare at a couple of them every morning in the mirror. But I stand before them now and bore into that darkness, unafraid, my quick tongue a flickering *sjambok*. I remember Beauty so vividly. Not the servant, but the avenger. I envision her wet, swaying black bosom heaving from the effort of vengeance. So mighty is the urge to smite my enemy, to force vinegar to her parched lips, that I could be Beauty.

"Damn you, Theresa!" I curse. "Cleo's dead because of you!" And just like Stompie, she doubles over, winded by my words.

When her eyes find mine, they are hooded. "I, too, have been looking for someone to blame," she wheezes.

∾

"DON'T LOOK, my girl," my grandmother insisted, tugging at my elbow after the cops had broken Beauty's nose. "You have seen enough for one night." But I still had to look, to see my father hobbling up to the group of farmhands, threatening and swearing till they dispersed into the bush; to see policemen clubbing at Beauty's back, her legs kicking out behind her till she had been shoved in the back of the van; to see how frantic my mother became.

I broke free from my grandmother's grip and walked toward my mother while the policemen hoisted Stompie's bloodied body into the back. "Perhaps we should uncuff them and let them at it," the one laughed.

"Save us the effort," snorted the other, and they tipped their hats at my grandmother before getting into the front of the van, as though she had baked them scones for tea.

"Mom!" I called, but she did not pay any attention to me.

"Beauty!" my mother cried, and in reply the face we all had come to love peered out from the barred back window. Just as the van pulled away she spoke to my mother, who had commenced a little jog to keep up with her words.

"Give us this day our daily bread," Beauty called out to her. "Give us this day our daily bread."

❧

IF THERE IS A HELL, it might well be a church basement parking lot and I will be assigned to it. Abandoned cars that the finance committee will not pay to have towed away, the piss smell in the corner next to the elevator, the rotting debris in the garbage cans that the custodian has to be reminded to empty. The scene of rushed lunchtime fellatio in red pickups by women who look to be twelve; drug deals, oil spills, spiderwebs the size of afghans, and fluorescent bulbs on the blink. Jenny finds me on my haunches next to her car, having heaved my breakfast at the tires of the silver SUV blocking her in.

"I am not going for another hour or so," Jenny says tersely. I stand up. "You will have to find your own way home." Her jaw is set just so, her hands on her hips, and I know she is expecting me to say something. What do I tell her, this friend of Easter? That you nail someone to a tree because you can't admit it should be you up there?

"I'll walk," I tell her, and turn to leave, but Jenny's anger wants an audience.

"There might have been a different time, Abbe. There was no reason for you to say it now."

"I expect you are right," I reply, turning to face her.

"You should have gotten that out of your system a long time ago; Lord knows she tried to give you the opportunity. But not now. Now it's time to move on. Do you understand me? Just move on before you change completely into someone no one can put up with."

"I am someone else," I say, but Jenny will have none of it.

"You *wish* you were someone else, maybe, but you're not. You are still Abbe and you are still going to have to deal with what's happened. Blaming other people is not going to bring her back."

I want to tell her she is right, so we can get this over with, but instead, I offer her only my obstinate silence.

She sighs. "We all miss Cleo, Abbe, and we all have regrets. We all wish we could have said or done something different so it didn't happen the way it did. But all the wishing in the world is not going to change anything. See, but you're still here and that's like having a piece of her. It's all we've got left. So please, Abbe, if there's any part of you that's going to change, don't let it be that part." When I still do not answer, she sighs once more, shakes her head, and walks away.

Jenny is right, but she also could not be more wrong. Cleo, every bit pure, held back none of her brightness from the world, and when she died, whatever sparks of it were in me went with her. I have only my own light by which to make my way, a light so dim it might as well be from that sick moon the night Beauty was taken away. The light that cast only enough of a glow to show how the slain were also the slayers, how the victims were also the villains.

PILGRIM IS ON THE DOORMAT when I get home, a lazy paw on the wing of a female cardinal struggling to flop away from his grasp.

"Pilgrim!" I shout, and slap him several times before he releases his prey. The bird's beak opens and closes in silent yelps. As I cup my hand around her I can feel her rapid heartbeat. She rests her head on the top of my finger, and I head out to the garage where the cage is stored.

I asked Greg to stop bringing injured baby birds home from the church after the fifth one died in my hand. It was too much to bear. From their nests in the big royal poinciana, they fell with such regularity you would think that the parents, after all that effort, would be a little more vigilant about their offspring. But the chicks plummeted to their crippled, exposed existence on the walkway, flapping around in the hot sun till a cat's claw or Greg's hand found them. He would put the baby bird in the cage, but it was I who removed it and placed it on my chest and chanted prayers to save its life. Not once did they work. "Leave them in the cage at your office," I told him finally.

I put this female cardinal in the cage. Hearing the phone ring, I leave the bird to die in peace, and head back inside to answer it.

"Hello?" I answer.

"*Mevrou* Elizabeth Deighton?" echoes a woman with a thick South African accent.

"Yes?"

"Please hold the line for Mr. Pietrus Slabbert," she instructs. A beep-beep, and then I hear my grandmother's attorney bellow across the continents.

"Elizabeth, how are you, *my klein blommetjie?*"

"Piet, you old *doring!*"

He laughs, never tiring of being called a thorn. "Good news: we have a buyer for the farm. I have an offer of eight million rand on my table," he says.

"For cow pastures?" I ask incredulously.

"Not for long."

"They know about the orchard and the soil?"

"These guys are developers from Johannesburg, *skattie*, they couldn't care how *vrot* the soil is as long as they can pack on top of it a ton of concrete and a flashy sign that says Kabbeljou Resort and Spa. We're talking five-star luxury here."

"Oh my gosh, Piet, that's great! What do I need to do?"

"Get Rhiaan to give you power of attorney and catch the next plane out here to sign the papers. They have given us a week."

"That's crazy—everyone's on spring break. Getting a flight any-time before Easter is going to be near impossible."

"Do what you can," he says before hanging up. I look around my house. "I might get to keep you yet," I whisper.

Supper is the avocado from Mrs. Chung's tree and a cup of tea, taken during my phone call to Rhiaan.

"Can't you go back and sign the papers?" I ask, but he tells me he is already behind his editor's schedule, that he has to be in New York with his agent and publisher next week to discuss a promotional tour for his new material.

"What's wrong with you going?" he asks.

"Two things, actually. First off, I don't have the money for a ticket, and second, I'd really rather not go and face all those old ghosts."

"In matters of finance I am only too happy to assist. Consider it a return on my investment. But as to the matter of ghosts, let me remind you of Dickens."

"What does he have to do with it?"

"In Dickens's stories, old ghosts always have things their hauntees must hear." ·

Before bed, I go out to the garage to dispose of the little bird. Quite incredibly she is sitting on the cage's perch. She looks at me without blinking. I'll be darned, I think, and return to the house to fetch her a little tray of water and a tiny piece of daily bread.

EASTER

SEVENTEEN

The occupant of 43A is the Easter Bunny! Just how many Easter egg confectioneries can she tuck under her arms? After she has shoved her load into the overhead compartment, she wedges her overblown girth into the seat next to mine and turns to give me an apologetic smile for the bits that spill over.

"They are for my grandchildren. Chocoholism runs in our family!"

My face must be doing something that is an indication for her to keep talking.

"Those duty-free shops are just the best, aren't they?" A ten-hour layover in a nondescript airport in a nebulous time zone can do things to a person, I tell myself, so make allowances. But then: "I bought me one of those fancy Chanel perfumes. Smell?" She thrusts her wrist into my airspace and all I can really make out is the need for a shower. "And a carton of Peter Stuyvesant only cost forty-nine dollars. Who can quit at those prices is what I'd like to know."

Seated across the aisle must be her husband, because after failing to get much more than a tepid response from me, she spans the gap with her huge arm and knocks him. "Freddie, how much you say that Bacardi cost?"

Holy Week, once again, has been a blur. Either it has raced by or else it has taken as long as a small-town parade, I can't decide which. Either way, time ceases to make sense. Upside-Down-and-Back-to-

Front Week, that's what they should call it. I slip the airline-issued blindfold over my eyes, an added precaution against any further conversations about chocolate-covered eggs or duty-free tobacco, and wait for Easter or touchdown, whichever comes first.

It is the captain's voice over the airplane's PA system that gets me started—the lump in my throat, then the tears. His guttural *r*'s tripping over one another in greeting: "If this is your first visit to the Cape of Good Hope, welcome; for those of you returning, welcome home, *welkom tuis*, and Happy Easter." As we make the bumpy descent through the clouds, twenty years vanish with the altitude. Table Mountain rises like the shin of the continent. Sprawled at its foot is the city of my birth, just beginning to stir.

Even before we land, the beat, the pulse, the drumming of Africa can be felt, the pennywhistle calling to join the dance. From a distance, the Cape is tidy and well behaved. There are no battle cries, no signs of spilled blood on the doorstep of Africa, no phalanx of people *toyi-toying* its way through dry riverbeds. Have the swords been beaten into plowshares? Does the lion lie now with the lamb? People say it is a different Africa, this one to which I return. Unrecognizable even. The captives have been set free, debts have been forgiven, land returned to its rightful owners. The Land of Jubilee, you might say. Or, on this early Easter morning, the Land of Resurrection. We will see, but for now, for me, it is an Africa of ghosts. I take a deep breath, pinch my nose, and blow to relieve the pressure.

∾

THE FACE of civilized suburban society opens the door. With a pair of pruning shears in one hand, a quick apology on her lips, and a trail of corgi dogs behind her, she is understated wealth. My God, I think, the Queen.

"Sorry, didn't hear the doorbell . . . I'm pruning the roses out in the back," she says, her voice surprisingly high for a woman who is at least a foot taller than me and twice as wide. And then, "Can I help you?"

"I called earlier," I say to the overweight canines that have begun their business of smelling my legs.

She shakes her head slightly, gray curls bouncing to and fro, and looks at me quizzically.

"About your ad in the Visitors' Guide," I explain. Bredenkamp B&B was featured last in the list of bed and breakfasts in the pamphlet at the concierge desk. I called it first because it was the cheapest.

"Oh yes, of course! It has been in there for months, but nobody has ever inquired. Ladies!" she snaps, and I realize she is addressing the dogs, which instantly duck and retreat behind her.

"It is still available?"

"Well, yes. As a matter of fact you will be our first guest! Let's go take a look. Hold on a mo'," she says, and she hurries into the house. She turns back to me and beckons. "Come in, come in while I get the key before you catch your death."

She leads me into her kitchen, warm and thick with the redolence of stew.

"*Molo mama,*" I greet her maid, baking at the stove.

"Good morning, missus," she replies in perfect English.

"My manners! Forgive me—that's Delia, and I'm Susannah Bredenkamp, and this is my mother, Antjie du Toit," she says of the stooped pale old lady entering the room, birdlike hands clutching a cigarette.

"How do you do. Elizabeth Spenser—Abbe for short," I say, surprised that I am using my maiden name, and shake hands with everyone. The Queen Mother takes note of me shaking Delia's hand. "Funny time to show up, isn't it, on Easter Monday?" she asks.

Before I have a chance to answer, Susannah, who has been mumbling "Spenser, Spenser," says, "You're not related to Harry and Louise Spenser, are you?"

"Yes, I'm their daughter."

"Oh my—what a small world," she replies.

"Lord Almighty! A prodigal, I should say," adds Mrs. du Toit.

"You knew my parents?"

"Not very well." She turns to the old lady. "Mother knew your grandmother quite well, didn't you, Mom?"

"A difficult man, your father," Mrs. du Toit answers with the luxury of bluntness only advanced years afford. "Don't know how Edith's girl put up with that kind of nonsense."

"Mother!" Susannah chastises.

The old woman continues, "Yes, well. Your mother was very kind. Donated a lot of books to the children's center before she died—a shame to go that early. Of course your grandmother's contribution helped fund the project from the get-go."

"Mother is one of the benefactors of the little day care center for children with learning disabilities," Susannah explains to me.

"Bloody government wasn't going to do a thing about it," she grumbles, and I see Delia nodding. "As usual. Fingers up their bums, the bloody lot of them!"

"Scoundrels, madam," adds Delia.

"You must excuse my mother," chuckles Susannah. "She has very strong opinions that she thinks are a waste if kept to herself."

"Better than having no opinions at all, like some people around here," she retorts. "Delia, when you get a minute, bring me in a cup of tea," says the old woman, retreating to the outer room.

"Nice to meet you," I say hastily, hoping to have heard her speak more of my mother and grandmother, but she is already gone.

"Doesn't hear too well anymore," says Susannah, and then changes the subject.

"Your brother, then, is Rhiaan Spenser, isn't that right?"

"Yes, he is."

"A champion of the underdog," she continues. "The voice—or the pen, rather—of people who felt the way I did back then."

She reaches for the shelf and brings down an old coffee tin and extracts from it a small key. "Just going to show Miss Spenser the *kaia*, Delia, won't be a minute."

She leads me out the back door and along the path that goes around the side of the house and down the hill to a tiny cottage. The aloes are chest-high, their blooms long since spent.

There is a padlock on the green Dutch door that takes some jiggling, but it finally unlatches and Susannah pushes it open and brushes away the cobwebs.

"It is really quite small," she begins apologizing, "and rather musty. My husband got a bee in his bonnet about having a B&B, as if the shop isn't enough of a headache." Susannah explains that her husband is the proprietor of the local grocery market, which also serves as a post office and a feedstore, and although he employs a manager to run the day-to-day operations, he spends many nights trying to make the columns of his profit-and-loss balance. "I don't know if it is suitable for your purposes," she tests.

"I'm here only for a week—to wind up my grandmother's trust," I say. "I don't need anything fancy."

I step into the dark single room and immediately feel it is the right space. There are two small windows, each no bigger than a shoe box. Beneath one window is a single bed with a faded patchwork quilt and a bedside table with a crocheted tablecloth and a small lamp. On the other side of the circular room is a Formica table with two chairs. A cupboard with two doors is mounted above the sink—a porcelain bowl set into a matching pinewood cabinet. There is a single picture in the room, a rendition of Jesus with hippie hair and blue eyes contemplating the left corner of the ceiling. I follow his gaze, but there is nothing to see except a few spiderwebs and a brown stain in the shape of a shoe. An exposed bulb hangs from the middle of the pitched ceiling. I pull on its chain and it sends its artificial yellow glow a few feet around the room.

"This used to be the maid's quarters back in the old days," says Susannah.

"Yes, there was one just like it on my grandmother's property," I say, recalling the paraffin lamp in Beauty's window.

"Is it her farm that is going to be sold? I heard there are plans for a luxury resort near here—I hope it isn't hers."

"Actually, it is."

"Put my foot in it, didn't I? You might not mention it to my mother. She's bound to persuade you otherwise."

"Oh?"

"I don't go to the council meetings, but from what my husband says, most of the folk want the Paarl area to stay the way it is. They don't want it to be turned into one of those glitzy atrocities plaguing the rest of the Cape, and they are all a bit put out that the developers prevailed—or rather, money prevailed."

"Well, things do not stay the same, do they?"

"So they tell me. I'll give you a few minutes to look around. Take your time and come up to the house for a cup of tea when you're done." And suddenly I am alone in this small space with its smell of a thousand wood fires, an incense luring memories of another *kaia* from another time.

∾

IT WAS NOT for something particular I was looking, the morning after Beauty's arrest, when dawn first poked its head over my windowsill and I could keep from fidgeting no longer. I can't even be sure if I was looking for anything at all. Anything concrete. Perhaps I was just hoping to find something that could explain why the man with yellow eyes had come to the farm in the first place, something that could explain why the tight space of Beauty's *kaia* could not contain their fight, what it was that had sent her into the puddles of light with a *sjambok* in her hand and murder in her voice.

Instead of shrunken heads on spikes or a shrine of witch magic, Beauty's was a room as conventional as any bedroom in my grandmother's farmhouse. There were no clues, no signs, no big black book of curses and spells. And I might have been convinced that it was just a room with a bed on bricks next to a washstand and a table if it weren't for the unmistakable odor of mystery among the scent of clothes laundered with Lifebuoy soap. The odor of something unknown, something that had reeled in the little man, that had turned Beauty upside down and shook her until, dislodged, all the anger spilled out. It was the smell of *knobkieries* and long knives, of secrets and chants, of *toi-toi*, of anarchy. A smell that made me linger and want to run at the same time.

It was a punishable offense to go snooping about in other people's business, corporal if the snooping took you to the off-limits quarters of black people. There were laws governing the freedom of movement of people between white and black neighborhoods, and I felt I was breaking every one of them when I walked around Beauty's room lightly touching each object: lamp, tin cup, television. Her kitchen was a table with a basin, a jug, four stacked cans of beans, and a bread box. I opened the lid and in it, upended, was half a loaf of stale brown bread.

Give us this day our daily bread. Isn't that what Beauty had recited as she was driven off in the police van? Had she meant *this* bread? Flipped like a shiny coin, the thought spiraled wildly. Heads or tails? I held my breath and picked up the loaf. Immediately I saw the thing that convinced me that Beauty's last sentence had not been a prayer but an instruction, for hidden in the gouged-out center of the loaf was a small glass vial.

A rose wants picking, as does a scab or a secret—you cannot help it—which is why, when my mother surged into the tiny room, I was prying from its yeasty bed the little bottle.

"Put that down! PUT THAT DOWN!"

I looked at her, bewildered.

"What in God's name do you think you are doing, Elizabeth!" she demanded, snatching from me the bottle and then the loaf. "Did you open it?" she yelled, but I was too busy staring at the spectacle of madness before me. "DID YOU OPEN IT?"

"No," I bleated, but she asked again and a hundred times more. "I didn't, Ma, I swear."

After replacing the bottle and the bread in the bread box, she yanked me by the wrist outside and around to the back of the *kaia* where the faucet was. Turning it on full blast, she held my hands beneath the torrent, and rubbed and rubbed with her nightgown till we were both soaked.

So aghast was I by my mother's uncharacteristic show of emotion and so embarrassed that I had been caught in the unpardonable act of riffling through someone else's private belongings that I began to cry. Not to mention the matter of a secret I had discovered, a secret I had been inches away from tasting.

"Don't you ever, ever, take things that don't belong to you," she scolded.

"But I wasn't—"

"Or touch anything that doesn't belong to you. And don't you ever, ever go back in there again! Do you hear me?" I nodded. "I said, do you hear me?"

"Yes."

She shooed me back into my bedroom and then, trembly and psychotic, went to the bathroom to throw up.

◆

AND HERE I AM AGAIN, touching things that don't belong to me. I walk back out of Susannah's *kaia* into the pea soup of the Cape autumn. Around the back of the hut is a double sink with a cold-water tap. A few paces away is the outhouse. I open the door and see the toilet on a wooden box and the doll doily covering the spare roll. The peacocks flutter out of my way when I step back outside. Parading royally down the driveway, they make a sharp right and head for the gap in the fence that divides this property from the neighbor's.

The bush covering the hillside of the Bredenkamps' property is singing with insects, a kettle boiling. The hoopoe birds call to one another from telephone poles, and the aroma of my youth, the smell of *renosterveldt* and dung, rises up from the soil. The memories rise up too—my grandmother's front porch, knitting needles, and the sharp smell of rooibos tea. Only the ghosts slumber.

After heading up the hill to the main house, I go toward the back door like one who has been coming here for years. Susannah looks up from her rosebush and I say, "I'll take it," before she asks.

"A hundred rand a night sound fair to you? That includes breakfast," she asks. "Right, then," she says, seeing my nod, "Delia will give it a dust and put new sheets on the bed. She will also stock the shelves with a few dishes and pots and cutlery, and we'll move in the coffee machine and the electric heater so you won't freeze to death in the evenings. And don't worry about the outhouse—Etienne treated it the other day. The only thing is, you will have to take showers in the main house. And you can do that whenever it suits you, except on Sunday mornings, which is when Mother and I go to church and Etienne goes off to the bowling green."

We drink tea in her kitchen and Susannah asks about living in Hawaii, tells how most of her friends have moved to Canada and Australia. A few luckier ones have moved to Florida.

"My sons are thinking of emigrating and I won't stop them. It is harder for the younger ones who are just starting out. I keep reminding Etienne that we left when we were their age; we moved to Singapore during the construction boom and Etienne made an indecent sum of money. But we were desperately unhappy and homesick and moved back here after four years. You never know, it might be the same for the boys. Bloom where you are planted, that's the most important thing, don't you think?"

"It certainly looks as if that is what you and your family are doing here," I muse.

"I don't know if one could call it blooming, but we are certainly planted," Susannah says. "You are planted in Hawaii, then, or are your roots still here?" It is an unfair question, and instead of answering I look at my watch. If I am to make it to the Perlemoen Hotel, where I checked in for just one night, get my luggage, and make it back here before being charged for another night, I must hurry.

"Where's your car?" she asks when she escorts me out the front door.

Rental cars are for people with budgets; budgets are for people with money. I don't say this but rather, "I took the bus most of the way and walked the rest."

"Well, it's better than those wretched taxis. Etienne calls them kamikaze taxis. But you shouldn't walk these parts alone, you know. There have been several incidents recently." I thank my new landlady, encircled by her panting, chubby dogs, and head down her driveway. I turn back before the tall pine trees obstruct the view of her house, and she waves imperially once again. I step into the shade of the trees and head off to the bus stop.

HOTEL RATES ARE HIGH in Paarl's city limits, even for a crusty, outdated relic like the Perlemoen Hotel. I am eager to check out and make my way back to the Bredenkamps' home on the town's outskirts. It is not quite two miles from the bus stop to the Bredenkamps' cottage, but it is all uphill and there is no break from the biting wind once I turn onto the main road. The two-way street is wide. Sidewalks must only exist in America; here gravel flanks the road, quickly wearing holes in children's Sunday shoes. The traffic is occasional and only a few pedestrians are out this afternoon. A woman in a white robe with blue trim, the uniform of the African Zion Christians, smiles at me and I bid her *"Molo mfazi"* as we pass each other. Farther along, on the other side of the street where it crooks like a fisherman's hook, is an African boy, not more than ten. He is running, one hand on the raised-wire steering wheel of his homemade car, his breath smoky-cold. He doesn't see me stop for a rest, switching my suitcase to the other hand. My arms, once accustomed to hoisting Cleo's thirty-pound frame, have turned to glue.

I have not gone more than a mile when a pickup truck slows down next to me and what looks like the Pillsbury Doughboy with a tan and a safari suit asks, *"Skies tog, het jy help noodig?"* I tell him no, I don't need help, that I am just walking up the hill to the Bredenkamps' place. And he switches quickly to English, heavily accented, and says, "Hop in, let me give you a ride. Too bloody cold to be walking about." He leans over and pushes open the passenger door. I heave my suitcase into the flatbed and get in, only to hear my mother say, You don't get in the cars of people you don't know. Least of all men.

"Karel van der Walt," he says, rolling his r's and shaking my hand with vigor. His heavy Malmesbury *bry* gives him away as a transplant from the Swartlands. "Pleased to know you."

"Elizabeth Spenser," I say, trying not to stare at his front tooth that is no longer there.

He grinds the truck into first gear and it lurches up the hill obediently.

"So you are family of Susannah and them?"

"No, I am renting their cottage."

"You not from here?" And then he apologizes, "Sorry for my questions."

"I used to be, but now I live in Hawaii."

He whistles, "*Jislike! Hawaii Five-O!* You hula-dance?"

"No." I smile.

"*Ja.* I suppose so. Just like all the foreigners think we have lions and elephants in a *kraal* in our backyards."

He slows, rolls down his window, and thrusts his hand out to indicate his intention to turn. "You can just drop me off here," I say. "I can walk up the driveway."

"No, I take you all the way," he insists, and we bounce up Susannah's potholed driveway till we are greeted by the yapping sausages.

Karel jumps out and retrieves my suitcase before I can get to it, and I hear him belt out, "Stupid bloody animals of yours, Etienne; when you going to make *lekker* kebobs out of them?"

Etienne Bredenkamp, a baobab of a man, lumbers toward the car. His immense torso is carried by trunklike legs and his arms are up shading his eyes from the sun.

"Quiet, hounds," he admonishes, and the yapping miraculously stops. To the kind knight of the rusty pickup he says, "Not until your wife makes mincemeat out of you, van der Walt, which I hear from the villagers will be pretty soon!"

"*Ag,* no need to get personal!" Karel chortles, and they shake hands. Etienne Bredenkamp bends down and says in his perfectly clipped upper-class accent, "And who, may I be so bold as to inquire, are you?"

Before I can answer, Karel says, "*Jislike,* man, she's your new tenant, all the way from Hawaii Five-O—"

"Abbe Spenser," I interrupt. "Your wife is expecting me, I believe."

"Yes, of course," he says, and extends his hand, which smothers mine. "Etienne Bredenkamp at your service. Please come in. You too, Karel, only if you promise not to eat my dogs."

"No, I'm on my way to the shop to pick up a lemon tart for Lavinia—she's having the preacher over for tea."

"I am glad to see you have reformed," says Etienne.

"She says if I am not going to church, she is bringing the church to me."

"Heard you scared off a couple of burglars from the Venters' place last week? Well done, lad." Aside, Etienne explains to me that Karel heads the neighborhood watch association.

"Those two scallywags didn't scare easily, man! Tell the truth, I don't think we've seen the last of them." He gets in his pickup, leans out the window, and says, "Good luck, Miss Hula," and then, to Etienne, "Give my best to Susannah," and he is gone with a cloud of dust following him.

"Please, this way," Etienne says, and he ushers me through the front door and into the sitting room, which looks as though it has been transplanted from a castle. Filled with antique furniture and pictures hanging in gilded frames, the room is host to half a dozen cats arranged around a paraffin heater. I am afraid to sit in one of the Queen Anne armchairs, so I stand awkwardly.

"Susannah is resting at the moment. She has not been feeling up to snuff this afternoon, I am afraid." He goes off to call her and I walk to one olive-green wall hosting a series of oil paintings of First World War airplanes. They are all originals, Allied planes flying between golden clouds. One picture captures the triumphant swoop of a plane emerging from a cloud, while below, in the bottom right-hand corner, a fireball trailing a dark line of smoke hurtles downward.

"My grandfather fought in the Royal Air Force," Etienne says, returning. "He was missing in action, but, I am afraid, his love of airplanes lives on in me."

"These are quite striking," I say. "I can't make out the artist."

"Yours truly," he says. "Painted more than thirty years ago. Before I realized I had to make a living, and canvases and paintbrushes weren't the tools with which one typically accomplishes that."

"He could have made a living at it," says Susannah, sweeping into the room wearing a persimmon and black kaftan and cooling herself with a sandalwood fan even though it can't be more than sixty degrees inside. "But he thought an architect would impress my father more than a struggling artist."

"Well, now that you have had a brief lecture in the history of the Bredenkamps, my dear," Etienne says, "let me officially welcome you to this our humble abode. You are going to have to put up with our rather eccentric ways—"

"Not to mention my menopausal moods," interjects Susannah.

"—but we trust your stay will be a good one." I half expect him to give a small bow, and as I say a quiet thank-you, Mrs. du Toit hobbles into the room from the adjoining dining room and says, "Etienne, my pipes have stopped working again."

"Good Lord, Mother, no!" he says in mock horror, and he and Susannah snicker.

"Oh for heaven's sake, grow up! I'm talking about my *water* pipes," she barks, shaking her cane at him. They both crack up, Etienne with deep guffaws and Susannah snorting through her nose.

"This is the third time my sink has blocked up, and if you cannot fix it once and for all, I'll evict the bloody lot of you, so help me!" But I can see she is straining from the effort not to smile, even though she has her right hand raised as if before a judge. She looks at me and says, "Oh yes, the Spenser girl," and then does a U-turn and exits before I can say anything. Etienne follows her and Susannah bids me sit.

"Delia!" she crows, "tea please," and I hear cupboards opening and china being set down in reply.

"My mother lives in the adjoining granny flat," Susannah explains, "but this used to be her house. She conveniently forgets she sold it to us fifteen years ago, and uses it now as leverage to get Etienne to do her bidding. Not that he wouldn't anyway."

"You seem very happy," is all I can think of to say.

"Oh, we get along all right; it's when the boys come home that all hell breaks loose."

"The boys?"

"Our children. Well, they're not boys anymore. Neville is forty-one and Toby is thirty-three. The one lives in Jo'burg—Neville—he's an architect like his father. And Toby hasn't settled down anyplace particular yet, so he often ends up crashing here between adventures."

"Very English names," I comment.

"Well, we are all English, I guess, except in surname. Etienne's mother was straight off the boat from Southampton, and she married an Afrikaans farmer from Parrow, hence 'Bredenkamp.' Etienne got his father's Afrikaans name but his mother's breeding and the best private education sheep's wool could buy. And we du Toits haven't been anything other than roaring Lefties since the Boer War. Both my mother's sisters are still alive, but Mother swears my father's kin all died off because God was doing target practice on the Nats."

I smile, and when Delia walks in carrying a tray of tea and home-made meringues, I try not to dwell on how it is that a left-wing democrat can be employing an old black woman to make her a cup of tea she is perfectly capable of making herself. I forget the dichotomies of Africa, the double standards, the layers of life and politics, and how sometimes they intersect and sometimes they do not.

As if reading my mind, Susannah says, "You remember Delia. She is part of the family and practically raised our two sons single-handedly, didn't you, Delia?"

"Yes, two very naughty boys, madam." She laughs.

The air is so comfortable between them that I half expect Delia to sit down on the Queen Anne settee with us and take the cup of tea that Susannah pours and offers me. But she doesn't. Traditions bind us together long after naughty boys grow into men, after constitutions are written and enacted. Instead, she heads out to the kitchen, and Susannah picks up the milk jug and says, "White or black?"

THE DOOR TO THE COTTAGE is open, and I notice a window box mounted on a ledge beneath the front window. It is filled with brown soil, and Susannah explains how she just planted daffodil bulbs, hoping they will "cheer the place up a bit" come spring. The watering can is next to the front door, and if I want to give them a bit of water each day, that will be lovely, she explains. It seems ridiculous to be so over-whelmed by the responsibility for something growing, so I issue a hasty "Sure."

The room looks different. Although its thick walls and small win-dows reminded me earlier of a cave, it is now caked with cheer. An enamel pitcher of protea is centered on the table. The faded quilt has been replaced with one of bold fall hues. The single lightbulb now has a beige shade on it, and when Susannah turns it on, a warm glow fills the room.

"No need to hang on to Jesus," she says.

"Excuse me?"

She points to the faded picture of the carpenter's son hanging above the bed. "It's been up there forever, but take it down if you like and we will find something else to hang in its place." She shows me the bowl of chocolate Easter eggs on the bedside table. "Should you choose to indulge.

"And we changed the lock; here's your key. It is the only part of the property that doesn't have an alarm, unfortunately."

I give her five twenty-rand notes and thank her, and she turns to go, then thinks better of it.

"I hope it's comfortable enough for you." After a pause she goes on. "I sense you want your privacy. You will find us to be a rather private bunch ourselves. But I want you to know you are welcome at the main house anytime, should you need something. Even if it's just company." And then, quite unexpectedly, she puts her arms around me in a quick embrace, and before I can respond she flutters away. Her kaftan sails behind her so that she appears to be a moth.

I unwrap a chocolate and look at Jesus daydreaming. "So. How's Easter working out for you?" Which makes me wonder how Greg's Easter went. His first without a pulpit. Did he miss proclaiming the mystery this year or did he miss planning the coronation more? If Greg had been a first-century disciple, he might not have outrun Peter to the grave site after hearing Mary's incredible news, but he most surely would have arrived with his clipboard and tape measure and digital camera. Perhaps it is unkind to say the details of the Easter event capture Greg's interest more than the event itself. But Greg is not one for apparitions; an incorporeal Jesus who begs not to be held suits him less than this more sensible rendering still averting my gaze. "Think we can get along for a few days?"

I unpack my suitcase and arrange a framed photo of Cleo and the windup alarm clock on the bedside table. Cleo's blanket goes at the foot of the bed and her bunny she got for her first Easter goes at the top. And I look around, eyes finally resting on Jesus. There: home.

EIGHTEEN

I wake up, disoriented, to the crowing competition between roosters and peacocks. Turning on the small electric heater to dispel the chill of Paarl's April morning, I stumble out the front door into the tepid sunlight and mark time to keep the seeping cold of the cement floor from making too much progress up my legs. The mauve light of dawn stretches out beyond the darkened pine trees lining the Bredenkamps' driveway. The morning mist is lifting above the town, brushed in a golden glow. Somewhere to my left is the faint sound of gospel music. Walking around the side of the *kaia*, I locate the boom box perched on top of a rusty petrol can. Next to it is Delia, hanging her madam's washing on the line behind the garage and singing along in the clicks and clacks of the Xhosa language, a typewriter's hammering keys. Between hanging up her boss's pants and reaching into the basket for the next item, she lifts her hands and bounces them heavenward as though she were propping up the sagging contents of a top shelf.

When I return from the outhouse, I sit down on the red vinyl backseat from some long-gone car and watch the century-old tradition of a black woman hanging white people's laundry. When the line between the tree and the end of the garage roof is full, Delia lifts her basket to the top of her head and reaches for her boom box. She sees me and shouts, *"Molo, m'faan, kunjani?"*

"*Molo*, Delia; I am fine, thank you," I reply.

She walks toward me, her free hand steadying her basket on her head. "*Ow*," she exclaims, "madam not feeling all right?"

"Just the outhouse, probably, and I ought to eat breakfast," I say.

"I'll bring you some," she offers, and then turns to walk up the path with her renewed purpose.

"Delia," I call, "please don't go to any trouble. I can go to the shop and pick up something there." The local grocery shop that Etienne owns is only half a mile down the main road and is flanked on one side by a petrol station, and on the other by a pub named Ye Olde Aardvark. Painted on the store windows in white shoe polish are advertisements for such local delicacies as ostrich *biltong*, sausage rolls, and *samoosas*, all of which sound strangely tempting for seven o'clock in the morning.

"*Aikona*, madam. No trouble. I'll be back *chop-chop*." She grins, and I notice she is missing all her front teeth. Delia is not a beautiful woman, nor is she young. Her fierce face has sunken cheeks and her small black button eyes are set too close to her wide, flat nose. She wears a *doek*, which covers her hair, and I can't decide if she looks more like a pirate or a warrior. Her skinny frame recedes from me, seesawing with a limp. Looking down past the hem of her dress, I notice how her right foot drags a black boot with a two-inch platformed sole.

The back of the Bredenkamps' property is interspersed with aloes, pelargonium, and vygies. Africa is aromatic this morning—a cross between bush tea, thyme, and cat pee. The Cape canaries call to one another from their lofty perches in the Port Jackson trees, the *piet-my-vrous* joining in the chorus. It is good to be back; fancy that.

I fetch a glass from the cupboard, fill it up with water from the tap at the sink, and return to my backyard throne just in time to hear Delia's "Helloo, madam!" Setting down the laden tray on the seat, she tch-tches, "Madam must eat. Madam is too skinny. Not good for a woman in Africa to be so skinny." There is a bowl of granola, a banana, a soft-boiled egg in an egg cup, triangles of toast, and a mug of tea with a picture of Charles and Diana on it. Don't these people throw anything away? From the pocket of her apron, she extracts two apricots, "from Ou Miss Antjie's tree," she tells me, referring to Susannah's mother. "She says the apricots are not for the family, but I pick them anyway when she's not looking!"

"What does she do with them if you aren't allowed to eat them?" I ask.

"The Ou Miss gives them to the *kleintjies* at the children center. She only goes every other Tuesday, and then she has me or the boy pick them."

"The boy?"

"Pepsi. He's a *skelm*, that one." By way of an explanation for calling him a scoundrel, she says, "Too many girlfriends, too much gambling. Too much fighting. I keep telling madam that the Boss should send him away," she says, clicking her disapproval once more.

"The gardener?" I ask.

"*Ewe.*" She nods. "He works here Tuesdays, Thursdays, and Saturdays, but he is very lazy. *Ow.*"

Sometimes it seems that nothing changes in Africa. Delia has been a voting member of society since 1994, her political party goes on unchallenged more than a dozen years later, yet she serves me toast with the crusts cut off and uses the vernacular of the apartheid era with her talk of "the boy" and "the Boss."

"Thank you for the apricots," I say, and eat a perfect triangle. "Do you think it would be all right to use the phone?" I have forgotten the place where I am to meet Piet Slabbert.

She squints at me, mops her perspiring face with the dish towel she has draped over her shoulder. "Yes, madam."

"Please do not call me 'madam,' Delia. It makes me feel old," I lie. It makes me feel white, is what it really is. "Everyone calls me Abbe."

She shakes her head and mutters something in Xhosa.

"Excuse me, I think I will eat inside," I say, and pick up my tray and make my retreat from her disapproving frown.

KONSTANTIA KOMBUIS, the restaurant where Piet and I have arranged to meet for lunch, is set off the beaten cuisine path of downtown Paarl with its jazzy eateries, art stores, and gift shops. Rather, Drosty Street has a row of Cape Dutch homes, most of them converted to small businesses. One of them is this slightly decrepit café—its thatched roof worn, the shutters shedding their bottle-green paint, and its austere dining room empty. Instead of boasting the region's finest KWV wines like its more frequented counterparts on Main Street, it offers a special on Windhoek lager. I order a shandy and take in the decor, which is a mishmash of French colonial and tribal hut. Before long Piet breezes in wearing coveralls, a backpack slung over his shoulder, and a lit cigarette perched on his lower lip in defiance of the anti-smoking ban. The restaurant manager claps his back and says, "Piet! *Jou blerrie skilpad!* At your age you can't afford to keep such a beautiful woman waiting!"

"*Luister, ou pal*, instead of reminding me of my age, why don't you make yourself useful and pour me a cup of coffee—or has it been so long since you've had a customer that you've forgotten how to serve one?" he volleys back, winking at me.

When he approaches our table he is scowling as the smoke hits his eyes. "Abbe! What a pleasure to see you," he says, removing the cigarette from his mouth so he can kiss the back of my hand. "So long; too long."

"You still look exactly the same," I say, and he does, apart from the liver spots dotting his bald head and the mustache that is now white and thinning at the corners.

"And look at you, all grown up; *pragtig nes soos jou ma*," he says. People who knew my parents always thought my features favored my father's, but I take his compliment that I am pretty like my mother without argument.

We order the specialty of the day—kudu kebobs—and he pulls from his backpack a folder with the offer from the firm, five percent more than asking price, which Piet says he set deliberately high. They hope to finish construction of the resort before the winter rains next year, he tells me. A win-win, Piet concludes his report.

"I heard the local council members aren't too happy about the idea of another big resort," I say.

"*Ja nee,*" he confirms. "It's going to be competition for all the local establishments, but progress is progress. And none of those people who are so unhappy about this deal are offering to buy the place, so there you are." He drains his second cup of coffee. "Rhiaan still on board?"

I nod. "He has wanted to sell the farm for years. I was the one who wanted to hang on to it—you know, in case . . ." In case what? In case I ever stopped running away and returned? In case my mother was right—that it would all still be here waiting for me when I came back?

Piet leans over and holds my hand. "It was your home, I understand." After the waiter has set down our entrées, he says, "Perhaps we should take a drive out to the farm first, before you sign the papers, and clear the air, so to speak. After all, we're talking about your home."

"It was never my home," I protest.

"*Ag, skat,* but it is where you left your heart, *nê?*"

Whether or not this is true, it is still not a good idea to visit the farm. There is a deal to make, papers to sign. Maybe afterward, when the land with its withered fruit trees is the site of the Kabbeljou Resort, I can visit. When all the ghosts have been evicted. "I need the money, Piet, and I mean in the food-on-the-table sense. I don't want any nostalgia trips cluttering this decision. Let's just do it; the sooner the better."

"Yes, of course." Piet goes over the contract, the estimated settlement statement, the government transfer charges and the tax implications. The final number, after all the required adjustments, is staggering even when you divide by two.

He finishes his food in a dozen mouthfuls and lights a cigarette. "There is just one small matter to clear up, which, hopefully, can be accomplished by the buyer's deadline."

"What's that?"

"The school." Although initially supposed to educate twenty elementary-aged black children, the farm is now schooling forty, half of whom are staying on the property. Nobody quite has the answer for the number of children orphaned from AIDS, or the matter that nobody wants to go to school with kids who are infected. These little start-up schools pop up on farms and church properties everywhere, modest projects of the well-intentioned. But before you know it, there is twice, thrice the number of kids expected. "Quite frankly," Piet continues, "I am pleased we are going to be out from under the burden of liability." Piet goes on to explain that there is a state-sponsored orphanage closer to Cape Town that can take a few of the children, and he is hoping the Catholics might be able to do something about the rest. Suddenly the euphoria of inheriting a small fortune is sanded down by the realization that for some, for many, there is no relief, neither from poverty nor an early grave. What is to become of children without mothers, without teachers?

"What if I talk to Rhiaan and see about taking some of the money from the sale and establishing a trust? Something that can provide scholarships for a few of these children."

"That would be very generous indeed, Abbe. But you are not responsible for these kids, you know. You and your brother have already been more than generous, letting them use the farm."

"I wouldn't call it generous—we both know that no one else wanted anything to do with the place. But a scholarship fund—that's something my grandmother would have approved of."

"Indeed," he agrees.

"So when do I sign the papers?"

"Nine o'clock on Thursday morning we will meet with the developer and his attorneys at my office. After that we can go see Mr. Lam at the bank and get him to do the international transfer of funds and talk to him about establishing a trust fund, if that's what you and your *boet* want to do."

"I don't know how to thank you, Piet."

"*Ag, my blommetjie*, this is the least I can do. You have been through so much; if this relieves a bit of the suffering, I am honored to have had a part in it."

By the time we walk outside, the morning mist has dispersed, leaving the sun quite chipper. Holding open the door of his old Mercedes for me to get in, he says, "What say you we take a drive past your old house before I take you back to the Bredenkamps'?"

THERE IS NOT MUCH ACTIVITY on Vitry Lane this afternoon except for the African monarchs darting along carefully groomed flower hedges, playing leapfrog with one another. Lining the newly paved street with its blinding pedestrian crossings are postcard-perfect houses. Some are new constructions made to look a hundred years old, and some of the grand old ladies have been dolled up with modern amenities. The Mercedes comes to a stop in front of one of the few plain-Jane houses that couldn't care less about curb appeal. It takes a moment to realize that this is the house, our house. The yard has shrunk to the size of a postage stamp, and is dominated by the azalea bushes. The tree from which my father once hung one of his old truck tires in a zesty moment of paternal goodwill is gone. And instead of my mother's familiar silhoutte, there is an old lady watering her flower beds with a hose. Is it too late to say goodbye?

∾

IT WAS NOT a teary farewell, at least not for me. Or for Cindy Meyers, who insisted on carrying my suitcase and blowing huge gum bubbles till my grandmother requested she kindly stop. "You are oh-so-lucky," Cindy said. "American guys are so cute." My grandmother, who had driven us to the airport, said to keep my head on the books, not the boys. "Do us proud, my girl," she insisted, and seemed somewhat confident I would.

Only my mother cried a little, but I did not think she had the right. She had given up the right to cry over me the way she had given up the need for depending on me. After I discovered the bread and its secret bottle, I realized it was its contents that my mother needed. I wasn't a fool. I knew it was on Beauty's witch-doctor remedies—her drugs— my mother now depended, just as she had once done on Gordon's dry gin. It helped explain why when each time I saw my mother it was as though she thought her edges were more clearly defined. As though she were emerging from the background of a diluted watercolor and taking the position an artist will reserve for the subject.

Nevertheless, things dead center often cannot perceive what is going on around them. My mother, for instance, seemed not to know that just one word from her would keep me from venturing any closer to the departure gate of DF Malan Airport. She seemed not to know that my application to the student foreign exchange program had been a bluff, that what I wanted her to know (I could find my own way in the world even if it led me thousands of miles from her doorstep) was really about what I wanted her to *feel*, that is to say: bad. Bad enough to beg me to stay, to cough up all her secrets and to keep her promises. All she did, however, was hug me the way she used to when I was a gangly kid who had grazed her knee. She lingered so long in that embrace, sniffing through her proud tears, that I thought for sure those words, Don't go, would come. Instead, she called my bluff, dusted my jacket, and waved me off with one clearly drawn hand.

"I love you, Abbe-girl," she yelled. "I love you." I did not turn back, a decision I regretted before the airplane's wheels had left the tarmac.

By the time the airplane had made its ascent above the mountains of Devil's Peak and Lion's Head, I couldn't quite recall my mother's features. I snapped open my diary to the picture lodged among its pages: my brother and my father behind us, my mother and me seated in the front. Instead of her face, I looked at my foot hooked around her leg to keep me from falling off her lap and beyond her grasp. How had it become unhooked?

MY MOTHER FOUND my father dead on the kitchen floor when she got home from the airport, but it took almost two days of flying before I landed in California and heard the news from my new "host parents." I called her as soon as we reached the house, expecting to hear a frayed-nerves-mother talk of coming home.

"His liver shut down," she explained, dry as a bone. "The doctor said it is common for people who drink as much as your father did."

Even in the absence of any bereavement, hers or mine, what plagued me was a question for which there was no answer: Why now?

"He didn't look like he suffered much," she said, mistaking my silence for grief. "He was curled up on the floor as though he needed to take a nap." So my father's last gasp, then, was in the gleaming kitchen where a fire once burned and a table once splintered. "Sweetheart, are you okay?"

"What about the funeral?" I replied.

"Oh, there isn't going to be a funeral—your father didn't want one. We are just going to bury him on Saturday and go over to Muriel's for a small reception." As though she were reading my mind, she continued, "Listen to me now: you didn't go all the way to America just to turn around and come back. Not for something like this. No, we all think it best that you do your thing."

I would have argued, especially when she said Rhiaan was already on his way home, if she had not started coughing. "Asthma acting up again." She wheezed. "Every time the apricot tree starts budding." Except it was not her usual dry hack that heralded spring but something more resinous. "It's no way to start off your adventure, sweetheart, but you make the best of it," she spluttered. "I know you are going to do us all proud. We are all going to be all right now. And everything will all still be here when you get back."

And that was that. My father was dead and my mother was having high hopes.

∾

"WANT TO GET OUT?" Piet asks, but I shake my head. Instead, I roll down the window and wave shyly to the lady, who looks at us inquisitively. It is only then that I notice what she is watering: my mother's old rosebushes, back from the dead, blooming prolifically in the afternoon sun.

"I remember the last time I saw your mother," Piet says, driving on to the B&B. "She was always a beautiful woman, but the day she came to my office she was a vision. Hell's bells, she looked like an angel! I couldn't believe it when Edith called a few weeks later to tell me she had passed away. There was just no telling she was sick to look at her."

"But she was there about her will; didn't that strike you as odd?"

He shakes his head. "She didn't come to see me about her will."

"What then?"

His eyebrows are raised in surprise, as though I should know. "She came to see me about changing back to her maiden name."

Piet drops me off at the entrance to the Bredenkamps' property and I walk up the driveway. Delia is hobbling ahead of me with a bag of groceries on top of her head.

"Hello, Delia," I call.

"Hello, madam," she replies, pausing long enough for me to catch up. "Madam Susannah sent me to the shop to get some things for your kitchen."

"Oh, you shouldn't have gone to any trouble, but thank you— that's very kind." I unlock the padlock and let Delia enter the *kaia* first so she can relieve herself of her bundle. As she unpacks the groceries, I chat away as though she might be Jenny. What I want to talk about is why my mother would revert to her maiden name only a month before she died. Was she somehow divorcing my decomposing father in his bed of soil still freshly turned? Was she reclaiming her lost independence and trying to find her way back to someone she used to be? Instead, I talk about being back. "Paarl has changed a lot since I last lived here," I tell her.

She hums in agreement. "*Ewe*, but too much is still the same."

"What do you mean?"

"Many of our young ones are *skelms*, and the old people in the townships are scared of them. They steal from you, and if you try to stop them, *sshck!*" With her forefinger she draws an imaginary line across her neck.

"But what about the police?"

She shakes her head. "Some of them *are* the police."

And then, when I think I have heard it all, she says, "Sometimes I think it is worse than before. There are too many guns now, and too much of the AIDS. It was not like that before." It seems then that Africa will always be struggling, suffering, weighed down if no longer by imperial power, then by disease or crime or famine. "Money, money, money," she continues. "Everyone thinks money is going to make life better. Everybody wants to win the Lotto and be happy, but *ow*, money can only bring more sadness to one who is sick in the heart." By way of example, she tells me how Karel van der Walt's wife, Lavinia, won five thousand rand in last month's drawing; money quickly spent on a shiny pink couch. "Everyone knows Boss Karel cannot say boo to a goose," Delia says, "but the money made him crazy." Apparently, having discovered his battered old La-Z-Boy sent to the dump, Karel raised his hand to strike his wife of thirty-three years for spending money he had set aside for a big-screen TV. None of this would be known had it not been for the domestic, who, while ironing, witnessed her madam deliver a surprisingly hard blow to Karel's gut. All evidence, by Delia's account, that the love of money made everyone crazy—black and white.

In addition to the assortment of teas, a canister of coffee, sugar and powdered creamer, there is also a box of freshly baked hot cross buns. I lift the lid and offer Delia one just so I might have her company a few minutes longer. She grins as she takes one and positions it to the side of her mouth, where she still has teeth.

"Do you mind if I ask you why your front teeth are missing?"

"*Ow*." She chuckles, then covers her mouth with her hand. "That was for when I was young, for keeping the boys very happy."

I laugh too. "Aren't you glad we get older?"

"*Ewe!* Now I tell them all to *voetsek*; I don't want to see their snake or I will chop it off!" We laugh and it seems as though we might be able to stave off a suffering Africa yet.

Until a voice says, "Nobody wants to show an old lady his snake."

In the doorway stands an African warrior. Naked above the waist, he might as well have an *assegai* in his hand and not a rake. His broad, gleaming smile and the cocky tilt of his head does nothing to soften Delia's temper. "Pepsi! *Ndiya kubetha!*"

Undeterred by the old woman's hostility, he locks his eyes on me and raises his chin. "Howzit."

"You must be Pepsi," I say, extending my hand, which he shakes as though he were tugging a weed. "I am Abbe Spenser, pleased to meet you."

"Go back to work, Pepsi!" Delia barks.

"*Haai*, the madam is looking for *you*, old lady. Teatime," he mocks, pretending to ring a dinner bell at his ear. As she hurries off, he makes no attempt to leave and the tiny hut fills with the smell of sweat. His, and now mine. He sees the buns. "Can I have one?" he says, more a demand than a question. The smile has left his face now and he patrols the room, crumbs dropping in his wake, examining my things. I want him to leave, but there is a voice telling me that this is Pepsi's country now. He eats another bun although I have not offered, and then from the nightstand, with a sticky hand, he picks up the picture of Cleo. Somewhere near my knees a panic is mounting.

"Your daughter?" he asks as though he might sniff at her.

"Yes."

"She is a beautiful girl."

"Yes, she was. She died last year." Why did I say that?

He shakes his head, and then wipes his mouth with the back of his hand. "That's good," he says, and leaves me thinking he surely meant the buns.

"sunup?" Delia asks, setting down a tray of dinner Susannah has insisted on sharing. It will be dark soon, and after Pepsi's visit I am glad to have Delia back in my quarters for a few minutes.

"Do you know it?" I have told her about selling my grandmother's farm and how I hope to help some of the orphans through a scholarship program.

She nods. "*Ewe*. I know the maid who used to work there a long, long time ago."

"Beauty?"

"Beauty Masinama, that is her," Delia replies.

Beauty, who has been haunting my thoughts for a year with her chants and spells, with her *sjambok*. Beauty, who I had imagined died in a prison like so many of the others, who stands beside my mother and grandmother in almost every memory, still cannot be this side of the Jordan, can she? "Is she still alive?"

"*Ewe.*" She nods. "She is living in Langa with her sister's daughter." Langa is the oldest township in Cape Town, saddled between Jan Smuts Drive and Settler's Way. Although it is now popular for air-conditioned coaches to transport their paying European clientele through the streets for the requisite pictures of corrugated iron lean-tos, trash-strewn dirt streets, and litters of dog-eared children, Langa still evokes for me the old fears. The sum of Africa's darkness was supposed to be fenced in in places like Langa, even as we waited for when it would spill over into an orderly suburb or a tidy farmyard. Waited for the Stompies of the world, with their bloodshot eyes and vengeful stares, to bang on the back doors of our burglarproof houses.

"Do you think Beauty would see me?"

"You can go to her, yes. But Beauty doesn't see anything anymore, only her dreams."

She moves to the door; it must surely be past the time for her to go home.

"Delia?" She looks at me as tenderly as a shepherd. "Would you sit with me a little longer? I would like to tell you about my girl."

NINETEEN

All but two of the eleven people spill out of the eight-seater taxi van after it has skidded to a stop in front of Bessie's Cash 'n' Carry Store, decorated with burglar bars and Coca-Cola signs. Next to it is the local butchery—a "smiley" stand where severed sheep heads hang upside down, grinning madly with old-people dentures. An assortment of trash and cans collects at the curb where customers with handbags and shopping bags line up to take the warmed-up seats we have just vacated.

Langa was founded at the turn of the last century, when the bubonic plague first broke out in the Cape. Tourists might find it surprising that its name means "sun," given the squalor, but so many things in this part of the world are disguised with misnomers. What I find surprising is how the sun that awakens urbane Cape Townians in their plush colonial duplexes is the same sun that shines through the boarded windows of this shantytown. The same sun, rising for us all.

And it is an obstinately shiny day, the sun high enough already that even the shadows cannot hide the corners of the view—mud shacks, unfinished brick houses with steps going nowhere, storefronts with their collapsing roofs. Along the unpaved ghost-town streets are hand-painted signs of the millenium's new plague: COMMUNITY UNDER-TAKERS: FUNERALS FOR PENSIONERS, FAMILIES, AND SINGLES. NO PROOF OF GOOD HEALTH, 4 EZ PAYMENTS.

A street sign leaning at a forty-five-degree angle confirms Delia's carefully drawn map. I am on Washington Street. My instructions are to walk a block past the Tsoga Eco Center to the library on the corner of Mendi Street and turn left. She cannot remember how many blocks it is to the house, but it is the only one painted pink so I will not be able to miss it. At the very least I expect to be watched as I head in that direction, the only white person as far as the eye can see, but nobody bats an eye. The taxi driver assured me that times have changed: white people—especially the very white from Europe—pay good money to come to the Place of the Sun, more if their tour includes a beer at the local *shebeen*. "Nobody worries about the whities anymore." He had laughed. "We just take their money and say '*Enkosi kakuhla*, thank you very much.' "

Pinched between the mud shacks are a few houses splattered with color: one green with a blue corner as though the painter changed his mind at the last minute, one General Motors white, another mustard yellow. The home of the niece of Beauty Masinama, though, is pleasing on the eye, the color of a nursery room, its window frames and door-ways accented in powder blue. I have to duck beneath two rows of laundry to get to the front door, which, like all the others on this street, is propped open with a brick. There is no need to knock, be-cause I have been spotted by someone I assume to be the niece. I wave an awkward greeting as she steps across the patch of cabbages the size of footstools, carrying her spade. Wrapped around her skirt is a brown and red plaid blanket, the fringe brushing the tops of her blue sneakers. On top she wears a striped rugby shirt, and a paisley *doek* is knotted behind her head, framing her face, which is both frowning and smiling.

"I am the one who called," I explain. "I have come to see Beauty."

"Yes," she replies, laying the spade against the side of the house so she can shake my hand. "She is expecting you."

The room into which I step, lit by a single window, is no bigger than a bathroom. Its walls are papered with *Sunday Times* comics, and hanging from them are two framed certificates, one a high school diploma. In one corner is a table covered with a green plastic sheet, the orange crates just visible beneath it. On top is a portable TV, a kerosene lamp, a flask, and two cups. Next to the table is a wheelchair. On the opposite side is a cot with a gray blanket folded at the foot of it, and the entry to the kitchen. It is through this door and into the room beyond that the cabbage-tender now goes.

My stomach is having that first-day-of-school feeling. The visit seemed like a good idea up until an hour ago, but could well now be the product of miscalculation. With nobody's hand to hold, I glance back at the open doorway, tempted to flee, but the niece is back before I do, and bids me "come."

Beauty's eyes are eclipsed by a blue veil of cataracts and seem to bobble on little puddles on her lower lids. Her face, creased and collapsed where her teeth once were, is unmistakable. But will she recognize me? The niece bends over to her right ear and clicks away loudly in Xhosa, then briskly retreats.

"Many rains," Beauty says, "many rains have come and gone since my madam died." She seems not to address me but the draft blowing in through the small window at the foot of her bed. "And Miss Louise," she says of my mother, shaking her head.

"Yes," I manage. "They have all gone, Beauty."

"But not the *klein miss*," she says, swinging her head around to face me, gumming a smile, and extending her arms. I bow into them, and her grip, strong as a python, curls around me.

"*Yamkele ikhaya umntwana*, welcome home."

"I'm not an *umntwana* anymore, Beauty. I am all grown up." I smile.

"To me you will always be a girl; a strong, good girl," she says. With one hand she feels my face to confirm what her eyes cannot see. "You have come back after all these years."

"Only for a short visit, I'm afraid."

She frowns. "You are not living at the farm?"

"Actually, we're selling the farm; that's why I am here." Beauty is part of a generation who had been trained never to disagree with a white person. Contrary opinions, like chew tobacco, are best kept in the cheek, and matters of disagreement are best dealt with by changing the subject, which she does now.

"I hear there are children living in the madam's house."

"Orphans, yes." Beauty seems to stare right into my soul, but her face registers neither judgment nor criticism. "Hopefully, they are going to find a better place to go to school."

"You have children?" she asks.

"One child. A girl—Cleo."

She brightens. "And where is she so I can meet her?"

After a pause I say, "She died a year ago."

"That is very bad," she tches.

Beauty is quiet for a while. Facing the breeze again, she closes her eyes. She is like that for so long I wonder if she has nodded off, but she opens them when I shift my weight on the folding chair. "My children are with the ancestors too. My boy and the girl; both gone. I am too old. In this day, it is the young who die and the old people who live."

"Yes. It's enough to make you wonder if you are being punished for something you did wrong."

She wags her crooked finger. "The death of our babies is not our punishment, *klein miss*. No-no. We must carry our burden like the buckets of water the women carry on their heads. Most of them carry small buckets because their necks are not strong enough. But a few of the women, the strong ones, have to carry the big buckets. They have to carry more water; they have to walk a long way. Then, when the others have finished all their water and are thirsty again, the woman with the big bucket comes home. She puts it down and doesn't have to carry it again for a long time."

Before I can decipher her meaning, she calls out in Xhosa and the young woman enters with two steaming mugs. The one that is not chipped she gives to me. She helps Beauty sit up in bed, straightens her *doek* so that it covers the white tufts of hair, and smooths out her blanket. When the woman leaves the room and quickly reappears with two rusks on an enamel plate, I thank her. Beauty soaks her cookie in her tea before gnawing off a piece. "My body is going to the ancestors, piece by piece." She laughs. "My teeth were the first to go, then my legs, and now my eyes are leaving me. But I am still remembering. I am remembering when I used to bake rusks for you and the madam's teatime and you would sit on the *stoep* and leave one for your mother if she came."

"I remember." If my mother did not come to claim her rusk, none of us ate it. Instead, I would crumble it and feed it to the chickens.

"It was a good place, my madam's farm."

"Did you ever go back?" I ask. "After, you know . . ."

"They locked me up for a very long time," she recalls, shaking her head. "Many seasons went by, till I thought the ancestors would come and fetch me from that place. And then one day the man with all the keys said I was free to go. So I went to the farm, but they told me the madam had died in the winter. I was very sad I did not say goodbye to her."

Beauty tells me stories about my grandmother, mostly how she was after Oupa had left. The Christmas my grandmother bought Beauty a subscription to *Fairlady*, the country's leading women's magazine, and Beauty, in gratitude, covered each issue with brown paper to preserve it, but, as an illiterate, could not read a word of it. The time she had Beauty come into her bedroom and try on all her Sunday dresses that could no longer circumscribe her uncorseted waist. After Beauty had made her selection, my grandmother insisted she wear the prettiest and then drove her to the seaside village of Hermanus for afternoon tea in the poshest establishment. Even though the government had recently relaxed the Group Areas Act, everyone gave them harsh looks nonetheless, which my grandmother mulishly ignored.

"The madam was very good to me," Beauty concludes.

"Yes, and you were very good to her. Actually, to all of us." She shakes her head and I ask, "Tell me, do you still throw the bones?"

"Oh no, I cannot see where they land!" She laughs. "No, but I am teaching the one over there." She flicks her head to where the niece is listening at the door. "She is going to be a better *sangoma* than me one of these days."

Our tea gone, the rusks eaten, the reminiscing over, there seems nothing more to say. Beauty seems to recede, as though retrieving the memories has been a physically challenging act. If Delia asks, I will tell her it was a pleasant visit. I will not tell her I had hoped for something more, for Beauty to have somehow been the door through which I could revisit the last summer of my youth. I get up and carefully scoop the crumbs from my lap into my hand and dust them into the mug.

"I should be getting back and let you get your rest," I announce.

"Be a good girl and hand me my knitting," she says, pointing to the box in the corner. I can't be sure, but when I lean over to pick up the ball of yarn, protruding from it appears to be the very same knitting needles my grandmother once bought for her. These same needles that had paused when my father insulted Beauty on the porch all those years ago. Suddenly I am breathless with shame at the memory of it.

"Beauty," I say, placing the bundle on her lap, "I am so sorry for how he treated you." And she knows exactly to whom I am referring.

"I am sorry for you, *klein miss*, and your mother." She feels for the needles, and runs her hand over the stitches as though she were stroking a cat. "He was a bad man."

"Yes, he was. My mother should have left him. I could never understand why she didn't; why she left me and not him. Your children are your blood. You will do anything for them, even die for them, don't you think?"

"You think your mother was weak. But your mother was a warrior, a clever warrior." Slowly, deliberately, she spears the row of stitches with the point of one needle and winds the yarn around the other as if to throttle it. "The Boers were stupid; they always thought it was the *assegai*, Shaka's spear, they needed to be afraid of," she continues.

One purl.

Vaguely I recall a ninth-grade history lesson on the Anglo-Zulu War, but its relevance is lost on me now. "I don't see what this has to do with my mother."

Beauty nods to herself. "Your mother knew what the *impi* knew: the Boer cannot fight what he does not see."

One plain.

"I'm sorry." I frown. "I'm still not following you."

"Your father was a Boer, *klein miss*," she says, looking up, "and your mother fed him from the tip of Shaka's spear."

One purl.

The niece, who has participated in the conversation thus far only by casting her shadow from the doorway, interjects harshly. "*Aikona*, Ma!" Although I do not understand what she goes on to say, the cautionary tone is unmistakable.

Beauty nods slowly. "Nontlé is telling me it is getting late, and my tongue is doing too much running. I am sorry. It is time for you to go."

But Beauty has opened the door, has given me a look at a woman I barely recognize. "Beauty, please! Go on!" Around her wrist I wind my fingers as though she were a stubborn child I could drag to a place she does not wish to go. Pulsing from her wrist, through the vise of my hand, comes a tremor, shaking my memories like teacups from a toppling hutch.

"I am an old woman now. It has been many, many rains since I was living at Sunup; they have washed away my memories."

"That's not true! You *do* remember! Tell me! Tell me what you know about my mother that I don't know. She talked to you; I saw it, every time she came to the farm. You and she had secrets." Flashing in my mind is the money in the envelope my mother set aside for Beauty, the tins she said were for her nerves, the vial in the bread box. "What was she doing with that stuff you gave her? Was she getting high? Was my father getting high?" and as I say it comes the urge to scrub the idea, the way my mother had scrubbed my hands at the faucet behind the *kaia*. The way you scrub to get off germs, or blood. Or poison.

I gasp at the realization. "It was poison, wasn't it?" Beauty does not answer. "Wasn't it!" On the tip of Shaka's spear.

"It is not right to disturb the dead for their secrets, *umntwana*, and sometimes it is better to leave the past behind us."

"I am not an *umntwana* anymore, Beauty! She was my mother, he was my father, and I have a right to know!" This time I look at the niece. "Tell her! Tell her I have a right to know!"

After a long pause, Beauty takes a deep breath. "She came to the farm that day, you and her, and she was very afraid. But not like a hyena is afraid; more like a lion who has to protect her cubs. Boss Harry had murder on his breath, she told the madam; she said he would come for her, and for you. It was the madam's idea to telephone the police, but Miss Louise went pale like a snake belly. Men with uniforms think a good beating is the best way to teach someone a lesson, especially wives who they think are slow to learn. No, Miss Louise said she couldn't have the policemen come; she was going to think of another way. Your mother came to my door after the roosters had gone to bed. She said to me, 'I am going to kill him, Beauty; I am going to kill him before he kills us.' I could see only a mother lion on my doorstep, nothing else. 'I am going to need your help,' she said. In my tradition, when a lion comes to your door, you give it what it wants."

A *sangoma* trained in the way of the ancestors, Beauty tells me how she offered a remedy as ancient as the hills from which its ingredients were gathered. "I was happy to help Miss Louise, so she and you could be safe." Her words slide around in my head like tumblers on a ship captain's table, and a swell of nausea rocks my stomach.

"But he died of kidney and liver failure," I wanly protest, even while recalling the pestle and mortar on the kitchen counter, Beauty's medicine pouch. "The doctors would have known if he had been poisoned."

She shakes her head no. "*Impila* is a very clever little plant. It can fool the white man's doctors." Looking at Nontlé as though this were part of her required coursework, she says, "The only difference between medicine and poison is portion."

As Beauty explains it, the dose was meant to be administered every day in incremental drops at each meal. After a two-month diet of the deadly sap, my father's renal system would shut down in such a way as to mimic the results of a lifelong affair with the bottle.

"But it took longer than that," I say, trying to pick my way through the ruins of memories.

"I told Miss Louise, 'Leave the girl here; do not take her home with you; I have seen too many people eating from the dish meant for the devil.' But she missed you so much. She came to visit, but every time she did, your father had days to get better." Beauty's voice becomes softer; her eyelids close as though she is reliving an awful decision. "So you see, *klein miss*, it was my fault she left you; it was me who told her not to come anymore, not until the *impila* had done its job."

"That's why she brought him to the farm that day . . . so she could see me and still give him the poison."

"*Ewe.*" She nods, and sighs. "I should have killed him myself that night."

"The night you were fighting with Stompie?"

"*Haai!* That stupid *inja!* He needed to be whipped for all the money he took from me. But it was your father I wanted to kill, coming to the farm, bringing all his sick ways."

"And so when my mother ran to the police van and you said, 'Give us this day our daily bread'——"

She nods again. "I was telling her where I kept the poison so she could finish the job."

The tears finally come. *You will do anything for your children, even die for them.*

~

MY MOTHER DIED not even a handful of months after she buried my father. Standing between my grandmother and Rhiaan at her funeral, I felt like a stranger, unable to give the mourners who greeted me the show they expected. How could I tell them that I had been grieving my mother's absence for years? How could I tell them it was not comfort I was seeking, but a culprit, someone to blame for her death?

I would not have recognized the man who, on the other end of the phone, had made my mother laugh all those years ago. He might have shaken my hand anonymously and slipped by into the broad African daylight had it not been for his remark.

"My condolences to you, young lady," he said. "You and your brother were the world to her, you know." Quietly then, as an afterthought, he added, "And your mother was the world to me." Suddenly I saw my mother as I had never before seen her, as the beautiful pirouetting axis upon which someone else's world had rotated. Someone whose parting had caused the creases of sorrow on his brow, who had made his gray eyes thoroughly rheumy with grief but who could never-theless see her more clearly than I ever could.

My mother's lover was not at all how I imagined him to be. He ought to have been taller than this docile man, ought to have been broad-shouldered and dark-haired like the leading men of paperback romances. He ought to have been a man whose stature would have been a brash stand-up to my father's burly frame. Instead, the man with the gentle handshake and soft voice was sketched in pastels. He was gone before I could say anything in reply. Later, at the cemetery, when I found my brother reading the headstones of my mother's earthly neighbors, I asked him about the pallid man with the cane.

"Professor Colin Wellsley, my high school English teacher," he said.

"He's the one you dedicated the anthology to!" I suddenly realized, recalling the single line of inscription on the first page of my brother's debut book.

"That's right. In many ways, he became a surrogate father to me," Rhiaan added.

"But he's the one Mom had an affair with," I continued, and Rhiaan stared at me as though watching a movie rewind itself.

"Yes," he said sadly, and returned to the task of reading the head-stones. "I know."

The mourners gathered in the small living room of our old house, around side tables on which Auntie Muriel and Mrs. Folliett had set trays of sandwiches and cream puffs and meatballs on toothpicks. Their mouths, buttoned up earlier in church, now flapped in the breeze of clichés. I retreated to my old bedroom, after hearing gossip passed like napkins: "Did you hear they have to sell the house just to pay off the debts? The children aren't going to inherit a dime!"

The room was still the same except for my mother's jar of cold cream on the bedside table and a picture frame serving as a paper-weight for a thrift-store novel. The photograph was of Rhiaan and me at the Christmas table, both with lopsided grins and paper crowns. I didn't even remember the picture being taken.

It was my mother's scent that billowed out of the closet when I slid open the door. Among a few of my abandoned school uniforms were her dresses and coats, a hanger filled with shoes—all of them new. I searched the shelves for her old clothes, but all I found were more new clothes: slips still with price tags, sweet-sixteen lingerie, and a nightie a bride might wear.

People said it was such a shame; they said wasn't it just like life that my mother died so soon after my father. It's often the case, they said; one goes, and the other can't seem to find a way to go on. What rot! If her new clothes and the freshly papered walls were anything to go by, it was obvious my mother had found a way. She had found a way with Professor Wellsley, Mr. No-One-Friend.

I sat down at the desk in front of the window that blinked out at the apricot tree, the place where first Mrs. Folliett, then the paramedics, found my mother the day she died. Perhaps she had sat down to write a letter to me or Rhiaan, or perhaps she had just sat down to watch the tree, the way I had done many times before.

The tree had taught me about life, death, and resurrection better than any Sunday school class. After a season of endlessly producing fruit, it would lose all its leaves, and by the time the fluorescent lights stayed on almost all day it was just a bare rack. Blackened from the rain, its witchy branches would scrape against my window as if begging to be let in. Most days I wanted to scratch back, "It's no warmer in here!" And then, in spring, when I thought I could bear the goblin days no more, I would look out and see tiny pink-brown buds covering the tree. They would appear overnight, and although they did little to alter the mien of the broomstick tree, those buds promised sunshine and good cheer long before I saw them with my own eyes. A dozen winters I spent in that bedroom waiting for the buds, and always they came. If someone had to ask me to define faith, "the old apricot tree" is what I would say. If people wanted something to talk about, it should have been how my mother died when the tree was covered in blossoms.

❧

"SHE DIED three months after he did, you know?" I say.

Beauty nods.

"Nobody really knew why. My grandmother wouldn't let them do an autopsy."

"*Ai,*" Beauty says, shaking her head. "It was not right that she died so young. Miss Louise had life again; she had made her fist." Beauty raises her arm in the old salute of African power: *Amandla!* "I have often wondered what happened to the lion at my door."

"There's no way to know."

Beauty looks at her niece and nods her head. "Fetch the bones."

After she has set the parcel on the floor, the niece helps Beauty out of her bed. I take her other arm and the old woman eases down until she rests on her knees. From the parcel, she unwraps a buckskin, impala perhaps, and lays it out in front of her. She straightens up only slightly as Nontlé removes her *doek* and replaces it with a headdress of beads, bells, and feathers. Around the old woman's shoulders she places a colorful blanket, and my grandmother's old maid has been transformed into a sorcerer. When she says, "The ancestors can tell us things no one else can," I am surprised to hear the familiar voice and not something that sounds like a record played backwards. Swaying her head till the beads clack and the bells ring like wind chimes, Beauty nods at Nontlé, who empties the contents of the pouch into her wide, craggy hands. Once they are sealed between her fingers, Beauty raises her hands to the ceiling and shakes them, and chants in a tongue I do not understand.

The fragments land in a haphazard fashion, and I am surprised to see not only bones, which look as though they might have been pilfered from my grandmother's oxtail stew, but shells and stones and the claw of a bird. In Beauty's right hand Nontlé places a short stick, the end of which is bushy with horsehair, and immediately the old *sangoma* bends over to examine her wares. Unsatisfied, she begins to run her hands over the objects, Braille-like. Only once does she point to a shell and ask her niece, "Which one?" After she gets her answer, she straightens her back and sits quietly. After several minutes her pearly eyes find mine.

"The ancestors have answered about your mother's death," she says.

I nod, afraid to speak, afraid she will decide not to tell me. She makes to get up and Nontlé and I help her rise and get back into bed. The niece then removes her headdress and draws the blanket from her shoulders. While I stand next to Beauty's bed, the niece packs up Beauty's magic as though it were an abandoned game of checkers. Only when she leaves the room does Beauty speak.

"Your mother's death and your father's death are the same," she says, shaking her head. "I am very sorry."

"You mean . . ."

"She died from the poison, yes."

"But how is that possible?"

Beauty rubs her eyes, moist now. "Very, very dangerous is *impila*; even when a drop touches the finger it can find a way quickly to the insides. Your mother knew this; I told her. Miss Louise was not afraid anymore; she said if she was going to die, better from trying than from Boss Harry's hand."

It is claustrophobic, this little room with its caving ceiling and moving walls. "Beauty, thank you for helping me, but I think I should go now," I say, wanting, more than anything, to slip free of Africa's clutches.

"The ancestors have spoken of your death too, *klein miss.*"

Blood running cold, isn't that how the expression goes? The chill that has been blowing in through the window is now racing through my veins, and I recall Jenny's prophetic words, *They come in threes.*

"It is a warning from the great Qamatha, the One Above All," she continues.

"Please, Beauty," I say, "I think I've heard enough for one day. There is a lot to take in."

Ignoring my request, she says, "You are being poisoned too, *klein miss,* by your own heart."

"Please, I really must leave!"

This time it is her hand that grips mine. "You have the bird in your path," she goes on. "The bird is the messenger. Look beyond your immediate situation; the healing is on the horizon if you choose it. *Umn-*

twana, you are your mother's daughter; you now must be a warrior like her." Beauty releases my hand.

Suddenly in the dusty room the particles of light seem to merge so that I see what Beauty has seen all along. Whether conjured by her magic or my wishing-hard, my mother appears before me. Not the demure housewife with an apologetic slump of her shoulders or the mother who left her child on Africa's doorstep. Around her eye is not the violet smudge of a bruise but a stripe of red clay, and over her upright shoulder is not a shawl but a *kaross*. Standing before me is my mother the warrior, beckoned from the plains of Africa's ancestral grounds. She smiles and it is as though the sun has just risen. I smile back at her, this vision or ghost. And then she is gone before I can decide which. "Now you can go," Beauty says. "Now it is time for you to go home."

TWENTY

The taxi, before turning north, deposits me in front of the Bredenkamps' store. It feels good to stretch my legs, and I am hoping the half-mile walk to the B&B might do my head some good too. Only two cars are parked outside, and on the store's veranda is a huddle of old tribal men sitting on orange crates and smoking their pipes. I walk into the cool of the store and push through the small turnstile, hoping to put aside—at least for a while—thoughts of witch doctors, avenging mothers, and poisoned fathers.

"Good day to you," says a male voice, and I turn around to see where it has come from. "Up here," it says when I don't see anyone. Leaning out the window of an elevated office above the cigarette counter is a gray-haired man with a beaming smile and a cigarette-clutching hand waving in my direction. Etienne's manager.

"Hello," I say to the lined, friendly face.

"Just in time for sausage rolls, straight out of the oven. Four rand fifty each or twenty rand for six!" he says, cigarette gesturing to the right. I follow its direction and see the sign that says BAKERY.

"Thank you, I'll try one." I nod, before walking down an aisle of canned food.

I fill the shopping basket with two cans of ravioli, two cans of halved pears, and, on impulse, a jar of artichoke hearts—enough to get me through to Monday's airplane fare. I wander down the center aisle and take a furtive glance at the office window, and since the manager is no longer there, I take a U-turn down the wine aisle for Pinotage Cheap 'n' Nasty. Since it is to be a night of indulgences, why not candy too? I peruse my childhood favorites: Caramello Bears, licorice (still sold without wrappers), Smarties. It is my mother's favorites I reach for—a box of Wilson's Mint Imperials, its scent infamous for veiling the breath of liquor. At the produce section, I pick out a huge grapefruit and a couple of bananas, then head to the bakery. "One sausage roll, please," I ask the young girl in her oversized baker's jacket. She is too shy to look at me directly and, keeping her head bent like a Karoo sunflower that hasn't seen rain for months, pushes the packet toward me.

On the way to the checkout stand I lean over the stack of newspapers for a copy of this month's *Fairlady*. While the cashier rings up my purchase, the manager sticks his head out the window again.

"Find everything, miss?" he asks.

"Yes, thank you," I reply.

"Got one of them pies, did you?"

"Yes, I did, thank you."

"If it's not the best sausage roll you've ever tasted, come back for a full refund," he says cheerfully.

"Okay," I say, and hand the cashier two twenty-rand notes.

"Going to get your Lotto ticket?" he asks. "One million rand in the coffers and the big draw is at four o'clock tomorrow."

"Next time, maybe."

"Won't be a next time this big."

"That's okay, all the same."

When I walk out with my two bags, I hear him call "Goodbye," but the doors close behind me before I can turn around and reply.

THE ALARM CLOCK is missing. I notice its absence immediately, and the groceries drop as I rush to the bedstand and look under it. The clock is gone! Turning wildly, I notice that the apricots are gone too. Cleo's bunny is no longer at the foot of the bed and my boots, parked earlier on the floor beside it, are gone too. Sal's locket, which I took off last night and left next to the washbasin, is no more. I run outside and around the back of the *kaia*, searching madly for the culprit, and succeed only in startling a pair of guinea fowl, which shuffle into the bush. I rush back to the front door of the *kaia*, heart pounding, feeling the anger rise to my face. Idiot! You lock your doors in Africa, I chastise myself, noticing the padlock is missing too.

"Bugger!" I swear. "Shit!" And then I cry because I have so little anyway and someone has taken my shoes and Mrs. du Toit's pilfered apricots my mouth was all set to eat. And Cleo's Easter bunny.

"Thieving bastards!" A nameless black face comes to mind. "Thieving bastards, the lot of them," I can hear my father say. "Thieves and murderers!" I almost nod in agreement. Why are they always black faces, the ones with the hands that wrench wallets from pockets or pies from windowsills? The hands that stab farmers and their wives on the moonless nights. Hands that grind mountain plants into hemlock.

Picking up my handbag, I race up to the main house. The door is open but the burglar gate is locked.

"Susannah!" I call, jabbing the doorbell, hearing it ding-dong down the hall.

Delia is the first to the door. "What is wrong, madam?"

"Someone has stolen my things!" I say through the bars.

Susannah approaches. "Dear God!" she exclaims, pushing Delia aside and unlocking the gate. The hounds, late in detecting a guest, are all fired up and barking, and rush down the driveway as though leading a cavalry charge.

"What's missing?" Susannah asks, huffing beside me. "Are you all right?"

"Yes, I'm fine. I just came back from Langa; the alarm clock is gone, and my shoes, and a few of my daughter's things."

We crowd into the little *kaia*, dogs too. "Off!" shouts Susannah when one of them jumps on the bed.

"I left early this morning, but I could have sworn I locked up," I say.

"Is anything else missing? . . . Money? Passport?"

"No, I had them with me in my handbag," I answer, and then sit down on the bed with my head in my hands, exchanging composure for a cry. "They took my necklace, and the apricots," I say between sobs.

Susannah pats my shoulder, "There, there," then hands me the tissue she has balled up in her sleeve. "It's clean."

"I go get some more apricots," says Delia, but before she leaves she adds, "Pepsi, madam! I know it was Pepsi!"

Susannah seems irritated at the suggestion, as though she is tired of refereeing two bickering children. "But he's not even here today, Delia; it's his day off." Pulling a chair from the table, Susannah sits down on it and pats my knee gently. "I am so sorry, Abbe. We will get to the bottom of this, I promise you. People talk around here."

"My alarm clock," I cry.

"Of course we will replace that, and whatever else you need."

"No, it's my alarm clock from my home." And she doesn't understand. She cannot know how it has measured my breath and tears, my longing for Cleo. My favorite clock because it had all its numbers printed on its face, not like the others carelessly skipping numbers— 12, 3, 6, 9—as if certain segments of time could just slip by unnoticed. She cannot possibly know what I now admit to myself, that the clock kept a vigil for me while I lost track. Since leaving Hawaii, the hours and days have stacked up without my counting. Other ghosts have elbowed their way in and a youth left years ago has been around every corner.

My tissue-bearing, knee-patting landlady sits in front of me, "there-there-ing," while I try to find solid ground. "My daughter died," I say, looking up and into her face. "She got hit by a car over a year ago and that clock is about the only thing that's kept me company."

"I am so terribly sorry," Susannah responds. "What an awful loss to bear."

I wipe the tears and snot with the back of my shirtsleeve, her tissue soaked and crumpled next to me. "It's supposed to get easier, isn't it? I mean, that's what everyone tells you: it gets easier. But when? When, exactly, does it get easier?" I know I am not going to get the little alarm clock back, just as I am never going to get Cleo back. Not the farm, my grandmother, my mother—they are all gone. Everything and everyone goes, yet nothing, other than grief and despair, steps from the wings and takes up even a little bit of the empty space.

There are no more words now. There is nothing to say. We sit in the coolness of the round hut and I wish the thief had taken my heart too, useless as it is. Steal it, I shout in the hollows of my head. Take it all! After you have gathered up the goods, lean over and dip into my chest and take that beating, faceless clock too. The one that will not stop ticking and ringing and waking me up to anemic days. Take it, you thieving, faceless coward! Rip it out and begone with you!

"You are going to be okay," she says after a while. "You are tough—I can tell."

I pat my face and nod as Delia appears at the door with an apron full of apricots.

"The Ou Missus saw me picking these, madam, and started swearing," she warns Susannah.

"I better go tell her what happened," Susannah says, excusing herself. "Delia, you wait here with Miss Abbe."

As soon as she leaves, Delia issues verdicts, judge and jury all in one. "Pepsi and those friends of his always go crazy when it is lottery time. They drink too much and gamble all their money, and get into fights. That Pepsi is a *skelm*," she says emphatically. "The madam and the Boss won't fire him, but one day it is going to be too late."

Too Late is the eighth day of the week, one with which I am well familiar. Tomorrow I will sign the papers and then I can leave behind the *skelms* who rob the poor. I can leave behind Beauty and her spells, leave her to dance upon the graves of my people. I will leave behind a farm lying fallow in curses, a land in its eighth day.

I DO NOT KNOW what time it is when Susannah pounds on my door, but when I sit up on the bed and look out at her serious expression catching the late sun, I know evening is fast approaching.

"Sorry to wake you," she apologizes.

I wave her in. "No, it's good that you did."

"I spoke to Yvette Dickson from next door and she says she saw a couple of men loitering about this morning. She did recognize one of them as Pepsi's cohorts. Etienne will talk to Pepsi when he shows up for work tomorrow, but for now the police are handling it. Not that that will do much good, I'm afraid. But," she continues, "we want you to join us for dinner tonight—Delia's doing a roast chicken—and we both think you should sleep in our house tonight." She opens her palm and offers me a miniature grandfather clock. "And this is for you. I got it as a present from Toby last Christmas, but my eyes aren't good enough to make out the numbers," she says. "I hope it can do the job, at least for now."

I thank her.

"So is that a yes? You will be our guest tonight?"

"Yes, I think I will."

"How about a nice hot bath for starters?"

"Sounds good." I grab my towel, my toiletry bag, and purse. And then, remembering the wine, I grab the bottle and offer it to Susannah.

"I'll trade you," she says, handing me the new padlock with which I lock the door.

We walk out into the cool evening just as the crickets begin to sing. The sun takes its sweet time to set in southern Africa in the summertime, but come autumn it slips away quickly, between blinks, tugging behind it a dark cloth. While the sky is ablaze, the foreboding clouds race in from the west as if bidden to come put out the fire. By the time we reach the kitchen door, Delia is getting on her coat and putting up her umbrella. Susannah gives her a twenty-rand note from her pocket for the taxi, thanks her, and hurries to see what Mrs. du Toit is calling about.

"I never did get to thank you for helping me find Beauty Masinama," I tell Delia.

"Was it a good visit?" she asks.

"It was and it wasn't, but it cleared up some things for me."

"We have a saying in Xhosa: Your past is always with you—be friends with it and it will help you find a good future."

"Well, we'll have to see about that. But thank you."

"I am very sorry for your daughter," she offers.

I nod in acknowledgment as she continues, "My youngest boy is going to die," she says, wiping at her eyes with the heel of her hand. "He's got AIDS."

"How long does he have?" I ask, reaching for her hand.

"Not many more summers, maybe two."

"I am so sorry, Delia."

"In October he will be twenty-seven," she continues. "He has three children." All we can do is nod respectfully into the voids of each other's pain. Our children are lost to us, and yet we have to keep from becoming lost to ourselves. Quickly, her stringy arms wrap around me with the ferocity of a desperate mother. "God give you strength," she says, and then, putting her bag on her head, she sets off down the dark path, having inadvertently cracked the crust around my heart.

BLOODY DOGS! is the last rational thought I have, stirred from a pleasant dream about Cleo by the high-pitched yap-yap-yapping of the Bredenkamps' dogs. A thought wiped so quickly from my mind as though from a blackboard when their barking is interrupted by three chilling, thunderous claps. Bolt upright in the Bredenkamps' guest room bed, peering into the clotting dark, I know it even though I have never heard it before. Gunshots.

Just as quickly come the screams and the men's voices shouting orders. At the other end of the corridor, words flare from a fitful speech like struck matches: "fucking," "kill you," "shoot," while my brain tries to catch up with my body: You're awake, it is the middle of the night, act quickly! As if to underscore the thought, the sound of Susannah's sobs parenthesize my options. The windows next to my bed are barred; there must be a way out, a way to call for help. How long can it take to get to the neighbor's? How long before they find me in this room?

The door makes no sound when I open it, a detail for which I am disproportionately grateful, and the passage is dimly lit from the lights blazing at its other end. While the unfamiliar men's voices get louder, shouting over Susannah's raving appeals, I steal inches of corridor, edging against the wall, praying, praying to God that I will make it to the front door, swung wide like a dislocated limb. Twenty feet away might as well be China, but then it is surely only eight, and now where the light from Susannah's room is bright enough that I am illumined, exposed, I have only two feet to go. Just one big step and I am outside. There is a loud male voice approaching from the west end of the house. I can make it. Hurry! I watch the living room doorway and for the shape that is surely to take its place any moment. Now! I take one last step, but my foot catches something large, warm. A footstool? I reach for the coatrack to correct my fall, but it collapses and the crash brings the gun to my temple. *"Daar's 'n vierde een!"* "There's a fourth one!" he yells. To my ear, he threatens, "One sound and it's finished and *kla!*" Looking down, I see next to my left foot the bullet-blown shape that was once a corgi.

Susannah's Victorian bedspread and matching headboard is splattered with so much blood I am sure it is not just the dogs that are shot. Susannah is sitting in her wingback chair next to her dressing table, nightgown exposing her plump white thighs, her body shivering against the fright. Her hands are tied behind her back and her eyes, pleading at me, are saucer-wide with terror. She watches as I am pushed into the corner on the floor beside her by the man with beaded dreadlocks that clack like Beauty's headdress. You read about these things happening all the time. You read about how the homeowners fight back, how they find a way to outsmart their captors. It is now for that way I search my mind.

Pepsi, his gun stuck in the back of his work jeans, is swearing his frustration at Etienne, uncoiling the coat hanger and then twisting it around his employer's thick wrists. One of Etienne's eyes has already swollen shut, his lower lip burst like an overripe granadilla. Taking the tie from Etienne's rack, Pepsi balls it up and stuffs it in his master's mouth. In beige monogrammed pajamas, sitting on the edge of his bed, Etienne looks more like a schoolboy awoken from his boarding-school bed by bullies in some wicked initiation rite. I feel as though I have stumbled into a private moment, and the shame of seeing him so helpless, of him seeing me witness his shame, is awkward. I avert my eyes and resume the business of watching Susannah's toes clench and un-clench the carpet fibers.

We hear the third intruder before we see him, shrilly shouting that he has the old woman, laughing that she may not need a bullet after all. When he pushes her into the room, he is a scarecrow no older than eighteen. "Grandma looks tired, Boss," he says to the captor with dreadlocks. "How about I put her to sleep?" Mrs. du Toit is straining with the effort of breathing. "Mother!" Susannah cries, for which she receives a blow across her cheek with Boss's gun-clenched hand. By the time Susannah revives, Mrs. du Toit has her arms bound tightly to her body with the telephone extension cord and has toppled over on her side from the inability to right herself on the edge of Susannah's di-sheveled bed. Another coat hanger has been retrieved from the cup-board for my hands, and before long the prickle that comes with a lack of blood circulation covers my chilled hands.

Pepsi and Boss rush out of the room. "If anyone makes a sound, shoot them, Lucky," orders Boss, leaving our guard to ponder his ques-tion aloud: "Who do I shoot first?" Pointing his gun at each of us in turn, he ends on Mrs. du Toit. "Pow!" he shouts. "Pow, pow!" The old woman flinches and he laughs brutally, but just as quickly the grin is gone and his sneering face spits into Susannah's, who has let out a bloodcurdling cry. The barrel of his gun presses up into the folds be-neath her chin. "Make one more fucking sound and you lie with your dogs tonight!"

While Lucky plays with his gun, reloading and recocking, we listen to the sound of the Bredenkamps' house coming apart at its seams. Maybe there is a way to overpower him. He is a scrawny kid; we can take him; can't we take him? Etienne and I? Etienne is making his own calculations—scanning the windows, the floor, the faces of his women. There must be something, some one thing that can get us out of the nightmare. When Pepsi passes by the doorway he is eating a drumstick from Delia's leftover roast. Under his arm is the sherry bottle that had only hours ago stood on the Bredenkamps' elaborately set dining table. Soon it will be over, I think—an attempt at rationality; they will have their loot and leave.

Or will they?

By the time Susannah's clock chimes for the third time, the two come back with their duffel bags stuffed beyond zipping and Lucky is clearly fed up with restraint. They talk to each other in their language of clicks, making arrangements about our lives we cannot understand. Mrs. du Toit is pulled to her feet, leaving a damp spot on the coverlet to which Lucky points and laughs.

"You won't get away with this," she scolds as Lucky pushes her out the door and into the living room.

"*Staan op julle!*" Boss shouts at us to stand. And Etienne, Susannah, and I are tugged and pulled and pushed out the front door and down to the garage. Pepsi hands me the keys. "You drive!" he says, and opens the driver's door of Etienne's Volkswagen minivan. He unwraps the coat hanger wire and I slide onto the cold seat. We now know what Pepsi is really after—the safe in the manager's office, the safe that has all the last-minute bets for tomorrow's lottery draw.

"Why don't you just take me, Pepsi?" reasons Etienne. "There's no need to involve the women."

"Fucking shut up!" Boss shouts, shoving him and Susannah in the back. After getting into the passenger seat, Pepsi looks at me and barks, "Drive!" With his free hand he retrieves the thing in his back pocket that has prevented him from sitting comfortably. It is the padlock to my *kaia*. Around Pepsi's neck, glinting beneath the edge of a soiled collar, is Sal's locket and the face of my little girl hidden within it. Pointing the gun at my temple, he sneers, "No fucking funny business."

The car sputters at first, protesting the cold, but I pump the gas and it jerks to life. I lean on the stick and pop the van into reverse without looking over my shoulder. After bumping down the driveway, the car turns into a deserted street.

∽

"LET'S GO FOR A DRIVE," my grandmother said the Sunday after my mother's funeral. When she turned left out onto Klippoort Highway in her beige Morris Minor and cruised past the wheat fields and the wine farms, never leaving third gear, I wished she would keep on driving. Driving till we crossed the border into a different life.

"It hasn't been easy for you this past year, has it?" she remarked.

I shook my head, rearranging her knitting on my lap.

"It's a hard thing to lose someone you love," she said. For a while the only sound was the motor straining for fourth. "Your mother had a sister, you know," she announced.

There are things, I had come to realize, I would never know about my mother. That she had a sibling is one thing for which I am completely unprepared. "I thought she was an only child."

"No." My grandmother shook her head. "There was a baby who came after her—six years after her. We named her Rebecca. The sweetest little angel you ever laid your eyes on. And good. Oh my, she never so much as made a peep."

"What happened to her?"

Recited was how her answer sounded. "She died one night in her sleep—cot death, is what they called it. She wasn't even six months old, but I might as well have loved her all my life."

"Why didn't Mom ever tell me about her?"

"People deal with difficult circumstances in different ways. Your mother was always one for keeping things close to her chest. Like her father, that way. I think she always felt responsible, that Rebecca's death was some sort of secret she had to keep. To your mother, keeping secrets was a form of survival, not betrayal."

"But you've never said anything before either!"

"Quite right. Quite right."

"So what happened?" I asked.

"Well, for a while I wasn't able to face the world. I thought I was never going to get over losing my baby. And I was right. I didn't get over it, I just got past it. But it took another child to help me find my way."

"My mom," I said.

She nodded. "She came to my bedroom door one day—oh, maybe four or five months after Rebecca had died. She had her doll with her and one of its arms was missing. 'Can you help me fix her, Mama? She's broken,' she said. I got out of bed and helped her mend the doll, and from that day forward I realized what I was called to do—what we are all called to do." Without glancing at me, she said, "You, me, everyone. We're menders. Mending the world is the only way we are mended ourselves."

She stopped the car on the road between Paarl and Franschhoek, where the mountain stretched out like a lady's ballroom slipper, and got out. "Your turn," she instructed. "It's about time you learned." And over the fifty kilometers that we sputtered and jerked and stalled home, she took up her knitting and never once glanced at the road to see how I was doing.

⁂

PEPSI DOESN'T watch the road either, but stares at the side of my head where his gun is aimed. Only when I turn right into the store's parking lot does he look forward and instruct me to park on the left side of the building, in front of the ramp leading to the loading entrance. He tells me to keep the car running but to kill the lights. At the word, we all stiffen. Susannah is out of the car first, then Etienne with Boss pointing his gun and ordering them to the side door where the alarm keypad is located behind the security gate. Pepsi calls out the window to Boss to come retrieve the keys. For a moment I can see what Etienne is thinking—can he make it to the bushes, ten yards away? Is this our only chance? But the answer is too late in coming and his captor is back to untie his hands. Etienne fumbles with the keys, drops them, picks them up, and sifts through them till he finds one for the gate. Is he stalling? Does he have a plan? Please, God, tell me he has a plan? Boss takes several paces to the side, gun still leveled at the couple in their pajamas, so he can scan the back alley for late-night revelers on their way home. "Hurry the fuck up!"

It is not the casualness with which Pepsi whistles that gets me—as though he has done this a thousand times before: watched people soil themselves, listened to the pitiful pleas, relished the indisputable power that a gun affords—it's the tune. What *is* that tune? I know that tune . . . There seems little room for anything but the sharp edge of fear, but bidden, like a well-trained Labrador, come the words Pepsi could only have learned in a church:

Ooh, ooh, come Sunday,
Oh, come Sunday, that's the day.
Lord, dear Lord above,
God Almighty, God of love,
Please look down and see my people through.

"I know that song!" I tell Pepsi.

"Shut up!"

"No, I know that song—I do. Duke Ellington: *I believe that God put sun and moon up in the sky. / I don't mind the gray skies, / 'cause they're just clouds passing by . . .* That's the one, isn't it?" But he is watching Etienne swing open the security gate, taking the final step to the alarm box.

Boss yells at him to hurry up.

"What?" Pepsi says, turning to me with a sneer. "You think your gray clouds are going to pass by?"

"Aren't they?"

For a moment Pepsi seems to forget he is a gangster, which makes me forget about giving up. "Please. Please don't hurt those people. They are good people, Pepsi."

He considers this, then looks at Boss, who is shooting a menacing look in our direction. "People don't get breaks just because they are good," he declares, and I know suddenly our fates are to be issued with the speed of nine-millimeter bullets. It must register in some noticeable way, because Pepsi says quietly, "I'm sorry; at least you will see your daughter again."

They say your life goes flashing by the moment it is about to end. They say from childhood through adolescence into adulthood, it flicks by one frame after the next like a slide show, carrying with it perfect detail you thought you had forgotten: how your mother's face looked the time you fell off the bunk bed, your arm hanging at a funny angle; your boyfriend's groan of delight the first time he reached in your blouse; how tight the wedding band felt when it had to be shoved on your swollen finger; what your baby's face did the first time she tasted solid food; how it felt when the old maid told you your mother had poisoned your father. What they don't tell you is that it gets stuck on one particular frame and keeps replaying that same scene over and over. For me, it is not the scene when Greg held up Cleo's newborn face to greet me. Nor is it the one where I held Cleo's stiffening body on the hospital floor, although it should have been—God knows that's when I thought life had ended. The frame that sticks with me is of the spectral woman in Beauty's *kaia*, her arm raised in a fist. Her voice a call to arms: Do something! Don't just let it all happen to you! To hell with dying! Act! Live!

To let the events, now certain, take their course without hindrance is to chance seeing Cleo again. Haven't I traveled a liturgical year to the brink of this moment? Is this not truly the kind of Easter for which I have been waiting? Let it happen, I tell myself. But my mother's command is a sharp stick poking at my ribs. I have wanted to die for more than a year, wished it, and now the hour is at hand and I want it no more.

Susannah has collapsed in a puddle of disarray beside the gaping security gate, and Etienne, with resigned shoulders, pushes open the unlocked door. Boss orders him then to kneel next to his wife and exchanges a look with Pepsi, a conclusion at which each of us has already arrived—dead people don't point fingers. Etienne reaches for his wife's hand, a gesture so tender, so brave. Not a deathbed gesture but a proposal, a promise of a happily-ever-after.

There are no pauses now between heartbeats; just a single ceaseless vibration goes off in my chest. I cannot tell whether it is tears or beads of sweat blurring my eyes, or rain. Everything is tilting, the world sliding off its plate like unset Jell-O. There is a click—one ear tells me it is the hammer of Pepsi's gun drawing back, preparing to slam the bullet forward. But the other identifies it as the sound of a Kodachrome slide dropping from the carousel into the viewfinder. It is raining hard, River Street is flooding. Suddenly a flash of yellow darts in front of me. The flash of a kite as it hurries out of the reach of a little girl. She will be following it. To avoid her, I slam the gearshift into first, stamping my foot on the accelerator and swerving sharply to the right. The van surges up the ramp, avoiding one collision and targeting another. My eyes fix on Boss, who has spun around to face me. I steady the wheel and head for the brick wall on the other side of his root-bound body.

There is a ringing in my ears, the ringing of church bells, or an alarm clock, clanging deafeningly over Pepsi's hysterical scream. It is still there at the first impact. I do not remember the second.

TWENTY-ONE

At times it feels like I am soaring, parting the clouds with each turn. Weightless, I am at last unfettered from the mangled scrapyard below and giddy with the relief of it. As though I have no body. A kite, or a feather; perhaps the detached wing of a butterfly. There is everything to see from up here; everything and nothing that stands still. Spirits, dreams like puffs from a pipe, wishes and beams of sunlight. And so quiet; it must surely be Elysium.

But then I turn, perhaps too sharply, and the sting of it brings me back to the hard hospital bed, to its newspapery sheets and cardboard pillow. Back to the brokenness and bandages, to a stomach sick on pharmaceuticals, to the horror of what somehow was not a dream. Boss's face, the one contorted in fear, is seared on the inside of my eyelids. I am awake. Go easy. I coach myself through the shift from back to left side. Opening my eyes is harder than flying, and when I do there are no puffy white clouds, only shapes that mutter, pressing their cold fingers along my flesh.

I squeeze my eyes shut again till the black dots appear and my body floats up out of its pupa and takes to the skies once more.

SOMEONE PUTS the clothespin back on my finger and tightens a band around my arm while things go beep. The annoying voice is back, the one that speaks in question marks. "How many fingers do you see, Mrs. Deighton?" I tell her not to call me Mrs. Deighton, but all I hear is a pot bubbling over.

"Do you know where you are?" she orders.

"Fwhumpl," I tell her.

"That's right, you're in the hospital. Do you know what day it is?"

I shake my head, and when I do the pain is back. *"Aaagh,"* I moan.

"Tell me about it! Half the time we don't know either. It is Friday," she announces. "Your second day. Doctor says he wants you up by this afternoon; can't have you sleeping through your five-star stay with us, now can we?"

My mouth is parched and I mumble for a sip of water, but nothing resembling sense issues forth.

"Don't try to sit up by yourself just yet, Mrs. Deighton. Your collarbone isn't going to appreciate that."

To signal my request, I lift my hand to my mouth and it feels as though it is dragging the weight of a ship's anchor with it.

"Doctor said you are only to take small sips; remember what happened last night?" She inserts a straw into something that used to feel like my mouth as I try to recollect what happened last night. Did my baby just die? Did someone else's baby just die?

"You don't want to start vomiting again. That's not pleasant for anyone, is it?" She answers her own question by removing the straw before the desert has received little more than a drop. "Remember, you have this button; you just click it twice when the pain is too much. Think you can do that?"

When she leaves she takes the light with her and all is dark again. Click, click.

RAGE AND SORROW roll up into a wrecking ball, its swinging arc speeding down on a single black face superimposed on a brick wall. His face is sneering, not smiling. No, wait, he's crying. "Stop!" I hear him scream. But it is too late. And now it is Cleo's face on the wall, and still there is no time to stop. Bits of glass and brick and bone splinter and careen till the earth is raining gravel. Then I am a thousand bits of shrapnel falling, falling; from the falling there is no relief.

It is a warm hand that beckons me this time, soft and reassuring, bidding me from my nightmare. Through slits I see two figures, fuzzy yet familiar. The paler, plumper of the two whispers, "Abbe? Abbe, dear, are you awake?"

It is only when from my bandaged hood I groan that they smile: Yes, this is the right room; see, I told you, it *is* her. Susannah, red-eyed, dabs her cheeks with her free hand; the other one is still pulling me from the wreckage of my terror. "We made it," she whispers. "*You* made it."

"Etienne?" I croak.

"He's fine, everyone's fine. We all made it!"

No, I want to remind her, we didn't all make it. Someone didn't make it.

"The others?"

Delia and Susannah exchange looks. "Don't worry about that now. Look, I've brought you something . . ."

Delia, holding her madam's handbag, grins at me as though seeing propped-up mummies were a regular occurrence.

"What day is it?" I ask.

"Saturday. Saturday, the twenty-second of April. Your brother will be here day after tomorrow—we talked to him again last night; he's very anxious to see you." To Delia she turns and retrieves from her handbag the framed photo of Cleo. "I brought some of your things from the house; I thought they might be a comfort to you here." She puts Cleo on the bedside table, along with the little clock. In my lap she places Cleo's fluffy bunny. "They found it in Pepsi's house, along with your other belongings. There, that already cheers the place up."

"Thank you," I say.

She starts to tear up. "We are the ones who should say thank-you. You saved our lives, Abbe; you risked your life for a couple of strangers you only just met."

I shake my head. How to tell her? How to tell her I was saving my-self. And not just from death. There are things worse than death. Guilt, for one. The shallow grave of what-if. Waiting, too, is worse. If there is a hell, it is surely entered only after a long bout in a waiting room. Waiting for doctors to bring pronouncements of death, waiting for children to climb up out of their graves or waiting for one to open up so you might climb in. Waiting for a trigger to pull or a husband's touch or a mother's return. How to tell her I could wait no more?

"No, really. Everyone is saying so." Delia hands her the newspaper, which she holds up for me to inspect. Pointing to a headline, EXPAT RISKS LIFE, THWARTS LOTTO THIEVES, Susannah gushes, "Everyone is calling you Paarl's hero. The mayor—Etienne plays bowls with him—says they are going to give you a plaque, and Simon Wessels, you know, from the *Tribune*, is doing a full-page feature on you. He's going to interview you as soon as the doctor gives the go-ahead."

Susannah rambles on, answering questions I do not ask, filling in the blanks so a picture emerges. Etienne, she tells me, triggered the shop's silent alarm before disabling it, even though he knew it would take the armed-response team ten minutes to reach them, ten minutes he knew they did not have. But he was thinking of his mother-in-law and the hyena boy who had her tied up. The alarm, sounding both in the police station and the bedroom of the neighborhood watch association's chief, was not only zoned for the shop but also for the house. Two patrol cars were quickly dispatched. The first, arriving at the Bredenkamps' home a little after 4:00 a.m., surprised Lucky, who, expecting the return of his cohorts, opened the door to find Karel van der Walt and his partner in no mood for talking. No one is quite clear how it happened, since there were no signs of resisting arrest, but the bullet Lucky had been so eager to discharge found its way into his own kneecap. Mrs. du Toit was untied from a chair in the dining room, and although unharmed in any outward way was taken to Green Valley Hospital to be on the safe side. "It took the wind out of her sails. But she's a tough ol' bird," says Susannah. "She will be all right."

The second patrol car got to the shop after Etienne had managed to pry open the driver's door of his minivan with a crowbar from the shop's hardware department and was in the process of pulling a semiconscious driver from her seat. By that time Susannah had run to the nearest neighbor and returned with Hendrik Swanepoel and his twin teenage sons, all of whom brought rifles and were ready to shoot at anything that moved. Nothing apparently did. Etienne, Susannah, and I were loaded in one ambulance, the two burglars and a police escort in another. When the manager opened shop at seven o'clock on Thursday morning there was nothing to indicate the ordeal of the early-morning hours other than a sprinkling of glass and a stain on the side wall. Which is not to say that nobody was aware of what had transpired. By noon the city editor had received two dozen different calls about the incident and had already assigned his top journalist to cover the story, and at the end of the day Etienne's manager reported record sales on everything from pepper spray to sausage rolls. I drift off as Susannah tells me about the journalist's visit to their home.

THE NURSE pushes a button and my bed sits up obediently. She steers toward me the tray of mush she calls "lunch" and tells me she wants to see it all gone by the time she returns. "You are a celebrity now; can't be looking like a scarecrow when your visitors come, can you?"

I feel the need to salute.

Each time the visitors come, it is with a little gift: Susannah brought a nightgown from Woolworths, lipstick, a few tabloid maga-zines. Etienne, on his visit, brought his gratitude, tied with a bow of stuttered sentences. Mrs. du Toit, too weak to venture farther than her own bed, sent with Delia a bag of apricots ("the last of them"), even though my jaw does not like to process much more than pulp. I have asked the nurses to eat them before they go bad, and occasionally they stand in clumps, juice dribbling down their chins, talking about noth-ing to do with cars or windshields or dead men. Bless them.

The guests have also left the newspapers folded in thirds where the stories are featured. The stories of that night. "Self-defense" is what my role has been chalked up to. At least by the police. But the good people of Paarl won't have any of that. *"She saved their lives,"* the neighbor Yvette

Dickson is quoted in Mr. Wessels's column. *"That makes her a hero in my book."* Some of the local clergy, along with several other activists, have taken it as an opportunity to lobby even harder against lottery organizers. *"They serve only to heighten a sense of disparity, encouraging others to act in such desperate ways,"* a spokesman for the Dutch Reformed Church is quoted as saying. In response, the paper does not run a feature on the Lotto's winner, just prints her name on the second to last page (Mvr. B. T. Naude of Franschhoek). Others are calling complacent neighbors to action, to form more "neighborhood watch teams" that will patrol the streets at night in shifts. But nowhere in the article and on no one's lips is the word that seems, if not obvious, equally relevant: murder.

When my nurse comes back and inspects my plate she is clearly displeased. My punishment is a sponge bath on the wrong side of luke-warm. When she is done and my skin is pink and goosey from her efforts, I ask for my hairbrush, but instead of handing it to me she begins brushing my hair. "Long hair is back in style again, isn't it?" she says. "In my day, a woman cut her hair as soon as her baby could yank on it, and it stayed that way forever-amen." It seems years, possibly forever-amen, since I looked in a mirror, longer still since I took the shears to my head. How is it my hair has grown long without my noticing? "Let's put it in a plait, shall we, that way it won't get so tangled up." She hands me a small mirror when she is done and tells me not to worry, it will be the same old face I will see in the mirror once the doctor removes the bandage. Not one that will win any contests on Halloween, she assures me.

As if on cue, the doctor with the turban comes in and flips through my chart. "Could have been worse," he says, as he has done every day. "Could have been a whole lot worse." He never elaborates as to how, and I never ask. Instead, I just nod and smile: Yes, yes, a lot worse. For dead does seem worse. Certainly it is worse for Boss, as it will be for Pepsi down the hall, who, they tell me, is losing his battle. And if dead isn't worse, then being a skinny black boy with a girlie smile and a name like Lucky in a crowded prison certainly is. Barely Dead and About to Be Dead are clearly not states of advantage. And this is still a novel thought for me. My mind runs over it like a tongue finding the tangy ditch in my gum where a few teeth once were.

Dead is also worse for the mothers whose wombs bore those two men. And though we will never meet, I can't help but wonder if we will forever be tethered by the same filament of grief at losing our children. Headlines with "hero" have done nothing to assuage the sense that I owe these women something. A debt I will never be able to repay. Wasn't that what Greg said of Mr. Nguyen? Are the old Vietnamese driver and I tethered now too? Mr. Nguyen has been on my mind a lot in the past few days. The old man killed by accident, and I called him a murderer. I killed on purpose, yet people call me a hero.

It is these unseen visitors, the ones who use my conscience as a stage, who point to such things as murder and blame. The hobo who had once hobbled up to the mike that Sunday morning confessing to murder and how the Man had, as Ezekiel had prophesied, put flesh on his bones and breathed new life—he revisits me with his words: "You take away someone's life, whether you're thinking about it or not, and your own life goes with it too." I know what he means now. With Boss has gone what was left of my old life. The Abbe who had given up, perhaps in part even before Cleo died. The Abbe whose only act of being was to wish for death. And in her stead is this other Abbe. Can't say I know her very well, but she has long hair and an idea that being alive is something good. Her old bones are being patched together and padded with flesh that feels like it can put up one more fight. And with a sudden huff and a puff her lungs are filled as though they might, someday, give out a whoop.

THEY STAND and eat Mrs. du Toit's apricots by my bedside, the visitors and the staff, at various times throughout the day. These moments of communion where nothing much happens except the savoring of leftover summer. The nice policeman who took my statement ate one when I insisted, as did Piet Slabbert, who ambled in last night. "If you want to talk to me, you have to try one," I said.

"Didn't know you could get them so late in the season," he replied, selecting the ruddiest. After he was done, he pocketed the pit and wiped his mouth with his handkerchief. "Don't suppose they allow smoking in here anymore."

"They don't allow anything much more than a grueling regimen of something called 'health care.' "

"Sounds too exhausting for me." He chuckled. "And speaking of exhausting . . ." The deal is still on, he told me. The developers, eager to move ahead with their plans, are still waiting for the papers to be signed.

"They are letting me out of here in another week," I told him. "But Rhiaan arrives tomorrow; maybe he can sign them."

"They can wait another week; it's not going to kill them." He cringed at the word. "Sorry!"

"What about the kids? Have you found them a place?"

"We are still working on it. But you leave that up to me and get on with the business of 'health care.' " I waved at his suggestion as though it were a fly about to settle on something rather perfect.

"YOU LOOK GOOD, sis," is the first thing Rhiaan says, his face spelled out in relief.

"For a mummy, you mean?"

"Actually, I was thinking more along the lines of a Mary Shelley character."

Cicely knocks his forearm with the back of her hand. "Stop it," she says, and bends down to give me a gentle hug. "I am so sorry for what you have had to go through."

Rhiaan ignores his wife's sentimentality. "It's the nurses I feel sorry for; from what I understand, you are giving them a lot of uphill. Nurses make terrible adversaries, didn't anybody tell you that? They have access to some really long needles."

"It's not the needles you have to worry about; it's the sandpaper they call 'sponges.' "

"I brought you a quilt," interjects Cicely. "A little one for the airplane." She spreads it out on the bed.

"Now you not only feel like a granny, you will be equipped with the quintessential granny accessory!" says Rhiaan.

"Did you fly ten thousand miles to torture me, or did you have some other objective in mind?" I ask my brother.

He scratches his head, eyes scanning the ceiling. "Was there something else?" he mutters. "No, just torture," he says finally.

After Rhiaan returns with an extra chair, they sit next to my bed while Cicely catches me up on the news. Jenny would like for me to call her—she has tried the hospital several times but always has the time difference wrong, so it usually ends up being in the middle of the night when only the nurses like to wake the patients. The animals are fine and Mrs. Chung is keeping an eye on the house and collecting the mail. The people at the magazine have been informed. "An awfully bossy woman by the name of Jean asked whether a travel story on Cape Town might be in order, and I told her it most certainly would not be—I hope you don't mind."

I smile gratefully. "And you told Greg what happened, I assume," I ask.

Cicely looks at Rhiaan, who nods. "Right after we heard from Etienne Bredenkamp."

"And?"

"He was shocked, of course. Wasn't he, Rhiaan?" Cicely rushes.

Perhaps part of me was hoping Greg would hurry to my bedside, read from a stack of my favorite books, dispel the hours of boredom. By the looks on Rhiaan's and Cicely's faces, perhaps they were expecting this too. But it is too late for white horses and on-call knights.

"He has called a couple of times to find out how you are doing," Rhiaan answers, his banter and chattiness having stalled. "And he sends his best wishes for a speedy recovery."

"It's funny," I say. "They all call me Mrs. Deighton in here. But I haven't been Mrs. Deighton for a very long time." Cicely leans over to pat my hand. "It's my own fault. I stopped making the effort long before it even occurred to Greg that he needed to make more of one. He's not going to now, and who can blame him?"

Blame. I had such high hopes for Blame. Wasn't it going to sort out the good guys from the bad, and then dole out to each their just desserts? A stand-in for God, really. But Blame has been scrambled now. Who can tell one yoke from another? It's good only as a serving to a world with no teeth.

Cicely tells me they are staying at "a darling little inn" just around the corner, which makes Rhiaan clear his throat. "The Biltmore," he corrects. They will be here to visit every day, she says, but Rhiaan has promised her a couple of excursions.

"There are the papers to sign—maybe that can be one of your outings," I suggest.

Rhiaan shakes his head. "You and I will do that when you get out of here."

"I went to see the old house, maybe you can put that on your list."

"How was it?" Rhiaan asks.

"Small," I tell him. "I didn't remember it being so small."

"What about the farm?"

I shake my head. "I didn't go there." When Rhiaan raises his eyebrows, I say, "The truth is, I have been avoiding it."

"Why is that?"

"I don't know. Maybe I just didn't want to face what happened all those years ago. Maybe I didn't want to be reminded of Mom leaving me there."

Rhiaan is thoughtful for a while. "I think we should go—you and I," he says.

"Me too."

Rhiaan leaves the room to answer his cell phone. "When he's not in New York, he's on the phone to New York," explains Cicely.

"But that's good, right?"

She shrugs. "Don't tell him this, but I can't see what all the fuss is about with the new poems. Not that they are bad; they are just such a departure from his other work."

"Maybe he needed a departure."

"Maybe." She smiles.

"Things seem better." *Between you*, is what I have not said, but she gets my drift.

"Better, yes."

THE NURSE COMES IN to take my blood pressure and temperature, and announces that the doctor will be in soon to take off my face bandage. "How many fingers do you see?" she asks, and I roll my eyes. "Okay, bad joke!" she says. "What are you going to do without someone asking you what day of the week it is and how many fingers you see?"

"Right. How am I going to know who I am if I don't have someone asking me my name every five minutes?"

"You will just have to look at that fancy plaque of yours, won't you?" she replies, glancing at the little frame with the mayor's seal propped up against a vase of wilting flowers.

"You're going home today," the doctor announces, scurrying into the room with his clippity-clop shoes.

"Technically, I only go home on Tuesday, but yes, I am leaving here today."

He peers over my chart. "Right," he says, snapping back the cover. "I expect you will want to leave your bandages behind, then."

"Yes."

"The moment of truth," he says, speaking as though in capital letters. "You ready?"

I nod.

The nurse hands me the mirror. Steadying it in front of my head with both hands, I wait while the bandage is peeled away.

❦

CLEO'S FIRST GAME, her favorite game, from the time she was an infant till the day she died, was peek-a-boo. Hands down. It beat ring-around-the-rosy, hide-'n'-seek, follow-the-leader. She would even drop the cat for a game. And every time I closeted my face behind my palms, peeking through the cracks, her face would turn from glee to concentrated expectation. Pursed mouth, saucepan eyes, breathing barely at all, Cleo waited for however long it took. And when the moment did come, her face registered as much surprise as the very first time we played. "Peek-a-BOO!" I would shout, and she would answer with a grin that would split her face in two. "Aden!" she would insist. Each time my face retreated behind its doors, it was as if she feared it had gone for good. Added to that was the possibility that if it were to reappear, it could just as easily be a monster as her mommy. Which made the delight even more acute when it turned out to be the latter.

The day before the roof leaked, the day she caught me in the laundry room sealing Hershey's kisses into plastic Easter eggs for Sunday's hunt, we played peek-a-boo for what turned out to be the last time.

"What are you doing?" she demanded, tiptoeing to see the contents on top of the washing machine.

"I'm getting ready for Easter, now go and play."

"Can I have one?" she asked, puppy eyes on her prize.

"No, they're for Easter. Now please: go and play; I'll be done in a minute."

"Mommy, what's Easter?" Stall tactics. I was about to say, Go ask your father, because if, in fact, it was an explanation she wanted, I could not think of any easy answer that wouldn't make the Lord sound like a lemming.

But instead, I put the eggs down and sat on my haunches so that we were eye-to-eye. "Easter is the day Jesus came back to life," I said. And then I told her how Jesus had died, how his friends wrapped him up in blankets and put him in a cave and rolled a big stone in front of it. I told her they were sad because they were never going to see him again. But then one morning, his best friend Mary went to the cave and she saw the stone had been rolled away, and instead of Jesus, there were only those dusty old blankets on the ground, and an angel. The angel told her that Jesus wasn't dead anymore. And then Mary saw Jesus, hiding behind the bushes.

I could tell I was losing her attention with too much explanation.

"It's like this . . . Watch." I covered my face with my hands. "See, the stone is rolled in front of Jesus. Jesus is gone." Her face dropped into low gear. " 'Where's Jesus?' says Mary. 'Where's Jesus?' " And then I opened my hands. " 'Here I am!' says Jesus. 'Here I am!' " Cleo clapped in delight. "See? Easter is like playing peek-a-boo with Jesus."

"Aden!" she said. And we played three or four more times till I gave her a Hershey's kiss and told her to run along.

∾

"EASY DOES IT," the doctor mutters to himself. And suddenly there is a chin and a cheekbone peeking between the peels. "Easy does it." The soft cotton pads are coaxed from their obstinate surfaces. And all at once, there I am: peek-a-BOO! Not Mommy, but not a monster, either.

"The scar will fade after a few weeks," he says, "but the wound has healed beautifully, even if I do say so myself." He admires my face as though he were preening in front of his own reflection. There are other pronouncements, and when they have all been made and acknowledged with my nods, he and the nurse leave me, my mirror and my face with its perfect X.

Across my brow, originating where a left eyebrow once demanded plucking into a neat bow and escalating into my hairline, is the visible reminder of that night. The point of impact etched across my forehead; the intent and the result written in the same decisive stroke. Cross-hairs. As if I would ever forget who and what had been set in them that night. Or what, in a shattering moment, I had become. And what I had un-become.

I stare at my purple scar. It is the taking of someone's life, plucked as easily as low-hanging fruit, that dials you into the life coursing through your own veins, animating your own heart. I scarcely can admit it to myself, but there it is, staring at me in the mirror: only in those brief moments, hell-bent on sending two men to their graves, did I feel as though I were resurrected from one myself. A more truly alive instant I cannot recall. Nor one for which I am more sorry.

It is not just my face peering back at me from the mirror, but that of my mother, the warrior.

There is a voice outside my door, and I tilt my head to listen carefully. It belongs to Cicely. I look at the mirror one last time. This time, with my head still cocked at an angle, the purple scar is a cross.

RHIAAN HAS MY BELONGINGS slung over his shoulder in the hospital-issue drawstring bag. Cicely wants to take the flowers, but I tell her to leave them. Only one apricot is left in the bowl on my bedside table. I pick it up and follow my family out the door. The nurse is writing the name of a new patient on the board, no doubt in the vacant space where my own has been erased.

"Well, would you look at you," she says, turning to me.

It is a spectacular performance, me shuffling along in house slippers, and I bow graciously.

"For you," I say, handing her Mrs. du Toit's last apricot.

"Thank you."

"Thank *you*. For everything."

We head for the door marked EXIT just as she says, "Goodbye, Elizabeth Spenser; don't forget who you are."

TWENTY-TWO

The oak trees lining the gravel driveway look as though they have been torched by the fire of Pentecost, a startling contrast against the green and yellow patches of field on each side. Before Rhiaan's rental car reaches the end of the driveway, the white farmhouse with its green corrugated roof is visible, and a century slips in between. Half expecting my grandmother to walk out onto her red *stoep* to see who has come to visit, toweling her hands on her apron, I hold my breath in anticipation.

Rhiaan pulls up in front of the steps and turns off the ignition. We are both quiet. The place is more beautiful than I remembered. Blistering along its torso, the house has covered its face with ivy and the *kopje* behind it is closer, as though it girded its loins and crossed the valley to come and console it. When Rhiaan and I get out of the car, the faces of African children compete for space at the bay window where my grandmother's parlor used to be, where my own face used to look out for my mother's car. The sign above the front door, the one that used to hang at the entrance to the driveway, says SUNUP. Someone has written beneath it in a black marker, SKOOL. For a while all I can do is stand and smell the dust and the fields, and stare at my past miraging beneath that sign.

To my left is Beauty's *kaia*, also in need of paint and a new roof. Unlike my grandmother's house, which is garnished with loops of flower beds, the *kaia* is unadorned, Leah rather than Rachel. Beside it is the now-vacant chicken coop, poles with swaths of fence missing. It is impossible to look in this direction without thinking that the *kaia*, if anything once an excerpt, is now the chief volume of my story, and contained within its bare walls are all the secrets and sacrifices. It keeps its silence, though, even when all has been told.

I don't know in what direction Rhiaan is looking when he says, "Some things never change."

"It's *all* changed," I counter. This is a different place, not just because it is inhabited by schoolchildren rather than relatives, but because what I know now does not line up with my memories of it. The girl I left behind has a different mother from the one she imagined deserted her. In fact, each of the women who once sat on the *stoep* years ago are not the ones I know today. And that cannot do anything but alter it all.

Still reluctant to step up to the front door, I scan the property rolling out to the west where I can be reminded how treacherous a place the past can be.

"I don't believe it!" I exclaim, wondering if it is possible that I have remembered wrong. Or could the orchard have switched sides?

"What?" Rhiaan asks, following the spoor of my astonishment.

I point to the orchard. "Those are the apricot trees, aren't they?"

The fruit trees, so long glabrous, rustle their boughs in the morning breeze like ladies sashaying from a hair salon. I hurry out to the field, crunching underfoot a mat of spent leaves, and watch the trees as they shake their heads and shed their curse.

"Well, I never," mutters Rhiaan, who grazes his hand along one of the trunks and inspects a branch.

"They are back from the dead," is all I can say.

"Lazarus trees," he muses. "Do you suppose they produced any fruit?" He crouches to the ground and cranes his neck to look under the trees. Shaking his head, he examines the leaves. "This is quite possibly new growth."

"What do you suppose it means?" I ask.

"Several possible explanations. I would hazard that someone has gone to the trouble of taking care of them." We both look around expecting to see someone step into the path to take credit, to ask, *Whom do you seek?* Nobody does. "Come on, let's go ask inside; ten-to-one the teacher will know who is responsible." Rhiaan strides along the beam of solving a conundrum while I draw back into the shade. Life has found a way to trump death. Again. It seems silly to cry now, even a little. It is sillier still to believe in curses, in curses being broken. Perhaps the tears have nothing to do with curses but the recognition of a great act of mercy: that someone cared for and took pity on these trees, and in so doing overcame disease or, worse yet, neglect. Someone who loved something not because it was theirs to love, but because it was a thing of beauty. It was a thing of beauty even when all there was to see was twisted piles of kindling.

Someone is calling my name. Just for a moment I wish it were the gardener. "Abbe! Come along! We don't have all day," Rhiaan hollers, and I hurry up to the front door, which he holds open. A tall Ndebele woman walks from the parlor into the hallway to greet us, a petticoat of students encircling her to have a look at who has come to visit. She introduces herself as Teacher Mavis, and Rhiaan apologizes for disrupting her lesson.

"It is an honor to meet you both," she says, although her tender eyes seem to be saying something else. "We have been waiting for you, and the children have prepared a gift to say thank you for the years you have let us stay here." She invites us into the classroom while the children scramble back to their desks. She addresses them in Xhosa, and in reply several children come to the front of the room. Dressed in clothes that are either too small or too big, they huddle against one another in front of the blackboard and giggle shyly until the tallest girl at the back taps her shoe against the polished wood floor and starts the song. The others answer antiphonally, clapping hands their only accompaniment. It is a traditional Zulu song about the children of the village running to meet their mothers, who are returning from the town with treats they have traded for their crops.

When the children have finished their song, Rhiaan and I applaud. While they return to their seats, one boy remains. "This is Bumlani Mabele," Teacher Mavis tells us. "He has been with us for three years." The boy, who looks no older than eight, stares at his leather sandals, scuffed and worn. His trousers, while clean, end two inches above his ankles. His knitted sweater, with sleeves rolled up several times to his wrists, is tucked in neatly at the top of his pants. *"The Owl and the Pussy-cat went to sea in a beautiful pea-green boat,"* he recites, staring beyond us as if to some boat that has left without him. *"They took some honey, and plenty of money, wrapped up in a five-pound note."* Teacher Mavis smiles fondly at him and I cannot help but think these orphans, mismatched and without flocks of their own, are owls and pussycats and piggy-wigs sent packing out from under their pea-green roof.

As Teacher Mavis takes us through the other rooms—three with bunk beds packed tightly together, the fourth a makeshift clinic—there is very little to remind me of the months I spent in this house. But reminded I am, not by furniture and the faces of people long gone, but by the views—those outside every window and those that dance across my mind.

"The places the children are moving to—are they good schools?" asks Rhiaan. Teacher Mavis nods, again with her sunset eyes. "Yes, they are very good. It is only sad the children will be split up. Some of them have been together many years; they are like sisters and brothers to one another." Rhiaan's face is suddenly blotted with guilt—we are breaking up a family.

In the kitchen at the stove is a second staff member who attends a large stainless steel pot already bubbling with stew for the children's midday meal. One of her feet is pumping an invisible organ pedal so that her entire body rocks to and from her pot. "This is Nomsa." Teacher Mavis introduces us, and Nomsa wipes her hand on her apron before giving us each a clammy handshake, still rocking. "Stay for lunch, stay for lunch," she says, eyes fixed over our shoulders, grin off-kilter, before returning to her organ pedal and pot.

"Nomsa used to be one of our special students; she has been here from the very beginning," explains Teacher Mavis.

Rhiaan tells Teacher Mavis that we will probably wander around the property for a little while longer before we leave for a noon appointment in town. Piet is expecting us to arrive at his office to sign the final contract before the buyer's representatives show up with any last-minute requests.

Just before heading out the back door, I turn to her and say, "By the way, who is the person who has been taking care of the apricot trees?"

She shakes her head. "Nobody, *nkosikazi*."

But from her pot, Nomsa disagrees, *"Qamatha, Qamatha."*

"What is she saying?" Rhiaan asks.

Before the teacher can interpret, I answer, "God. She is saying God has."

Nomsa smiles and nods.

The back veranda has two large trestle tables pushed end to end, and functions as the outdoor dining room. It has a commanding view of the overgrown clump of wattle trees and the *kopje*, which serves more as a milieu than a backdrop.

"I don't think there was ever a time when I came to the farm that I didn't hike up there," Rhiaan says wistfully. "It always made me feel like I had climbed to the top of the world."

"You want to go up there now?"

"Are you up to it?"

"Sure," I reply. "If I get tired you can give me a piggyback."

He shakes his head. "Unless you weigh what you did when you were eleven, I think that option is out of the question."

"If you know what's good for you, brother dear, you will steer clear on matters of a woman's weight."

We head out on one of the well-trodden trails, and it winds its way through the knee-high *fynbos* to such a degree that sometimes we are headed in the direction of the hill and sometimes we appear to be switching back to town. After twenty minutes of walking from one grasshopper conversation to another, we begin a gradual ascent that becomes suddenly steep. Rhiaan hands me the bottle of water as we pause to catch our breaths. Even from halfway up the view is commanding.

"You can't say you've ever seen Paarl if you have never seen it from the top of Grandma's *kopje*," Rhiaan announces.

I want to correct him; it is Beauty's hill, not Grandma's, if it is a hill at all. More like a dispensary is this place, rationing out, as it did, *muti* and magic, cures and curses.

After ten minutes we arrive at the summit, which is strewn with boulders the size of shopping carts. Rhiaan scrambles to the top of one and belts out a throaty yell. "My God, it feels good to be up here."

I find a boulder for a bench that overlooks the valley. The farmhouse with its green roof looks like a model. To the south, the town of Paarl sprawls out like a picnic on one of Cicely's quilts. Beyond are the mountains of Du Toitskloof. Rhiaan sits down next to me and hands me a fistful of Cape daisies. "One forgets how beautiful it is here."

I nod. "I wish Cleo could have seen this."

"She would have loved the farm; can't you just picture her playing hide-'n'-seek in the orchard?"

"Bossing all the schoolkids around, more like it!"

"That too." He chuckles.

"You never brought Frannie and Claude here, did you?" I ask him.

"No."

"Why is that?"

He shrugs. "I can't say for sure. Partly because it is always a bit painful coming back, to the empty nest, so to speak." After a pause, he continues, "But I suspect part of it is that this place represents a time in my life of which I am not entirely proud."

"I think you can be proud of what you did, Rhiaan. You took a stand; most people weren't that brave. *I* wasn't that brave."

"I ran away, sis; one can hardly construe that as bravery. Everyone thinks of it as political exile; I wanted to believe it myself. But I always wonder if things might have been different had I stood up to Dad, had I stuck up for Mom."

It occurs to me that this brother who I thought saw my mother more clearly than any of us also sees her in part. I consider adding the piece that might bring her closer to being whole for him. "It wouldn't have mattered. Mom had to learn to stick up for herself."

"You may be right," he says, sounding as though he means the contrary.

"I am, and she did."

"She did what?"

"Stick up for herself."

Whenever we disagree, Rhiaan pulls rank, and he does so now simply by shaking his head. My two-mindedness tapers into a pencil-sharp point.

"Remember Beauty, Grandma's maid?"

Rhiaan shrugs. "The one who used to pilfer Grandpa's scotch."

"No she didn't!"

He laughs. "Come on, Abbe—don't tell me you still believe all that nonsense about her being a *sangoma* and brewing up magic potions in Grandma's kitchen. She was an alcoholic who qualified for Grandma's charity."

His condescension is irksome. "She was a *sangoma*, Rhiaan, not a drunk. In fact, I found out she is still alive, and I went to see her the day before the robbery." My brother's response is to retrieve from his pocket his pipe and tobacco pouch. "She knew things about our family I didn't know, stuff I bet even you don't know."

Holding the lighter to the nest of tobacco, Rhiaan tokes on his pipe till a spindly coil of smoke dribbles from his mouth and disappears. There seems to be a danger of Beauty's story going the same way, so I say, "It's something I think you *should* know."

Rhiaan's response is to raise one eyebrow lazily, as though this statement doesn't warrant the energy of raising both.

"She told me she helped Mom poison Dad." There.

Shock, I expect; at the very least, speechlessness. Maybe a denial, a call for evidence. But not laughter, which is how Rhiaan now responds.

"It's true!" I protest.

He gears down to a smile and tries to rub my head before I pull away. "Come on, Ab."

"It *is* true! I saw it, back then. Beauty had a vial of poison stuffed in a loaf of bread in her *kaia*. Mom was using it to kill Dad. Beauty says that Mom got sick from handling the stuff, that she ended up dying from it herself."

I recount the story, a single cord braided with strands from both my own memory and Beauty's recent account, and conclude with the vision I had of our mother as a warrior. I see immediately it is a mistake to include this part. Although Rhiaan has been quiet throughout the telling, he gazes over the farm. If he is convinced of anything, it is my slant toward melodramatics. "You don't believe it, do you?" I ask.

"It's not what I believe that matters."

"What's that supposed to mean?"

Rhiaan takes another puff of his pipe, exhaling patience. "I don't know that it matters how Dad died or how Mom died or who was to blame for what. They died. End of story. What seems to me to be the issue is how the rest of us are going to live our lives."

"Of course it matters! It matters what Mom did because it changes who she was. And who she was influences who *we* are, how *we* act. Or at least how *I* act. Realizing that she finally took charge of her own destiny, instead of being pulled along by one current or another, is what made me do what I did the night of the burglary. It's as though Mom was telling me: You have two choices—you can die, or you can die trying. It's in the trying that she lived, and it's in the trying that I feel I started living again."

"What you did, Abbe, is not because of who Mom was, but because of who *you* are. I don't think you can give credit to other people for things going right in your life, any more than you can blame them for when they go wrong."

It seems futile to continue arguing, particularly when we notice two pickup trucks pull into the farm's driveway, spewing up dust in their rush. Along the roadside, across the street from the farm's entrance, stops a dirty-yellow bulldozer, its mandibles coming to rest in front of it.

"Who are they?" I ask.

Shielding his eyes from the sun, Rhiaan stands up and squints into the distance. "It looks to me like the developers."

"But our meeting is at Piet's office, isn't it?"

He nods.

"Then what the heck are they doing here?"

"I don't know. Let's go find out."

Slimy from perspiration and bothered by the lazy flies looking for a free ride down the hill, I arrive at the farmhouse substantially more agitated than when I left it. It has nothing to do with my aching collarbone or my fatigued muscles, and everything to do with the particular way the man with the red cap is gesturing with one hand, swinging it from the plans rolled out on the hood of his car to the fields. Rhiaan, on the other hand, is composed concern.

"May I help you?" he asks several feet before we are face-to-face. The pickups are company trucks, BOLAND CONSTRUCTION, INC., according to a sticker on the car door.

"Sorry, who are you?" The man with the cap is peeved at the interruption.

"Rhiaan Spenser, and this is my sister, Elizabeth. We are the owners of this farm."

"That's not what I have been told," he says. "Hammerson and Sons—that's who owns the place now. Bit of a *kakhuis*, if you ask me, but I—"

"I'm sorry, but what did you just say?" Rhiaan is clearly vexed.

"I think he just called our farm a 'shithouse,' " I tell him.

"Look here, sir, I'm going to ask you kindly to leave. As of this minute, the property on which you stand is ours and you don't want to be in the unfortunate position of trespassing," orders Rhiaan.

The man with his cap turns to the other two men and snorts. When he faces Rhiaan again, his contempt is a hazard sign. "Listen, mister, when you start paying my salary, then you can tell me what to do. Until then, you can kindly *piss off* and let me do my job." This brings titters from his two cohorts.

By now a brood of children have assembled on the *stoep*, Teacher Mavis pecking at them to stay together while Nomsa grins madly and waves at our shadows.

Whatever ground Rhiaan imagines he did not stand in the past is now bearing the full weight of his umbrage. "I'd say you are dangerously close to not having a job."

"Excuse me?"

"Let's not do this, Rhiaan," I interrupt. Rhiaan glances at me while the man with the red cap mutters an instruction to his associate, who flips out his cell phone and punches numbers. My brother knows, as he so often does, what I am thinking—this time that I do not want to sell the farm, that I cannot sanction the eviction of orphans any more than I can allow a concrete parking lot to replace the orchard, especially with its bushy boughs. To my questioning eyes, Rhiaan nods his consent: *Go for it!*

When I look at the man with the cap, he snatches the phone from his colleague. I take a step closer to him. "What my brother is saying is, you don't have a job, at least not this job."

In response, he raises an index finger requesting a minute, but it is not the voice on the other end to which he must now pay attention.

"No," I tell him, "you can't have a minute. What you can have is two minutes; two minutes to get into your trucks and get the hell off this property before I call the police. And you can take that monstrous contraption parked on the road with you. There won't be any digging over here. Not today, not tomorrow, not ever."

ASCENSION DAY

TWENTY-THREE

Cleo's first word contained two distinctly different syllables: *tuhr-til.* We were at the pet store buying dog food when I took her over to the little glass tank on the floor with teeny baby turtles barely distinguishable from the rocks on which they were sitting. "Turtle, Cleo." I pointed and she repeated the word back to me as clearly as the Queen of England might have done. I yelled across the store, past the ferret-looking cashier to Greg. "Honey! She said 'turtle'!" He came rushing while Cleo stood with her index finger pushed against the glass, saying "turtle" over and over. She was only ten months old and we looked at each other for the thousandth time, with raised eyebrows and fly-catching mouths as if to say "Star."

First words. They are recorded in baby books, are bragged about to parents who for the life of them cannot recall what your first word was, and are the subject of press releases sent to everyone no matter how remotely related. Those with pulpits may very well do what Greg did: announce it in church. Just after the congregation had hollered its lethargic "aloooo-ha" to the first-time visitors who had been bold enough to introduce themselves, Greg boomed, "This week, there is only one announcement not printed in your bulletin worth highlighting."

People looked up.

"Cleo said her first word yesterday." While the little old ladies cheered, he came down the center aisle to the pew where I was holding Cleo, picked her up, and carried her back to the chancel steps. He held out the jade turtle pendant Jenny always wore around her neck and asked, "Cleo, what's this?" She peered at it, then at the congregation waiting for a pin to drop, then grabbed the microphone and took a big, slippery bite out of it, making the speakers crackle and everyone laugh. "Today," he continued, "is Turtle Sunday. It is not on the liturgical calendar, but it's a day of great import nonetheless. This day we thank God for all shelled creatures, from the ones snapping in mud ditches beside the roadside in Ohio, to the great green sea beasts that inhabit our Hawaiian waters, to those that inspire babes to utter their first words." On cue, the organ bashed out the opening bars of "All Things Bright and Beautiful" and we all stood and sang as though all things were.

But what of last words? Not the ones we the surviving kin inscribe on gravestones or send off to the obit editor, but *theirs*. The ones who speak no more. Nobody came to ask me about Boss's last words, which I like to think were more benedictory than blasphemous, that in his terminal wail ("Jesus!") the summoned Lord had indeed rushed to meet him—gun unfired, sins forgiven, no harm done. Surely someone wanted to know—a mother, a brother, a girl waiting at home with his baby at her breast. And yet they never came to ask.

The subject of Cleo's last words has been the same way—like a bone, at first buried for lean times, now possibly irrecoverable. If I concentrate hard enough I can still conjure Cleo's voice, and slowly then will the edges of her chubby face emerge, and I am as sure as ever I could pick her out of a crowd. But just as she opens her mouth to speak, the edges blur and she fades away as swiftly as a shadow on an inclement day. I once thought we had never inquired about her last words because it was easier living with what each of our sainted memories conjured for us—parting words bestowing favor, as Isaac did on the wrong son. But now I know it is because last words require an act of community. Retrieving the buried treasure cannot be done alone. Someone has to help, someone who may be responsible for there being a dry bone in the first place.

On the knuckle of Ascension Day, surrounded by boxes in my hilltop house where the echoes run freely, I am unable to bear the un-knowing any longer.

THERESA AND HER CHILDREN are living now on the other side of the island with her sister, Loma, who I take to be answering the phone.

"May I speak to Theresa, please?"

"Who's this?" she asks abruptly.

"It's Abbe."

A beat. "I don't think you have anything more you need to say to my sister," Loma hisses.

"Please, it's important."

As though she has not heard, she continues, "They are all ghosts now, okay?"

"I'm sorry?"

"Ghosts. They are gone: your daughter; Jakes. We talk now of the living."

"Please," I repeat, feeling the burn of defeat. "Please, let me talk to her; it won't take a minute."

After a hundred years go by, she relents. "She is almost a ghost her-self, you know."

When I first saw the Grand Canyon I was surprised there were places where anyone could walk up to its edge and look miles down into the deep crack in the earth without the security of railings. Where the drafts billow up heat and wild taunts of jumping. At great heights, the soles of my feet tingle as if they want to sprout roots and my lungs shrink as if the merest of sighs could disturb my balance. This is what I felt at the joist of the Grand Canyon and what I now feel as I clutch the phone and listen to the pat-pat-pat of Theresa's feet carrying her body to the phone.

"Hello?"

"Theresa."

And she says resignedly, "Hello, Abbe."

"There's something I want to talk about and I was hoping we could meet . . . It shouldn't take long."

"Okay," she agrees. And it is as simple as that. "When?"

"I could come now, if that's okay."

She gives me the address and hangs up.

I spend fifteen minutes looking for a pair of shoes. In the three weeks I have been back Jenny has applied first-grade pedagogy to packing so that there is a system of boxes all color-coded and labeled in A-is-for-apple letters. Still, it does not help me in the matter of last-minute necessities like shoes, or for that matter, guts. When I at last find a pair of flip-flops in a laundry basket along with the dustpan, an extra toilet roll, and the dog leash (I have my own system of packing too!), I am no nearer to being ready. Still, I head for the garage.

Sitting in the driver's seat, I stare in my rearview mirror at the blank space where Cleo's car seat used to be. It is a full five minutes before the urge to vomit passes. When I shift the gear into reverse, sweat trickles down the sides of my body though it is at least ten degrees from the midday high.

Theresa's sister lives in Waimanalo, which means I have to take the highway over the Pali Mountains. Along the roadside there are a few makeshift memorials for those who did not make it all the way over, conspicuous with their gaudy bouquets. I slow down near one of them—"Aloha Kanani"—to catch a glimpse of the girl's photo. The other cars ride up to my bumper and then surge ahead. One carries a face frowning its disapproval: Why don't you drive, lady! I pull over. Surrounding Kanani's face, smiling as though nobody's had the heart to break the news to her, are words of farewell and pledge: "We will always remember you"; "The world will miss you"; "Till we meet again." Nowhere to be found are Kanani's last words to the world.

The house is on the old Waikupanaha Street, where the locals live and sell their produce in front of abandoned cars rusted into flowerpots. Not many *haoles* live in these parts, but as in Langa, they are frequently bused through in air-conditioned coaches for "a taste of old Hawaii-nei." Just past the hand-painted sign advertising "apple-bananas" is the turn for Loma's driveway, and as I approach the Hawaiian ranch house I notice half a dozen wild-haired children piled like puppies in a stained old bathtub in the middle of the front yard. Tess, at the top of the heap, is laughing and brushing her long hair out from the corners of her mouth.

I pull up to the house and nobody is outside, just two half-starved mongrels too hot to bark. Before I get out, my mind announces what my loosening bowels already know: it is too late for second thoughts. For one horrible minute I think I will have to knock on their door just to use their toilet. Suddenly there is a thump against my door and I see little Tess shouting at me with excitement, "ABBE! ABBE! ABBE!"

I roll down the window and smile. "Hello, Tess."

"Abbe! I remember you!"

"I remember you too." Gone from her features is the poodle-cuteness of a preschooler, and in a glance I can see all the promise of her becoming.

"Did you come from your house?" she asks.

"Yes."

"Are you coming to my house?"

"Yes, I am; I have come to see your mom."

"Is Cleo coming?"

She has forgotten, then remembered all at the same time, and I reach down out of the window to rub her head. "No, love, Cleo isn't coming."

She whisks around as she hears her mother call. "Go on in the house, Auntie Loma has haupia pie for you," Theresa says, and Tess dashes off, but not before waving. "Bye-bye, Abbe."

"She's grown so much," I tell Theresa as she approaches my window. But here is a woman who needs no reminding of how time is fashioning one daughter and not another.

"Yes, she has. Are you going to come in?"

I shake my head. "I don't think I can. Would it be all right if we talk in the car?"

"Okay." She shrugs and heads around to the passenger side as I stretch over to unlock the door. Her heavy frame eases into the seat.

"This may turn out to be a mistake," I say, finding the equilibrium between words. "I haven't rehearsed—no, that's not true; I haven't rehearsed as much as I would have liked."

Theresa responds with a smile and we sit quietly side by side.

I look over at her. "I am sorry about Jakes."

"Thank you," she says politely.

"He was a good man. I should have said that at the funeral."

"Yes, he was. And yes, you should have."

My mouth has gone dry and I think about Kanani's poster board. "The world will miss him."

"Jenny told me what happened to you," Theresa interjects, and I know she has seen the scar.

"Other than the heads of states in a few backwater nations, I think she told everyone."

It is not her body that is a ghost but her smile, so faint I want to rub my eyes to make sure it is there. "I was sorry to hear about it."

"Don't be. It all turned out for the best, I think."

We are quiet again. I catch myself praying for a way forward.

"Today is Ascension Day," I say.

"Is it? I haven't been going to church lately, so I've not really kept up on all that stuff."

"Well, I haven't either. But Jenny's asked me to go to the service on Sunday, and I thought it might be a good time to say goodbye to some of the folks."

"She told me you are moving back to South Africa. Are you going for good?"

"I don't know about 'for good' anymore. 'For now' is as far as I plan these days."

She nods. "I know what you mean."

To the eavesdropping ladies of the women's auxiliary this might well be quaint afternoon chitchat, no need for a teapot even, but to two mourners this is a truce creeping up on no-man's-land.

"The thing about Ascension Day, if you think about it, is that it's about last words." I might as well have pulled out a revolver and aimed it at Theresa's head. At first her eyes dart madly, as mine must have done, looking for a way out. Finding none, they spray with tears.

There is a packet of tissues in my handbag, but I am afraid to reach for them and give her one, afraid the smallest gesture will make her bolt from the car. "I am so sorry to do this to you; I know you have been through a lot. It's just that I can't go to a service about Jesus' last words and not know the last words of my own daughter."

Theresa lifts the bottom of her T-shirt and wipes her face as a small child might do. She takes a few great gulps of air and then turns to face me for the first time. I look at her, at her black eyes rimmed with red veins. "She was singing," she says.

Out of all the sentences and words I have imagined Cleo saying, in all the possible ways she might have uttered them—a shout, a screech, a whisper, a yell—I have not imagined a song. And it seems that I did not know my child as well as I should have. Tess walks out on the porch, the corners of her mouth bearing the remnants of pie. Behind her, in the doorway, Loma glares out at the car.

"Do you remember what she was singing?" I ask.

And she nods. "The mommies on the bus go 'shh-shh-shh.' I remember because at the hospital, when I could hear you crying way down the hall, that's all I could think about."

In Cleo's version of the song, the bus driver goes "move on back," the children go "up and down," the daddies go "I love you," and the mommies go "shh, shh, shh." The actions accompanying the mommy verse involve staking a sharp finger to pursed lips and potting atop an equally uncompromising scowl. Daddy, the melody of unsung adoration; Mommy, the rigid rule. Sometimes I would sing it, shuffling the words so Daddy ended up the disciplinarian. But it never worked. Cleo would stop me immediately. "Nononono, the *mommies* go shh-shh-shh." Just once I argued, "But the mommies can go 'I love you' too, can't they?" Who could forget Cleo's perfect mimicry of her mother's exasperated tone? "Mo-ohm!" she said, and I relented, but perhaps I shouldn't have.

"She knew I loved her, didn't she?" I quaver. Can it be that this is what the blame has been about?

It is a priestly hand that finds mine. "Yes," my friend says. "Yes, she did." To her emphatic squeeze, I echo back my thanks, and in that fleshy Morse, forgiveness offered and accepted has traveled unnoticed by anyone but us.

"I'm going now," she says, drawing away.

What I want to say is, Don't, and she is halfway out when I remember. "Wait!" I fumble for my handbag, rummaging through a warehouse till my fingers find the folded envelope. "I want you to have this."

Taking the envelope, she nods, thinking perhaps it is one of my silly letters, a poem, a photograph. She lifts the flap and, seeing nothing, peers in. What she sees resting at the bottom like alluvial gold is the weight of the world: a blond curl tied with a cerulean bow.

EVEN BEFORE CLEO DIED, I began to think of life as a rather long procession of goodbyes. What started it was a traffic jam on Alakea Street when I glanced at myself in the rearview mirror and saw that a net of wrinkles had been cast over each eye. "Up until yesterday I was young," I told Greg, who called it vanity at first, then melancholy when I pressed the matter. (Greg was the only person I ever knew, besides dead Greek philosophers, who used the world "melancholy," as though a cupful of bloodletting leeches would do the trick.) But I believe it more than ever. No sooner have you met the love of your life than he is headed for the door, or you are wishing he would. Friends betray, disappoint, or move to someplace cold, and you are back at the window, waving away. Children come as seeds and just as flighty, dandelion-like, flit away with the first big puff. A beloved tomcat, the only show worth watching on TV, the last empty lot in town: valedictories to all of them. Goodbye to the neighbor who never waved, the house you swore you would die in, the memories you rehearse like times tables; hope the gerontologists are right: that they will return one day when all anybody requires you to recall is whether you had a bowel movement. Hope to God you will remember, instead, the precise smell of your mother's eau de cologne and the words she spoke when she daubed it behind your ears one night, or your little girl's squeal of delight when she found the first hidden Easter egg.

The house still has relics of parting even though the movers have taken away all the boxes. The FOR SALE sign is still on the curb, and Solly keeps one eye on me and the other on the pet carrier he hopes isn't for him. Mrs. Chung and Gillian Beech's entirely impractical yet tender gesture at goodbye is already dotted with mold even though there is only one perfunctory slice missing from it. Can't pack cake, but I haven't the heart to throw it out either.

Even the answering machine, once so adept at hanging up on people, now insists I call everyone back with detailed goodbyes. Greg I do, even though it is mostly to talk about when the pets will be arriving and to give him the details on the portable storage unit. "Take anything you want," I offer, and though I mean it to be kind, he bristles. "I will write," I tell him—it is an easy promise, easier than "Goodbye," easier still than "Forgive me." But those will come. I rub Solly's ears. "Not yet, boy," I assure him, and head for the front door. As I glance back, the house seems gone already.

WHEN I SLIP into the pew fifteen minutes later, Jenny hands me her open hymnal while the congregation sings Isaac Watts's beloved hymn "Jesus Shall Reign":

> Jesus shall reign where'er the sun
> Doth his successive journeys run;
> His kingdom stretch from shore to shore,
> Till moons shall wax and wane no more.

A time when there will be no more moons—good or bad—waxing and waning is the best description of heaven I can imagine. I join in on the second verse, looking up between breaths to see the familiar heads.

Petal, with Blossom tied to her in a sling, waves from across the aisle and mouths something incomprehensible. Jenny says it's her last Sunday too, that she is headed back to England next week. Mrs. Scribner's new poodle is looking over her mistress's shoulder like a distracted child although no doubt she is expected to follow along where Mrs. Scribner's finger keeps track of the notes. Next to her are Rita and Frank. Frank has his arm over Rita's shoulder, a sign perhaps that a wedding is on the wind. During the next two stanzas I am able to locate Sylvia Horton in the choir loft; Althea Worthington and her great-nephew in the middle pew, pulpit-side. Carolyn Higa, who is not singing but casting around to see who's doing what, is seated next to two people wearing military outfits and henpecked expressions. But there are also a number of heads, come to think of it, that I do not recognize. In fact, the crowd seems to have swelled since we left, a point I will omit from the letter I will one day write Greg.

After the hymn, Pastor Penny (as she likes to be called) bounces to the Plexiglas lectern, a new addition to the chancel, below the newly erected PowerPoint screen. Tucking a few impertinent curls behind her ears and sliding her spectacles back up her ski-slope nose in one deft move, she enjoins us to greet one another in the name of Christ. Dutifully, we turn and pass the peace, some with hugs, others with handshakes no less hearty. There is a good deal of crossing the aisle, and a general chaos emerges so that the sanctuary resembles a tailgate party. Bumped along from one congregant to the next, I am suddenly face-to-face with Kelsey Oliver. His hesitation is unmistakable, but my hand, in the momentum of gripping and shaking, extends toward him. "The peace of Christ be with you, Kelsey," I offer.

"Um, yes. Indeed," he stutters. "And with you." For just a beat I don't let go, realizing all that pomposity is nothing but a scared, sweaty palm.

"Okay, friends," laughs Pastor Penny. "Back to your seats, please. We do want to be out of here before Denny's closes for lunch."

Flashing on the screen is today's Scripture—the text taken from Matthew's final chapter. I close my eyes and listen. Perhaps never before, not in the fervor of conversion or in the sit-up-straight duty as the preacher's wife, have I been so attentive. It is the awkwardness of goodbyes that makes us do what we should have done all along: listen instead of speak. It could be Chicken Little, clucking her warning, for all I care. The ceiling could cave in under the weight of a collapsed sky and I would not care as much as I do for the grace of knowing Cleo's last words. Among the rhythms of old come finally the Lord's: *Lo, I am with you always, even to the end of the age.* All through the town.

"ARE YOU SURE you want to do this?" Jenny asks, putting on her turn signal. River Street always comes up quickly, and it is easy to miss the turn. Not something Jenny will want to do when there is a plane for me to catch and a schedule to keep. So as not to distract her, I fire out a quick "Yes," although the truth is to the contrary. Is there a name for the fear of tight streets? Counting by the calendar, fourteen pages have flipped over since Greg and I last drove down this street. It is both yesterday and a different century.

Someone is painting the door of 121B fire-engine red, the same someone who must have hung the geranium-filled window box in front of what used to be Theresa's living room window. "Those aren't going to last long," Jenny remarks, crossly because she has to be so upbeat about my departure.

"But they look pretty," I say.

"True," she retorts, pulling over to the curb across the way. "If you have money to waste."

Someone else is setting out a trash can. The new door, the geraniums, the discarding of trash are small acts of hope. Before, I used to think living on River Street was like serving a prison term; now it seems more like an act of faith. All anyone can ask of a memorial, I suppose.

"We're not stopping here, go on down to the end," I tell her, and when she does there is one small space slurred with an oil stain. "Park here."

"What are you doing?"

"Park here. I'm going to see if anyone's home."

There is a mound of good sense Jenny wants to shovel at me, but I get out quickly and ring the doorbell without looking back. Please, please, please, I find myself praying again.

Sadder than my mirror is the hollow face behind the widening door. Sadder than a leak, a puddle, a skid mark in the road no one notices.

"Mr. Nguyen?"

If his eyes are telling the truth, I have knocked at the door of a cell, perhaps upon the lid of a coffin. He seems not to hear, so I repeat his name, and suddenly his lips crack in concern, with old-people fear. It is a fear of pirates coming to loot leftovers, when all that is left is borrowed time.

"I am Abbe Deighton," I announce.

One fear passes and another, like a swelling tide, rushes in to take its place. "The little girl's mother," he croaks, his cheek perhaps recollecting the last time we met, because his veined hand feathers it.

"Yes."

The door gapes as he gestures for me to enter. Fear recedes for resignation. "I thought you would come a long time ago."

Wearing polyester trousers, a collared shirt, and a tie, the old man is dressed as though he has been expecting company so long his attire has grown tired of waiting. To the lacquered dining room table he shuffles and pulls out a chair. He pushes aside a half-lost game of chess and takes the seat at a right angle to mine.

"Would you care for some tea?"

I shake my head. "No thank you; I have a friend waiting for me in the car. I can't stay long."

"I see."

I glance up at the ceiling, searching for the words; it sags as though heaven is closing in on us.

"I miss her," I begin. "I miss her so much."

"Yes." He nods, staring at his lap.

"I wish there were a way for her to stay intact, to stay whole in my memory, but I keep losing little bits of her, you know. I have to fight for the memories, even of the little things. Every day it is a fight."

He nods, probably expecting one now, and his silence makes room for more of my words. "I thought I could never forgive you. I thought as long as I didn't forgive you, the ending wasn't written in stone. You see, I didn't want it to end, not if it was going to be where someone didn't pay a price."

"Price. Yes," the old man repeats. There is no indication from him that he is impatient for this to lead somewhere, sitting, nodding, yessing like he was waiting for wax to harden. Everything in the room is beige, the palette of someone with but one sorry memory. A dear price, perhaps, has been paid.

Jenny sounds the horn. "I learned something a few weeks ago about blame," I tell him. "I figured out that for everything that goes wrong in the world, if it's a baby dying of AIDS on the other side of the world or a car crash outside my friend's front door, there's blame. But here's the thing: either we are all to blame or nobody is to blame." Mr. Nguyen looks at me for the first time, but I can't be sure it is with the light on. I can hear the car door open and close, Jenny's voice calling my name; time to go. "What I'm trying to say is, I didn't come here to blame you, Mr. Nguyen. I came here so we can help each other with the ending, and the only way I know how to do that is to tell you I forgive you." My voice is almost a whisper now. "And what I am asking you, Mr. Nguyen, is to forgive yourself."

It is the swift movement of the day that hardwires us for quick change. Shadows chase themselves around corners all day till they can do nothing but lie down in long, languid paths. No sooner have the flowers yawned and stretched out their petals at sunup than they are wrapping up again with the evening's cool shawl. Things change quickly in a day, and how we have grown accustomed to this. Mr. Nguyen, neither shadow nor flower, shows no notice of how the sun has shifted. I could stare at him for hours, as one might watch a sequoia grow, or a turtle rest upon a rock, and still not see the effect of my words. Perhaps forgiveness, then, is more like compost than the sun so quick to snap heads this way or that. Partnered with the wormy work of penitence, forgiveness is the victuals, the daily bread that nourishes what is buried in the dark, one molecule at a time. Someday its good might be perceptible to the naked eye, maybe in an nth of an inch gained from this man's unfurling stoop. But not today.

"I must go," I announce, getting up. Mr. Nguyen walks me to the front door without words, and on the way I notice the forlorn bookshelf and its one tiny patch of color. A fuzzy blue bear, the kind a machine claw might catch if fed enough quarters. Seeing my glance, the old man reaches for it and thrusts it at me. "Please," he says. "Take this."

"Oh no," I reply, "you keep it. Blue was my daughter's favorite color."

But he is adamant. "Please. Maybe one day I try my luck again."

DESPITE JENNY'S CONCERNS that we would arrive at the airport late, we are half an hour ahead of schedule. Instead of entering the air-conditioned departure terminal, we find a bench outside, where the soft, fragrant breeze brushes up against me one last time.

We watch a group of tourists, identifiable by their matching leis, wrestle their luggage to their designated coach.

"You're going to write every week, you hear?" Jenny says.

"They have telephones in Africa too, you know; if you're very good, I'll even call."

"I'm not laughing. Do you see me laughing?"

"And you said you were going to visit," I remind her. "Your next tax return, right?"

She nods. "As long as you know I'm not staying in any maid's quarters." She tries to laugh, but she chokes on her tears instead.

"Come here," I say, folding my friend into my arms.

We have promised not to say goodbye, so when Jenny withdraws from my embrace, she pats her face and picks up my bag. "Come on, we're not going to drag this out any longer." Seeing Mr. Nguyen's fuzzy blue bear sticking out the top of it, she asks, "So what are you going to do with this little fellow?"

"I'm going to give it to the boy I told you about, Bumlani." The child who had knocked at Beauty's *kaia* even though the door was open. Past his scrawny frame I had been able to see Rhiaan at the car talking on his cell phone, no doubt to Piet. Everyone had witnessed the spectacle, watched the pickup trucks spin their wheels and sputter down my grandmother's driveway, heard the growl of the bulldozer disturbed from its lair. But it had been the owl-and-pussycat boy who followed me to Beauty's *kaia*, stirring in me the familiar sense of being caught red-handed. Except I had held nothing in my hands, just the tremble of something akin to hope. The hope that a group of mother-less children, those who came with death certificates, somehow stood more of a chance by our holding on to the farm. More of a chance than one little girl who had once chased a yellow kite.

It was only when Bumlani stood in front of me that he asked his question. "Are you going to help us?" There is a saying in Africa that Qamatha casts a wide net. It was in the boy's question that I felt gath-ered up in the catch.

"You know," I tell Jenny, "I never did ask Bumlani what he needed help with. Who knows, maybe it was simply to help move a table or serve the stew, and here I am giving up everything to go do something I'm not sure I am going to be any good at."

"Oh, you'll be good at teaching," Jenny says. "I've always thought so."

"And why is that?"

Without hesitating, Jenny gives her answer. "Because you learn from your mistakes."

❧

MY GRANDMOTHER used to say if it was rainy on Ascension Day, the crops would do badly and the livestock would perish from disease. There wasn't much anyone could do about it, even Beauty with her an-cient spells. But if it was sunny, the summer would be long and hot, the farm productive. Now, at takeoff, the day could not be more glorious. For just a moment, it seems the airplane might catch up with the sun on its way back home. Sunday skies, having parted for the ascending Lord, stretch out for a bit of undisturbed peace and quiet. A hot, long summer, then.

ACKNOWLEDGMENTS

I am indebted to my wonderful agent, Emma Sweeney, who went from reader to advocate with supersonic speed, and yet still found time to answer all my questions.

To my publisher and editor, Sarah Crichton, I offer my appreciation for her guidance and clarity, for bringing to the manuscript a light touch and the weight of her expertise. Credit also goes to her assistant, Cailey Hall, who provided invaluable help along the way. To all the people at FSG, particularly Debra Helfand, Michelle Crehan, Susan Goldfarb, Charlotte Strick, Abby Kagan, and Laurel Cook, I am much obliged.

For her medical expertise, I am grateful to Dr. Ranjini Kandasamy, a fine pediatrician and friend.

My appreciation goes to Hilary Saner and Anthony Peckham. It is no simple task to be both friend and critic, yet it is one they accomplished with distinction. The book is better because of them.

Thank you to Helena Ogle, Carol Saggese, and Margie Hubbard, who spent almost as much time praying for this as I did writing.

Emily, my Halley's Comet of a child, has a myriad of ways to remind me what really counts—singing at the top of her voice while I was editing was the most effective. Thanks for the music, Ems.

It is with deep love and gratitude that I thank my husband, Robert

Morley. This book would not exist if he had not said three magical words—*Write it down*—and then provided a lifetime's supply of encouragement as I did. Without his insight, counsel, and commitment, I would be adrift. He is both anchor and sail to me.

And to the Wind for sending a gust this way, thanks.

DISCUSSION QUESTIONS

1. At its heart, *Come Sunday* is a tale of joy reclaimed. What is the source of Abbe's resilience? Which small moments gave her the grandest glimpses of hope?

2. Isla Morley portrays the experience of parenthood with a blend of unflinching candor and wise tenderness. How was Abbe's identity as a woman shaped by her relationship with her own mother? How was her brother, Rhiaan, affected by his father's shadow? How does the relationship between mothers and daughters compare to that of fathers and sons?

3. Discuss the novel's two locales. Do they share any similarities? What traces of South African culture does Abbe miss the most? Who is her greatest source of comfort in Hawaii and in South Africa?

4. What made Greg and Abbe compatible in so many ways? Why was it necessary for her to let him go? In what way was this decision destined to bring peace to both of them?

5. In chapter five, Abbe compares Greg to Sal, commenting that Greg is comparable to a playground sandbox, while Sal is like a

merry-go-round. "It is hard to get hurt in the sandbox," she says. "After my father, it was all I ever wanted in a man." By the end of the novel, how does she feel about trust and love?

6. How is Abbe healed by returning to her homeland? How does she define "home" at various points in the novel, from the modest house she shares with Greg to the restored, fruitful farm of her youth? Where have you felt most at home, and most restored, throughout your life?

7. What were the most lasting lessons that Abbe learned from Beauty, both as a child and when she returned later in life?

8. What transformations took place in Abbe after she began to see her mother as a lion who would do anything to protect her children? What images best capture the spirit of your mother?

9. In emotional terms, what did it take to bring about the reunion with Abbe's brother, Rhiaan? What accounts for their very different approaches to life?

10. Near the end of chapter twenty, in the midst of the attack, Abbe hears Pepsi sing the words that give the novel its title. What does Sunday come to mean for Abbe? How do the media's depiction of the crime differ from the way Abbe experienced it?

11. What is the effect of the first-person voice that drives the novel? What is special about Abbe's perspective on the world?

12. How does Abbe combine rational thinking and faith to call into question the nature of God? Ultimately, what answers does she find?

13. In chapter twenty-two, Abbe and Rhiaan debate whether their mother's secret actions affected them. Abbe argues that "who she

was influences who *we* are, how we act." Rhiaan thinks that's a moot point: "What you did . . . [was] because of who you are." Who did you side with in this argument? How much is your identity influenced by family lore?

14. As the author introduced you to South Africa, her birthplace, what surprised you most about its history and culture, and about life there after apartheid?

15. What aspects of hope are captured in the novel's structure, tracing the journey from Good Friday to Ascension Day?

16. How did you react when Abbe initially rebuked Greg for forgiving Mr. Nguyen? What leads to her change of heart? Describe the greatest difficulty you ever experienced with forgiveness.

17. What were Cleo's greatest gifts to those who knew her?